Pauline Taylor was born in a little mining village in what is now South Yorkshire. She was the youngest of three children.

Pauline left school at the age of fifteen with no qualifications and went to work in a factory. She got married and had four children by the time she was twenty-seven.

During her life she had undergone many hardships, including being bullied at school, work and by various people through her married life, plus her husband being taken ill at a young age.

She looked after her husband, brought up her children and passed her nurse training to become a Registered General Nurse, even though no one really believed she could do it.

In 2008, Pauline was taken ill herself and over the next five years she would retire early from the job she loved, lose her husband, meet her new partner and have to go through all the stress once again of him becoming very ill and her taking on the role of 24-hour carer.

Maldwyn's Quest is Pauline's third book and although it is sometimes hard to find the time to write, she knows that writing, for her, is the best therapy she could have had.

She has had a few knocks with her writing, none more than the rejection she received from the ladies of the writing group she used to attend, but she tries to put that behind her.

But with all that has happened Pauline is still looking forward not back and already has two more books in the pipeline.

MALDWYN'S QUEST

Pauline Taylor

MALDWYN'S QUEST

Vanguard Press

VANGUARD PAPERBACK

© Copyright 2018
Pauline Taylor

A CIP catalogue record for this title is
available from the British Library.

ISBN 978 1 784654 65 8

*Vanguard Press is an imprint of
Pegasus Elliot MacKenzie Publishers Ltd.*
www.pegasuspublishers.com

First Published in 2018

**Vanguard Press
Sheraton House Castle Park
Cambridge England**

Printed & Bound in Great Britain

Acknowledgments

I would like to thank the artist Paul Horton for creating the wonderful collection of Wizard artwork that gave me such inspiration to create the story of Maldwyn.

Paul tells stories in his art work and leaves it up to the viewer to input their own interpretation.

I acquired four of his limited prints when I was in a dark place in my life, I am sure that bringing Paul's characters to life and going with them on their journey through the story, helped me to overcome my fears at that time and come out the other end a lot sooner than I would have.

He then, very graciously, gave me permission to use his characters for the inspiration for the story I had to tell, and after it was written he offered a copy of one of his art works for the book cover.

Due to his generosity the characters of Maldwyn and his companions come to life before the reader even opens the book.

Thank you Paul Horton I will be forever grateful.

Preface

Everything and everyone has a story. It does not matter who you are or where you live, from the moment that you are born your story begins.

As you walk along the path of life you will encounter many things, and many people. There will be many trials and tribulations that you have to deal with and overcome down the path that you take.

If you are lucky, you will, in the course of your journey meet people, or a person that you can call a friend. People just like you, people that want the same things in life and have the same goals to fulfil.

All our encounters down the path of life will lead to some positive and some negative outcomes, but it is a path we all have to take until inevitably we are snuffed out like a flame on a candle.

So it was with our small intrepid band of companions whose story this is. They all set off down their respective paths, only to meet along the way as if fate had willed it.

In the great scheme of things, they were an insignificant group, and some would say strange bedfellows, but they were a brave truehearted company.

None of this group was who they appeared to be and taking this into consideration I will tell you a little about Maldwyn and his companions.

Maldwyn

Maldwyn was a man of science, a man of learning, an alchemist. Some called him the 'Wise One' as he was a man of learned reputation. But he was for want of a better word a wizard.

Maldwyn was a very good wizard. He was kind and caring to the people in the village, and he was always on hand if they needed help or assistance with a problem.

Maldwyn dressed in the traditional garb that wizards or 'wise men as they were known in some villages' had worn in the Empire of Sandina for centuries.

His long frock-like garment dropped to the floor with just the tips of his shoes visible beneath it. This garment came with a matching hat and it would never do for a mage of Maldwyn's calibre to be seen with a mismatch of hat and gown. The hat was a conical shape and had a small rim around the base where it clung like a limpet to Maldwyn's head; it was a tall hat that twisted as it went up to a point at the top.

His hair was shoulder length and pure white, as white as the snow before any footfall was put to it. His beard was magnificent as far as beards go; it too was as white as snow and longer than his hair, in fact it was nearly to his waist. It was shaped into a v shape and trimmed to a fine point. Everyone was in agreement that Maldwyn had a beard to be proud of.

The colours of his garments were also fixed by tradition.

Grey was the colour for everyday use, going to market or for a walk or an informal visit. If he were going on a long journey that would take him away from home for more than a day, then he would put a belt around the robe and hang a leather pouch and numerous other items from it.

Rich vibrant blue was the colour for special occasions such as meeting the Empress and dignitaries visiting the castle.

Brown or a dull red was the colour of work robes.

White was for meeting other wizards at official gatherings and for officiating at weddings or high ceremonial occasions.

Maldwyn was as most wizards are, a private man, a reclusive individual that did not venture out of his house very often.

Maldwyn was a benevolent wizard.

PYEWACKET

Pyewacket `real name Sorona` was a cat or in magyk terms a familiar, or was she?

Maldwyn had found him on the doorstep one evening two years ago meowing to go into the house. Maldwyn had taken the cat in and he had been there ever since.

Maldwyn had made the presumption that the cat was a male and it had wandered out of the village chasing a mouse and got lost, thus finishing up outside his house. There were quite a few feral cats in the village; it was not strange to see them walking about at all times of the night and day.

He had been very taken with the cat. It was friendly, clean and well behaved, but there were a few strange things about Pyewacket that you or I would have been suspicious of, but not Maldwyn.

Pyewacket could not only talk but he could also articulate and often assisted Maldwyn with intricate alchemy problems. He was a very clever cat as most cats are and these traits would have seemed strange to anyone but Maldwyn.

He had again falsely presumed that because his house was enchanted, that any creature that came inside would have the power of speech and be capable of doing all sorts of wondrous things.

The first thing you should understand is that Pyewacket did not just randomly wonder over to Maldwyn's house. Secondly, he was a she and thirdly she was not a cat! But she was on a purposeful mission.

Pyewacket was a hybrid `mixed race` being. Her mother `Peri Truckle' was a faerie creature that was herself a hybrid and descended from a fallen angel. They are known as the `Peri`.

Her Father `Gastak` was a `Ghillie Dhu`, a shy faerie-type creature that guards the forest, but mainly birch trees.

These two beings were very attractive therefore it would follow that they would not only have a child with extraordinary talents but a child that would be extraordinarily beautiful.

The only problem with this in the land of magykal creatures and faeries is the jealousy that can emanate in other beings.

This was the case with Pyewacket, and she found she had to escape along with her guardian Christano before they were captured and killed by the evil Sheela.

WINSTON

Winston was Maldwyn's small brown owl; he also was not what he appeared to be. Yes, he was a male and yes, he could talk, but again Maldwyn thought this was the power of the house that was causing this phenomenon, but he was not an owl!

Winston's real name was Christano, and he was both friend and guardian of Sorona, or Pyewacket as she was now known.

Owls are thought to be very intelligent creatures but the reality of their intellect is very different. In fact, owls are very stupid birds and the only thing they think about is food and where the next meal is coming from. The folklore that has been built up around owls could not be farther from the truth.

Maldwyn again did not take this into consideration when he realised that Winston was a very clever bird. He again thought it was the house, but had he stopped to think about it and apply some of the science he relied on so much, Maldwyn would have come to the conclusion that something was going on with these two creatures.

The house may have been enchanted enough to help them talk but not to talk in the eloquent way that they did. And it was certainly not enchanted enough to give them the very high intelligence that they both obviously had.

Winston also had piercing blue eyes because some changes in their transformation could not be made.

Maldwyn had found Winston perched on the uppermost windowsill of his house on the very same night as Pyewacket had been found on his doorstep. He was cold and shivering and Maldwyn had felt sorry for him; but not once did he think it strange that not one, but two creatures would turn up on his doorstep looking for shelter on the same night.

THE THREE

And so it was that these three individuals met at a crossroads in their life and started down a path that was going to be both dangerous and life changing.

CHAPTER ONE: THE BEGINNING

❖

Maldwyn left the castle and made his way down the winding path towards the great forest of Sandina.

The snow had been falling gently for hours and Maldwyn's footfall was making deep impressions behind him. He stopped just before he reached the forest. He turned to look fondly at the castle perched high on the hill silhouetted against the moonlight. He looked at it with fondness and affection. Maldwyn had grown up there, and as a boy he had enjoyed exploring the castle and most of its secrets.

His father, a very renowned alchemist called Hubert, was the court wizard, his mother had died at Maldwyn's birth and to be honest Hubert never spoke about her. Maldwyn thought it was because it was too painful for him but the truth was yet another story to be told at a later time, as Maldwyn was in fact adopted.

He had just visited the castle for his monthly meeting with the Empress Alyssa; he looked forward to these meetings as the Empress was as charming as she was beautiful. She was also very wise, a trait she had inherited from her late mother, but again that is a story we will not be telling at this present juncture.

The castle had a great lake that ran past it on two sides. The lake was a serene, tranquil place and the creatures that lived in it were happy and unhindered. It was the largest lake known in the land.

From the uppermost vantage point of the castle at its rear, if you looked straight out over the great lake, land could only be seen as a distant fixture on the horizon.

To the left of the great lake were the wastelands and the Morby Mountain, which no one in their right mind would ever venture near without purpose.

As the lake flowed down past the wastelands and mountain it slowly became narrower. It carried on in this way moving over rocky terrain getting smaller and smaller for a few miles before it eventually became a tiny stream that fed filtered drinking water to the village of Trask, at the base of Morby Mountain and Sandina's outer most village on the very edge of the Empire.

As the stream left the village it carried on a little way until finally disappearing underground to join other streams that fed the many caves and potholes that lay under the mountain.

To the right of the castle were hills that overlooked valleys and small towns. These towns were numerous and of different sizes. The Empress's chancellor had an appalling record of trying to collect taxes and carry out census, mainly because the people kept moving about and towns kept expanding. But the chancellor, good man that he was, did not have the qualities required for that particular post.

To the front of the castle lay the windy path that led to the village and the forest. This was the way Maldwyn had taken.

He turned and continued on his journey home, his staff in hand to steady him. In front of him was the forest. It started off as many forests do with a typical scattering of trees here and there as you approached it. These trees slowly became thicker and denser so that before you knew it you were in the thick of the forest.

Maldwyn was not afraid of the forest or the creatures that inhabited it, unlike the people of the village who would not venture near. He respected the forest and always stayed on the path. But if he so wished he could have ventured into the thickest of trees unimpeded.

It was a cold winter's night but Maldwyn felt warm enough in his robes. He lit his lamp and waited until it started to glow a calm yellow colour then set off on his way down the path to home.

Maldwyn enjoyed the solitude of these walks. The forest was so beautiful, silent and calm with the snow hanging on the branches of the trees. He got so carried away with all these tranquil thoughts that he forgot all about Pyewacket and Winston, who were waiting at home for their master's return so that he could give them their suppers.

He remembered them both as he reached the clearing at the end of the forest path that was the approach to his house. This was not because he had a good memory, but more to do with the creatures sitting in the upstairs window peering out at their master.

He hurried down the winding path now aware of their hunger, quickly unlocked the door, walked in and bolted it behind him, and then made his way straight to the kitchen to prepare the evening meal.

There were some peculiarities about his pets that Maldwyn had never found strange. One of these peculiarities was that both these creatures ate normal food; well normal for a human anyway, with a slight exception from Winston who preferred his meat raw not cooked.

After he had given his charges their supper Maldwyn prepared his own. He was not an ostentatious man: he was simple and led a simple life as far away from the limelight as he could get; he lived the way of a hermit at times.

Maldwyn's supper consisted of three slices of the best bread the village could offer and a small truckle of cheese given to him by a grateful villager for ridding his vegetable plot of some very large ugly slugs.

Maldwyn had taken his food upstairs and was sat in his favourite comfy seat near the fire. After he had finished he put his plate on a small table and looked around the room.

It was a relaxed room with a warm glow coming from the fire in the hearth. He smiled as he picked up his books and glanced at his small friends. Pyewacket was washing herself near the fire while Winston was reading a book on alchemy. Maldwyn thought he would try to decipher an algorithm on shape shifting. In fact, it was a very typical night for the three friends.

It was nine thirty when Maldwyn stood up from his chair and went over to his bureau near the window to put his work away for the night. The moon was bright and casting shadows through the trees and as he looked out of his window Maldwyn thought he saw someone or something moving on the path.

He stared and concentrated on the path looking intently for any further movement. Yes, he was right there it was, two small figures hurrying along the path from the village towards Maldwyn's house. It was difficult for him to see who it was, and from the size of them he thought at first it could be faerie folk. But it was almost never known for them to leave the safety of the forest and, if they did, it would be for a very good reason and a bad one.

As he stared at the figures and they came closer to the house he could see they were in fact two small children; they looked to be about eleven or twelve years old. There seemed to be a boy and a girl but what were they doing out at this time of night?

Maldwyn watched until the children were nearly at the house then he turned and walked to the top of the stairs and waited for the knock.

There was much whispering outside the door and Maldwyn decided he should go down and open it as the children were obviously a little frightened. And who wouldn't be when they were knocking at a wizard's door?

Winston immediately flew on to Maldwyn's shoulder and Pyewacket walked serenely at the side of him in the way that cats do as if she did not have a care in the world. Which of course she had.

As they reached the door there was a light knock, so light it would not have been heard upstairs by human ears. Maldwyn opened the door to the sight of the two younglins looking up at him with expectation in their eyes.

He still had his reading spectacles on that were half glass, which only made him look stern as he peered over the top of them. He said, "Now what are two younglins like you doing out at this time of night? Where are your parents?"

The girl burst into tears and sobbed persistently until the boy put his arm around her then she calmed down a little.

The boy answered with a shaky and nervous voice. "P... Please, sir, your honour. My name is Stephann and this is my sister Doras. We have come to see you on a matter of extreme urgency, my lord, a matter of life and death."

Maldwyn looked at the children. This boy was obviously distraught, he kept stuttering and his sister could not stop crying. Maybe he should invite them in and find out just what was bothering them.

Maldwyn was just about to ask them to follow him up the stairs when Pyewacket said, "Meow, isn't it time you invited the poor wretches in, Maldwyn. It is a cold night and I for one am very cold." She had a very precise speaking voice when she decided to speak, which always showed she had good breeding.

Maldwyn was a little annoyed with his furry friend. He said, "I was just about to do that when you once more interrupted me, Pyewacket. Please children come in and I will make you some hot chocolate."

They followed him up the stairs and sat down on the comfy sofa as he had indicated for them to do. They sat very still just moving their heads around the room to take in their new surroundings.

Maldwyn nodded to his two companions to keep an eye on the children while he went down to make the cocoa.

What Maldwyn did not know was that his two companions and his two visitors knew each other, and as was said before none of them were what or who they appeared to be.

As Maldwyn came up the stairs he thought he heard talking coming from the upper room but as he opened the door with the tray of drinks and cake there was no sound, which for a second or two he found a little strange, but soon dismissed it when the girl started to cry again.

He looked at his guests then at his companions with suspicion: he did not know why, but he thought there was something very odd about this meeting.

Maldwyn put down the tray and handed the children a drink and picked one up for himself. He sat opposite them in the large chair near the fire that Pyewacket sometimes favoured. He drank his cocoa from a large mug, both hands cupped around it studying these younglins with care.

Maldwyn said in a very gentle voice, "There is no need to be nervous, youngers. Just finish your drinks and tell me what it is you want from me!"

The boy sat silent while he finished his drink, then said, "As I have already told you, sir, my name is Stephann and this is my sister Doras.

"We do not know if you can do anything to help us, your Honour, but we can only tell you our story and then it will be

22

up to you to decide if you can do anything to help, your worship."

Maldwyn was starting to realise that the boy was wise beyond his years and he was also suspicious about the identity of these two, and for some reason the identity of his two companions. Now that he saw them all together there was something odd that he had never seen before.

Maldwyn held out his hand to the girl but she pulled her hand back from him; it was a definite sign that they were hiding something. Maldwyn would have known with one touch if they were really younglins or if so human younglins.

They could all see Maldwyn's suspicions and thought it was best to make a clean breast of it.

CHAPTER TWO: STORIES TOLD.

↑

Pyewacket and Winston went to sit behind the children on the sofa which Maldwyn took as a sign of support. Why had he not noticed before all the incredible things that these two creatures could do? He should have known; what a fool he had been!

"Well," he said, "I think I deserve some sort of explanation especially from you two." He gave Pyewacket and Winston an annoying glance.

"If I can explain, your worship?" said the boy.

"Yes, I think you had better explain, and do not think I don't know you are not human kind, because I sense things you could only dream about. I do not need to touch you. Then it will be the turn of my two faithful foundlings, will it not? Pyewacket and Winston." He looked from one to the other.

Maldwyn was angry. It was a feeling he did not like because his father had always told him an angry wizard is a dangerous wizard, and the world has too many of those to start with, without adding to them.

The boy Stephann started, "We are Bucca; people think that Bucca just exist but that is not the case. We have parents and we are born just like any other living being but not exactly in the same way.

"We are known for shape changing and for being a little mischievous but we are basically good creatures and only like to help when we can.

"That was the case with our parents. They wanted to help their old friends, a Ghillie Dhu called Gastak and his mate a beautiful Peri Truckle whose name is Emily. They had an enormous threat hanging over them and they did not know what to do.

"They had a young daughter that was so beautiful everyone either stared or averted their eyes as they had never seen such beauty; but there had never been a mixing of these two magykal creatures before so something special had to come from this union.

"So worried were her parents that they enlisted the help of a guardian, a wise one that was one of the Seelie Court race of beings. This guardian was to watch over her and guard her with his life."

Maldwyn interrupted, "And did this guardian turn out to be the trouble you speak about?"

He replied, "Oh no, your honour, he did not. In fact, he suffered the same fate as Sorona the beautiful girl of whom I speak."

"And what prey was that fate, younglin?" Maldwyn asked getting a little impatient.

The boy looked sad. "Why this!" he said pointing at Pyewacket and Winston.

"This was their fate, but the magyk forbids them to tell anyone what or who they are."

Maldwyn stood up as the realisation dawned on him and walked over to the window. He stared outside into the darkness thinking about his companions and the torment they were going through and indeed had gone through. They were not able to confide in anyone about their plight, even with him who loved them dearly.

He turned and walked back to the chair, sat down and placed both his hands on the edge of the chair arms gripping them tightly; he turned to look at his dear companions that were sat around the sofa.

He sighed. "I am so sorry, my dear friends, that I spoke a little harshly earlier. I should have waited until I was better informed before I made such judgments; it was not very generous of me.

"It must have been so difficult for you both not being able to confide in me. I suppose I had been on my own for so long I was glad when not one but two new friends turned up to live with me: an alchemist's life is a really lonely one. So, what is it you want me to do reverse the spell?"

The boy and his sister both said in unison, "No, no." The boy continued, "You cannot do that, your honour, you must hear the entire story before you make a decision."

Maldwyn answered, "I will listen to your story then we will, as you suggest, Stephann, work out what will be the best course of action."

The four friends nodded and Stephann started to tell his story.

He began, "It all happened just over a year ago a long way from here deep in the dark forest. It was so deep that no man and no wizard has ever been there, as they have had no need to.

"There came to the forest a Frau Berchta, her name was Sheela and in her natural form she is the ugliest hag ever seen, as the true nature of a being cannot be hidden for long. But in her preferred guise she is a beautiful woman with long white flowing hair and a long white flowing robe to match.

"She leads the hunt, hunting for mortals and magykal creatures alike with a pack of Hell Hounds that are as hideous and evil as she is. Her kind only usually go on the hunt on the sixth day of the New Year cycle, but she is different – she is more evil.

"Sheela had been gaining ground over the past few years and collecting a following of foul creatures on the way."

Maldwyn interrupted, "What do you mean by gaining ground exactly, Stephann."

Stephann continued, "She has waged an unofficial war against the good entities and creatures of our world, and she wishes to rule it in its entirety.

"She already controls some of the villages on the far side of the forest and I would say a good quarter of the forest too.

"Frau Berchta came to our part of the world after hearing about the beauty of a small child, and through some sort of twisted jealousy she was determined to find that child and deface or kill her. Well that is how it started out, now she wants everything.

"But as I said before, your honour, the parents of the child gave her a guardian in the form of a Seelie Court that went by the name of Christano and through his cunning and determination they nearly outsmarted that foul creature, but she threw a spell before they could escape and it caught them both behind.

"Because it was only the tip of the spell. A faerie godmother whose name was Jessica the Gentle threw her own spell at them, and although she could not counteract Sheela's spell she could and did lesson the effect."

Maldwyn said, "A Seelie Court eh? Well I am honoured, Winston, or should I say, Christano? I have heard of your race but never in a million years would I have ever thought I would meet one of you."

Maldwyn turned to Stephann and Doras. "Have you ever heard of the code of the Seelie Court? It is what these brave faerie live by. Now if I can remember it is something like:

- **Death before Dishonour**: A member of the Seelie Court would protect his or her honour to the death. Honour was the single source of glory for the Seelie, the only way to attain recognition. A true Seelie would rather have died than live with personal dishonour, and would never bring dishonour to another of the Seelie.

- **Love Conquers All**: For the Seelie, love was the perfect expression of the soul. It transcended all other things. Though romantic love was considered to be the highest and purest form of love, platonic love was also encouraged.
- **Beauty is Life**: Beauty was one of the first tenants of the Seelie Court. To belong, a faerie had to be beautiful, and all beauty was to be protected. The Seelie were known to go to war to protect beauty, whether it was a beautiful person, place or thing.
- **Never Forget a Debt**: This tenant worked in two ways. The Seelie were bound by their code of honour to repay any debt owed as soon as was possible. This included both favours and insults. The Seelie would repay a favour in a timely fashion. At the same time, they would exact vengeance almost immediately.

"Is that right Christano?"

The little owl who could not speak about it flapped his wings and jumped up and down as a gesture of yes.

Maldwyn carried on, "And if I am not mistaken you are also in love with your ward Christano, as Sorona is with you! But in my excitement I have digressed. Please, Stephann, carry on with your story."

He nodded. "Well the owl or Christano had to think quickly to get them out of the way of this hag so he being made of Seelie magyk grew larger and larger until he could pick the cat up gently in his claws and carry her away from the danger. There were spells flying everywhere but the hag could not catch them, but she is still looking.

"They flew straight to the centre of the forest where we reside but could not tell us who they were or why they had come to us as the spell forbids them to tell anyone.

"Luckily the faerie god mother, Jessica, had followed them to our area of the forest and she told our parents the story. It did not take them long to get their packs together and set off to help Gastak. They knew that Sheela was dangerous: her reputation was already reverberating around the forest dwellings.

"We had word back a few weeks later that Sorona's mother, Emily, had been taken hostage as leverage to get Sorona back in Sheela's clutches. Gastak had engaged in battle with Sheela and her army of misfits. For three days he battled but in the end he too was captured along with our parents.

"The rest of their allies were put to the sword as a warning to others not to defy Sheela."

It was at this point that Doras again started to cry. She was obviously distraught at the thought of her parents being locked up and goodness knows what else was happening to them.

Maldwyn asked, "Firstly I need to know who brought you this news? Was it someone reliable?"

"Yes, it was," Stephann answered. "It was a Manitou of good repute that came to tell us the news; he had one horn missing: it had been severed in the battle and his wounds were great."

Doras spoke, "The poor thing had been tortured but through his pain he told us to take Sorona and Christano to the wizard at the far end of the forest near the castle. He said you would keep them safe and we were not to tell you anything until we got word from him to do so."

Stephann put his arm around his sister and said, "We had word yesterday that we should tell you everything but we also had some bad news that concerns you at this side of the forest. There is great danger, your honour."

Maldwyn looked at the children and said, "You know I will help in any way I can, even if it means my going on a journey and putting myself in harm's way. The greater good is paramount and this hag cannot be allowed to gain any more ground, so tell me what could possibly be of importance to this Sheela at this side of the forest?"

Stephann looked at Maldwyn. "Sheela lives somewhere in or beyond the Morby Mountain; nobody knows exactly where. It is said that as she was travelling over this land she spied the castle and tortured one of the locals to tell her all about this place and the Empress.

"Due to her excessive greed and jealousy she wants what the Empress has and she wants it as soon as possible. That will mean, your honour, that war is imminent. The hag's normal modus operandi is kidnap, killing and torture. She is ruthless in every way and will stop at nothing to get what she wants.

"I am sorry to say that even now as we speak she could be hatching a plot to kidnap the Empress and take over her dominion."

Maldwyn could not believe what he was hearing; his beloved Empress, his sweet Alyssa to be overthrown or killed! No that could never be allowed to happen.

He said, "As I have already said I will do anything to help you and your families in their plight, but first I must visit the castle.

"The first thing is to ask the Empress for her permission for me to leave the area of the court and go with you to find your parents and this fiend, and the second is to ask permission to awaken the sleeping wizards!"

The two Bucca children looked puzzled. Doras asked, "Who are the sleeping wizards, your honour? And how can they help us?"

Maldwyn smiled, Pyewacket meowed and Winston hooted. It was common knowledge in the house of a wizard and everyone or every creature that lived there would know about the sleepers.

Maldwyn informed them, "When a mage is very, very old he tries to not die, well not fully anyway; what he tries to do is go into a rest state prior to his death, but he has to do this early enough for it to work or he will die fully and irreversibly.

"I myself will do this one day I hope, but I have to choose an apprentice and train him before I go into rest sleep, otherwise there will be no one to carry on my work and keep my secrets."

Stephann asked, "Why have we not seen your apprentice yet, sir? Is he at the castle?"

Maldwyn laughed. "Oh, bless you, younglin. I have not chosen one yet. I have not met a child worthy to be my apprentice but when I do you will be the first to know, Stephann."

Stephann looked puzzled. "Thank you, sir, I think." But the two companions of Maldwyn gave each other a knowing look.

It fascinated Doras that there was such a thing as a sleeping wizard; she was intrigued. "Where are these sleeping wizards, your honour? Do you have to go on a journey to wake them?"

He smiled once again. "Bless you; it is good to have an enquiring mind. There is a room in the castle that is enchanted and only the Empress of the day and the wizard of the day can enter. This means that no apprentices can get through the enchantment, and also none of the Empress's or emperor's siblings or offspring can enter either.

"Even other visiting wizards cannot get into the room. It has been a system that has worked for thousands of years and on only three occasions previously has the room ever been entered in great need.

"In a time of crises, the wizards in rest state can be woken from their slumber to perform magyk once more, to protect him or her that sits in the high seat of the castle, and if what you are telling me is true, we need to visit the Empress and tell her what the threat is!"

Stephann asked, "How many are there, sir, and will they all awaken?"

"Twenty that we know of," he replied. "But only twelve will be revived as it takes hundreds of years to build the wizard safeguards because they cannot be put back to sleep and if they do not die in battle they will die of old age when the threat is gone. This is what will happen to me I hope, so that in the future I can still be of some service to the descendants of my Empress.

I also need to send messengers to all the outpost wizards that are scattered all over Sandina. They must prepare their apprentices and then come in person to help hold the castle if they are needed.

"The other dreadful thing is that if this old hag gets a foothold here and controls the castle she will be able to access other domains that none of us should ever cross into."

The children asked in unison, "Other domains?"

Maldwyn realised he had spoken out of turn. He said, "It is of no concern to you two younglins. We should really go to bed and get some much-needed sleep."

Stephann said, "I do not think we can sleep, sir; we have not slept for weeks."

Maldwyn went into the other chamber and brought out a thick mattress and some blankets. He put them on the floor and indicated for the children to rest. They did as they were asked and before Maldwyn had a chance to re-enter his bed chamber the two were fast asleep.

Pyewacket and Winston followed Maldwyn into his chamber and Pyewacket said, "Well now you know, and we still can't say anything. So, what do you think?"

He looked at his small charges with fondness. "I think I will be sorry to lose my companions and it will seem empty here without you both. But hopefully unless something dreadful happens, Pyewacket, I will have my apprentice."

She meowed, "Why are you still calling us by the names you gave us? They are good strong names but they are not ours."

He replied, "No they are not but they are secure names and that is what we require, security, so I believe it would be best to call you by those names while you are in this guise."

CHAPTER THREE: THE EMPRESS

↑

The next day Maldwyn let the children sleep even though he knew the urgency of the situation; he felt that these two required sleep more than the urgency of the situation, as it would take time for this Sheela to rally all her troops for an assault on the castle.

They woke up about ten thirty and were quite horrified to find they had slept as long as they did. Stephann thought that it was ridiculous, the Empress needs to have this information as soon as possible; he could not understand why Maldwyn would let them sleep so late.

Maldwyn, as if he knew they were awake, walked into the room carrying a tray with porridge and hot drinks on it. He set this down on a small table at the corner of the room, then looked at the children.

"I would get this breakfast down you, youngers, then we can set off for the castle."

Stephann was a little angry at Maldwyn's apparent indifference to the situation and he asked a little more abruptly than he intended, "Why didn't you wake us up earlier?" He looked at Maldwyn peering at him over his glasses and realised he had overstepped the mark, after all he was a powerful mage.

He continued in a softer manner, "But of course, your honour, will probably have a reason not to have woken us!"

Maldwyn smiled. He liked this boy as he had the makings of a good wizard and it shone through. "You do not have to worry, if I had wanted you up earlier I would have woken you.

"The Empress has always a lot to do in the mornings. There are certain matters of state that can only be attended to at that time, so you see we would have been waiting about anyway. No, it is best to wait until she has finished then we will go."

He could see the two were anxious, so continued, "We will set off as soon as you two are ready and not before, there is plenty of time."

By the time they had had their breakfast and everyone was sorted out it was gone noon. They knew this because Maldwyn had looked out of the window and announced the time. The children thought it remarkable that Maldwyn knew the time by just looking outside but the truth was he had one of the earliest timepieces known to man outside in his garden. Maldwyn had created a shadow clock which was basically a tall tree with stones strategically placed around it to form a sundial.

They wrapped up warm and the five set off on their journey to the castle. As they walked towards the forest, Maldwyn said, "When we get to the castle, younglins, you must try and remember castle etiquettes; please do not speak unless you are spoken to and sit where you are told to sit. It does not matter if you make a mistake or two as the Empress is of kind heart, not like the tales of some of her predecessors, she has a forgiving nature and a sense of humour."

They walked in silence, the children feeling a little nervous, their Bucca confidence and mischief making not yet fully grown in them as they were after all only young.

As they walked up the forest path the children were holding hands, walking just behind Maldwyn, Pyewacket at his heels and Winston on his shoulders; they looked a very strange company indeed but they all looked relaxed with each other as companions do that have full trust between them.

They carried on through the forest until they reached the clearing at the other end, they stopped and looked at the magnificent sight before them. The castle in its pearly white form stood on the small hill with the sun catching every beautiful shape and colour that the structure had to offer.

No wonder Maldwyn was always talking about it with reverence in his voice. The Bucca children were stunned for words; they just stared at the castle in awe of its beauty. But Winston and Pyewacket were not as impressed as the others, coming from the faerie community and as such they were used to living in castles far more beautiful than this. But they could see why the humans and other creatures of the forest thought of it the way they did.

Maldwyn led the way up the path and pulled the rather large metal bell pull that was fastened to the stone wall at the side of the enormous gate.

A guard opened the large gate after peering through a spy hatch to see who it was and he said, "I am sorry, your honour, I did not think you would be coming back today. Is everything all right, sir?"

Maldwyn answered, "I need to see the Empress on urgent business and I mean urgent. Could you please inform Dimone that I am here and wish to speak to him please, Hubert?"

The guard Hubert had the same name as Maldwyn's father and because of the close relationship of both their fathers, Maldwyn's father was named protector for the child at his naming ceremony. Hubert nodded and hurried off to find the Empress's adviser while the guards at the gate 'as was protocol' kept the visitors in the gate room until permission had been given to let them enter.

Hubert came back to escort them into the great entrance hall of the castle where Dimone would meet them, but before Hubert left, Maldwyn said, "I think you had better let Godwin know that we may need him in this meeting too, Hubert."

The guard looked worried: this could only mean serious, serious trouble; he nodded again and went to find Godwin who was the commander of the army.

Dimone walked towards Maldwyn his arms stretched in greeting. "What brings you back again today, old friend, and why so serious?"

"Please, Dimone, we have something urgent to discuss with both you and the Empress and I hope you do not mind but I have also sent for Godwin," said Maldwyn.

Dimone looked at the party one by one. He was a very astute man and knew when something was not right. He said, "Of course, Maldwyn, I will tell the Empress Alyssa of your arrival."

Dimone disappeared once more through the door he had just come out of which was the main reception room for receiving guests. He informed the Empress of the urgency of the situation and he was soon back in the hallway and asked them to follow him.

The Empress had decided that if Maldwyn had come all the way back to the castle the day after his monthly visit, then it must be important and she would see her visitors in her private sitting room.

They were just leaving the hall when Godwin arrived. He came hurrying across to them wanting to know why the commander of the army was required at a meeting with animals and children.

He said in a rather indignant tone, "What is the urgency? I was told it was a matter of national security. I cannot imagine what you mean by that."

Maldwyn looked at his old friend and said, "Godwin, I am very sorry my old friend. I know that anything out of the ordinary that upsets your routine is not something you like to happen. But that is exactly what it is, and I have come to also ask permission to awaken the sleepers. I know that will upset you even more but you must listen to what we have to say before you start getting upset about things."

Godwin looked at him and grunted. He was not happy but he would listen, after all if Maldwyn was involved it was not likely to be a falsehood.

Dimone gasped and said, "Surely not, Maldwyn, surely it is not that serious that it should involve the sleepers?"

He looked sympathetically at his two friends. "If it was not that serious I would not be even contemplating the ceremony, Dimone."

They followed Dimone through an archway that led from the entrance hall and down a long well-lit corridor; the corridor turned at the end to the right and carried on for a further few yards before reaching an ornate door with intricate carvings in the panels.

Stephann and Doras stared at the door as if they had seen something wrong in it but said nothing. Dimone knocked on the door and waited for the Empress to answer. He opened the door and announced the party in his loud official voice as if he were announcing dignitaries from a distant land.

Maldwyn walked in followed by the four companions with Godwin and Dimone bringing up the rear. The two Bucca children were so fascinated with the door that they felt compelled to touch it on their way through, which, did not go unnoticed by Maldwyn.

Alyssa stood up as they walked into the room. She always loved to see her much loved alchemist: he had taught her so much on his visits over the years about the stars, nature and the magykal creatures that lived in the forest.

Alyssa walked towards him. She could never wait until he reached the sitting area. "Maldwyn," she said, holding both

38

her hands out for him to take in the traditional greeting of Sandina.

Maldwyn took her hands and very slightly bowed his head in respect and in accordance with the high status of the Empress.

She looked at his stern face. "What is the matter, dear Maldwyn? Please come and sit with me and we will talk of your troubles.

"Who have you brought with you, Maldwyn? Your pets and some children – this will be an interesting story."

Empress Alyssa looked younger than her years; her girlish stance and looks masking her forty-two years. Alyssa came from a long line of special people that aged slowly, due to one of her great grandfathers many, many years ago being married to a Dryad and of course the gene of longevity past down the female line for over six generations.

Alyssa only looked eighteen at most and usually acted accordingly, thus increasing the speculation that she was much younger; although in matters of state she had a good head on her shoulders.

They sat down and made themselves comfortable with Pyewacket jumping on Maldwyn's knee and Winston on his shoulder, while the Bucca children sat like statues at the side of Maldwyn.

Alyssa indicated for Dimone and Godwin to be seated also. They did as she asked but they were not feeling very comfortable with the idea as they rarely sat in their Empress's presence.

Alyssa organised some drinks of hot chocolate for them all as that was the main drink of Sandina, then she sat back in her comfy chair to listen to their story.

She said, "Now we are settled will you please tell me what this is about, Maldwyn? You would not be here if it was not serious." She tried to sound very official but it was 'as she wanted it to be' an informal meeting.

Maldwyn gave a weak smile. He did not know where to start so he did what Maldwyn often did, he started in a muddle. "These two younglins came to see me last night with such a tale as I have ever heard. They talked of intrigue, anarchy, deceit and cruelty on a scale that has not been heard of since the Empress's great, great Uncle Seth tried his hand at a coup all those years ago.

"Her mother has been kidnapped. Her father has gone in search of her. The younglins' parents have gone missing and her protector has been rendered to a certain extent inert! It is all very upsetting."

Alyssa as well as Dimone and Godwin looked puzzled at the wise man. What was he going on about?

Alyssa said calmly, "Maldwyn, you are a clever shaman but your mind runs way too far in front at times. Please either start at the beginning or let the younglins tell their story to me themselves."

It was decided that Stephann would tell the story again as he was very articulate when relaying the facts of a tale. After he had finished there was silence in the room and all eyes turned to Pyewacket and Winston which made the pair feel very awkward.

Alyssa was very sympathetic to the plight of these magykal creatures, after all they had lost almost everything they held dear, and now they were here to inform her that she may do the same. It was grave news indeed.

She addressed Pyewacket and Winston first. "You poor dears, this is terrible news for us all but especially for you, as you have had to live in this guise for all this time not knowing where your family are and not being able to ask for help."

She then turned to the Bucca children. "And you two also, you have gone through much in your devotion to your parents' friends. We have to do something or this will get out of hand. It is terrible."

"What do you suggest, my mage?"

"Well," said Maldwyn, "I suggest that we make ready for a full siege on the castle and awaken the sleepers to protect it, with your permission, my Empress."

Godwin interrupted, "But that will be too soon. We need to awaken them if and when we are under siege so that they do not get spent too quickly."

"That makes sense. Why do you want to awaken them now at this early stage, Maldwyn?" Alyssa asked.

He answered, "Because, my Empress, I was going to ask your permission to go with these four on a quest to find their parents and gather intel about the hag Sheela. And as for the question of the sleepers being raised too early, that is a false assumption that was put about for the benefit of our enemies.

"The sleepers will live for as long as they are needed. You forget, my friends, that we are talking about etemmu here! Not full living beings, and magyk etemmu at that.

"They can walk, talk, speak and fight and because they were wizards when in full life, they have the powers and understanding they had then; you can hold informed conversations with them but if you touch them they are cold and a dreadful fear will rise in you.

"They are the walking dead and I am very glad they are on our side."

Alyssa looked at him kindly. She knew his concerns for her and the castle were true, and she also knew he would lay down his life to protect the innocent, but she had to think like a leader not a girl and that is precisely what Alyssa did.

She addressed her loyal commander and her advisor. "We must gather all the senior security personnel and the heads of household, and I mean everyone down to head cook. If

41

there is to be trouble, everyone should know about it and I wish them to be at the meeting.

"I will consult with my trusted advisor Dimone and we will set out the plans at the meeting. Now, Godwin, I wish you to try and get everyone there in two hours please. We will use the large war cabinet room as that will be more fitting, and as it has not been used for hundreds of years, it is due for an airing.

"Could you please tell the kitchen staff we are ready for lunch, Dimone, our guests will be joining us today."

She turned to her guests. "I was running late with the castle duties so I have not eaten yet; please join me."

A footman walked towards them as if out of nowhere and asked them to follow him while Alyssa had a conversation with Dimone.

They followed him down a small corridor and approached a large wooden carved door that had depictions of dryads, sprites and other faerie creatures all over the panels. The doors were opened and they stepped inside.

It was a light airy room which had a large picture window that overlooked the lake. On a bright day you could see the horizon very clearly. It had started to snow; it was a light flurry that drifted gently down and kissed the windowpanes as it fell, only to melt on the glass with the heat from the fire in the large fireplace.

The maid came in to serve lunch. The Empress beckoned for them all to be seated. There was not much formality as this was Alyssa's private dining area and it gave her a sense of normality to have their meals in there.

The table was a plain wooden affair made out of oak with intricately carved patterns on both the table and chair backs; the patterns depicted sprites, dryads and faeries dancing in the forest in celebration of something.

Doras put up her hand rather sheepishly. The Empress smiled kindly at her. "Yes, Doras, did you want something?"

Doras swallowed, her mouth dry. She did not know if she should be speaking to the Empress of Sandina or not, let alone asking her a question. She eventually plucked up the courage and asked, "I was just wondering, these chairs and this table, your Empressness, are they faerie made?"

The Empress smiled at the way Doras addressed her. She had never been called your Empressness before. She answered, "Yes they are, how very clever of you to know that. One of my ancestors was a dryad and these were a wedding present from her family."

"Oh," Doras said. "Thank you, your holiness, I just wondered how you came to own such pieces as they are usually only given to faerie kind. But if you are part faerie and that is the reason I am sorry for the intrusion, my Empressness."

Maldwyn looked at Doras in horror, and he was not happy with what Doras had just said.

Alyssa noticed his anxiety and said, "Maldwyn, we are not formal in my chambers, and the youngling was right to question things. You must not dare to chastise her."

Maldwyn bowed his head at his Empress but still he thought that Doras was out of order and she had not listened to what Maldwyn had told her about castle etiquette.

CHAPTER FOUR:
ORIGINS AND TRUTHS

ק

After lunch the children along with Pyewacket and Winston, went to the nursery with the maid who had been put at their disposal. Meanwhile, Maldwyn accompanied the Empress to the meeting of the head people in the castle.

The nursery was once Alyssa's many moons ago, and she had left it pretty much the way it had been when she was a child. She had once commented that no decor would be changed in there until she herself had children; then it would be re-decorated to her style, not the style of the past. So, for now she thought it would do. It was often used by visiting dignitaries' younglins, to keep them from running wild all over the castle.

Pyewacket headed straight for the comfy chair and jumped onto the plumped cushion, pulling it down and padding it to make it a little more comfortable. The only trouble was the cushion was one that Alyssa's grandmother had embroidered with roses and forget-me-nots, and Pyewacket had pulled numerous threads right in the centre.

The cat did not mean to do this and she knew it was wrong, but it was what cats did and she could not help herself. Winston, seeing her distress, flew over to her and whispered in her ear that he would fix it when the maid was not around. The maid saw this gesture and thought the owl was kissing the cat, which caused her to remark 'awe, bless him'. This in turn made the Bucca children giggle: they thought it very funny.

Winston flew onto a large wooden candle holder that was placed at one side of the room. It was an elaborate affair, about seven feet tall and could accommodate five candles, but as these were not lit Winston had thought it a good vantage point to observe his charge. After all he may have been turned into an owl but he was still Sorona's defender and he was Seelie Court.

The Bucca children went over to the toy area to investigate the things that human children played with. There was a table in the centre of this area with four smaller chairs. These chairs were too small for Stephann and Doras but they still sat on them and thought they were wonderful.

The table had numerous games, jigsaws, books and pencils, the like of which they had never seen before. There was also an assortment of jelly, sweets and cakes on a small table to the left side of the larger one. The Bucca children were having an exceptional day and they were going to make the most of their new experiences.

Meanwhile, Alyssa and Maldwyn went to the meeting chamber to join the others and get the meeting started. The prospect of informing the people living and working in the castle that they may be invaded or even killed at any time was a daunting thought, but that seemed to be the dark cloud that now hung over the castle.

Dimone opened the meeting and Maldwyn (his nerves of public speaking gone) told the gathering of the impending trouble. Godwin and Keatin both kept interrupting Maldwyn with questions about their particular area of expertise, so the information that Maldwyn was trying to pass on took rather longer than expected.

Keatin said, "If we are to believe what these children have told us about this hag, and the fact that she has kidnapped some, well what sounds like highly influential people. Then where are the two that escaped? This Sorona and this Seelie Court faerie, where are they? And what are they doing to help get her parents back? It seems to me that they have run off and left it all to these poor Buccas that are ill equipped to deal with the situation."

Alyssa interrupted Keatin. "My dear lord Keatin, please do not be harsh with your words. The two you speak about are hidden and while in the guises they are in have done much to help with the intel we may need. But for security reasons we cannot say where they are or what guise they represent."

Desmy spoke, "If we knew where they were, my Empress, we could help to protect them."

"No," Alyssa said in a firm voice. "It is better this way for all concerned."

Keatin apologised and informed the Empress, "Well if it comes to an assault, Empress, my aeronauts are ready. They are accomplished flyers and we have been practising with an Ariel projectile weapon that we can release over the heads of our enemies.

"The eagle core are also doing well and are nearly ready for some action. We use the lighter of our men on their backs and it does appear to be working."

"What is this?" Alyssa said.

Maldwyn answered Alyssa, "It was just a thought that my Lord Keatin and I had a few months ago about the eagles that live on Morby Mountain. They have, of late, been having a tough time due to the harsh winter and the lack of small mammals. Their number was dwindling and more than half have died. Neither we, nor they, can explain the lack of small mammals but there has definitely been a decline in them.

"The solution, or should I say one of them was to ask them if they wanted to live on Sorby hill, which as you know is as high as a small mountain. Basically, we were offering them a

46

place to live and a good supply of food with some extras thrown in. All they had to do was work for us as flyers and carry a man on their backs. They were very willing to do this, as eagles, especially the giant talking variety, they get so bored just sat about.

"I went into the forest to talk to the gnome king who lives under Sorby hill, after all we could not just re-locate the eagles there as the hill is part of the gnome's kingdom. The gnomes were miserable because of the litter that the humans left there, and one man was actually going to build a house on the hill. They were more than happy to accommodate the eagles; the eagles do have the power of speech but as you know it is limited due to their anatomy; but, they can communicate in other ways and they are very much aware of situations and what is being said to them.

"The gnomes have even built a number of eyries for the eagles and a rubbish pen for all their waste products. The gnomes use this and recycle it in their subterranean gardens. It is truly a symbiotic relationship.

"Anyway, my Empress, it appears to be working and the eagles may prove to be a great asset in any forthcoming battles."

Alyssa smiled at the way Maldwyn had gone into great detail about the project and said, "I am very pleased that an amicable arrangement was reached, Maldwyn, and I am sure that Lord Keatin and his men will work well with the eagles to help seek an end to this problem.

"Now, what are we going to do about this Frau Berchta? And more to the point how are we going to do it? She needs stopping and from the sound of it she will not give up that easily. Therefore, we need to set plans in motion before she sets them in motion against us."

Dimone who had been listening to the opinions of everyone said, "I agree with Alyssa, we should start making plans right away before there is any danger to the castle. We must be ready!"

There were more than a few gasps around the room at hearing Dimone call the Empress, Alyssa; it was not heard of for a servant to do such a thing. They all knew that Dimone and the Empress were close but this went way beyond his brief.

Alyssa laughed at the reaction. She thought it very funny that her lifelong friend could not call her by her Christian name, (as he often did in private). She thought she should give them an explanation and shock them even more.

She said, "Well the cat is out of the bag now! My consort Dimone and I are to be married tonight when the moon is at its highest as is the tradition of my ancestors 'the dryads'.

"As most of you know we have been close friends from childhood and were betrothed by the time we were eight years old. The extra special thing about this arrangement is that we have loved each other for as long as we can remember; but we decided to wait until I had grown out of my girlish ways a little more and had started to grow up. But time has run out and we have to get married tonight so that we can prepare for war.

"The ceremony goes back thousands of years and is always at high moon. It does not have to be a full moon but it does have to be high. So it was with my forebears; Suki, a dryad and Carlton a human, they had to be married as tradition dictates so that Suki's power could grow."

Desmy looked puzzled as did most of the congregation. He said, "If I may be so bold, my Empress, what do you mean by you have to get married for your powers?"

Alyssa laughed and replied, "As I have already stated, we have both known for some time that we would eventually get married, but for the sake of our people and the unity of the bond, we had to be strong and deny each other the love that we felt. For the wedding day or should I say the wedding night is the time when a female dryad comes into her own and her powers are at their greatest for one full year.

"Yes ,I will keep my powers but they will not be as strong as they will be for the first year of wedlock. So, you see, my Lord Desmy, if this threat is true and there are certain dangers that must be overcome then the time is right for me to accept my responsibility and leave my girlish ways behind me, for the sake of our people.

"In a way I am not unlike the sleepers except that I hopefully will live on after all this, but they will not."

Dimone spoke for the first time. "What some of you do not know is that I was not the son of a simple household servant. Yes, my mother worked at the castle as a nanny to the Empress, but my father..." Dimone smiled at what he was about to say. "My father was and is the Tuatha De Danaan; he is the keeper of the magykal cauldron and the sword of light. He is still very much alive. Even though my dear mother is past there is not a day when he does not go to her grave and speak to her, such was their love for each other.

"My father lives many miles from here in a very secret and magykal location as there are always dangers when you are the keeper of such highly prized relics. The main thing you all need to know is that I, being a male, have inherited a good number of my father's attributes and powers so I too can help Alyssa in the fight for our continued freedom."

Maldwyn spoke, "I always said that you were special, my friend, but I could never quite reach inside you and find out what it was. Were you purposely blocking me out, Dimone?"

Dimone laughed. "Of course I was, Maldwyn; even you could not know who I really was until it was necessary, but Alyssa knew, she knew from the beginning when we were children."

There was a silence in the room as the company digested the implications of all the information they had just been given. Once more the castle and its residents were throwing up new revelations that no one knew about. How many more surprises were there going to be?

The meeting went on for a further two hours; they discussed everything from battle strategies to stocking the pantries up with food and water. But it was decided that the in-depth planning would be better achieved within small groups and by the heads of the departments that those groups dealt with on a daily basis.

One of the commanders laughed at the thought of the head cook or the head of household planning strategies but this was met with a sharp rebuke from Alyssa.

She said, "May I say before this gets out of hand and we get into a high status in fighting battle, that none of you are better than anyone else. If you think that then just see how you would manage without each other, and every head of every department must plan strategies on a daily basis, albeit not military strategies.

"We need the armed forces and the armed forces need to be fed, and clothes need to be washed and the castle needs to be cleaned and the gardeners need to provide fresh food and the sewage workers need to clean the drains. Do you want me to go on? In other words, we are all here as a team to provide a service for each other. No one is better or worse or above reproach. We have gone through this before, my Lord Godwin. Please do not ask us to go through it again or I may get very cross indeed.

"Now, that's over, Scoot, you will look after the provisions and start stocking up with fillers and essentials, Dimone will give you a list of the spare rooms near the kitchen area that you can use for storing food; we are not sure yet how many of our subjects we are going to have to take in.

"Taryn, you will liaise with Dimone and arrange as much accommodation as you can for the people if they have to seek refuge within the castle walls.

"Sophia, you are now the head of the maids and I will require you to make sure they know what their objectives are, such as getting the bed linen and towels in order and creating new rotas of work. You know better than I what is required. As do all of you, so let's get on and do it, shall we?

"If you think of anything else either speak to Maldwyn or to Dimone they are both here to help. Oh, and Sophia, the next in line after you is Taryn so please keep her up to date with what you are doing as she is after all the housekeeper.

"Taryn, there is no disrespect to you but you have a lot to do without concerning yourself with housemaid work so that is why Sophia will be your right hand on this occasion."

Taryn and Sophia both nodded and understood the reasons for collaboration, which was more than Godwin did.

Alyssa continued, "Lord Godwin, you will need to ready your army and get some of the, what should I say, the more portly of your men into shape."

Alyssa grinned, and still smiling suggested that Godwin himself could do with a few laps around the castle.

She composed herself and continued, "Lord Desmy, you will ready the ships and liaise with the mermen and the creatures of the lake so that they can ready themselves to protect their homes if need be.

"My Lord Keatin, your men's training programme needs to be brought forward and the eagle squadron brought up to their full potential."

They all bowed their heads in respect to their Empress but before they had left the room, Dimone suggested that they really needed to inform the wizards on the outer reaches of the kingdom about the situation as soon as possible. They would need to get ready for the oncoming battle; if there was to be one, and also ready the people for evacuation if it was required.

He said, "It would possibly be a good training exercise for your eagle squadron."

Alyssa asked, "Would that be conducive to you, my Lord Keatin."

"Yes, it would, Empress; I will attend to it right away." Keatin answered.

Maldwyn asked, "And the sleepers, My Empress?"

She replied, "We will perform the raising ceremony in the morning, Maldwyn. That is when I will be at my most powerful."

She said this with a slight blush to her cheeks as her thoughts drifted to the wedding night.

The war cabinet finally broke up and everyone went their separate ways to make plans and inform the rest of the castle about the impending threat. But not before Maldwyn had for the umpteenth time told them to be vigilant and watch for odd behaviour and spies.

Dimone went with Taryn to help her and Sophia explain to the household staff and also observe for any odd behaviour that could mean a spy was in the castle.

Alyssa walked with Maldwyn to the nursery, talking as they went, mainly about the upcoming wedding.

Maldwyn thought hard about the wedding. He said, "Due to the wedding being the auspicious occasion that it is, I will need my best robes, my Empress; I will take my leave and go back to my house for—"

Alyssa cut his sentence short and touched his hand. She said, "My dear mage, there will be no need for you to journey back to your abode. Tradition dictates that the same robes should be worn whenever possible for all the Royal weddings.

"Can you guess, Maldwyn, who the robes belonged to?"

Maldwyn looked at Alyssa puzzled, then he gasped and replied, "Not the great mage himself, not Myrddin? But they are a myth! A legend! Surely not!

"Why did I not know about them? Oh dear, I am sorry, Empress, I am asking far too many questions. You are the head of the human state and I am as always your servant."

She smiled and replied, "They are very special robes as you know, Maldwyn, but when you put them on, I would like you, at some time in the future, to tell me what you felt as you put them on. They are very beautiful and also enchanted, not everyone is able to wear them, Maldwyn, but I believe you should have no trouble."

Maldwyn asked, "Where are they now, Empress, in one of the tower rooms?"

She looked at him gravely. "No. That would be the first place a thief would look and so would the dungeons. But a room linked to the head of states chambers; they would probably not think to look there.

"And anyway, the room is enchanted, not just anyone can enter but that is another thing you will be aware of when you enter the room."

"Can I ask another question, my Empress?" Maldwyn asked.

She smiled at Maldwyn's formality. "Of course, you can, my mage, what is it?"

He looked at her thoughtfully. "Is it true that Merlin or Myrddin is in the high tower with the sleepers?"

"In truth, I do not know the answer to that, Maldwyn. I have never been given that information. If he is, then I would have thought I would have been told before I was handed the reins of my office. But I was privy in part to some information and soon I hope I will know the rest."

CHAPTER FIVE: OLD HISTORY

ק

They had reached the door to the nursery, but as Maldwyn put his hand on the door handle Alyssa stopped him.

"You know, Maldwyn, those four companions of yours are very special, and they will, if they survive to the end of this, be key players in this war, as will you.

"But they will need to know the truth about where we humans came from, and why we came here."

Alyssa looked seriously at Maldwyn. "I know that you disapprove of me telling them anything about the old history, my mage, but believe me they do need to know this information, and they need to know that they are not only fighting for this world but for the world of our ancestors: the world of man."

Maldwyn did not look pleased, and he was just about to argue his point when she said, "Shush, my mage, and think on what the consequences would be if they did not know all they were fighting for. No, dear friend, they need to know."

He put his hand back on the door handle but before he opened it he asked, "Are you sure, Empress? Do they really need to know the old history? After all there are only two people, well two humans anyway, that are privy to that information. And that is you and I!"

Alyssa nodded her head to say yes, and that was enough. Maldwyn opened the door. He found his young charges inside very relaxed with their new surroundings. The two children were playing games at the table, games that they had never seen before, and Pyewacket and Winston were just pretending to be an animal and a bird. This was because the maid was still in the room.

Alyssa addressed the maid. "I do not require anything at the moment, Susie. Please go and get some food for yourself. Then I would like you to help the others with the wedding preparations."

Susie replied, "Yes, Empress. But if I can be so bold as to ask, who is getting married?"

"Oh I am sorry, Sophia, you do not know," Alyssa replied. "I am going to marry Dimone at the high moon tonight."

Susie curtseyed again and left the room giggling whilst Maldwyn's companions stared after her.

Maldwyn looked at them. "It is a long story and it will have to wait as the Empress has something more pressing to tell you."

Alyssa sat opposite the two Bucca children at the table and Maldwyn sat at the side of her, which was quite unimaginable under any other circumstances, and Maldwyn was not very comfortable with it.

Alyssa started: "There is something that the four of you, more than anyone else, need to know; and that is the origins of the humans in this world. None of you are humans and you may think it does not concern you but alas it does; it concerns everyone in Sandina but they do not realise it and I hope they never will."

Now that they were alone, Winston spoke, "But Maldwyn is human and yes you are half human, Empress, therefore it does concern us as you are our friends and speaking as a Seelie Court we look after our friends, Empress." Alyssa smiled at the small owl that was speaking to her in such an eloquent fashion.

She replied, "What I am going to tell you stays in your ears only and is not to be repeated unless, like in this case it is required. Thousands of years ago there was a great mage, a wizard of such powers who could visit almost any land he chose to in an instant.

"He was also a great alchemist and for a time assisted the inventor of an item called The Philosopher's Stone. That stone was said to be like a large ruby but it had magyk in it and its powers became legendary in more than one world."

Pyewacket interrupted, "Meow, more than one world, Empress? I do not understand, meow."

Alyssa answered, "I will get to that later Sorona, but first is the history." With Pyewacket really being a princess in her own right Alyssa thought it more polite to use her real name.

Pyewacket gave another furtive meow and settled down to listen.

Alyssa continued, "The stone could turn metal into gold and when used with water and a certain spell, could produce the elixir of life. This, it was said, was how Myrddin as well as his friend managed to live for thousands of years. The noted Myrddin was born into the world of man, of humans. He started off as an apprentice to a wizard, but it was a short-lived apprenticeship, after he had an accident whilst making a strong potion to encourage intellect, to help him get through his tests with the wizard.

"He took the full brunt of the potion's explosive properties and was unconscious for over two weeks. When he came around there was no one to rival him in intellect, negotiations, magyk or planning.

"Myrddin changed his name in his own land and became a legendary mage. He called himself Merlin and after a rough start using his skills in a less than appropriate way he started to work to help people, but not all people just the innocent men that he came into contact with.

"He fought in many battles and helped millions of people over many millennia, but eventually as he was nearing the middle age of his life, there was an evil that even Myrddin could not vanquish; an evil so bad that it was relentless and led to a war that involved every land in his human world.

"Myrddin could not help all of the people that were being slaughtered and persecuted at the hands of this evil, and believe me they were in their millions. This tyrant did his research well, he sent his men to the far corners of the world to find anything with strong dark magyk within its makeup, and he used what he found to wreak more havoc in the world and conquer more people.

"There was a particular race that he took great exception to and he set out to systematically annihilate them. Myrddin was appalled by this and saved many from the camps that were built to house them, but it was not enough and when he heard that there was to be an increase in the extermination of the people he decided that something had to be done. So, he set out to find a way to bring some into the world of Nirvana."

Pyewacket meowed and yawned a long drawn out yawn, then she said, as if it was matter of fact, "I thought humans had always been here. I did not realise they were brought into Sandina by a wizard, but I did wonder." She stopped as if in thought and stared at the floor.

Maldwyn was quick to say, "Not just any wizard, Pyewacket, but Myrddin, the great wizard from whom all wizards have found their trade."

Alyssa needed to get on with her story and did not need any more interruptions, after all she was getting married that night and time was of the essence.

Alyssa interjected, "Well back to the story. Myrddin could get into this world himself with no problem and could even bring inanimate objects through the portals, but to bring thousands upon thousands of people through was a monumental task.

"Many years before this he had experimented with bringing some humans through the portal that were in fear of their lives; this was done to save their lineage.

"He brought just a few with him, well four to be exact, they were my ancestors. They had been brought through the portal from a very cold country that had gone through a revolutionary upheaval.

"They were cousins of the royal family who unfortunately had been slaughtered, except one and she was said to have had true royal blood. Her name was Anastasia and she was the mother of all the humans' royal line in the faerie world.

"Realising that he had done this once with a small group he thought he would try it again with a larger one. As I said before, there was a cruel dictator and he built the camps to exterminate people like you would exterminate a plague of rats. The crises were getting worse and Myrddin knew that if he was to bring thousands of people into the Nirvana he would not only need help, but also permission to do this as it was not his world, so he went into the forest for a meeting with all the magykal creatures.

"The great council in the forest, after much negotiation said yes but there were embargoes; but I will talk about these later.

"After everything was agreed some of the faeries and dryads came to the castle, which at that time was a much smaller affair. They came to talk to the human royal family and came to some agreement as to how this was going to work.

"By this time Anastasia had married her cousin and they had a son. It was not an easy thing for anyone here to contemplate. Taking in thousands of refugees when there is no infrastructure at all in place is problematic at the best of times; but here there were no houses, no factories, no schools or shops, as this was not the way magykal folk lived.

There were just the trade markets that were deep in the forest and even the royal family never went there."

Doras asked in her very simplistic girlish way, "Where were they going to live, your holiness? And what were they to eat?"

Alyssa smiled. She liked the Bucca children and she knew she would miss them, especially Doras when they left. While the boy seemed to understand almost straight away what the content of a conversation was, Doras needed to know more and she asked questions about the things that others would not have even thought about.

Alyssa continued, "The council wanted to keep these humans in order as they had a reputation for aggression and fighting, and this was where the embargo came in. There were many things to consider, many different races of people, different colours of skin, with different cultures and beliefs. The council did..."

Doras put her hand up yet again. Alyssa stopped mid-sentence and smiled. "You have a question, Doras!"

Doras looked sheepish, she knew that Maldwyn was displeased with her interrupting but the urge for clarification was great in Doras. "If it pleases, your Empressness, I do not understand about the different cultures and colours. Do they paint their faces and bodies like the trolls of Morby Mountain? I heard they are painted a horrible green."

This time Alyssa could not contain her laughter. She did not mean to be unkind but it was a delight to hear the questions this younglin asked. "Oh, Doras, you are a delight and I hope that we will see you again in the castle after all this is over.

"Now, how to answer your question let me think? The belief thing, well you believe that the sun and moon and earth and water and fire are special as they give you life and help maintain that life, in other words you believe in nature and all that it encompasses.

"Well these people believe in a similar thing to you but they believe that a deity, a powerful being made all of nature, and they worship that being. But to complicate things, dear Doras, they do not all believe in the same powerful being, and that alas is what causes a lot of wars in the land of men.

"Now the coloured part is more complicated but still has a lot to do with nature. People born in the very hot countries where the sun beats down relentlessly usually have a very dark brown skin. And the people born in the colder areas usually have a very white skin. And everyone in between that has variant shades of skin colour but this can also depend on diet.

"This also causes trouble because some men of certain colours think they are better than others and this also leads to wars. As I was saying the council decided on an embargo or a simpler way of putting it is restrictions. I will now let Maldwyn take over and tell you about these as he understands them a lot better than I do, and I need a hot drink. All this talking has made me dry."

Alyssa poured herself a cup of chocolate from the large pot that was on the table and sat back to listen to Maldwyn.

Maldwyn studied his charges, then said, "Although I am greatly known for my patience I really do not want to be interrupted if it can be at all avoided please, we do need to get on.

"What you need to understand is that humans are not only an angry, violent race, they are also bigoted and jealous, so the prejudice and violence that this tyrant doled out to people that he considered not to be like him, was relentless and fuelled others prejudices too."

Stephann said, "We have all kinds of different creatures here and some are considered evil like this Frau Berchta but we would never kill them because of any difference of opinion that they may have. They have to be planning or have done something really bad for any law to be used against them.

"Even the trolls of Morby do not get persecuted."

Maldwyn looked seriously at Stephann. "I know it is hard for you to understand but this man took a large continent and turned it upon itself in a very short time. Neighbours turned on each other, relatives would report people in their own family if they thought they were not pure bred or were plotting against the state. They were dark times indeed and not for the first time in man's history, the will of one man was being pampered to by the multitude.

"The council said that Myrddin could bring the people through but they had to have a certain clearing of the mind, not a full clearing but the bigoted religious, colour and creed memories, so that no one would start calling names and fighting in this world.

"The other thing that Myrddin asked for was permission for the humans to bring some of their technology into this land, but the elders on the council were against it.

"They decided to let them bring in things like building materials and the means to produce them, textiles, food production, and all the things that you would need to keep thousands of people in relative comfort and in gainful employment. They had to be self-sufficient and it was imperative that they think they had lived here all of their lives.

"The magykal creatures of the forest built the villages and factories, planted crops and tried their hardest to keep families together in one village. This was all carried out in one week by magyk and they did not rest until it was done.

"Then came the hard bit: the humans came through about two hundred at a time and were asked to sit in the community hall of the nearest village, which was Satina as this was ground zero. Once they were there they were put into a deep sleep with a hot drink laced with certain herbs, then their memory was cleansed. But as I said not all of their memories; they kept their personalities but not the aggressive warring part, that was erased forever.

"They were taken to their relevant villages, and there were six villages in all. They were given a choice of house after being told their own homes had been burned down in a terrible fire. They were allowed to pick their own furnishings also as Myrddin had helped to replicate the type of furniture they were used to.

"Most of the people he brought here had skills and those that did not learned them very quickly. It was not long before there was a thriving industry in each village which led to trade and more industry and towns sprang up. But the council are always watchful and they will not tolerate too much technology after all this is faerie land and nothing should spoil that. It is the human's sanctuary not the magykal creatures'. This is their home and they will dictate the rules.

"They were allowed to also marry who they wanted with no regard to colour or religion because they did not realise that there was any past discrimination. That is why we now have no dark skin, no light skin just a nice mix of in between because once you take away all prejudice people will live harmoniously.

"Their churches were once for religious worship but are now for singing and giving thanks for our lives and good living. A meeting place, and although we say we are getting married no one can remember the ceremonies concerned with that, so our marriages are blessings but they are for life as in the olden days.

"The thing is, if there really is an all-powerful being that created everything he would probably be pleased at the way the humans in this realm conduct themselves."

Maldwyn took a drink from his cup and grimaced. The cocoa was cold and he obviously did not like it.

Alyssa said, "If you would be so kind as to finish here, my mage, I will go and get ready for my wedding and I will ask for a hot pot of cocoa to be brought to you."

Just at that moment, on cue, Dimone appeared at the door. He had come to escort his future bride to her chamber for her dress fitting where her maid was waiting for her.

Alyssa took Dimone's arm, smiled and walked gracefully out of the room.

After she had left, Stephann asked Maldwyn, "Why have we been given this information, your honour? Of what relevance is it to us exactly?"

Maldwyn looked grave. "This hag cannot be allowed to find out about the existence of other worlds, it does not bear thinking about, and she could destroy them all with her evil."

It was Winston's turn to look astounded. (And if an owl could ever look astounded then Winston just did.) He said, "Do you mean there are other worlds besides these two and how many?"

Maldwyn looked at his little friend and wondered if he had said too much but the Empress was right they did need to know. "Yes, there are many worlds; or at least that is what Myrddin hypothesized. Well from what we know it was not him but a scientist friend of his called Schrödinger. Our world and the world of man are but two worlds of many, although I do believe from Myrdden's writings that his friend's work was about parallel worlds not different ones."

Doras put her hand up and asked, "Please, your goodness, what is a palllallel? And what happened to the wicked man? Does he now rule the land of humans? "

Maldwyn could see the concern in Doras and said kindly, "Oh bless you, a parallel universe is a place where other worlds exist in conjunction with ours. For instance, according to this theory we all exist in these other worlds but some people call them multiverses. It means that another person could live in all these worlds that are named Maldwyn and look exactly like me, but their paths may have gone down a totally different road to the one I have taken.

"And the bad man! He does not rule the world of man. He was defeated but not before he killed thousands upon thousands of people. He would have killed more if Myrddin had not saved thousands more.

"They said he killed himself but some people said he was too much of a coward and he faked it and lived to a ripe old age, but it's of no consequence any more. Time is so different there. It has been over a thousand years since man came to Nirvana but in the human world it has been less than a hundred years. I do believe that by now the man will be dead."

Pyewacket said, "Meow, I always wondered where all the noisy industry came from and those odd flying machines, because there was no mention of these in our magykal history until just over a thousand years ago. It does answer a lot of questions, meow, but I do agree we now know how important it is to keep this old hag away from these secrets. Purr."

Pyewacket had snuggled down on the cushion again and was throwing one paw down then the other, in turn padding and pulling at the embroidery. She looked worried (if a cat can look worried), she knew she should not be doing this but it was now her nature.

Maldwyn, feeling sorry for the cat, waved his hand with the second and fourth fingers extended and muttered a spell; immediately the cushion repaired itself and the cat looked less stressed and the padding stopped. Maldwyn knew that it was a little-known fact that cats usually pad for comfort when they are worried or stressed more than when they are happy. The more Pyewacket padded, the more mess she made and therefore the more she padded.

Pyewacket immediately jumped down and started rubbing her fur along Maldwyn's robes, which depicted how grateful she was and how fond she was of Maldwyn.

Maldwyn bent down and stroked the cat, then the pleasure purring came from her throat, she was very happy at this moment in time.

Maldwyn said, "Well I must take my leave, my friends, and put my robes on. I suppose Dimone has it all in hand."

Maldwyn walked over to the door to find Dimone just walking in with a pot of hot cocoa. Maldwyn took the pot and put it on the table and said, "Help yourselves to the cocoa and wait here for someone to come and get you, I will not be far."

As Maldwyn turned to the door once more, Dimone announced, "I think Susie is coming to take you to your chamber, you will not be forgotten."

CHAPTER SIX:
THE WEDDINGS AND THE
COMMANDING TRUTH

ᚼ

After Maldwyn had left the room the children and their companions talked about the information they had just been given. It was a shock to them all to know that other worlds existed and you could get to them just by walking through a portal as if you were going to the other side of the wood, which sometimes happens with advanced magykal creatures.

They were not alone for long before there was a knock at the door and the maid came in, and said, "I thought I heard more voices as I approached the door! I could have sworn you had someone in here with you."

She looked around then laughed. "Unless the cat and the bird can talk, which is highly unlikely." She laughed again and continued in a condescending way, "Well if you are ready I will take you to your room, children. You have a nice room overlooking the lake, and the Empress has had some lovely clothes put out for you, and a nice new collar for your cat. The thing I do not understand is the small charm for the owl. What is he going to do with that?"

Stephann replied hastily, "Oh you know what it is; he belongs to a wizard, so he does not act like an owl. He sometimes thinks he is a maglethief – he loves shiny things."

"Oh that is so cute," she said, stroking Winston under the chin. He wanted to peck her as he felt insulted but he knew it came from a genuine caring nature, and she did not know what a high-ranking Seelie Court he was.

The maid gathered up the pot of cocoa and the cups, then said, "Well, follow me and we will get you ready for the wedding breakfast."

Doras said excitedly, "Ooh, are we going to stay up all night. That's exciting! Although I have done that a lot recently without my mother to send me to bed." A tear came to her eyes, then she remembered that it was all a big secret and she must not talk about it.

The maid looked concerned, then asked, "Why? Where is your mother?"

Stephann once again jumped in and said, "We came to stay with the mage as he is a good friend of our father's, and it was thought we would learn something from our visit."

The maid felt for Doras as she was young to be parted from her parents. She tried cheering her up by saying, "The wedding breakfast, my dear, it is just a meal that is given to guests after the wedding. It's just a name because it is the first meal after the start of their new life.

"It's nothing but a grand feast that's all, it will be held tonight after the wedding."

"Oh," said Doras, feeling a little foolish. She had never been to a wedding before and was not sure what happened or what to do.

After they had gone to their bed chamber and the maid had left, Pyewacket jumped on the bed and walked over to Doras who was sat on the bed looking unhappy.

Pyewacket also felt sorry for her and rubbed her fur against Doras, then allowed her to stroke her back. Pyewacket actually found this very pleasurable and could not help purring. She said, "Meow, it is a good thing to ask questions if you do not know something, Doras. That is the way we learn and you are still very young, there is a lot you do not know and a lot of questions that you will need answered. Please do not ever feel bad at asking questions.

These few words from Pyewacket put Doras at ease, and she thanked her for explaining, but she still felt silly.

There were two extremely large beds in the chamber and they looked very comfortable. It was not long before all four were curled up on one of the beds fast asleep. It had been a long day and they needed rest if they were going to the party, as Doras called it, after the wedding.

They had not noticed another door leading to a room that had several choices of clothes for Doras and Stephann, plus the collar and charm that the maid had talked about. They were so tired that looking at new clothes was the last thing they had on their minds at this time.

The next few hours were full of hustle and bustle around the castle. Servants were rushing about in every direction making preparations for this very hurried wedding and always carrying something from here to there.

Maldwyn on the other hand was having a small adventure of his own; Dimone had taken him to the secret vault which was built by the first wizard of the castle.

Dimone took Maldwyn first of all into Alyssa's mother's old bed chamber, then from there down a secret passage all the way to the vault. It was deeper under the castle than any of the other vaults; it took a good five minutes for Dimone to get into the lock as there were multiple locks and multiple combinations.

Maldwyn asked, "I do not understand why I was not told about this vault? Did my father know about it? I really must protest that this was kept from me; why Dimone, why was myself and my father, who was the castle wizard, not told of this? Could we not be trusted?"

They entered the vault and walked towards a large chest.

Dimone felt sorry for his old friend and said, "In answer to your questions, my dear friend, you were not told because it was never necessary. And in answer to your other question, no your father did not know. He knew there was a vault but not where it was. The last one is more life defining, why you and the castle wizard were not told. Because Hubert, who you called father, was not your father, Maldwyn."

Maldwyn stared in horror. What was Dimone saying to him? Hubert was not his father; how could that be?

Dimone asked, "Are you all right, Maldwyn? I know it is a big shock and this was not how I wished to tell you but you were asking too many questions and I find that the truth is normally the best answer.

"Come sit." Dimone pointed to four smaller chests in the corner of the vault.

Maldwyn followed Dimone in silence and sat down on one of the chests. He asked, "How can that be? Hubert was my father, my mother died when I was born and he brought me up on his own; but thinking about it now it was strange that he never talked about her, and no one in the castle can remember her. Is this a nightmare I am having, Dimone? Is this vault enchanted and causing you to say these things?"

Dimone felt really sorry for the mage. He wished that there could have been a better way of breaking it to him but there was not. "Maldwyn. You have got to understand that Hubert was the best father you could have had, and you do not need me to tell you that.

"Your mother did die just after your birth but not before one of her most loyal companions had rescued you."

Maldwyn looked up. "Rescued me? Who from and why? What are you saying? Who am I?"

Dimone sat at the side of Maldwyn. He said, "I can only tell you what I know; and before you ask I was told by my father and sworn to secrecy. As the son of Tuatha De Danaan I was privy to a lot of information about a lot of people and all that information is still and always will be with me.

"Not even Alyssa is privy to most of it but she does know about you as Hubert, your adopted father, needed help and confided in her parents.

"Your mother was of the faerie people and your father was Merlin who you know as Myrddin. That is why you are good at your craft; did you not ever wonder why you were more advanced than your father, did you not think it was strange?"

Maldwyn stared at the floor as he took in the enormity of his lineage. Was he really half magykal creature and half human, but not just any human. Was Myrddin the greatest wizard that ever lived, the metaphorical father of all wizards, was he his real father?

Dimone continued, "The story is that Myrddin as defender of the poor and downtrodden made some influential enemies while he was in the world of man. He was arranging the rescue of a group of humans when his wife gave birth to their son a good month early. It was you Maldwyn!

"Myrdden's enemies came looking for him but as Myrddin was not there they decided to leave him a message. So they killed his wife, your mother."

Maldwyn said, "But why, why would they do such a thing and why was I not killed, after all leaving a son alive is dangerous as revenge can be sought in later years. And it will be if you tell me who did it, Dimone, I swear, please, Dimone."

Maldwyn was feeling anger well up inside him that he did not know he had. It was the type of anger that his adopted father Hubert had always tried to quell in Maldwyn, the kind of anger that bad wizards let in to eat them up with grief and darkness, the kind that Maldwyn did not really want.

Dimone was again sorry that he had to let Maldwyn know this but he had good reason, and it was not just the vault. "I know this is painful, old friend, but you must listen. I told you that your mother's friend and companion took you to hide you for safety. Your mother was faerie and she knew she was dying; it is a risk they take when they fall in love with a human. What very often happens to a faerie when she gives birth to a half human child is that she will forfeit her own life. But she also knew that there were people on their way to kill her.

"These people would have no hesitation in killing her new born and your protection was paramount in her decision.

"When Myrddin got back he was mortified to find his love had been murdered; but as I said, Maldwyn, she would have died anyway so she had nothing to lose personally but she would not let them harm you. That was not an option, because while you lived a part of her could go on living.

"Your mother's companion had fled into the woods where an old hermit lived. He was a friend of your mother's and he hid you until he could return you to your father.

"Myrddin buried his wife back in the land of the Nirvana, in a traditional grave with the whole family and magykal creatures watching on.

"He brought you, the hermit and your mother's companion back with him so that protection could be given, but Myrddin was a man in pain, a man who could not rest. He was a man in love with a dead wife and blaming himself for not protecting her.

"He visited the scryer and looked into the future. He saw that the castle during this timescale had a very talented mage that was kind and gentle. This mage, your step father Hubert, was a widower. His wife had died some years before and to their great regret they were childless. It was suggested by the elders of the council that you be deposited with the said Hubert and brought up as his son to ensure your survival."

Maldwyn interjected, "You make me sound like a lump of gold being deposited with the banking gnomes of Sandal."

Dimone laughed. "Sorry, my friend, but you still do not understand it, do you? You are Merlin's son and you are more precious than any gold bar; I feel you are one of the main players in this story and I, no we, need you to focus.

"The other thing you do not understand is that your mother died hundreds of years ago and so did your father."

"But how can that be, how?" Maldwyn said.

Dimone explained, "The elders did a scrying session as I have told you, to look into the future to see where the baby would be better placed and protected, as no one was ever to know that you were the son of Merlin until the time was right. Using their combined powers, the council elders and Merlin turned a portal to the future and brought you here to the best father that you could ever have had.

"Now should we open the chest and get you ready before I miss my own wedding!"

Maldwyn gave a weak smile. "Of course, my old friend, you have been both courteous and kind with the news and it is not so bad. I had a good father, as father he was. Hubert was the best father any wizard boy could wish to have, and if I grumbled about my upbringing it would insult a good man.

"Now where are these famous robes you have brought me to see. I have a blessing to officiate at."

Dimone tried to open the chest but it rejected his advance. He gestured for Maldwyn to try, and immediately the chest opened with such gusto they both jumped back. They looked at each other and burst into laughter; it had been a shock but one of those shocks that would first surprise you, then when you find out there is no danger the relief causes laughter.

After they had settled down, Maldwyn reached in and removed the most handsome robes he had ever laid eyes on; these too, as with a lot of things in the castle, were obviously faerie made.

As Maldwyn picked up the robes, he felt a pulse resonating from it. He felt the residual power surge through the robes and into his body.

Maldwyn held the robes at arm's length to admire them. He said, "I do not feel worthy to wear these robes, Dimone. I am not anywhere near the level that Myrddin was."

Dimone smiled. "You must be worthy, my dear Maldwyn, otherwise the chest would have remained locked; and are you not forgetting something? You are the true son of the great mage himself!"

Maldwyn let himself smile a little at this thought, then said, "I will go and get changed into the robes, Dimone." He carefully folded the robes, but as he did so he felt something hard in the pocket of the lining. He fumbled about to find the pocket and pulled out a magnificent ring.

The ring, that was obviously magyk, was heavy and pure gold but yet was light for whoever wore it. It had an intricate pattern around the sides but the top was plain; it was just a flat piece of gold and it looked very odd as if something should be seated on it.

Maldwyn showed the ring to Dimone who said, "It was obviously your true father's; therefore, you must put it on, Maldwyn."

He did this very thing and another surge of magyk, much greater than the one he had already experienced, shot through his whole being. Maldwyn felt energised, he felt youthful. He smiled and followed Dimone to his chamber to change for the wedding.

The chamber was next to his small companions' bed chamber and he wanted to check on them. After he had placed the robes carefully on the bed, he went next door to check on his charges. They were fast asleep so he went back to his room to get ready.

After about half an hour there was a knock at the door. It was a servant sent to escort Maldwyn down to the chapel.

Maldwyn could never understand why humans wanted to get 'married' when it really was a blessing. The problem, if problem it was, seemed to start when the royal family came through the portal; as there were only a few of them the elders on the council did not exclude their beliefs from their minds but did ask them not to participate in any religious practices.

They were allowed to build a chapel but it was for thanksgiving of a bountiful crop and the joining of genders and eventually community meetings. The elders on the council would not and will not let any of man's old ways contaminate the peace they have. Humans had too many differences, too many differing views and too many religions.

Maldwyn walked into the chapel. He was surprised to find that there was only a handful of guests; there was Dimone's half-sister Cusan and one of Alyssa's aunts named Blossom who was a dryad. There was also a very old man who Maldwyn did not recognise. The old man; whose name was Silus, was one of Alyssa's grandfathers many times removed and one of the oldest dryads.

Maldwyn knew Alyssa had no human relatives left alive so they had to be magykal folk.

Maldwyn took his place at the head of the church near to the community table. He felt like a different person in the robes that belonged to his true father; but then his life had changed in the last two hours more than he could appreciate, and at this moment he was a very different person.

Alyssa and Dimone walked down the aisle with dignity and reverence as befitted their station in life; Alyssa looked very beautiful in the long flowing faerie-made dress that her ancestor Suki had worn for her wedding to Carlton.

The ceremony was plain but poignant, with both of them pledging their allegiance to each other and the peace in all the magykal lands. There was a lot said about peace and showing kindness to people and creatures that they will meet along the path of life together.

Then the bonding ceremony came around when they both held out their forearms and the oldest dryad, Silus, wrapped a garland of magykal ivy around both their right arms interlocking their fingers with each other and the ivy.

They whispered some magykal words to each other. This was as the roof of the chapel was cranked back to reveal the high moon. There they stood, lit by the moonlight with a magykal aura about them. Only Silus and Maldwyn could hear what they had just chanted and they would never tell. The two kissed and as they did the garland fell to the ground, its job of bonding the two together done.

The ceremony over they made their way to the banqueting hall where the Bucca children, Pyewacket and Winston were awaiting them along with a multitude of guests.

Alyssa and Dimone did their duty and went around their guests, but after about an hour they made their way up to their chamber to be alone, leaving their guests to enjoy the party.

Doras thought the party was a grand affair. She was sad when it drew to a close and she had to go to bed. It was a party that she would never forget: the people, the gowns, the food and the faerie folk. They would always be very special in a young girl's eye.

The next day was a late start for most of the castle's inhabitants and Maldwyn and his small group were no exception, although Maldwyn himself was up earlier; he had the sleepers in mind.

At roughly nine thirty, Alyssa and Dimone walked into the small dining room that overlooked the lake to meet with Maldwyn; the snow had stopped falling and the lake was now in full flow once more. Spring was on its way but there were still a few weeks of unpredictable winter weather left; and more snow, while not impossible was very unlikely.

Maldwyn smiled and said, "Good morning, my Empress; and good morning to you, my Emperor."

Dimone gulped and said, "What? Are you making a joke, Maldwyn? Why did you call me emperor? I certainly am not that." He laughed trying to make a joke of it and hoping it was not true.

"Well," Maldwyn replied, "That is your rightful title now, my Emperor. You have married the Empress so therefore you are the emperor; but protocol does dictate that you can have the title Lord instead if you prefer."

Dimone looked at his new bride, his face showing the horror of the responsibility he had taken on. He had thought that he could just carry on being Alyssa's consort but he was wrong.

Alyssa laughed and kissed his cheek. "Oh, my love, did you not think that things would change once we were wed and you would all but become my equal?"

Alyssa sat down and patted the chair next to her. "Oh, my Dimone, please come and sit with me, as Maldwyn rightly said you are now second in the castle and if anything should happen to me it would be up to you to carry on and keep the royal line going as you are now part of it."

"But!" said Dimone in protest, "You cannot be serious, my love, we have not been married a day yet and you are telling me that I should do whatever I have to, to keep the royal line going if you fall in battle. No, my love, I will not speak of it and that is an end to it."

Alyssa laughed again and looked at Maldwyn. "Do you hear that, Maldwyn. My new husband is laying down the law already! What a bully."

Dimone then saw the funny side of it and the mood lightened.

Maldwyn thought that it was obvious these two were right for each other and always would be.

CHAPTER SEVEN: POWERS

ᛋ

While the other members of Maldwyn's party were kept entertained by the maid, Maldwyn, Dimone and Alyssa discussed the awakening of the sleepers.

Dimone asked, "As the awakening has only been carried out once before, that anyone can remember, how do you two know what to do? Or are you only guessing?"

Alyssa replied, "I have no idea what I am going to do! But I am presuming that I will when the time comes.

"How do you feel, Maldwyn? Are you puzzled about this thing we are about to do?"

Maldwyn replied, "Yes I am, Empress. I have no idea what my role will be or how things will play out when we get to the chamber of the sleepers, but I am hoping that I will know once we are there.

"Before we talk further on this matter, can I please ask why you did not tell me of my lineage, Empress? I thought we always had a good working relationship?"

She looked sympathetically towards Maldwyn and said, as she took hold of his hands, "A good working relationship is not the way I would describe it, Maldwyn. We are friends. You, Dimone and I have grown up together. You may be a little older, but not that much, and we have always been close. Is this lack of familiarity what it comes down to when you feel betrayed, Maldwyn?

"We are on our own yet you call me Empress, please do not let the dark nature of the wizard find its way through or we will all be lost. You were not told because, as you yourself have already said, Hubert was your father and if this crisis had not happened you would never have known about it.

"It was both your fathers' wishes that no one who knew about it should speak of it; they tried to protect you, that was all it was, dear friend.

"You were not always as calm as you are now, and the fear was that as you got older and just past your youngling years you would seek retribution and find the portal to the other world but time is different there, as you well know, Maldwyn, and the people there that you seek are no longer alive."

Maldwyn thought for a while on the explanation he had been given, then answered the Empress. "Thank you for explaining, and I am sorry for any thoughts of malice that I did harbour. I do not fully understand why but I have to try and put myself in their shoes; would I have done the same?

"Anyway, back to the problem; have you noticed any new powers yet, Empress?"

Alyssa and Dimone smiled a knowing smile at each other. "Well, yes we have, but I was definitely not in full control, Maldwyn." Alyssa said.

"I was reading something this morning and not really concentrating. I was thinking about the trouble we have found ourselves in and a feeling of dread came over me.

"The next thing I know there was a crushing sensation on my head and when I looked up, it was the ceiling."

Dimone said, "We nearly sent for you, Maldwyn, but luckily as soon as Alyssa realised what was happening she started to fall, a little more quickly than I would have liked.

"I dropped everything I was carrying and rushed to catch her; the odd thing was I needn't have worried because when Alyssa was a foot off the floor she came to a dead stop, then floated slowly onto the carpet.

"It was so scary and made me realise that Alyssa may not be in full control of her abilities and could use some help."

Maldwyn replied, "I would much rather Alyssa learned that skill from a fellow dryad. I presume your kin are still here, Empress?"

"Yes, Maldwyn, they are," she replied.

"Then I will speak to them immediately if that is conducive with you, my dear wife," Dimone said.

She gave a faint smile and once more took her husband's hand. "Of course it is, my love, that is an excellent idea. Thank you, Maldwyn, we should have thought of it ourselves."

They joined the children for their breakfast and sat down with them to chat about the wedding the night before. Doras was very chatty; she was telling Alyssa all about the beautiful dresses and the ladies with long flowing hair intertwined with flowers and ribbons, and the music, and the food.

Doras was fascinated with the whole thing and as she said she would never forget it, it was the highlight of her stay in the castle.

The day was pleasant but cold. There seemed to be calm over the castle and everyone in it. Most people did not let the impending trouble dampen their spirits; this was partly because nothing had happened yet.

But mainly it was due to the thought of the protection they felt they had with having their own wizard and an Empress that now had some limited powers.

After breakfast the children went for a walk around the castle with the maid and one of the guards. This was because the castle was in a lock down situation and they had to stay within the confines of the castle and not outside. Not even Alyssa could get out at the moment.

The maid took her young charges into the maze; the aforesaid maze had been created by one of Alyssa's earliest ancestors. The party spent a further two hours in the garden playing hide and seek before they went back into the castle.

When he left the breakfast table, Dimone went, as he had said he would, to see Alyssa's aunt and grandfather. After all the niceties and ritual of respect that was normal at a greeting and meeting between two races, they settled down to talk about the problem that Alyssa was experiencing, and hopefully finding a solution to her problem.

Alyssa and Maldwyn were walking slowly and deep in conversation about the problems of the day. They were also not quite sure what they were going to do when they reached the tower room that housed the sleepers.

It was one thing to talk about awakening the sleepers, but another to actually do it; neither had given the problem much thought as they presumed that it would become clear when they were both stood side by side outside the door.

They approached the large ornate door to the tower room where the sleepers lay; there was nothing, no knowledge as to what spell they needed, no knowledge as to what ritual was required.

Maldwyn said, "It looks like we are going to have to research this little problem, my Empress. I fear we have procrastinated too much and in so doing we presumed that it would be relatively easy to awaken the sleepers, and the answers would somehow automatically come to us.

"I suggest that you, Empress, talk to Dimone and find out if the dryads are willing to help. I fear that your powers are not under your control and may need to be nurtured a little before we can do anything about the sleepers."

Alyssa asked Maldwyn, "And what of you, my mage? What are you to do?"

Maldwyn was worried but he was a sensible wizard and his thoughts were of what his father would have done: his real, adopted father, Hubert. Maldwyn was still having problems with Myrddin being his father; he knew it would take time to accept his biological father but they were thoughts for another day.

Maldwyn said, "I, my Empress, will visit the old wizard library in the bowels of the castle. I want to see if I can glean any answers from my father's writings." He paused in thought. "But if I go back further to the journals of the wizard Ramsey, who as you know, Empress, was the last wizard to perform the rising ceremony, I may find the answer there."

"Good," said Alyssa, "and while you do that I will beg your leave, my mage, and go to my husband and my dryad kin to see if they can be of any help with the problem."

With that said they both went their separate ways to hopefully find the answers to the problem.

***

Alyssa walked into the guests' sitting hall, where the three were waiting for her; she approached her husband and the two dryads like a nervous child on her first day at school. The human part of Alyssa found it hard to accept she had to be schooled at her age; but the dryad part that was always seeking knowledge knew she would have to accept the teachings of the elder dryads.

As she approached the three, Dimone stood and walked towards her holding out his hands in greeting. Alyssa took her husband's hands and smiled, the smile was a weak one and she knew it.

She said, "Dimone, Aunt, Grandfather, have we got a plan or is it futile to think we have the knowledge to awaken the sleepers?"

Blossom spoke, "We knew that it would be difficult when you suggested it, but not impossible."

She looked at her niece intently, then took her hands. "Alyssa, you were named after one of the most beautiful and most intellectually perfect dryads that ever lived, and I have observed that you have also inherited a lot of her traits.

"You wish us to give you tuition so that you can hone your powers to their full potential, but it will not be that easy."

Just as Alyssa was going to ask why, Silus interrupted. "What exactly do you expect of us, Granddaughter? If it is instant answers and instant fixes then I have to let you know they do not exist.

"What you ask comes with practice and perseverance, not haste, therefore you must be patient, Granddaughter."

Alyssa said with panic in her voice, "But I cannot wait, Grandfather. We cannot wait; the castle cannot wait. It is imperative that I help Maldwyn to raise the sleepers and we do not know how to!"

Blossom suggested that Silus put Alyssa into a deep trance state in order to bring her powers to the fore, but only a small portion of them.

"Alyssa, my granddaughter, please come and sit by your grandfather," said Silus.

Alyssa did as she was told; once more she felt like a small child. There was more than a vague recollection in Alyssa's mind of a time long ago when she was taken to the great forest and was passed around the elders to be blessed, to learn, to observe and to listen.

That was how all dryad younglings learned their trade and Alyssa's trade was to be an Empress.

Silus looked his granddaughter in the eyes and after about two minutes he said, "Blossom was right, you do look like your namesake, especially your eyes and your smile."

Silus drifted off into his own thoughts; he was extremely old and it was not unusual for him to go off into past events.

Alyssa stroked her grandfather's hand gently. She said, "Grandfather, can you help me please? I really do need some answers and I have not got time to wait, I need to know now, Grandfather."

Silus looked thoughtful at his beloved granddaughter and asked, "Has Maldwyn been told of his lineage, Granddaughter.

"Yes," she answered, "he has, Dimone told him."

"And what was his reaction?" Silus asked.

Dimone answered, "As we expected, my grandfather, he was shocked and he kept saying that Hubert was still his father, his real father, and no matter who sired him Hubert would always be his father. But I think he is getting used to the idea."

Silus considered the answer "As I predicted, my Grandchildren, Maldwyn is a very wise man and will not slander the good upbringing he had. He judges a man by his acts not reputation or what may have been. As far as Maldwyn is concerned, Myrddin or Merlin, is just a fictional character until such time that they meet and then he will still respectfully look on Hubert as his father.

"Now let us try and solve the immediate problem of the sleepers, then we can get on with your education, my child."

Silus faced Alyssa. "Now look at me and let us see how much power you really have! Give me your hands, Granddaughter; now relax and close your eyes. I want you to think about the sleepers' chamber. Now imagine that your mind is a labyrinth of small chambers and vaults, each with its own secrets and stories to tell.

"This labyrinth is in the shape of a circle and has a well type feature at its centre. You want something from one of the chambers but you cannot reach it, therefore you must physically float to it as it is too deep."

Silus looked at Alyssa and knew that by now his voice would be having an echoing effect on her mind: she was deep within his spell.

Silus continued, "You step out into the void but you do not fall; instead you float down very gently, passing along the way, other chambers that you will need at another point in time. Each chamber has writing upon the top of the door giving indication as to what lies behind; you will remember these chambers as you will need each one as your life progresses.

"It is as if you are on eagle's wings and you find the sensation pleasurable; you float serenely to the bottom and land on the soft ground that is covered with the mist of the morning dew. Can you see the deep vault that you are looking for, Granddaughter?"

She answered, "Yes."

Silus thought, this may just work. "You reach the door. It is beautiful and is faerie made, so I wish you to look at the door and tell me what you see."

Alyssa smiled as if it was a pleasure for her to see the door. "The door is the most beautiful door ever seen, and it is more beautiful than the ones in the castle. It is inlaid with silver and gold and some precious stones I do not recognise. There is a circle in the top part of the door; it is made out of silver and has a raised silver knot in the centre. I am taking the knot, it is coming off in my hand.

"I put the knot into someone's hand; he is standing at the side of me. I know him, I feel him but I cannot see his face."

Silus said with his voice very low and almost singing, "Look at the man's face, you recognise him! Who is it, my Granddaughter?"

Alyssa turned her head to the side as if she was looking at someone and said, "Oh I know him, he is my good friend the mage; it is Maldwyn. Oh, he is doing something with the knot of silver."

"What is he doing, my granddaughter?" Silus said in his haunting voice.

She turned and looked at her grandfather again. "He is moulding it of course. He has cupped his hands around the knot and he is speaking the ancient words. My mage has opened his hand. Oh, it is so elegant, so beautiful, such intricate patterns and runes are on the key, I have never seen the like!"

Alyssa stopped talking. She was smiling, and as with her speech over the past few minutes, her smile was also childlike.

Silus said, "Tell me, Granddaughter, what is he doing with the beautiful silver key?"

Alyssa smiled once more. She said in a dream-like voice, "Of course silly, it is simple, he is putting it in the lock."

Silus squeezed his granddaughter's hands and quietly said, "You will now very swiftly raise your body to the top of the void and again stand looking down at the vaults and chambers. Now you will take a pace back and turn to face the opposite way."

Silus then whispered something into his granddaughter's ear and she woke up. Alyssa looked around at everyone and asked, "Did anything happen?" Then followed this with, "Oh, yes, it did, I remember. Oh, Grandfather, it worked, you did it." As if still under his influence she hugged her grandfather as she had as a child.

"Yes," he said. "But it was only a quick fix. You will have to learn and work at the rest of your tuition. This was a once only, my granddaughter."

***

Meanwhile, Maldwyn had made his way down to the wizard library to look for the information he required; it was imperative that he got into the tower and raised the sleepers before he left, to find his companions' parents and solicit more magykal help to stop this hag Sheela taking over their world.

He walked into the wizard library and looked around with fondness. His father Hubert had first taken him there when he was but four years old and he could remember it as if it was yesterday; the sheer joy he felt when he was allowed to touch the books and read them was the best memory from that day.

Even at four years old Maldwyn could read complicated spells and perform small ones, like turning an apple purple or levitating a chair; he had a brilliant mind and he was proving it even at that age.

Before Maldwyn could do anything, he had to ask permission from the resident librarian, a spectre named Rame. Rame was the first librarian and did not wish to leave after his death. Maldwyn went from one book to another touching them fondly, with memories flooding through from his younger years. He walked along row upon row of bookcases but could not find what he wanted. That was when he remembered all wizards kept journals of special spells they performed and the reason for using them, and on their death all these journals were locked away because of the content of the spells.

He approached the small strong box that was hidden behind one of the bookcases and started to chant an opening spell that he did not even realise he knew. It was the box that gave him the knowhow as it recognised that Maldwyn was the castle wizard.

When the box had fully opened, the journal that once belonged to Ramsey moved and shuffled until it found its way to the top and gently floated out of the box and into Maldwyn's hand.

Maldwyn said, "Well, little box, you are very clever to know what I was wanting from you. Thank you very much. I will not be long and you can have the papers back."

Maldwyn settled down at the large library table to read the papers; he was about a third of the way through when he found a sealed parchment. The sealing wax was the usual red colour, but what was unusual was the raised dragon that Maldwyn presumed was the writer's stamp.

He put his hand down and touched the dragon; it looked so real. The dragon immediately reared up, opened its wings and sprayed fire onto the wax seal, breaking it up and giving Maldwyn access to the contents.

The dragon that appeared to be alive, was a very small dragon. He or she was only approximately half an inch high: it was indeed strange magyk. The dragon very slowly walked over the parchment and then the desk until he reached Maldwyn. He looked at the mage as if he were searching for something or for a recognition of the person in front of him.

Maldwyn, feeling no malice coming from the creature, held out his hand. The dragon gave one large leap 'half jumping and half flying' and landed on Maldwyn's ring; the one he had found in the robes. The dragon settled down in the centre of the ring and looked up at Maldwyn over his wing that was shading his eyes, then dismissed him and went to sleep. It was to Maldwyn very much the same way as he had seen Pyewacket curl up on his bed.

He observed the creature for a few minutes, then said, "Well, my small friend, I presume you are a guardian my real father put in place to protect me, but if you are real, and I feel you are, why would he perform a shrinking spell on you. I will have to now think of an appropriate name for you, my small friend."

The dragon appeared to be comfortable so Maldwyn returned to the task in hand. He unfolded the parchment, which was very old, to see just what it was that the dragon was protecting.

The only thing that was written on the parchment was a spell, but the spell was written in some kind of ancient runes. Maldwyn instinctively knew that it was part of the ancient Draco language; but this had not been spoken for many millennia.

Maldwyn read the title out loud, then realised he should not go any further as this was a whisper spell. Some wizards performed whisper spells under their breath and they were the most secret and the most dangerous of all spells.

The spell said:-

ᛏᚺᛗ ᚱᚠᛎᚺᛎᛏᛪ ᚠᛈ ᛏᚺᛗ ᛗᚠᚷᛗᚺ.

Which meant:

The Rising Of The Mages.

Maldwyn was not sure how he knew this but he could now apparently read ancient runes fluently.

Maldwyn silently read the spell and stored it in the part of his mind that he called his archive; others would call it their memory but not Maldwyn. He noted where it was and what it was for so that when he wanted it, in an instant he could retrieve it.

He was just going to fold the parchment when he noticed that the words had faded. There was now no protection on the parchment, therefore it was not safe to be seen by anyone and Maldwyn was the only one that knew the spell, apart from the dragon that is.

He re-sealed the parchment and gave it back to the little box, knowing that one day when he truly wished it to be so the words would re-appear as before, then he put it back where he had found it and thanked the spectre of the library as he left.

CHAPTER EIGHT: SLEEPERS
ᛗ

Maldwyn climbed the many stone stairs until he reached the main castle area, then made his way to the nursery to meet with his companions. They were having a much-needed drink of hot chocolate after their little excursion around the castle grounds.

The maid, seeing Maldwyn approaching them, poured Maldwyn a drink also. They were seated near the fire to warm up. "Hello, my friends! Have you had a pleasant morning?" asked Maldwyn.

Doras said excitedly, "Oh we have had a lovely time playing a game called hide and seek; it was really funny, I do like that game."

The maid then said, "I have never known a younglin that did not know how to play hide and seek, I really have not."

Maldwyn was worried at the way the conversation was going and thought he had better say something. "The children have had a very strict and sheltered upbringing, they concentrate on the sciences rather than play. That is one of the reasons they are staying with me: to learn how to play and be children for a while.

"You are doing a very good job, Susie; it is Susie, isn't it?"

The maid, who was a little taken aback that an important wizard would know her name answered, "Yes, your worship, it is and it is a pleasure teaching them; they are very good children."

He smiled at the girl. "Thank you very much, Susie. Now will you be so good as to take the children to the small dining room. The Empress will be waiting for them to start lunch.

Oh, and please inform the Empress that I will be along directly."

Susie made a small attempt at a curtsy; she was very young and new to the castle which consequently made her nervous. She took the children and closed the door behind her.

Winston waited until she had gone then asked, "Did you find any information in the library about the sleepers, Maldwyn? We are running out of time."

Maldwyn looked with fondness at his small feathered companion, then at his loving Pyewacket. "Yes, I did. There is a spell that must be spoken in a certain way. But the language that the spell is written in has not been spoken for many millennia."

His companions were very curious. Winston asked, "And what language would this be, Maldwyn?"

Maldwyn replied, "Well in a way it is faerie and it is magykal, but not easy. It is dragon."

Pyewacket sat up from washing her paws. "How can this be, there have been no living dracos for thousands of years, they are extinct."

Maldwyn held out his hand to show them the ring that was now inhabited by a living breathing draco, albeit a small one. The dragon moved his body gently up and down to the pattern of his breathing but no sound came from him. He was deep in sleep until he was needed.

The two companions were in awe of the magyk required to make such a thing happen. To shrink a draco was a feat in itself but to tame one was a whole other sort of magyk.

Winston said, "That is ancient magyk you are messing with, Maldwyn. I am not sure it is safe or even allowed any more. The mage that cast that spell was very powerful indeed."

Winston paused then had a sudden thought, "More to the point, Maldwyn, why has the draco let you handle it? Did it just give itself to you or have you had to win it in some way?"

Maldwyn smiled. "My friends, what I am about to tell you both goes no further than this room, well for now anyway. It is so outlandish and impossible to believe that you may have trouble believing it as I did. But if I needed any more proof this little fellow was it.

"It all started when I went to the dungeons with Dimone." Maldwyn went on to tell his friends all about his real father, then the library and finally the draco.

After he had finished he said, "I should not have told you but when the time comes and my power increases I may require you two to give me strength and help.

"I am also very sorry that this play acting has to carry on and I cannot show you both the respect you deserve by calling you by your names, but it is too dangerous.

"It seems we are all being deceptive these days and only ill usually comes from that road."

Pyewacket meowed, "That would account for a few things then, Maldwyn, you being Myrdden's son I mean."

He looked at the cat puzzled. She carried on, "Well you have always been able to do things better than the average wizard. Look at last year when you moved all the snow from the village in one swift movement, moving it to the water storage tanks.

"We commented at the time that there was more to you than we understood; you needed great power to do what you did that day and you were not even worn out with the effort because there was no effort was there!"

Winston interrupted before Maldwyn could say anything. "Do you think the draco will one day return to his normal size, Maldwyn? After all we do understand what it is to be something you are not."

He replied, "I do not know my friend; it is hard to say with such ancient and powerful magyk. We have no idea how old the draco is or if it is male or female. All these things could have a bearing on the outcome. But I need a name for the draco, and as yet his name eludes me.

"But for now, I suggest we meet the others and have some lunch, the Empress and I have some unfinished business in the tower."

As they left he looked at his friends and said, "Good, you received your charms. You are going to need them. Hopefully, they will help you to get your true forms back and keep them. Never take them off. I put every protection and reversing spell I could find into those charms and I hope they will work as well as I hoped they would, but you may not require them."

They left the nursery and met the others in the dining room. Alyssa had told the servant to serve the meal so they were already eating when the others arrived.

Alyssa commented, "I hope you do not mind, my mage, but I thought it best to start without you as the children were hungry and I was not sure how long you would be."

Maldwyn answered, "That is not a problem, my Empress, the quicker we get the meal over the quicker we can climb those many stairs once more." He had a slight grin on his face as he said this, knowing that Alyssa also had aching legs after the last climb.

She grinned at Maldwyn but did not chastise. They ate their meal in relative silence, even the Bucca children, being of magykal stock, could tell something of enormous reverence was about to happen in the castle.

Maldwyn asked what his companions had in store for the afternoon, but they had had such a tiring morning they were all going to relax in their chamber.

Truth be known, not being in the forest was having a strange effect on the younglings and they were starting to act more like human children. They would never become human but the small idiosyncrasies that they were adopting were worlds apart from that of a Bucca child. So, the children went to their chamber with the maid to have a nap.

Pyewacket and Winston waited behind to talk about how they could help in the fight against Frau Berchta. They needed to take stock of what exactly they could and could not do with their now limited powers.

Dimone went off to make sure that the plans for the protection of the castle were on target.

And Alyssa and Maldwyn made their way up the spiral staircase to the tower rooms. They walked up the stairs solemnly; they had both over the last few days been subjected to some very profound experiences and unforgettable changes. These changes in turn had made the pair more serious in their outlook and it was very visible.

Maldwyn was acting more like a forty-five-year-old, which was his age, instead of the old man he was becoming before all this started, and he was less forgetful, but Alyssa put this down to him now having purpose to his life.

They reached the top of the steps and walked over to the door that they had approached earlier. It seemed larger, more ornate, but at the same time more threatening. The patterning on this door was of such beauty it was indescribable.

Alyssa looked at Maldwyn and said, "Well, my mage, I trust you have good news!"

Maldwyn smiled. "Of course I have, my Empress, and you!"

"Yes, Maldwyn, I have, but why have you taken to calling me by my title and not my name? We are not in public," she replied.

He smiled again at his old childhood friend. He thought of Alyssa more as a sister than his monarch. "I will continue to do so until the end of this trouble, my Empress. You have to keep your authority and the only way to do that is to also keep the respect of your people.

"My calling you by your first name may be interpreted as disrespectful and you may lose support for not being a strong leader in times of trouble."

She answered, "Ah, politics. You are right as usual, Maldwyn. I will not take offence at that particular salutation for the duration of the trouble, as you call it. But after, if we ever get back to normal, I will take offence.

"Now what have you to tell me?"

Maldwyn looked grave. "I, my Empress, have found the spell of the draco. I have read it and understood it and I know how to utter it under my breath to minimise any causative fallout. It is of a very ancient magyk, one that should be told in stories but has been long dead. It could do untold harm if I spoke it out loud, of this I must be mindful.

"But first I need to get into the tower room, so please tell me you have found a way!"

Alyssa smiled as she did often. "I have, my mage, and it was found in a strange experience. I of course had help and that will not happen again, so I will have to learn to hone into my skills as I cannot always rely on others to be there.

"Tell me, my mage, have you noticed anything about the door in front of you?"

He looked at the door then back to her. "Yes, my Empress, I have noticed the intricate patterns that could only be faerie made, the precision of the carvings, but as I studied them, and the harder I stared at them, they appeared to come to life. Why? Is it of some great significance?"

She grinned and answered, "It is of no consequence, my mage, I just wondered if you had noticed, but of course you have, you are Maldwyn, son of Hubert and son of Myrddin.

"Now, you see that circle of silver in the centre of the door?"

"Yes," was his reply.

"Well that had something on it and now it has gone. It may seem bizarre or even silly but during my strange experience I saw you take that in your hands and mould it. If you look in your robe pocket you should find the item that you made, Maldwyn," she replied.

Maldwyn laughed, he thought she was joking. He had not moulded anything from the door! But to humour his Empress he put his hand into his pocket and immediately found a long metal object. He pulled it out and stared at it for a few seconds, then said, "But how, when...?"

Alyssa interrupted the perturbed Maldwyn. "I think, my mage, that this is indeed old powerful magyk and we must accept it and not question why! There is no time for inquisitions, Maldwyn."

Maldwyn still amazed at finding the key in his robe pocket, put it in the lock and turned it. He gave one small push on the door and immediately it swung inwards with a very loud creek.

This door had not been opened since the last rising when it was opened by the wizard Ramsey. Hubert, Maldwyn's adopted father, was the last wizard to find a place in the chamber of sleepers, but as with all wizards that had taken that path, no one had put them there, and no one knew how they got there, only that they were there.

The thing that people in the castle did know was that once a wizard was near to death and had made the decision to join the sleepers, with his last breath his body was consumed in a serene halo of light. He would be raised from the bed and his materiel body then disappeared in an explosion of colour.

During this process the wizard's body was transported to the sleeper's chamber to await resurrection. The chamber that Alyssa and Maldwyn now both found themselves in.

The chamber was dark at first but after speaking the luminosity spell it became bright with a white light that lit up every corner of the chamber.

All around the walls there were bodies laid on plinths that were suspended from the wall somehow. These plinths were nine high on every wall. Alyssa realised that the room was not square but more like a hexagon shape. No one really knew how many wizards there were as no raising had been carried out since Ramsey hundreds of years before.

Alyssa said, "Now what, my mage? What do we do and which do we choose?"

Maldwyn answered solemnly, "First of all I do not believe we choose any. I believe the choosing will be done for us.

"I think it more likely that the oldest will rise first and if that is right I will not see my father Hubert whom I dearly loved."

There was a sadness in Maldwyn's voice as he said this; he really was hoping that he would see Hubert. "I will now say the spell that the draco gave me. Let us hope it works, my Empress!"

Maldwyn stood back from Alyssa. He chanted words that made no sense to her, ancient words that had not been spoken for many millennia. Then he started the second half of the spell. He raised his arms into the air and uttered the spell under his breath. He turned to every side of the chamber as if he was talking to every soul that was in there, but still he uttered under his breath.

He put his arms down and dropped to the floor, exhausted after the intense work he had put into the spell. Alyssa ran to him and helped him to sit up. He said, "I am all right, my Empress, it is just a very tiring spell and one that needs a lot of concentration."

They heard a noise and looked around them as one by one the wizards sat up on their plinths, floated to the floor and stretched. They looked at their hands and shook their legs, and it was as if they were making sure they were all there.

They lined up as if they were waiting for something but Maldwyn and Alyssa could not think what! They had just realised that there were only eleven wizards and not the traditional twelve, when they heard a grinding noise.

A stone slab that was in the floor in the centre of the room slowly started to rise up. As they watched, the stone lifted as if it was a lid and, underneath, was the body of a wizard.

The body of a tall thin man with a long white beard and hair started to rise from the floor. He was horizontal at first but gradually tilted until he was vertical and stood in front of the others.

He stretched and examined himself just as the others had done, then he looked around to take in his surroundings. He looked for all the world like an older version of Maldwyn.

Alyssa and Maldwyn should have been frightened, but they were not. These wizards looked alive. Their clothes were a bit dusty but apart from that they looked normal as if they had never died, which they never really had. There was not even the smell of death that Alyssa was frightened of, in fact there was nothing to say that they had just been resurrected.

The sleeper that had just risen looked at Maldwyn and said in a croaky voice, "Maldwyn, my son, so you survived, of this I am so pleased."

Maldwyn knew instinctively that this was Myrddin, his father. He walked over to the mage and looked at him in great detail; for Maldwyn it was a bit like looking in a mirror.

Maldwyn enquired, "How did you know it was me, Father? How could you tell?"

Myrddin replied, "I would have known you anywhere, my son, you remind me of your dear mother so much." At this thought a tear came to Myrddin's eyes. "You must forgive me, emotion is a side effect of the long sleep but it does not last long."

Myrddin looked at Maldwyn's ring, "May I?" he said as he reached over to hold Maldwyn's hand. Maldwyn nodded and offered his father his hand.

Myrddin said as he stroked the dragon on the ring, "Ah I see you found Sunstar, well of course you did or you would not be here, she is a faithful guardian."

Alyssa decided to be brave, after all it was her castle. She walked past the other sleepers who followed her with their eyes and she went to stand at the side of Maldwyn. She was shaking but she also knew that as the custodian of the castle she had to introduce herself.

"My lord Myrddin, I am the custodian of the castle and I am happy to see you are all revived well but could I please ask, what happens now?"

Myrddin faced Alyssa. "Ah, the new Empress; you do look very much like a dryad I once knew. Her name was Alyssa. Is she by any chance a relative of yours?"

Alyssa blushed. "Yes my lord Myrddin, she was and my name is also Alyssa. You are the second person in as many days to comment on the resemblance."

"Ah," he said, "it is to be hoped that you have inherited some of her traits too, my child. Determination, honesty, bravery and fairness were some of her best attributes. The rising of the sleepers is never carried out lightly, and I fear you are in dire trouble if you have considered this action. So then, if you will show us to our chamber we can refresh and then you can tell us why we have been summoned."

She replied, "My lord Myrddin, we have not prepared a chamber as we did not know what you would want!"

He grinned and so did most of the other wizards in the tower. "To start with, will everyone please stop calling me Myrddin. My name is Merlin and I like it very much. Myrddin was the name I used to evade my enemies.

"Now maybe you require some explanation. We need a chamber that is large enough for us all. We do not need beds just large comfy chairs. While it is true we do not normally sleep it does not mean we cannot, in fact we do like forty winks now and again, but we have to be forever vigilant about the oncoming danger."

Maldwyn said, "We apologise, Father. We did not realise you would all look so well and there is no written information about what happens once you are risen. I mean none of you look dead."

There were a few smiles around the room, then one of the oldest wizards called Romley spoke. "You have probably been told that the sleepers would be cold to the touch 'zombies if you like' and that if you touched us you would never forget the cold feeling you would experience.

"You have also probably been told that we only fight and speak and nothing else. Well that is not strictly true. We can speak and hold a good conversation. We can eat and drink; again, we do not have to but most of us do like to taste our favourite foods once again, so we choose to do this. In fact, we are as if we were never dead. Come feel my hand, Maldwyn."

Merlin interrupted, "No feel my hand, my son." He lifted his hands towards Maldwyn.

Maldwyn did as he was asked and soon realised that his father felt warm, but something else also happened; in those few seconds that Merlin had his hands on his son's, he passed on a lot of the knowledge and spells that Maldwyn would need to win.

It was old knowledge, old magyk and Maldwyn fell back slightly as his father released him.

Alyssa went to his aid. She was concerned for her old friend. "What has befallen you, my mage? What has happened?"

Maldwyn recovered himself and said, "I am all right, my Empress, please do not be concerned with this, I will explain later."

Merlin looked at Alyssa and said, "My son has a good friend in you, Empress, and he will need friends before this is through, as you will."

CHAPTER NINE: COUNCIL

✝

Alyssa and Maldwyn paid their respects and went out of the tower to arrange some accommodation for the wizards. They had made a request for a long dining table, with an array of certain foods, clean robes and twelve easy chairs in which to relax and doze.

Alyssa asked, "Maldwyn, are you pleased that you met your real father?"

"Yes," was his reply but he said no more; he still wished that he could speak once more with Hubert who he called father.

It took the best part of two hours to arrange a chamber large enough to put a long table in and twelve easy chairs, but eventually with the help of a little magyk it was done.

Dimone who was by nature very curious, was charged with going to get the wizards and bring them to the chamber. As he walked in he was greeted with gusto by a wizard named Marlon.

Marlon walked swiftly up to Dimone and held out his hands in greeting. he said, "Dimone, son of Tuatha and of Gladwyne, I am so pleased to greet you. I hear you are now the husband of the Empress Alyssa; I feel that to be a good match, Dimone."

Dimone was puzzled. "How do you know me, my lord?"

Marlon smiled. "I am sorry, my boy, in my haste I have not introduced myself correctly. I am one of your ancestors. Your mother was my niece many, many generations removed. We wizards have the ability, once we have slept, to recognise all our kin and I am duty bound to acknowledge you, whether you are good or evil."

He paused then. "Now, where would you like us to go?"

Dimone could not wait to inform his bride about this encounter. He was over the moon that one of his ancestors was a wizard. He asked, "Could I ask your name, my lord, then I will show you and the rest of your company to the chamber that has been prepared for you."

Marlon told Dimone his name and suggested that they talk at a later time about Dimone's history. Dimone then showed them to their new accommodation.

He took them down the stone staircase and to the left on the first landing. This was where the large chamber was awaiting them as far away from prying eyes as possible. There was, as promised, a long large table set with all manner of foods that the wizards had enjoyed in their heyday, and twelve comfy chairs as requested for them to sleep on or as Maldwyn had called it meditate.

By late afternoon the sleepers had tasted their favourite foods and drinks, had a change of clothes and while the mess on the table was being cleared away they settled down in their comfy chairs to rest and await the Empress and the explanation for their rising.

Alyssa, Dimone, Maldwyn and his companions made their way into the wizards' chamber at about six p.m. After introductions they carried some chairs from the table and sat around with the wizards to talk about the trouble they were in.

Stephann and Doras were in awe of the wizards that sat before them. They looked normal, like real people; it was not what they expected at all. But Doras for one was very glad that they were so normal as the thought of a living dead person was frightening, even though Maldwyn had explained that the wizards had never actually fully died in the first place.

They settled down to tell their stories about why they thought the castle, and especially Alyssa were in danger from the hag Sheela.

Pyewacket and Winston gave their version of events, then it was the turn of Stephann and Doras to continue with the tale. It was obvious that most of the wizards were taking this very seriously because more than a few had heard about the exploits of the Frau Berchta, plus her misdeeds when they were the castle wizard.

The ones that had not would rely on the council of their peers, so they too were in no doubt things were serious. Dexter, one of the wizards, had been a great strategist in his time and he was the one that asked the next question.

His mind was not exactly clear about certain details that had been mentioned, or not mentioned, which he found perturbing as he liked everything to be mapped out in order.

He said, "Now let me get this straight, the hag tried to kill you as she was jealous of your beauty, and I do believe she has done that before. She is ugly in her true form but she is also the most beautiful of maidens in her guise. Now you say she kidnapped your mother, the faerie princess Emily, and your father, the Ghillie Dhu called Gastak, but your father escaped. Is that right?"

Pyewacket started to whimper in a small cat-like voice. Being a cat she could not cry but she did manage a tear in her eye. She snuggled into Winston's feathers for comfort and it was he who had to answer Dexter's question.

"Sorona's father only escaped for a short while. He was recaptured again within the day, but not before he had inflicted great losses and harm to the enemy's forces.

"He was giving me a chance to get his daughter out of harm's way but we were pinned down and finding a safe line through the carnage was difficult. I had just said to Sorona that I was going to join in and help her father when he was captured.

"I felt low in the heart. I was charged with saving Sorona but in doing so I had let her father be captured and did nothing to stop this from happening."

Winston stroked Pyewacket with his wing; he was feeling very sad thinking he had betrayed her father.

Alexo said, "There was nothing you could do, my dear owl, you are Sealy Court and you were charged with looking after the princess. You did your duty, to have done otherwise would have had more serious consequences. You both could have been killed."

Winston carried on with a sadness in his voice. "I know, my lord, but the guilt is still there. Anyway, I decided that while all the confusion was going on we should make a run for it, but we were seen and the hag threw a spell and here we are, a cat and an owl."

Dexter was still puzzled. "But I thought the whole point for this hag was to kill Sorona so why were you turned into an animal and bird and allowed to escape?

Winston hooted a hoot of acknowledgment. "Oh, I am sorry, I have not made myself very clear. She did try to kill us both but as the spell flew towards us and could not be stopped, Jessica the gentle stepped in, and just before the spell hit she cast another spell and it altered the outcome.

"We were turned into the shapes you see before you. Sorona was stunned but I, as a Sealy Court and a warrior was ready for any outcome. I saw the frau striding towards us in a fury and rage and I used what magyk I had left to make myself bigger. I scooped my dear Sorona up in my claws and spirited her away to the other side of the forest where I knew her father, Gastak, had friends.

Dexter stroked his beard. "Then that was where your parents came into the plan?"

"Yes," Stephann replied. "As we told you they decided to go and help their friends, but we have heard since that they too were captured. We can only hope they are all still alive."

Stephann cuddled his sister who was sobbing by this time and Stephann was trying very hard to be brave for her sake.

"Before they left, they instructed us to take Christano and Sorona to the kind wizard at the edge of the forest as soon as they sent word for us to do this. We were to let him give them new names and not to let him know who they were until word had reached us from my parents, then we should pass whatever message we got onto the wizard.

"We eventually got the word from a Manitou who was badly injured bringing us the news, and that is when Maldwyn took charge of our friends here. Then a few days ago we got the news from Jessica the gentle that we should come and tell Maldwyn everything right away."

The wizard Alexo spoke. "According to my calculations I have been asleep for roughly four hundred years. I seem to remember Jessica the gentle being around doing her good deeds then. How long can this faerie live? I did not realise she was one of the long Gevity faeries!"

It was now Winston's turn to be puzzled. "You are right, she is not one of those, and she is still very young looking and beautiful. You do not think she is something more, do you? I mean she is so good and helpful, are you saying she is not what she appears to be?"

The wizard Mylo commented, "Yes, I remember Jessica, she must be over seven hundred years old; how can that be?"

Merlin stood up to address his fellow wizards. "Do not concern yourselves, my brothers, Jessica is what she seems, but yet she is not.

"What I am about to tell you must not leave this room, so you two younglins will not say any of what you hear to anyone ever."

Merlin waved his hand over in their direction as if he was dismissing them but to the trained eye it was obvious he was casting a spell. His fingers put in a certain formation as he uttered the spell under his breath.

He continued, "Now you will not be able to ever tell anyone the secret, not even each other. But you will remember it.

"Jessica is the last of her race. She comes from an ancient gentle race that is not immortal and can die like anyone else; but they have a very good trick for living for many hundreds of years.

"I think most, if not all of you, will have heard the story of the fabled Phoenix; how just before they die they burn in a cold flame, and from the ash a new life is re-born and starts again until it is once more extinguished with another burning. Well that is what happens to Jessica. She is from the original race of Phoenix. Has no one ever wondered why she has red wings?

"The other thing you may not understand about the form she takes is that it protects her. To all intents and purposes, she is a good faerie not a Phoenix. But when someone is dying in battle, or when someone is dying prematurely for one reason or another, Jessica can turn back into the Phoenix and save them with her tears."

There was gasps around the room. Jessica a Phoenix, could this be true?

"That is why it is imperative that this knowledge stays a secret and that Frau Berchta does not learn of this as Jessica too will be in danger. After all she will not want Jessica healing the men as fast as they fall. That would be a great advantage over her army."

"That is so true," Alyssa said. "Do you think we should bring Jessica here to the castle for her protection?"

"I think we should ask her Empress; but be warned, she will not come if she thinks it is for her good. I suggest that you ask her to come to help with the wounded if a battle does ensue.

"We should send a courier right away to ask her."

Winston hooted, "I will go and ask her. I can be quick in this form."

"No," said Dexter. "It would be more prudent if the new eagle squadron that I was told about went for her to inform her that the Empress requires her council. In fact, if you could take a quill to scroll Empress it would make it more official."

Alyssa smiled. These wizards did show their great age when they spoke of things that had not been used for hundreds of years. Even wizards were now using books made at the paper factory in the town of Linton, and pens that had ink flowing through them called biros: an invention brought from the land of man by the relative of a man who was escaping the camps. These had been in use since Merlin first brought the humans from the camps of the great upheaval in their land.

But there were still a few wizards on the outer edges of the empire that still used quill and parchment.

There were a lot of things that were modern in faerie land now, but there also was a lot of things that were not allowed. The technology was a mismatch of every era from generations that had immigrated to this magykal world to evade conflict and death. This immigration did not happen any more as Merlin was the one that had brought them all, but that was hundreds of years ago and the few things the humans were allowed to bring were built on and replicated until there were now thriving communities with factories and shops. It all went unhindered as long as they did not break their treaty with the magykal creatures.

They were allowed to have a printing press, but that was as far as the written word went. There was no talk of revolution or uprisings as there was no need, they all lived free and every book was well bound and special.

Maldwyn answered Winston. "You are needed elsewhere, my little friend. You and your companions have a path to tread that you have only just put one foot on, and it is a long path. You are needed to help find the younglins' parents and those of Princess Sorona."

Merlin agreed. "They are all of high status in their communities and Sheela has been known to use blackmail on more than one occasion." He turned to Alyssa. "We all know of your benevolent nature, Empress; you would give yourself up to save their lives; but alas the truth of the matter is that she would kill you all anyway.

"There is nothing else for it, Maldwyn and his companions have to start their journey into the unknown and try to carry out a rescue."

He turned once more to his son. "You, Maldwyn, must be strong. You have good company and loyal too. You have Sunstar as your guide and protector."

"Sunstar?" asked Dimone.

Maldwyn held out his hand so that he could look once more on the ring. "That is her name, Dimone, Sunstar."

At the sound of her master saying her name she rolled her eyes up, but seeing there was no danger she settled back down to sleep again. She reminded Alyssa of Pyewacket when she was dozing off.

They had gone a little off task thought Dimone, so he tried to get them all focused again. He told them he would speak to Keatin, the commander of the Aerials, as soon as he could and get an eagle out to Jessica.

Gregmot, who was once an advisor wizard to one of the Empress's ancestors had a suggestion for Maldwyn. "I believe it would be prudent for you to start at the Morby Mountains and seek advice from the Golem. They are not as bad as people think they are, but they can be crafty and need watching, by that I mean they talk in riddles.

"It is the Green Man you really need to speak to. He knows more than anyone, but the Golems are probably the only ones that know where he is at the moment."

Maldwyn thanked Gregmot for his council. "We will do that very thing if you think it is the correct course for us. Now if there is nothing else here we must prepare for our journey."

As they were leaving the chamber Merlin called to Maldwyn to discuss his journey. "My son, you have grown well, Hubert did a good job with you as we knew he would. I hope that you now forgive me as I had no choice: your life would have been in grave danger had I kept you with me. I with all my tricks and magyk would not have been able to save you and it was imperative that you survived. I owed that much to your mother Casandra." Maldwyn held out his hands to his father. "I have had a good life with my father Hubert, thank you, Father. Casandra, so that was my mother's name, I always wondered what it was. Was she so very beautiful?"

"Oh yes," he replied.

He took a gold locket from his pocket and gave it to Maldwyn. "This is a likeness of your mother. Please take it with you, you will need it. That is all I can give you, Sunstar for protection, your mother's spirit for council. Just open the locket and she will come to you, but no one else can see her; and a special shrinking spell to help you carry all the provisions you will need in your journey, the one I used on Sunstar."

Maldwyn asked, "Does this mean that I do have to enlarge Sunstar at some point?"

"No, my son, Sunstar has the ability to do that herself. She will be there when you need her, and if need be she will carry out the starburst.

"It was her choice to become so small. She found me and asked for help to get away from the Draco slayers, so we made her disappear as an ornate ring. As yet she is the last of her kind.

"The spell is for your journey. You cannot possibly carry all the items you will need for your journey, but along with that is the rest of the spell that can reduce living beings. You must be vigilant, my son, because as you know it is strong ancient magyk and in the wrong hands can shrink armies.

"You can open the locket when you are feeling unsure about anything and your mother will talk to you and try to guide you. Her spirit is still in the locket but be warned it has limited use so please do not waste it. Only you will see her or hear her, unless you wish them to; be very aware of who is around you when you use it."

Maldwyn asked, "What is starburst?"

Merlin replied, "You will see one day soon I am sure."

Maldwyn thanked his father and turned to walk out of the room. Merlin said, "Maldwyn, I may have expired by the time you get back, but please know that I have always loved you and I will always be proud of you.

"And know this, your faerie grandfather who was a great seer, predicted that while you were on your travels you will meet three sisters; one of them will have hair so golden that when the sun dances on her hair a halo of light hovers all around her head. She has deep magyk, deeper than even she knows, and you will fall in love with her. She is called Olivia."

Maldwyn's eyes opened wide and the Bucca children giggled at the thought of Maldwyn getting married.

He once more thanked his father and awkwardly put his arms around him in a last farewell, tears in both their eyes.

This was not an emotion either of the wizards were used to but one that would have a profound and lasting effect on both men.

***

Alyssa and Dimone kept council with the other wizards for a further hour. They brought them up to date with things that were happening within the castle and the people in charge of the various departments that were on the war council.

Zamor spoke, "Would it not be more prudent, Empress, if the council met here in this chamber? We are still recovering our strength and it may take a further two days for us to be in full strength.

"But we also may be better off here as we do not want to become a side show, do we?"

Alyssa once more seemed a little puzzled. "My Lord Zamor, I am sorry but I do not understand; recovering your strength? None of you appeared to have suffered any ill effect from your time as a sleeper, and come to think of it, how do I know your name?"

He replied with a smile on his face that did not suit him at all; it looked like a grimace. "Empress, you have got to understand that we have been asleep for a long time, some of us for thousands of years. And while it only takes a matter of hours to recover our physical strengths it can take days for the magykal strength to fully come back to us.

"Even our facial expressions have not yet fully recovered. I still find it very hard to smile, Empress. And the answer to your other question is simple; you are the head of the castle, the Matriarch, the Romanova if you like. You are supposed to know everything that is going on in the castle, well most things anyway and names of your people are one of the things that should come automatically to you.

"This is a good thing because if you flounder and cannot recall someone's name then it is either because you have fallen ill with the mind sickness, or that the person does not belong in the castle and therefore is potentially dangerous at this time and could be a spy.

"You have to stay vigilant at all times."

Dimone looked around the room and said in amazement, "But I also know all your names now, why is that?"

Marlon addressed his young decedent. "You are married to the Empress and therefore you have the right to that knowledge also. As Zamor has pointed out, this could be a great boon for you to wheedle out any potential spies among us."

Zamor continued, "I know you are going to arrange things for a later meeting and I must admit we do need to meditate, but one last thing, Empress, I have kin in the castle but I am not recovered enough to know what he does or if he is a good man. His name is Desmy."

Dimone smiled. "Do not concern yourself about Desmy, my Lord Zamor. He is on the council and you shall see him later. He is the commander of our Navy."

Zamor was delighted. "Oh! I am so pleased, but not surprised, the sea has been in the family for many, many generations."

Alexo, who was known for his common-sense arguments and level headedness in a crisis said, "I think, Empress, that I personally require some meditation so if I can take my leave I will sit in my chair to recover my strength."

Alyssa spoke kindly, "We will leave you now Lord Alexo and let you recover in peace. We will be back at ten a.m. with the council."

As they left she said to Dimone, "I always thought it was strange that I knew everyone's names in the castle. This has happened ever since I became Empress, how strange."

CHAPTER TEN:
THE JOURNEY BEGINS

↑

Maldwyn and his companions had retired to the children's room to plan their journey. Winston asked, "What is the plan, Maldwyn, or should I say, have you got a plan?"

"Oh, yes I think I have now, but only with the help of my paternal father, Merlin.

"Without his help I was struggling to know where to start," said Maldwyn.

He continued, "We are to go high up in the Morby Mountains to seek the help of the Golem. Gregmot seems to think that there are still a number of Golems up in the mountains but we know this is wrong: there is just a young one now. He is a solitary fellow who is not used to the company of others. Therefore, we will have to tread carefully if we are to glean any information from him."

Winston hooted. "Then he is a lot like you, Maldwyn; you were a solitary figure until recently!"

Maldwyn smiled, he supposed that was exactly what people must have thought of him.

Pyewacket asked, "Is this Golem dangerous?"

Maldwyn grinned. "No. I do not believe he is, he is just grumpy. I have never met him but my father Hubert did once. I believe it was just after the Golem's inception.

"All the Golems had gone, all struck down by the Golem slayers after they had played havoc by fighting near a village on the far side of the river. They were so strong and so relentless when they were fighting that nothing else mattered to them. The fight spilled over into the fields and a full year's crop was ruined in a matter of minutes.

"There was nothing for it, the Emperor of the time had to send in the Golem slayers to eradicate them all; there was not one left. I am afraid they brought it on themselves.

"Alyssa's grandfather, who was the Emperor, had to feed the village for a whole year out of the grain store. Everyone hoped that there would not be a flood that year as no food would be available."

Pyewacket was still concerned. "How then is there one left if they all were slain?"

He answered, "Ah, well, my father Hubert, told me that there was an old hermit that lived in Fallingwell wood that needed a way to reduce the fly population that was plaguing him. He was human and had only limited magykal ability.

"He thought it would be a good idea to make a Golem so that it could do the job for him. But the process is precise and also banned due to the ferocity of the creatures when fully made. As he collected the clay people realised just what he was trying to do and reported him to the Justice so they went out with the slayers to see what he was up to.

"Unfortunately for the young Golem, he was already made but not finished and that was the problem. No one had the heart to destroy him so they exiled him to the caves high up in the Morby Mountains. He was grumpy and full of threats but had no harm in him: he was just an unhappy clay man.

"The poor thing is neither inanimate nor human. He was made so wrong that even known magyk could not fix him. He is a pitiful creature."

There was sadness in Maldwyn's voice; it saddened him that he could not help the Golem. "We must talk to him as there is nothing much that goes on at that side of the mountain that he does not know about, therefore it follows that he may know where we can make a start.

"He will probably know who we need to contact first to find Sheela's stronghold."

Stephann asked excitedly, "When are we going on our journey, sir? How many days will it take to prepare?"

Maldwyn looked at his companions. He was very aware how young the Buccas were and it worried him. Also, they were a secretive breed and not much was known about them.

"We are to set off first thing in the morning, Stephann, at sunrise, so be ready and waiting for me; I do not want any delays. And, Stephann, please stop calling me by those ridiculous names. I am Maldwyn that is all, Maldwyn."

"I am sorry, Maldwyn, I will remember in future. It just seems so disrespectful to call you by your name, and I thought it was forbidden to speak it!" he replied.

Maldwyn said kindly, "Yes, it is forbidden to say my real name but be assured, no one knows that only me.

"I am going now to prepare the provisions we will need, along with spare clothes and other things that may be useful on our journey, so please get some sleep. I will fill three pouches then we can each carry one. That way if one gets lost we still have food and water to last us."

"Pouches!" Doras exclaimed. "Do you not mean travel packs?"

He smiled at Doras. Maldwyn was finding that he smiled a lot recently. "My father also gave me the reducing spell that makes things extremely small and light." He patted the pouch on his belt. "You would be surprised what I have in here. This is how wizards have carried things for thousands of years; but this ancient spell that has been given to me makes things even smaller.

"But it must stay a secret: no one must know that I know this ancient spell. Now get some rest."

As he left Maldwyn waved his hand at Doras who thought he was saying goodnight, but he was actually stopping her from speaking about anything they had discussed, as she was the weak link, the talkative one.

**

The next morning, checks carried out, Maldwyn was at his companion's bedchamber bright and early. They were just finishing up their breakfasts. Alyssa had arranged for them to have it in their room. Doras ran to him and put her arms around his middle giving him a big hug. The human characteristics were really coming out in Doras now. The quicker she left their influence the better in Maldwyn's view. But he had to admit to himself that he loved the thoughtfulness of it all.

He allowed himself a small bowl of porridge while they were getting everything together and giving Doras and Stephann a pouch to fasten to their belts, and with staff in hand, they started their journey.

They said their farewells and started to make their way up the path that led to the mouth of the estuary where the water met the great lake. There was a small landing platform and jetty where the ferryman, Anton, would pull in to pick up his passengers that wanted to cross to the far side near the Morby Mountains.

Anton was half mermaid and half man. If it had been the other way around he would have had a fish's tail but because it was his mother who was one of the sea creatures and his father that was human, he had legs. But he had tremendous strength like his ancestral mermen forebears; he also had gills behind his ears and flaps to his human ears so that water did not penetrate them. His eyes were also strange in colour and they had a membrane that automatically came down

117

when his face was submerged in water, just like the merpeople.

Anton was a good soul and he was legendary for his sense of humour because he did not have one. Whatever traits he had received from his father, laughing was not one of them.

Anton slowly came across the estuary to pick them up. His house was halfway across, and that was usually where he waited for his passengers to call him, then he would set off in his barge as he had this time.

Payment to Anton was usually food, grain, wine or books; in fact, anything that you could afford he would barter.

They loaded themselves onto the barge and settled down for the ten minutes or so that it took to transport them across the water. When they got out Maldwyn gave Anton a large gold piece. This was far too much but Maldwyn knew that Anton did not normally get money from the customers and he needed to go to market to buy things in the winter months, so he gave it him on the understanding that it was also payment when they got back if they required his services.

They made their way back down the side of the estuary to the point just before it goes out to the great lake. This was where the hidden path was that led to the Morby caves at the far end of the mountain.

Doras looked up. "That is a long way, what if we fall?"

"You will not fall while you are with me," was Maldwyn's reply.

They set off up the narrow path. It was a winding path which was overgrown with nettle and bindweed ready to scratch or trip you as you tried to negotiate your way through. They eventually came to a clearing that had a small freshwater pool cut out into the rock. This was fed from a small trickle of water that came down the side of the mountain.

Doras turned around and gasped. She was seeing, as they all were, the lake in all its magnificent glory for the first time. The air was fresh, there was a feeling of invigorating healthiness about this place and you could see for many, many miles. Doras said she would like to live up here in three years' time, when she was old enough.

Maldwyn did not understand until Stephann told him that Bucca girls seem younger than they really were for a good many years, then at the age that Doras is now she would start to grow up rapidly and in less than three years she would be able to marry or leave the family, but if Doras so chose, she was old enough to do that now.

Pyewacket asked, "How old are you, Doras?"

She answered, "Oh I am nearly twenty-one by human standards, and we marry as you call it or leave home at twenty-three so this could be my last chance at being a younglin. But some will make that choice at eighteen."

Maldwyn stared at her. "That explains a few things about the human traits you have been exhibiting."

"I suppose it would," she said.

They all had one last look at the view over the lake and continued on their journey up the mountain trail. This part was not as steep but it was longer as it wound around like a snake instead of zig zagging like the first half of the path.

They seemed to be travelling for a long time when Maldwyn suddenly stopped them and said, "Up there, that I think is the Golem's cave. Please be quite as we do not want him to come out and start throwing rocks at us."

"Is that likely?" asked Stephann

"Well it is for the proper Golems but this one I am not sure of. I must confess I do not know what we are going to face," he replied.

They carried on as silently as they could until they reached the cave entrance. They slowly walked inside, with

Maldwyn's staff pointing forwards ready for trouble if there was going to be any. The cave was large and very high. It made them wonder just how big this small creature was? They walked forward and around the corner, but there was nothing, nothing to be seen but another cave that went deep inside the mountain.

They followed this cave for nearly a mile going back on themselves and all the time moving slowly upwards within the cave system. Pyewacket, who was strapped into a kind of carrying papoose on Stephann's back meowed, she needed the toilet and her now animal nature would not let her be discrete about it. Maldwyn lowered her from the harness and she ran off, tail and head held high as cats do when they are focused on something. She ran behind a boulder at the corner of the cave.

Doras laughed in her childlike innocent way and said, "I think Pyewacket needed the ladies' room."

They had stopped so it was decided that they should have a drink and something to eat. Maldwyn opened one of the leather pouches and hovered his hand above the opening; immediately, the food and drink they required came out of the bag and settled on a cloth on the floor. After they had taken refreshments and had a small rest they set out on their journey once more.

It was a further hour before they eventually turned a corner and were confronted by a small house built into the mountain. The door was made of wood but no trees grew up here which made Maldwyn think that the Golem had either ventured down the mountain or the house was already there and he was making good use of it.

The house was straight across from them and the door was large. It looked to Maldwyn as if it could at one time have belonged to a mountain giant. These creatures were now extinct. They were so gentle they were blamed for a lot by the humans and persecuted to extinction.

The door was painted red and the door knocker was silver and very impressive.

Maldwyn said, "I will go first but please be quiet and stay behind me. After all we do not know this Golem, he is an unknown species."

Stephann asked, "How is he alive if he is not alive?"

The wizard looked sad. "It is because he was not finished. The hermit did not know what he was doing and he also got interrupted by the Justice as they took the hermit into custody. There was an unfortunate number of mistakes made with this poor creature."

Stephann was still curious. "Will he get any older, Maldwyn?"

The mage answered, "No, I do not believe so, he was never given a special name, and a name even if it is given as a means of slavery is still a name. A name shows you are good for something even if that something is cruel. With no name you are good for nothing. There is a lot of magyk in a name, Stephann."

Doras had a tear in her eye. "The poor thing, he has no mother and no father and no one that cares for him. There is no wonder he is miserable, I would be. It is so sad. Can we do something for him, my lord?"

"I promise that as soon as we find your parents I will come back here and try to help him, but what help I can give I am not promising," Maldwyn answered.

She smiled and thanked him, then followed him as they crossed to the house and went through the open front door. The rooms in the house were very high. It was really a cave that had been turned into a house by its previous occupant.

They heard mumbling from the room ahead of them. They cautiously walked through the doorway and hoped that the Golem was indeed friendly.

The Golem looked up and shouted, "Goes away, you pesky creatures, you's not wanted."

They stopped dead in their tracks. The Golem was sat on a bench facing them. They all looked at the Golem's face especially Doras who just stared and stared at the Golem's forehead. The Golem had a number of runes deeply carved into his clay forehead. Doras wanted to cry feeling the pain that he must be feeling.

The Golem glared back at them. "Tis rude to stare ant nobdy telled you, yer pests, shoo, go away."

"Now don't be like that, Golem, we apologise if you think we are rude, but the younglins are very curious at this age and they have never seen a clay man before," Maldwyn said.

Doras said, "I was not being rude, Mr Golem, I was just wondering who did that to you? Does it hurt? What does it mean?"

The Golem grunted, "I don'ts want to speak to pests. I don'ts have to. Told yer don'ts want to."

He shuffled on the bench and turned to face the wall folding his arms in protest. He looked so funny that it took all Maldwyn's willpower not to laugh.

Doras on the other hand was very concerned about the clay man. "Dear, Mr Golem, could I ask, are you in pain from the marks on your forehead? I mean they do look very deep."

"Course I ams silly, you'd be in pain if you'd had this carved into your forehead wi a blunt knife, not even had the decency to sharp the thing first. But then I don'ts matter, I'm only Golem," he moaned.

Doras walked around the bench to face the Golem and she looked at his face. He lifted his head, still grumpy. "What you wants, pest?"

Doras raised her hand and put it gently on the Golem's head. She said, "You poor thing, no wonder you are so grumpy. Why did they do such an awful thing to you?"

Something strange happened as Doras touched the Golem's head; he actually looked as if a small smile had touched his face and it seemed to hurt him. "What yuz done, my mouth moved, it hurt silly, what magyk yuz done?"

Doras answered, "Well, that is better. If you smile, Mr Golem, you will find that you are less grumpy. Have you got a name? It seems rude to keep calling you Mr Golem."

He looked at her as if she was an idiot. "No! Silly, told yers, he not gid me a name, that why it urts."

She did not fully understand but felt so sorry for the creature she put her hand back on his forehead and with eyes shut started to trace the runes with her finger, and as she did she said, "I will give you a name. I will call you Mark! That way you will never forget that you were named after the marks on your forehead."

Now two things happened simultaneously. The first one was that Maldwyn shouted, "No," at the top of his voice. And the second was that the Golem stood bolt upright, raised his hands above him, threw his head back and screamed as loud as he could. The noise was one of great pain but also one of great relief.

As they looked on at the sight before them the clay started to crack and as if it was a cocoon it crumpled to the floor, but the Golem was not destroyed. What stood before them was a tall, well-built muscular, handsome young male with extremely white hair and pale skin.

He sat down on the bench and sobbed as he put his face in his hands. Doras picked up a piece of sacking from the floor and wrapped it around the creature to cover his naked flesh. Then she sat down at the side of him, arm around his back, trying to console him.

Doras spoke softly, "Oh, please do not be sad, Mark. You are very handsome and you are now human. I did not do it intentionally it just happened."

He lifted his head and looked at her. He felt his forehead with his now strong lean hands; the runes were gone and so was the pain. He tried to speak but found it was difficult at first. Eventually some words would come out that made sense but for now they did not. Doras cradled him in her arms as he continued to sob; the poor thing was in shock.

Maldwyn was the first to speak. "Doras! You have grown, you are a young woman! How? Why?"

Stephann answered as Doras too was feeling very fatigued. "Doras, what have you done? I told you that this happened to Bucca girls, didn't I? She is womaning, she is three years earlier than it usually happens but it has been known for it to happen at this age. It is their choice. They seem to like being younglins longer than male Buccas do and some have to be forced to change.

"I wondered if something like this would happen when she started making speeches about how nice it was up here, and how she wanted to stay and live here. The only thing that can make them do this early is love. Oh, Doras, what have you done."

Maldwyn asked her, "Is this true, Doras, do you love this Gol... sorry I mean Mark?"

She looked to the side of her at the young man she was cradling. "Oh yes I do with all my heart." As Doras said this the final stage of her womaning happened as her hair grew quickly down her back; it was like summer sunshine and had a glow to it even in the cave.

Maldwyn went into his belt pouch and pulled out the spare clothes that Doras had given him. He enlarged them and made them bigger to accommodate the new body that Doras had acquired.

He handed them to her and said, "I think you should really put these on, young lady!"

Doras thanked him and gently letting go of Mark she walked into the next room to get changed.

When she came back the sobbing from Mark had stopped and he was still sitting on the bench staring at his masculine hands. Doras sat once more at the side of Mark. He looked up at this beautiful woman before him and managed to say, "You love, Golem?"

Doras stroked his face as she replied, "No, I love Mark that used to be Golem."

He sobbed once more and buried his head in her arms. "Pain gone, hurt gone, Mark my new name, Mark loves girl."

Doras smiled and said, "Doras! Mark loves Doras."

He lifted his head and said, "Yes, Mark loves Doras."

Even his speech had started to improve.

CHAPTER ELEVEN:
MARK AND THE BRONZE MAN

ᛗ

Now that he had found life and a woman he loved and who loved him, truth be known Mark just wanted to stay in his house with Doras and learn how to be human.

It took a further few days for Mark to remember all he needed to remember for them to set out on the next leg of their journey.

Mark, with Doras as his mentor, was turning out to be a very gracious host, but the main thing that the rest of the company could not understand was the intelligence of what used to be a very ignorant Golem.

They turned to Stephann for an explanation that even Maldwyn did not have. Stephann said, "When Doras used her magyk to ease the Golem's pain, she inadvertently must have given him a portion of her magyk and also of her intelligence, not only turning him into a man but also into an intelligent magykal man.

"Without someone like Doras to teach him at this stage he could become a very dangerous foe. But I also suspect that some of the good nature and empathy for others that Doras possesses may also have been transferred, therefore he may not have been as evil as he could have been without her.

"You have to remember that Doras gave all of this freely with no thought as to how it might affect her. Mark's knowledge will grow and if he is anything like my sister he will have a thirst for knowledge and want to read as many books as he can get his hands on to gain more knowledge."

Winston hooted, "I am glad I witnessed this as I would have never thought it possible!"

Stephann smiled. "There are many things about Buccas that are not common knowledge, and we do prefer to keep it that way."

The company respected this and did not ask any further questions about the matter. Maldwyn set to work, with Stephann's help, turning the spare clothes that Doras had and one of his robes into clothes for both Mark and Doras. He then made the bed larger and turned one of the sitting benches that were around the house into a table.

There were still pots and pans in the cupboards and a fire with cooking trivet that were left over from the previous owner of the house, but Mark, who at that time could not eat or sleep, only used the house as a base for his wonderings around the mountain.

Mark when he was Golem never went far and always got home before dark because, although he did not have any real human traits the one he did have was fear. As Golem he lived in fear all the time of the slayers.

By the time the friends had finished the house looked like a human home. Pyewacket had found a chest in a small cupboard that was bursting with bed linen, pots, ornaments and curtains. The later was surprising as there were no windows, but Maldwyn soon altered that, making two medium-sized windows with glass. These were in what was the long room with benches, but now was the eating and sitting area.

Before they sat down for their last meal together and Mark's seventh meal ever, Doras made an announcement. She told them, "I am sorry, Stephann, but I am staying here with Mark! I really want to see our mother and father and make sure they are safe, but you know as well as I do that I was always the weakest link in the chain and you just did not like leaving me behind.

"Fate had me come with you on this journey for a reason and that reason was Mark. I know he will not manage on his own. It would be cruel and inconsiderate to turn the clay man into a handsome young human only to leave him to fend for himself. He needs to learn about love and consideration for others, not hate through the betrayal and desertion of his benefactors."

"Well, Sister, that was quite a speech indeed. Who would have known that when we set off with that small younglin she would turn into an eloquent speaking young woman? I am very proud of you and I think the decision is just," Stephann said.

Maldwyn interjected, "We thought this would happen as soon as we saw the bond between you both. I too think it is the right decision for you but, we are not happy to leave you two on your own with all the obvious feelings and emotions that you have for each other.

"Stephann seems to think you will want to have a life blessing with Mark in a few weeks anyway, so we think you should do that now if that is what you both wish! I can do the blessing tonight."

Doras looked at Mark and took hold of his hand. "I think, well I think, yes I would like to marry Mark. I use the word marry as I like that word better. That is what the Empress Alyssa called it and so will I."

She smiled at him and then attempted to explain what a wedding or as their people called it, a blessing was, and that they would be together for life, which for those two would be approximately seven hundred years unless they were killed.

Mark was ecstatic with excitement: he could not contain his enthusiasm. At last he would never be alone and he had someone that cared for him and also most importantly whom he cared for.

They had their wedding and later sat around the fire to talk. Mark thought this a very nice thing to do and decided that in the winter he would do this a lot at night time.

Mark told the company what they needed to know. He said, "You need to speak to the bronze man; he will know the best way to the hag's layer. He patrols this mountain trail looking for his charge, a beauty he called Europa, but after centuries of trying to find her, he thinks himself a failure. We had a lot in common but I was not able to see that then."

Stephann was curious. "How do you know all this, brother? After all you were not supposed to understand anything before this happened to you!"

Maldwyn interrupted, "Let me explain. Mark, when he was Golem came in contact with lots of people and creatures; but being what he was at the time he could not make any sense of the tales he was being told, but now he can.

"The thing is he has a new perception and thinking process which helps him to remember all those conversations and all the information he was being told. Am I not right, Mark?"

Mark replied, "Yes, you are. I can remember that once on my travels up the mountain pass I came across the Bronze man. He challenged me but I was a rude Golem and I told him off. He laughed a deep growly echoed laugh and I told him he was a pest and he was rude. I was not scared of him because I did not understand scared, well only slayer scared, and this he could not understand.

"He realised I was clay and asked if I was Golem. I said yes and what did it have to do with him. He ordered me to sit down and told me his tale, but I still do not fully understand it even now."

Doras said as she stroked his head, "Do not worry, Mark, I can explain most things later when our guests have left." He smiled and carried on, "He told me that he was from an island, a beautiful island, in a sunny place and he missed it so much. He told me he was the protector of a woman, the fair Europa, and he circled the island twice a day to look for brigands so that he could protect her.

"One day while he was doing this, he walked right into an invisible wall. There was a blinding flash of light and he found himself here in the Morby Mountains."

Maldwyn stopped him. "This is very important, Mark, do you remember his name?"

"Yes, it was Talos or Talus, he said it funny, hard to understand. But he did say he was like me, he was made, but he was finished which was then unlike me."

Stephann addressed Maldwyn, "Have you heard of him, my mage?"

Maldwyn smiled. "Yes, I have. When the humans first came to Nirvana they brought with them many thousands of books and many stories and beliefs. One of those stories was from a race of people that came from one of the warmest parts of the human lands. This place was one that had many ancient beliefs about great gods that lived on a mountain called Olympus.

"From what I can understand from the tales I have read, Talus or Talos was made by one of the gods to guard a woman called Europa, so Mark was right, that was his job in life. If for any reason Talos (I believe that is his real name) could not fulfil that role then I suppose it would have made him angry and confused. There were many creatures similar to him but all supposed to have their origins in mythology and many believe that they did not exist."

"Yes, but that is what I am supposed to be, Maldwyn. I was a myth or whatever anyone said I was. But I was not a myth I am here," said Mark.

Maldwyn answered, "But you, my dear fellow, were made in Nirvana that is the difference. This is a very magykal place, the human world is not, well only for the chosen few that is.

"Anyway, Talos disappeared without a trace as did a lot of the other creatures. There were a few that were slain but on the whole they just disappeared. It is just making me wonder how many other creatures like him are here in Nirvana.

Winston hooted, "And it would answer the question of where the hag came from too. She originally was not of our world."

Maldwyn studied what he had been told. "Merlin said, he had conjured up many portals to get the humans here. What if he inadvertently set off a chain of events that would see these portals not only opening up all over man's world but also going back in time and opening up in any random era it landed in?"

Pyewacket stretched. "Meow, so you think he may have messed with time too much and it had an unstable effect on the two worlds?"

Winston asked Mark, "What do you think he knows, Mark? Will he know where to find the hag or where we go next?"

Mark thought for a while. He was still trying to recall memories that had no meaning for him at the time they happened but now may prove very useful. "I think so; thinking about it he seemed to know a lot about her: where she came from, her cruelty, I would think he would know."

Winston hooted, "I wonder if she is the same creature that some of the villagers talk about at the far end of the forest? They have books and verbal legends dating back to when their ancestor first came here from the dictator's camps in their country of origin.

"These refugees talk about a folktale of a hag that rode a chariot pulled by hell hounds. There are different versions but all are roughly the same."

Merlin said, "Well that could be so, but we will know more when we meet her I suppose. Now if there is nothing else I would like to get some rest, unless you can think of anything we should know about the bronze man, Mark?"

Mark was deep in thought again. He was learning very quickly but it was hard trying to process and understand everything. "The only thing I can say is do not be scared of him. He is not a bad man, but when I met him the first time he was confused and like me now, he was trying to understand what was happening to him. I did not have any thoughts before but he has and the thoughts hurt him terribly."

"You are becoming very perceptive, Mark. You were a good choice for the husband of a Bucca," said Maldwyn.

Doras took hold of Mark's hand and said, "He will be even better by the time you get back with our parents. They will welcome him and he will at last have a mother and a father. We are tired and will say goodnight now."

Mark walked into the bedroom with Doras not really understanding just yet the full implications of marriage, or even why she was going with him: he had a lot to learn.

The next day they awoke to the sound of Doras singing in the kitchen while she made them breakfast. She was happy, well mostly, but she was worried about her parents. She was no longer a child with the protection of childish thoughts and the seriousness of the situation was finally sinking in. Doras went into the house just over a week ago a child and now she was a young woman and married.

The company said their goodbyes and set off walking up the mountain pass. It was easy at first but it soon became clear that this was not going to be the case for long. About a third of the way up it started to become more difficult due to the small rocks and stones that had slipped onto the path.

The winter sun was warm, but they were under no illusions that they needed to find a sanctuary before night fall threw the bitter cold wind, snow and rain at them. They carried on climbing for a further two hours up the steep path before the top of the pass could be seen.

Maldwyn decided that they should stop and have a rest and a drink, but the others wanted to keep moving until they reached the top then they would stop, so onwards they went. By the time they reached the summit of the mountain pass they were cold, yet sweating, hungry and more than anything thirsty.

Pyewacket meowed, "Is it possible to stop here for a while, I need to stretch my legs a little, please?"

Maldwyn and Winston, both sensing danger, said together, "No."

Winston carried on, "There is something not right up here, I sense it, but what it is I do not know. Any ideas, Maldwyn?"

He replied, "Not yet but stay close to each other and have your magyk at the ready. I have a feeling that when it comes we will not have much time."

They walked cautiously, Maldwyn holding his staff slightly in front of him with Winston on his shoulders. They had only gone a further one hundred yards when a dark figure jumped out at them from an overhang in the rock and started an attack on the company.

Although they had had a feeling that something may happen in this rough lawless terrain, they had hoped that their feelings were wrong, and the sudden attack was a shock to them all including Maldwyn. None of them were ready for the nasty fight that ensued.

It took only a few seconds for more of these vile creatures to join the first one; they were grossly overpowered. There were sparks, curses and spells flying in all directions from Maldwyn and Winston but the creatures kept coming back for more; it was as if they had no sense of pain and continued to fight with big gashes and heavy bleeding to their torsos.

Stephann decided it was time he too became an adult and mustered up spells that he had practised with his father for many years; the air was electrifying, the blood from both sides spilling onto the mountain pass and the rocks. These creatures, whatever they were, had a relentless nature.

Pyewacket, who was still on Stephann's back when the first creature pounced, was thrown some distance away and landed behind a boulder, her small body battered and bleeding from the fall.

In a way, this was very lucky for Pyewacket as she was no match in her present form for the adversary that confronted them. She would have been eaten without a second thought. She would not have had, and did not have, any chance to muster her magyk. So, for now, there she lay battered and bruised and in an unconscious state, but safe, waiting for the battle to end.

The rest of the company were obviously losing the battle and there seemed no way they could win this one until some hope came in the form of a Samaritan. They heard a loud, dull voice boom across the mountain tops. The creatures stopped dead in their tracks. They leapt up from one rock to another to escape whatever had made the noise.

Winston announced, "Well at least something scares them."

Maldwyn and Stephann gave a weak smile. Everyone was hurt in some way. Maldwyn had managed to kill two of the creatures and injure many more but he himself had suffered a hefty blood loss through a bite on his leg. He worked his magyk quickly to stop the bleeding.

Unfortunately for the creatures, Winston had made himself larger and had swooped down at the creatures' faces pecking at their heads and their eyes. It was altogether a gory sight. This action had given Maldwyn just enough time to compose himself and confront the creatures with his staff.

Two of the creatures had fallen dead at his feet. Winston, who was by that time in the full throng of his magyk, had made himself even larger and attacked the beasts at an alarming speed; several of them howled and ran away to recover themselves, then they had come back for more.

Pyewacket was unconscious behind the boulder and as yet no one was missing her. Stephann had two large open wounds to his arm and face, but he was happy in the thought that he had given as good as he had got, taking the leg off one of the creatures, and killing another.

After the creatures had run off and the booming voice had become silent, they looked around them to see who had spoken. The ground was shaking and the voice was deep and loud as it asked, "Are you all, all right?"

A very large bronze man walked up to them and sat down on a large boulder with a thud. He looked down at the injured warriors. "And what exactly are you doing on this part of the mountain? You do realise it is dangerous up here!"

That was when Winston realised that Pyewacket was missing. He ignored the question from the large man and started to shout for Pyewacket as loud as he could. There was panic in his voice and the others could hear it. Where was his beloved Sorona?

Winston flew around the site looking for her. He felt she was here somewhere but what if she had been taken, that thought did not bare thinking about.

Maldwyn said, "Use your magyk, Winston, try to find her that way. If we do it together we may be lucky but your grief will prevent it from working, you must calm yourself. You know that as much as I do!"

Winston did as Maldwyn had suggested and tried to settle down a little. They both closed their eyes and concentrated on Pyewacket. It was not long before they saw her in their mind's eye. Winston turned and flew over to the boulder that was hiding her.

The bronze man looked over the boulder, reached down and gently picked her up; she was limp and cold but not dead. He put her down with such a gentleness that amazed them all.

Maldwyn immediately went to her side to see what was wrong and said, "The only thing we can do is wait for her to awaken on her own. She has banged her head and is in a deep sleep."

All this time the bronze man was sat observing the company trying to work out what they were up to.

Maldwyn eventually remembered him and said, "I am sorry we have ignored you for so long, my friend. We were very glad of your assistance; please accept our thanks we are most grateful."

The bronze man looked surprised. He boomed, "You do not seem surprised or scared to see me, Wizard, how is this?"

Maldwyn answered, "Because it is you we have come to see, Talos. You are legendary in the land of men, and with some of the humans that are here in Nirvana, but it is a long story."

Talos replied, "I have nothing else to do and you are awaiting your small creature friend's recovery. So please,

Wizard, explain to me how she is not dead and how the owl can speak. You know me but I do not as yet, know you. Therefore, I would really like to know just what you are doing on the mountain?"

CHAPTER TWELVE:
AN ENCOUNTER WITH THE TROLLS

↑

They lit a fire and prepared a meal. Everyone was surprised to learn that Talos could actually eat food; he could also sleep and occasionally required the little boy's room. Apparently, the deity that constructed him had made him as human as possible, so that he could have empathy for the innocent, but, as they all saw, his skin was not human.

Maldwyn was curious. "Why do you still continue to patrol the mountain as you once did in your own land?"

Talos looked sad as he replied, "It is only the pass that I patrol. That was my purpose to patrol and guard the sweet Europa but alas I do not do that anymore. I do not want to think about what may have happened to her since my departure.

"I occasionally save people from the Chimera and that is now my sole purpose, albeit one I have chosen and not my maker Hephaestus."

"Then the tales of you scaring travellers off and killing them are greatly exaggerated," said Winston.

He answered in a faraway voice, "Yes, but I have been known to intervene when travellers are attacked.

"I once saw three brigands attack a young family. Sadly, they killed all of them before I could intervene, including a small child, it was heart-wrenching. But they got what they deserved: the Chimera, hearing the noise, came to see what was happening and immediately attacked and ripped the men apart. I for my sins stood by and watched it all; but I feel no shame for that; they were all murderers.

"I tell you this: if I had got to them first I would have pulled their arms and legs off as if they were flies."

Stephann was sympathetic and wanted to know if the Chimera had taken the family.

Talos told them, "No, they will only eat what they kill. I took the family and I buried them on the upper most peak of the mountain so that their spirits can look down on everyone they know.

"I dare say I have got the blame for the disappearance of that family. They usually blame the bronze man in the nearby villages, well that is what used to happen in my own land. Why would they kill younglins, especially the ones so small, they are barely a mouthful for them, an appetizer?

"I will never know what it is to be a father, but if I was it would be the worst thing ever to see your younglins hurt. My maker said he would make a mate for me and we would have children and a family life on a deserted island. We could live a normal life, but that was never to be. But I am here; wherever here is."

Maldwyn told him, "You are in Nirvana, or as the humans commonly know it: faerieland. It is very likely that you came through a portal when you walked into the light in your land."

Talos looked puzzled, then said, "I only ever told one person that story and it was a creature, a Golem, how would—?"

Stephann interrupted and tried to explain. "That is easy to explain, my sister and I are Bucca, and—"

It was the turn of Talos to interrupt. "What is a Bucca?"

Stephann smiled and carried on, "We are one of the magykal creatures that inhabit this world and we have certain abilities, especially where love is concerned. The Golem is now human and his name is Mark."

Stephann went on to recall all that had happened to his sister and the Golem in the last few days, and why his name was Mark.

Talos listened intently to Stephann, then said, "Lucky, Mark. Can I be turned fully human? I mean human size,"

"I am sorry, Talos," said Stephann, "but it was sympathy, empathy and eventually love that caused this turn of events. It is very unusual for this kind of thing to happen."

Talos was sad; he looked at the ground and started to move the earth about with a stick, which was as big as a tree branch. He had hoped when he heard the story of the Golem that he too could be turned human and not have to march continuously up and down the mountain pass, but alas that would not be so.

Maldwyn had a suggestion. "You say you are normal, apart from your skin that is, and you would like to be of normal size and have a wife and a family?"

"That is so," he answered.

Maldwyn walked over to the giant and touched his skin on his ankle; it was remarkably soft and pliable. He said, "I have a suggestion for you, Talos, and if you agree you will be of normal size; but with this will come a great responsibility.

"I have a spell that can make you human size. You can stay that way for as long as you wish, but if you want to become large again then you would have to pick a focus word that will make you large again in an emergency.

"What do you say?"

Talos looked surprised. "Is that possible? Can I really be as you say, Wizard? But what of my strength, will that go too?"

He replied, "No! Your strength will remain, plus any other powers that you possess will stay with you, but I cannot take your bronze away, but I feel that this is not the issue; it is just your size."

Talos replied, "Yes, Wizard, you are right, but you do not know me, and I get the feeling that you are instilling on me a great honour, so why, Wizard, why?"

"Why?" Stephann replied, "Because you saved us from the Chimera, and Maldwyn can tell a good man when he sees one."

Just at that moment Pyewacket started to come around. She moaned in pain then looked up at her beloved Winston who had not left her side. "Where are we, my love?" she meowed. "What happened?"

Winston was beside himself with happiness. "You gave me such a fright, Sorona, I mean Pyewacket. In fact, you gave us all a fright. When we get back to normal I will ask your father for your hand in blessing and there will be no more wondering for you, just party and fun with the Seelie Court. I thought I had lost you."

Winston hooted as if he was sobbing, but of course owls do not sob.

The bronze man was amazed at the love and tenderness the two small creatures felt for each other, even with their obvious disability. Maldwyn was concerned about her concussion and his attention turned to the small feline. After he had examined Pyewacket and they had relayed to her the events that had happened while she was unconscious, their attentions once more turned back to Talos and his problem.

Maldwyn apologised, "I am sorry, Talos, for the interruption but I was concerned for my companion."

"Of course, you were; it is only natural," he replied.

Maldwyn carried on, "Where were we? Oh yes. Are you sure, Talos, that you want to go through with this; it is a big responsibility as I have said."

Talos appeared puzzled. "Why would it be a responsibility? What are you not telling me, Wizard?"

He explained, "The magyk I am about to use is extremely ancient and in the wrong hands could tip the course of any war in the favour of the holder. You must take a life vow that you would die rather than give up the secret, such as your focus word, or that I know the only spell that can do this.

"Here is my dragon companion, Sunstar. She is the last of her kind, persecuted to the brink of existence until she went to my father Merlin for help and he used the ancient spell on her to protect her."

He lifted his ring hand up to show Talos. The Draco, knowing what Maldwyn wanted her to do, raised her head dreamily and looked at Talos, then curled up again in a cat-like curl with her tail wrapped around her body and head.

Talos answered, "The dragon has a reverse spell? A focus spell?"

"Yes," was the answer.

Talos nodded, and Maldwyn using his staff floated up to the side of the bronze man's ear and told him his focus word, while speaking the spell silently in his mind. Until that point he did not realise he could do that with such an intense spell.

It was a dangerous spell and Maldwyn knew that if anyone else learnt of it the battle would be lost before it started.

As Talos started to shrink, Maldwyn slowly floated down to the floor. Talos had the physique of a tall man so Maldwyn decided to reduce his size accordingly to six feet eight inches; this seemed a reasonable size for such a big man.

Talos looked down slightly at Maldwyn, tears in his eyes. He was only four inches taller than Maldwyn now and could hold a conversation face-to-face for the first time in his life. He said with his eyes tearful, "I am so grateful to you, Wizard, I am in your debt. Please tell me what brings you up here into this land of vagabonds and brigands?

"If there is some small deed I can do to repay you in some way then please tell me; I am very willing to help you in any quest you are on."

Maldwyn said, "Come, my friend, let us sit and talk over a mug of chocolate then you can decide how you can best help us, Talos, and once we have told you who we are and what we are doing I think you will be more than willing to help."

They drank and talked for some two hours before all went silent while Talos digested the story he had been told.

He suddenly stood up and started to walk about looking at his small legs and then at his hands, like Golem he was in awe of his new form.

He said, "I thank you, Wizard, and for this I will repay you by joining your little band and pledging myself to your Empress Alyssa as you have, and I swear to help her rid this world of the hag Sheela.

"I suggest that you next visit the Green Man, as he will, I think, be able to point you in the right direction for this hag Sheela."

Maldwyn was puzzled. "I understood that you could tell us where her base is. Do you not know?"

He replied, "Well no I do not, but I do know she resides at the other side of the mountain range in a small castle hidden so well no one, unless they are looking for it, can find it. But I heard that the Green Man has seen it, or seen her spies or helper. No one knows what they are but they have been spotted outside the castle going in and out of the castle at will. But although he saw them going down the path to the castle and disappearing as if they had entered, he could not see any entrance."

Maldwyn thought for a while. "The only possible answer is an enchanted entrance that only her minions can see!"

"No," Winston hooted, "there is a further possibility, an underground entrance that slopes down and goes right

143

under the castle walls. In a siege that type of entrance is a lot easier to protect as the enemy has to come through the tunnel to attack."

Maldwyn answered, "Yes you may be right, I did not think about that: sometimes when you use magyk a lot you forget that there are alternatives."

"Whichever it is, it is well hidden unless you get too close for comfort; either way we do need to find the Green Man if, as I have heard, he has the exact coordinates," Talos said.

Pyewacket meowed, "I am well enough to set off now, Maldwyn. Should we start while we have the dark on our side?"

Maldwyn looked fondly at his small companion; she was battered and bruised and still wanted to press on and not hold them up.

He was just about to answer when Talos said, "I believe your plan is worthy of consideration little one, but I know these mountains roads and I am still as strong as I was before. So, I believe we should rest now and set off in the morning, after a good breakfast and a good night's sleep, no one will hinder us."

The others all agreed. None of them really wanted to set off in the dark and Pyewacket needed the rest. Maldwyn gave Pyewacket a herbal drink and told her to rest; which she did as he had actually given her a sleeping draught.

It was just gone eight a.m. when they set off the following morning. Pyewacket was almost fully recovered due to Maldwyn and her own internal magyk, and she was well rested and ready for whatever faced them on their new day.

Talos lifted Pyewacket into the sling on Stephann's back and took point with Maldwyn bringing up the rear. He led them on for what seemed hours, following the path that was winding up and down the mountain and occasionally turning back on itself.

By now they were all ready for a rest and some food, so they made camp on the path; from their vantage point they could see the estuary that led to the lake below, and just make out the turrets of the castle, but if they had looked further round to the right and leaned over slightly they would have clearly seen below them the cave of Dora's and Mark.

They had their food in silence, then after they had cleaned everything away, and were having a hot drink before setting off again, Maldwyn broached the subject once again of the next destination.

Talos said, "As I have said, we need the Green Man; but the problem is finding him. I know there are lots of magykal creatures in these mountains but I have not met all of them, only a few. We need to carry on along the pass and look for signs of others so that we can enquire about the Green Man."

They all agreed with the plan mainly because they did not have another and set off on their journey once again. About halfway up the section of the path they were following, they heard a scream. It made them stop dead in their tracks.

Winston hooted, "That did not bode well! Someone is definitely in trouble."

Maldwyn and Talos both said together, "Down there."

They pointed to the large rock fall that was just ahead of them. Talos then said, "Wait here, I will take a look."

Talos walked up to the rock fall, then cautiously and slowly down the slope. He had to be careful of the scree that was around the rocks; he did not want to alert anyone to his presence.

He was treading stealthily for a large man, not a sound came from his feet. The others looked on as he disappeared beyond the lower rocks; it was not long before he was back and ushering the others silently up the path.

When they reached a spot that was a safe distance from the rock fall and the sound of the distressed dismembered voice had faded, Talos told them what he had seen.

He told them that the rock fall was not natural but made by some sort of creature; there was an entrance to a cave which, he suspected was the reason for the rock subterfuge.

Talos continued, "I heard a deep gruff voice; it sounded like it would be coming from a large creature and that would tie in nicely with the height of the cave entrance.

"He was talking to someone. I suspect they were the source of the screaming we heard earlier as the person or creature was still sobbing. I also suspect there was more creatures in there, but of what variety I do not know."

Maldwyn asked, "What did he say to the other one that he had obviously captured?"

Talos said, "That was the odd thing, he said you will do my bidding and bring down the rock in one swoop where I say. We will find it and you will help, then you can retrieve it and form it for me.

"How would, what sounds like a small creature, bring down a rock?"

Stephan answered, "Magyk. Maldwyn could do it."

Maldwyn looked worried. "I can only bring down small amounts at a time to move what this creature obviously needed moving. I can only think of one creature that could do this! And they are extinct.

"Oh my word, we need to get in there, this is not good if the being I am thinking of still exists then the creature within it must not be released."

Winston said, "You do not mean the rock elementals, do you, Maldwyn?"

"A what," said Stephann.

Maldwyn explained, "There is a creature called a rock element. No one in living history has ever seen one. The

146

creature went into the realms of mythology hundreds of years ago. This creature can focus such a destructive power that it can bring down the whole of the mountain if it wished.

"It is said that these creatures are docile, in the main good and mild mannered. They are not vicious creatures but if the one within is brought out in anger and pain it shows no mercy until it calms and that can take a long time. As I said no one has ever seen them so I do not know what they look like.

"It is imperative that we find and rescue it as not to do so could be catastrophic. The creature could bring down the whole mountain and the people we care for on it. And the debris would probably reach the castle causing great damage and death there too."

Talos spoke, "Then we need a plan, we need to know what the creature is that is captured."

"I will go," said Pyewacket, "I can hide in the shadows."

"No," Stephann said, "I will go. One of my guises is a mouse. I can get in easy and you still need your rest, your Highness."

It was the first time in months that Pyewacket/Sorona had been called by her designation, as the princess was the daughter to another faerie princess, Emily. She gave a small meow and bowed her head gently in agreement.

Stephann quickly turned himself into a mouse and scurried away to do some spying.

Talos looked on. "You are all strange beings and not at all what you seem to be. I am glad I am on your side." He looked at Pyewacket. "Princess? Really?"

They waited and waited, but there was no sign of Stephann. They all thought he would be back within ten minutes, fifteen at the most but he was not. After nearly two hours Talos announced he was going in. He could not wait any longer and he was worried, as were they all about Stephann.

Just as he started to walk down the rocky path a small mouse appeared and started to slowly change shape as it scurried towards him. Stephann stood quite still for a few seconds to recover from his shape changing ordeal; it took a lot of energy to turn into something so small. And to keep that shape for such a long time was an even greater strain on his energy reserves.

When he could finally move without feeling weak, he walked over to his friends and said, "I hate that feeling." He looked at Pyewacket and Winston. "I hope the drain on you both is not as bad as mine. You have both been in these guises for such a long time."

Maldwyn asked, "Are you all right now, Stephann?"

"Yes," he replied, "but I need to tell you what it is that is happening."

CHAPTER THIRTEEN:
THE SISTERS OF FIRE

↑

Stephann was quite excitable by this point because he had seen a vision in the cave that he thought he would never see; he had seen a beautiful girl, and like his sister he thought that he too was in love. How could this possibly happen to the two of them within a few days? It seemed impossible, but here he was having feelings he was not sure of. He knew he had to pull his thoughts together and tell Maldwyn and the company just what he had seen so that the rescue of the three sisters could begin.

Stephann told them, "There are trolls in there, the nasty type that live deep within the mountain; they are different to the gentle mountain giants that live on the surface.

"There are two of them, Uhug and Erk. They have captured three sisters that they say can produce fire in rock just by thinking of it."

Talos was curious. "How did you know that? Did the trolls tell you?"

Stephann laughed. "No, they would have eaten me, not talked to me. It was the sisters that they had captured, who told me all this."

It was all starting to fit together now. Maldwyn was both worried and excited at the same time. He interrupted Stephann. "I am sorry to interrupt you but you say three sisters? And they can make fire in rock. Would one of them be called Olivia by any chance?"

Stephann grinned and answered a little satirically, "Yes, Olivia, Isla and Mille. I wonder, Maldwyn, how would you know that?"

Maldwyn answered, "It is true then, the prophecy that was told to me by my father; as my faerie grandfather foretold when I was born, I would marry one of three sisters and her name would be Olivia. It is probably nonsense."

Stephann still grinning replied, "Oh yes, I remember him telling you, Maldwyn." Stephann had not forgotten and Maldwyn knew that.

Maldwyn said, "Anyway, I think I may be right, and this Olivia may be one of the three sisters: a rock elemental. I do not think anyone even realised that there would be three of them, it was always assumed that there was only one. I am sure I am right! And if I am we must be cautious and try not to make them angry. They could bring down the whole mountain if they get too distressed."

Stephann started to speak and said, "No, Maldwyn, these three sisters are very gentle and will not do anything to endanger life; of this they assured me, it takes many hours of torture to get the fire elemental out of them involuntary."

"What do they look like? No one has ever seen them," said Winston.

Stephann smiled. "That is because they are a lot like the Bucca; they hide in plain sight. My family like to look humanoid, but these creatures do not have to, they are humanoid.

"I had a very good conversation with them and to be honest they are remarkable women."

Maldwyn asked, "You mean they are human?"

"Oh yes and very beautiful that is there real self. It is what they hide inside that is the secret," said Stephann

Maldwyn said, "So they are very beautiful, are they?"

Stephann laughed. "Yes, very. Maldwyn, did you think you were going to marry a monster of unknown origin?"

He replied, "Well I was not sure when it started to dawn on me, rock elementals and Olivia together; I thought maybe we would be incompatible, she could have been lizard-like in appearance.

"But first we have to free her along with her sisters, my future may depend on it."

"It would seem so, Maldwyn," said Talos. "We should make plans and after that I would really like to hear this tale of yours."

The company sat down and started to talk about their plans for a quick and easy rescue with little risk to the elementals themselves. The trolls on the other hand could be a casualty of war.

The plan was for Talos to creep in while the others waited outside, as his stealthy footsteps were legendary for such a big man. Stephann was to become a mouse again and go to the cave and tell the sisters what was happening. Then Talos was to creep into the cave and take the two trolls unawares, grab them, and throw them against the wall rendering them unconscious.

Maldwyn would stand by with his staff to cast a magyk spell if it was needed. Once the trolls had been rendered unconscious, the sisters could escape. But, as it usually is with most well thought out plans, the execution can be different to the planning. This occasion turned out to be no different.

Stephann turned his shape back into a mouse and scurried off to approach the three sisters to tell them the plan, but they were not totally happy with it. They had something to tell Maldwyn and that something was to do with the Green Man, but before Stephann could do anything about telling Maldwyn Talos had appeared and mayhem ensued.

Talos tried to grab the trolls but they were very quick for chunky creatures. One of them ducked, fell at Talos's feet and pulled on his ankles, but as he stepped back to get away from him, he fell backwards over the other troll that had crouched down behind him. Talos went crashing backwards hitting his head on the floor as he fell.

He was furious. He got up and flew for the one that had tripped him over but he was too quick. By this time Maldwyn had arrived and had realised what was happening; there was what you could only call a brawl in front of him.

He lifted his staff and said the spell under his breath. This caused Talos as well as the trolls to be frozen in time, just staring at each other where they stood. Stephann and Maldwyn had the two trolls leaning against the cave wall and out of trouble in no time. Unfortunately for Talos he too had to wait thirty minutes for the spell to wear off.

Talos was not pleased when he came around; he was very angry with the trolls and also himself for falling for such a trick. Maldwyn apologised to Talos; he was most upset but he had to concentrate now on the sisters and see if they could help them in their quest to find Sheela's castle. It would be greatly in their favour if they could have three elementals on their side during the battle.

Talos said, "I will be all right, I am just feeling a little dizzy at the moment, hurt pride I think, Wizard."

Maldwyn had decided to stay with Talos and help him to bind the trolls with ropes of magyk. The others went to the sisters' rescue. They had found the sisters in a smaller cave a little further in. Stephann, Pyewacket and Winston went into the cave to get the sisters but first they had to move the metal grid that was stopping their escape. This was the only part of the cave that could be used as a prison as there was only one way out.

When the company came back accompanied by the three sisters, Maldwyn was immediately struck by their beauty and was attracted to the one with flaming red hair; he had no sooner realised this when he remembered once again the prophecy.

The sisters told them that the trolls tried to kidnap them from their village where no one knew what they were; everyone in their village thought they were just three sisters, that were orphaned and were now all alone in the world.

They took in washing, dressmaking and made pottery to earn a living, but every few years they changed villages or went back to the cave in the mountains until people forgot they existed. They would reappear in a new village to live a normal life again for a further few years. How the trolls found out about them they did not know but the trolls did say that they needed to find the gold that was hidden in the mountain for their mistress.

They evaded capture and ran for the caves but the trolls eventually caught up with them.

The one called Millie said, "She's evil and we have heard that she is waging war on the rest of Nirvana. She is wanting to start with the castle that is near the great lake.

"She cannot be allowed to do this so we had refused to help, but the trolls started to use torture on us and we feared we may not be able to hold our powers at bay for much longer. If we had released them the whole of the mountain could have come down and we could have been responsible for killing thousands of people."

Maldwyn said, "We are from the castle by the great lake and we are searching for the Green Man so that we can find the hag Sheela. She is the one trying to take over the castle and Nirvana. We would be grateful if you would join us in our quest to bring her down and rescue the parents of the Bucca children and Pyewacket, my ladies!"

Isla looked confused. "I think we should sit and let you start from the beginning, my mage, then we will decide what to do."

They decided to stay under cover in the cave and talk about their histories. It seemed that they were now becoming a good-sized group, all with unusual powers that may be needed at some point during the final battle.

They all discussed their relevant stories starting with Winston and Pyewacket and ending with Talos and his heart-wrenching journey to becoming a normal-sized man, and therefore hopefully gaining a normal relationship with a wife and children. But at Maldwyn's request, Talos said nothing about the reducing spell, only that it was a one off and could not be repeated.

Olivia said, "I hope you do not mind me asking, Mage, but have we met before? I feel I know you."

Maldwyn did not like being put on the spot in this way and he did not feel comfortable with it, but he did realise at this point just how attracted he was to this redheaded beauty.

He answered, "No, I do not believe we have met or I would have remembered, especially with you being the fabled sisters of fire."

"You are right, Mage," she said, "I would also have remembered you." She bowed her head in reverence and then stood straight up at the side of her sisters, each with hands one over the other down in front of them.

Talos asked, "What are we going to do with those two?" He nodded at the two trolls who were trying desperately to wriggle out of their bonds.

Maldwyn smiled wryly. "We are going to let them go."

Talos was speechless, but after a long pause and everyone staring at Maldwyn, he said, "Oh do not concern yourselves, I am going to let them go but with a few alterations to their brain chemistry.

"In other words, they will have no memory of us, Sheela or where they came from. They will know they are brothers and they will know each other's names but as for anything else they will be completely ignorant to everything.

"I will make it so that they are docile trolls, and this should enable them to obtain gainful employment among any of the humans or the faeries."

Maldwyn walked over to the two trolls, lifted his staff and thought of the spell he required. Within the hour the trolls were meandering down the mountain path towards the great lake and a new life. They were laughing as they went and talking about all the help they could give people, and as long as they received food and lodging they did not require wages.

You see it never occurred to these trolls to ask the question of who they were or where they came from, or what they did before they took the journey down the mountain. They were so stupid that these thoughts would never cross their minds. The only two things now for certain was their names as Maldwyn had made sure they remembered those and the compulsion to help people and take care of each other.

By the time all this was done it was late afternoon and Maldwyn wanted to push on in search of the Green Man.

He said, "I think we could make a further few miles before dusk if we set off now."

But as they started to gather their pouches and cloaks up off the floor Isla said, "We have a better idea! There is a lower passage that runs under the mountain for a fair way. We know it well and it is on the way to the Green Man's area of the mountain. It may be prudent for you to stay in this tunnel."

Stephann asked, "Is it safe?"

"Oh, bless you, yes," she said. "Very safe; we use it all the time to get from one village to another. And all our household belongings are just down there in another cavern, we need to pick them up."

"Pick them up!" exclaimed Stephann questioningly.

Maldwyn laughed. "I think I am not the only one that has a few spells up my sleeve."

Stephann opened his eyes wide. "You do not mean that all your house can be put into a pouch?"

"No," laughed Isla, "we do not have the skills that the mage has, but we do have a reducing charm that our mother gave us. Millie is better at carrying out the charm's instructions than Olivia and I.

"She can reduce things but only to the size of dolls furniture, therefore we have to each carry a backpack."

He exclaimed, "Thank you for explaining." There was a pause then he continued, "Charm?"

"Yes," answered Winston. "It is well known that charms made by magyk, if used correctly, can work for many years but it takes a great wizard to do what Maldwyn does. Was your mother faerie?"

"Yes," answered Millie. "She was a wood nymph but our father was the Firestarter for our world. It was a weird combination but they loved each other very much. They were both killed in the last troll wars."

"But that was over a thousand years ago!" said Pyewacket.

Millie laughed. "Yes, we are quite old, but without intervention to our lifespan, we think we can live for two maybe three thousand years. We are new creatures; we are the sisters of fire."

Maldwyn smiled once more as he admired the tenacity of the three sisters, but with the urgency of the situation Maldwyn needed to get on. He said, "Please take us to your present home and I will see if I can make your belongings light enough for one of you to carry."

"Thank you, Mage," she replied graciously, and with a bow of her head she walked towards the back of the cave.

They followed the sisters through an opening; it was very tight but they all managed to get through it. As soon as they were through they were amazed by the size of the cave and the amount of furniture that was in it.

The sisters had made themselves very comfortable. It was like a little house but there was no upstairs: it was all on one level. The problem with the reducing charm was that it had to be put on every item that you wanted to shrink down, so the process of moving house used to take them a long time, sometimes up to three days.

Maldwyn knew this, as he knew the way that charms worked, so with one sweep of his staff and uttering the words under his breath of the reducing spell everything shrunk immediately. They had no need to take anything out of cupboards and drawers. Everything was left where it was but all the pieces of furniture were now on a smaller scale of less than half an inch for each piece of furniture.

Everyone proceeded to carefully pick it up and put it into one of the backpacks. The sisters were most impressed: one of them could carry all their household belongings and it only filled a quarter of the backpack. Maldwyn was concerned, so he cleared everyone's memories of how he had done this, just in case one of them got captured.

It was not normal for minds and thoughts to be stifled in this way, and it was frowned upon by the good magykal creatures of Nirvana, but in times of war to protect others it was sometimes necessary.

All this done, the sisters put on their cloaks and they set off on their journey through the caves. The cave pathway did not go straight, in fact it was harder going than the mountain pass above them, with its undulating floor and loose stones; it was not a well-trodden route, and in places was quite hard to walk upon.

One minute they were going up, and the next down. There were traces of mining: tools and buckets that were probably left a very long time ago by the dwarfs. They mined this side of the Mobby Mountains many years before the humans arrived, but the seams went dry, or so they thought, and now they mined diamonds under Sorby Hill.

Maldwyn said, "I do suspect that if they knew gold had been found on this side of the mountain they would be back.

"That is why they must not be told, and anyway technically speaking gold has not been found as you did not reveal any."

"There is always a chance that the trolls and their mistress were wrong," said Olivia. "This way."

They had just reached a point in the track that had a fork in it. Stephann asked, "Where does that go?"

Millie answered, "You do not want to go that way; there are many drops and loose stones near the edge. The sheer drop is terrifyingly deep, it leads to nowhere, only death."

They walked until they reached a further cave chamber which the sisters told them they had used previously when they were in hiding.

Maldwyn thought they had travelled far enough and suggested that they stop for the night; everyone was in agreement as they were now feeling quite exhausted because for some reason the cave system was harder and took more energy out of them than the mountain pass, but a lot of it was down to stale air.

As they sat around after the evening meal talking of their adventures and their past lives, Olivia walked over to talk to Maldwyn. She sat beside him and said in her soft demure voice, "So, Mage, the prophecy?"

Maldwyn blushed. "Now who told you about that?"

"Ah, a little mouse," she whispered.

He replied, "Well, if you know about it, what else is there to know?" He grinned.

Maldwyn had thought he had forgotten how to smile, grin or have a jest with anyone; but the Bucca children had changed all that, they had been as good for him as he had been for them.

Olivia also smiled. "Well, you like what you see, Mage? Or am I a disappointment?"

He looked at her terrified but soon realised she was teasing him; he could tell Olivia was a lady of high spirit and a lady that did like to jest occasionally. After a few seconds they both burst out laughing; it was the beginning of the courtship and somehow, they both knew it.

It was to be an uneventful night apart from the sound of a few rats scurrying around in the caves and the bats from another distant chamber: it was peaceful. The cave system was like a labyrinth due to the mining over thousands of years; first one part of the mountain then another had been excavated until the dwarfs thought there was no more to be found, but they left one saving grace: there were shafts for air that went right to the surface and without these the cave would have been intolerable.

It was these shafts that the bats used for their nightly excursions out into the countryside, making quite a lot of noise in the process. The shafts were good for travellers as the air, while being a little stale, was breathable and made it bearable to be down inside the mountain.

They continued on their journey the next day, the sisters leading the way to the next intersection. After about a mile they arrived at the intersection that the sisters had told them about, but it was not one of simple choice. This one had five different pathways leading from it and five different choices.

Maldwyn asked, "Well, which do we take, my ladies?"

Isla answered, "It is a difficult choice, mage. If we start at my left-hand side, the first path leads to a dead end and the nest of a sleeping Boggart; she has been asleep for many hundreds of years and we do not want to awaken her although there is a way out through there.

"The next path, we think, leads to the surface but it is treacherous and full of dangers.

"The one straight ahead we have not tried yet. There are sounds that come from the dark passage that make your blood run cold, and we were never brave enough to go down there to find out what lies within.

"The next one is one of choice, but again there is something dwelling in there, but whatever it is, it has never bothered us.

"Now the last one to my immediate right is definitely one we do not want to go down. It leads to a labyrinth of caves and tunnels. A creature walks its path the like of which we have never seen, a terrifying creature."

Isla shuddered, and Millie continued, "The creature is very tall and broad; we do not know its nature but it looks odd."

Maldwyn asked, "Looks odd? You have seen it? In what way does it look odd?"

She continued, "Oh, Mage, we glimpsed it briefly. If you were to see it, he only has one eye right in the centre of his forehead. Such an evil-looking creature we have never seen."

Talos laughed his loud haughty laugh. "Oh I know this fellow. He is from my land; he is the fabled Cyclops, that is if he is the same one. I always understood that there was only one as there is only one of me. I have never met him but if he got transported down here instead of to the surface I can understand why he's so grumpy."

Maldwyn asked, "So you have not been in that cave since? And you do not know where it leads?"

"No, my mage," replied Olivia. "We thought it best to leave the creature be; his anger is most real, he screams like the banshee."

"Or," said Talos, "maybe he is in pain due to the lack of food, the dark and the excessive cold and heat. Please, my ladies, do not dismiss the Cyclops as a daemon or monster, he's probably just a one-eyed man who is in pain."

"Then we will take that route and see if we can do anything to alleviate the creature's pain," said Maldwyn.

The sisters started to talk all at once; their objections were quite convincing but not to Maldwyn. He was not convinced and he held up is hand for silence. "Or the poor creature may just be frightened. In that case we should help the poor thing and he may in turn be so grateful that he may join us. He sounds like someone that we could use as one of our allies on our quest.

"And before anyone suggests he only has one eye, if it is the same creature that Talos is talking about and I have read about in the human books, then he is not violent, not without cause."

Pyewacket said, "Meow, we are all strange creatures to someone; this is because we are not all the same. I say meow, we should give him the opportunity to speak and have the benefit of the doubt." She continued licking her paws and washing herself as if the conversation she had just had was of no consequence.

Maldwyn was concerned: he knew that if Pyewacket did not take her true form soon she may never get rid of some of her cat traits.

Although cautious they decided they would go down that route, but that Maldwyn and Talos would go first with the three sisters following on. Maldwyn had wanted the sisters to take Pyewacket and walk behind Stephann as he had some magykal powers that were growing fast. But they objected saying that if needed they could produce fireballs in their hands for protection; the only reason they did not use these methods on the trolls was because they were still denying that they were elementals.

CHAPTER FOURTEEN: CYCLOPS.

ᚠ

The path that was taken was indeed hazardous with its fallen rocks leaving loose stones underfoot and sharp rocks sticking out of the walls. It was dark and had a very pungent smell, but as Maldwyn pointed out sanitation would be non-existent for this poor creature.

The company were lucky that they had Maldwyn as he had made sure a portable private cabin was available for their ablutions whenever they needed it; Maldwyn had tried to think of everything.

As they went further up the tunnel, torches in hand, they heard howling as if a creature was caught in a trap and in severe pain. The sound was a fair distance away due to the tunnel being so long and the sound resonating down to them like it would in a tube. Maldwyn asked them to stop as he wanted to take stock and see that everyone was going to be safe.

Talos switched off his torch to preserve the batteries as Maldwyn had illuminated his staff as they spoke. Talos was still in awe of this feat of human engineering and kept stroking the torch as if it was magyk.

Maldwyn, having observed this, said, "Yes, the humans did bring some intriguing little trinkets with them and a good amount of knowledge too. There are two small factories making these torches and other such items. These kinds of tools are not forbidden, it is projectile weapons that the magyk folk fear as humans are so volatile."

"Don't they worry that they may make weapons in secret?" said Talos.

"No, there is too much magyk involved, they are not that stupid," answered Maldwyn.

"Right, back to the plan. I think you should all stay here while myself and Talos go to talk to the creature. We will then, and only then, know if he is a Cyclops or not."

There were a few arguments as everyone wanted to play their part, but Maldwyn insisted and Maldwyn usually won when he knew he was right. It was no good them arguing with him; he wanted to keep them safe and that was uppermost in his mind.

Within ten minutes, Talos and Maldwyn were heading down the passage alone towards the creature's lair. As they got nearer they could hear crashing and banging, then there was silence and then came the sobbing. The creature had been hitting his head on the wall as he started to sob. It was a broken creature in a lot of ways: a pathetic figure.

As they approached he heard them coming and stared in their direction. He listened for a few seconds then shouted, "Who's there? If you have come to take me for food then so be it, but you will have to fight me first."

Maldwyn said, "Do not be afraid, we have come to help you, not to harm you. Let us come to you and we will talk."

Maldwyn was ready with staff in hand, while Talos was ready to administer brute force if necessary.

As they approached the creature they could see he was ready for them. Then he saw the light from the staff and he was blinded by it. He shielded his eye as it hurt so much to look upon the light after so long.

He shouted, "What magyk are you wielding to make my eye hurt so much? I have told you, you will not get to me that easily."

Talos shouted, "I am Talos, the bronze one. Are you Cyclops?"

The creature lifted his head. He was by now getting used to the light and could see the silhouette of the two figures behind it, and for all the fear inside him he was glad of the spoken word and the company of others, even if it was just before his death.

Talos shouted again, "Are you Cyclops?"

"Yes," he answered. "How do you know of me in this godforsaken hell, have you come to destroy me? Because if you have you are too late, I was destroyed in this place long ago."

It was Maldwyn's turn to try. "I am Maldwyn. I am a wizard, you may know me as a Shaman or a mage. We heard your cries and we are here only to help and take you from this place." The Cyclops started to sob again. Gone was the great fearless fighting machine, he was now a broken creature too long in the dark abyss, and he had been broken in mind and in spirit.

Maldwyn whispered to Talos, "My father went between the worlds with good intentions but at what price, Talos? At what price?"

Talos said, "It is not your fault, Wizard, you are doing your best, as he did."

The creature was staring at them by this time, and as they stood there he took a few steps towards them and they could see he was indeed broken. The beast was thin with long hair and bedraggled in appearance. The poor thing was indeed a pitiful sight.

Cyclops said, "Are you really Talos? But then that cannot be. You are a giant among creatures. How would that be possible?"

Talos replied, "Like you, my friend, I have been brought here from our homeland when I walked into the light, and many changes occurred with me also.

"Can we please come forth and help you; we are not your enemy."

The creature nodded. "It would not matter if you were, I have no strength left any more; I am a beaten miserable creature. I could not fight you."

They walked forward and the pity they both felt for the Cyclops was great. Talos helped the Cyclops to sit again while Maldwyn prepared a broth for him with healing herbs and a potion to give him strength.

After he had taken the potion he lay down and slept. He was exhausted and nearer to death than he had realised.

Maldwyn said, "Talos, will you go and relay what has happened to the others in our company and ask them to come here. We will camp for a few hours. I cannot leave the Cyclops now, I must ensure he is going to be all right."

Talos nodded and went down the long winding passage to bring his companions back to Maldwyn and the Cyclops.

By the time they got back to Maldwyn he had a small fire going and was bathing the Cyclops' head and upper torso with a healing bath. As soon as all of them saw the sight in front of them they felt sorry, and the sisters felt ashamed that they had not held their hand out to the creature when they first heard his cries.

Maldwyn, knowing what they were thinking, said, "You could have done nothing to help him. If you had come to him earlier he would have run you off or thrown something at you. Everyone has a breaking point and the Cyclops was no different. He needed to reach that point to allow us to help him."

"Thank you, Mage, but it does not make us feel any less guilty. He was asking for a charitable act and we did nothing.

If we had, he may have allied himself to us and the troll incident may never have happened," said Millie.

"Or," said Talos, "you could have been badly injured and died. It is not worth even starting to think that way, so please do not."

"And," said Stephann, "we may never have met you." He looked at Isla who blushed and felt a little embarrassment coming over her.

They did not know how long it had taken for the Cyclops to come around again but it was a long time. He kept drifting in and out of sleep. Stephann had said it was six hours.

Maldwyn had given him a wristwatch that he had bought some time ago at the village market but he preferred his cuckoo clocks and his large ornate grandfather clock that he had downstairs near the door.

The human side of Maldwyn liked anything man-made and tried to embrace their inventions, but he still looked out of the window when he was at home to tell the time with the tree clock that he himself had put together.

As the Cyclops regained consciousness he yelled out and tried to sit up. Talos put a hand on one of his shoulders and said, "Steady yourself, Cyclops, you are among friends."

The creature looked up at the faces around him, then back at Talos. "I thought I was dreaming. Please tell me, bronze man, that this is not a dream, and that my rescue is imminent. That is unless you too are trapped."

Maldwyn approached. "You were never trapped, my good friend, you could have got out at any time, but as you do not see very well in the dark you could not find your way out."

The creature was amazed. He looked such a pathetic sight in the light of the fire and torches: his face drawn, bags under his eye and his clothes hanging from his torso as if they had never fitted him.

What had become of the once terrifying creature he had been? He was now broken, all due to Maldwyn's father underestimating the power of the Vortex.

Talos asked, "Do you have a name?"

He replied, "No, I get called so many vile and insulting names and the stories of my birth are all wrong. I was a normal human child. The eye was a curse that was put upon my mother while I was in her womb."

Pyewacket meowed, "That is terrible, and your mother did not name you because of your eye?"

"No. I was nicknamed Cyclops after the mythological creature because of this terrible affliction I had."

Maldwyn gave him some more broth and told the others he needed to meditate; he went into a small corner of the cave and took out the locket and opened it to reveal a facsimile of his mother.

Immediately his mother appeared to him. "My precious son," she said, "you must be troubled to ask something of me. What is it my son?"

Maldwyn, tears in his eyes, said, "Mother, it is not for me but for the creature called Cyclops who needs your help. He is not the real Cyclops and I wondered if there is any way we can reverse the spell that was put on him while he was still in his mother's womb?"

Maldwyn went on to explain what had happened to the baby. His mother said, "My son, it is good that you ask my counsel in your concern for others. I am proud. Now you must ask Sunstar if she will go like the wind and fetch one of your faerie relatives and bring them back here, then you will know better if it can be done to make him whole again."

He answered, "But Sunstar will be at risk! And what relatives, Mother?"

"Sunstar will not be at risk, my son, she is very clever. She was my friend. She will stay her size and look to all the world like a moth, and for your other question, you are relative to most of the faeries in the forest," she said.

Maldwyn said, "Thank you, Mother."

She answered, "You are welcome, my son." But before she disappeared she concluded, "You have used this time wisely, my son, in the pursuit of others' happiness and this selfless act will not go unnoticed." She smiled and blew him a kiss as she faded away.

Maldwyn was too distressed to go back to the others right away. After all he had just been speaking with the mother that he had never seen and even though it was only her spirit, to him it was his mother and he greatly appreciated the time he had with her.

He lifted his hand to his mouth and whispered something in Sunstar's ear. She stretched herself and lifted off from his ring. She took flight and disappeared down the passage that led to the main path of the cave system.

Maldwyn got up and walked back to his family, as that is what they were to him now. The others could all see he was upset but it was only Olivia that had the courage to sit beside him and ask him if he was all right. She took his hand as if she knew what had just happened and said, "Sometimes the people we love get snatched away from us far too early. It is the price we pay for giving our love to someone. Please, my mage, please come back to us. We need you. Do not dwell too much on what may have been but on what is."

She looked towards the company of new friends. "They need you to be with them in spirit as well as physical form, mage. They all need you, I need you."

She once more looked at him and squeezed his hand. There was nothing else to say; he knew what she meant. He looked at her and smiled. "You are wise, Olivia, and of course you are right. I can see I am going to have to listen to you more often, my lady."

They went back to the others and had a drink. The Cyclops was feeling a lot stronger but at times still feeling that he was in a dream. He had been tortured in this hell cave for so long now, it was hard to believe that he was finally going to be free of it.

They had started to settle down to some sleep when Sunstar reappeared. She landed on Maldwyn's ring, looked at her master then curled up in a ball and went to sleep.

All Maldwyn could do now was wait to see what happened. After five or six hours they started to stir. Maldwyn re-lit the fire and the sisters set about preparing the porridge for breakfast. Maldwyn was just about to eat his when a voice from the side of him said, "Well, this is where you disappeared to, is it Mage?"

He turned to see who it was and saw Seth, one of Alyssa's great uncles many times removed, but also one of Maldwyn's grandfathers many times removed. He was accompanied by Newton who turned out to be one of Maldwyn's relatives, also many generations removed. They sat introducing themselves and were invited to breakfast, which they ate with great gusto while all the time looking at the poor Cyclops.

Eventually Newton said, "It's all a front. It is the crudest type of curse that is why it causes you such pain."

He turned to the others and one by one asked them how many eyes they could see on the Cyclops.

They all, with no exceptions, said that the Cyclops only had one eye in the centre of his forehead, just above his nose.

Newton said, "No, no, there are three, but one is not real but merely an extension of the other two. That is why you do not see well, my friend, and why you need plenty of light.

Maldwyn did not understand. "Three eyes?"

He looked at Cyclops. "Yes, when the curse was cast you were fully grown in your mother's womb. This meant that it would take a great sorceress to change you completely as you were protected as you were part of your mother."

"This also meant that the curse could only partially work. You are, my friend, a man with three eyes. You are like everyone else: you have your normal eyes, but the eye in the centre of your forehead and the wrinkle skin around it is not really part of you," said Seth.

It was not only the Cyclops that looked at Seth shocked; everyone thought this an incredible statement, and how could it be possible?

Newton explained, "You cannot take the prosthesis away but it is not you; underneath you are perfect and you see with both eyes but through the central one. Now if you give your consent, myself and my father Seth will attempt to relieve you of what is not really part of you, and I suggest that you think of a new name as Cyclops will probably not be appropriate after we have finished.

"But be warned, the process is painful and you will have to wear dark eye glasses for a further few days."

The Cyclops did not know what an eye glass was and was puzzled. Then emotion started to take over and he began to cry. He always felt that the eye was not right: he may have a sudden itch under his forehead or feel as if there was something in his eye but to the side of it; he now realised why.

The two faeries sat with the Cyclops and the older one, Seth, put his hands over the Cyclops' face. He sat chanting for some time, then Cyclops gave out a cry that was so agonising the others in the company wanted to cry for him.

Seth who had his hands on the Cyclops' face for the whole of the spell suddenly started to pull the Cyclops' face; it was a little like Pyewacket when she was padding her blanket. Very slowly he continued to pull gently at the skin on the face, pulling and kneading until the pain became so bad that the Cyclops' screams echoed through the cave.

The screaming got worse and his pain more intense. Eventually Seth pulled up the skin and the mask was removed. All went still, no one moved. Seth stepped aside to reveal a handsome young man with two eyes that were dark brown in colour.

They were the type of eyes that belonged to a race of people in the Mediterranean area of the human world: they were gentle but fierce with passion, and they were beautiful.

The Cyclops stared at them all, then into the mirror that Maldwyn had handed him. He started to cry once more but this time they were tears of joy. He said, "Is that really me? The face I have shown the world all these years was just a mask. I would have clawed it off myself if I had any suspicion that it was not my real face."

Newton answered, "You could not have done that without magyk as she had fused it to your facial tissue, and do not worry about the mild scarring it will go eventually."

"She?" said Cyclops. "You know who it was?"

Seth gave a knowing grimace. "Oh yes, I do. I had that information given to me when I removed the mask."

"Will you tell us who it is, my lord?" said Maldwyn.

Seth answered, "No I will not, but I will tell you this: the situation will be looked into when we get back to the forest.

"To hold a grudge against a woman is one thing, but her unborn child is another. She could not get to the woman so she got to her unborn; the woman did not suffer all these years, the child did, and that is against faerie law. It was not the child's fault and as I said it will be dealt with."

Maldwyn was suspicious. "And why would a magykal creature go all the way to the land of men for revenge?"

"Because," said Seth looking at the Cyclops, "her mate was unfaithful with a human woman. You are part faerie and you are not Cyclops. In fact, you, just as Maldwyn, are of my brethren and you should call me grandfather."

Stephann asked, "How many grandchildren do you have, my lord?"

He answered, "You have got to remember I am very old and grandfather to several generations, and I had at last count over a thousand grandchildren, great-grandchildren and so on."

Talos exclaimed, "That is a lot of grandchildren, my lord."

"Yes," he replied with a grin, "but they don't all visit at once, and it could be worse my father Silus has four times the amount I have."

Newton was anxious to get back as this business with Sheela had also caused a stir throughout the forest. "I think it is time to go now, Father. We have business to attend to."

Seth also thought so. "Yes, yes, so we have, well remembered. What is your name?" This question was directed to the Cyclops.

Cyclops looked at his new grandfather and shrugged his shoulders. "I do not know, I have never had one, sir."

Seth had a suggestion. "Then allow me if you will, my grandfather's name was Tiberius and I think it is a good strong name; it would please me greatly if you would call yourself Tiberius, my boy."

The Cyclops said, "Tiberius, yes that is a good name. Thank you, Grandfather. I may call you that, may I?"

"Of course, I said that you could. Now help Maldwyn all you can to beat this hag and show her we will not tolerate her kind in Nirvana. Goodbye, my grandchild."

They said their farewells to the faeries and they disappeared as quickly as they had appeared. The company stayed in the cave for a few more hours. They had a meal and a drink and talked about their plans to find the Green Man. Then they rested. It was all a ruse so that Tiberius could

173

recover his strength enough to join them on their journey; after all he had just gone through an extremely painful procedure.

CHAPTER FIFTEEN:
TROLLS AGAIN

ᚦ

They packed up their belongings, once more ready to start their journey; but which way to go? That was the question now.

They could go the way they had come in or the other way. They had found an alternative passage that was wider and higher than the previous one; it was hidden behind a boulder in the corner of the cave.

They decided to go the way of the hidden passage as there seemed to be plenty of fresh air coming in that one. So, they set off down the new route in high spirits. Maldwyn's thoughts recalled what had happened over the last few days; they had rescued a Gollum, a bronze man, three sisters and the Cyclops. What next are we going to meet? he thought.

These were thoughts he wished later that he had not had. They followed the tunnel until again there was a fork in the path but the obvious way was blocked by a large boulder. The problem that Talos and Tiberius had with the boulder was that it did not look right. After a discussion between the two men, Talos said, "Maldwyn, I think this is some sort of trap. This boulder looks like it..."

His words faded and he never finished what he was saying; there was a crash and everything went blank.

Fortunately, Maldwyn had pre-empted something like this happening in the labyrinth and had instinctively instructed his staff to become invisible at the first sign of danger, which it had done when they had been attacked. Only Maldwyn could see the staff when invisible and it would not turn back to being visible unless it was in Maldwyn's hands or in the hands of the mage-in-waiting. (Which he knew would eventually be Stephann, but Stephann did not know this yet, nor would he be able to see the staff yet either.)

They woke up in a dark cave where the air was stale and the feeling of oppression was all around them. Winston hooted, "I think we are way underground, a lot further than we were before."

"Of course we are," said Maldwyn in an `I knew this would happen sort of tone'. "It's trolls again. When this is over I swear I will zap every single one of their brains, vile creatures that they are.

"This will set us back days. I am not pleased. Where are the little monsters?"

Maldwyn was exceedingly angry. He knew that his staff was nearby as it would have followed him but he did not want to show his hand yet. Maldwyn continued, "Are we all here, Talos, Stephann, Winston, Pyewacket, my ladies and Tiberius?"

They all said `here' in turn as Maldwyn spoke their names. He was glad no one was missing. Winston said, "What I cannot understand is why Pyewacket and I are still here? They should have eaten us, as a snack."

Maldwyn answered, "They would have if they could have seen you, but as with my staff you two also have a spell upon your bodies, that means only the seven of us can see you. Plus, you can see each other, of course, no one else except probably the faeries.

"Pyewacket was brought here with Stephann and Winston with me. This way we are not separated, but as they cannot see you, then you could be our ace in the hole as the towns folk would say. That is if we need you to be, I think that is the saying anyway. Never mind you get the meaning."

Just then the cave started to light up slowly as a large troll appeared in the opening. He stared at them. "Well! You are a scabby lot I must say. Only two of you with any meat on your bones. It's a good job you are not for eating time."

Another troll pushed by him. "Will you move, Clot. Stop talking to the vermin, they have work to do for the mistress. This way, scum." This troll had a large whip in his hand that he was very willing to use.

Talos whispered, "We can get these two, Mage. There's only two of them; we could jump them as they go through this passage."

"No, we need to know the layout of the cave before we do anything silly, and we also need to know what they are up to! We will go with them and see where they are taking us," said Maldwyn.

They put their heads down and followed. Maldwyn used magyk to make them all look like normal villagers, even Talos looked human to them. They were taken to a large cave that was high enough for Talos to stand in at his normal height. All around them they saw an army of humans digging at the walls for the gems that lay within.

There were several large trolls wielding whips and using them profusely on young and old. If they dropped through illness or exhaustion they were killed, stripped of their clothes and taken for the trolls' next meal. There had been several reports of humans going missing over the past few months and it was a mystery as to where they had gone; but now they knew, the humans had been going for slave labour for the trolls and their mistress.

Maldwyn said, "Who is your mistress, Troll?"

He hit Maldwyn across the face with the whip. "Don't you talk, scum, you will not ask questions, you work or you will die."

They were taken to the far end of the cavern and marched up a slope to the wall of the cave about twenty feet up. There were four other humans working there. They were beavering away trying to get the precious gems out of the wall but with little success. It was a thankless task and with the trolls guarding them ready to use the whip at any time, it was also dangerous.

Luckily the ledge was roughly eight feet deep so there was not much chance of falling off. The troll in charge of them did not like heights and moaned profusely about everything; he was not liked by his peers and was given jobs on his own that no one else liked. Maldwyn thought that this troll, whose name was Grit, was the ideal troll to start turning to his way of thinking.

They beavered away at the rock to no avail, so every so often Maldwyn with great effort managed to loosen a large or a small piece of rock containing a precious gem stone. The others on this work detail were very happy about this as they regularly got whipped for not finding anything.

Truth was this cavern like most in the mountain was running dry of gemstones and that is why the dwarfs had left this mountain in the first place. Over the next few days Maldwyn managed to start manipulating Grit's mind and also instilling in him that he liked these humans and would treat them better. He would pretend he did not like them and he would pretend he hated them which he really did not; this was so that his fellow trolls would not know what was happening to him.

After a few hours when it came time for food, they always received bread and water. It was literally the convict's dinner; the only saving grace was that the bread was made daily by the human slaves that were allocated that duty with flour from a large storehouse within the cave system.

Tiberius commented, "They must have been planning this little scheme for a long time to have that many provisions."

Maldwyn, who had everyone's pouches concealed under his clothes, pulled out just enough meat to feed them all. This was after Grit had gone down to get his own food and left the slaves to eat their meagre meal. Maldwyn made a small piece of meat grow until it was large enough for them all on the work detail. He also made the other four in the detail swear to secrecy before he would even start to give them any food.

The workers started to feel stronger after having food and thanked Maldwyn. No questions were asked as to where the meat had come from, they seem to know instinctively that there was something different about this little band of newcomers.

This carried on for a few days. He wanted his fellow slaves on that ledge to become strong enough to fight with them and to overpower the trolls. If he could get to more trolls the way he had got to Grit there would be no need to fight, but for that he thought he may require the help of his staff.

Maldwyn should have realised that his powers were growing faster now and apart from when he was fighting, where a magykal staff came in very handy, he would rarely need to use his staff; from now on he was powerful enough without it.

Maldwyn worked his magyk on the troll that guarded them in the cave chamber where they slept. Then on the one that wielded the whip. His name was Cluts, and he was easier than Maldwyn had thought but then he was the most stupid as he resorted to brute force long before any of the other trolls ever did.

Five days had passed and the word was spreading to be ready. Maldwyn had made sure that over those five days as

179

much food as possible had got to the rest of the slaves so that they were strong enough to fight if needed.

On the sixth day as they walked with the other slaves through the main cabin, Maldwyn doubled over as if he was in pain. Cluts came to see what all the fuss was about and what was taking the humans so long to get going. Everything happened at once as it usually does in those situations. Talos grew to his normal size, which luckily was lower than the height of the cave. The sisters started to throw small bolts of fire that they had conjured in the palm of their hands, at the trolls' heads

The invisible Pyewacket and Winston did their bit, Pyewacket tripping the trolls up and Winston flying at their heads; between them they were using the little bit of weak magyk that they had to disable a few of the trolls while the slaves tied them up.

Stephann and Tiberius were fighting them with tools that were left by the miners, and as more trolls came running out to help their comrades, the other slaves, seeing that they had the chance to escape, also picked up tools and started to fight.

The whole thing was pandemonium; it lasted for nearly an hour. The trolls were not going to give up easily. Maldwyn, Stephann, Winston and Pyewacket were throwing spells at the trolls at every opportunity to try and slow them down. Talos was crushing them underfoot or picking them up in his large hands and slinging them against the cave walls.

The battle was rough and deadly, but it was a battle of necessity. As things started to calm down and everyone began to realise that they had won, loud cheers went up, but as with all battles there came a time when they had to count the dead and the wounded. They counted a hundred and five trolls altogether, and ninety of them were dead, the rest had their minds altered by Maldwyn while they were injured and unconscious.

But the human toll was great. Out of five hundred men and women there were over two hundred dead and many more injured. The only thing was that the trolls had not captured children and they were not strong enough to work, but Tiberius did find out after that some children had died as their parents were snatched.

Talos by this time was back to his now normal size and no one seemed to notice that he had been any different. Only their small band knew that there had been changes in Talos, this again was due to Maldwyn's magyk. As Maldwyn looked at the sight of devastation, he thought that there was no glory in battle, and no celebration for the victors, as the cost was too high, but one that had to be paid for freedom.

Olivia approached. She took Maldwyn's hand and said, "How many more lives will be lost because of that hag, my mage? How many?"

She nodded her head in disbelief but knew that this was not the end; there was more to come and more deaths and maybe their own, they did not know at this point. They left the trolls where they were. The Troll survivors would not be going back to their mistress as it would mean certain death and trolls by nature are cowards. With any luck Sheela would continue to think, for a while anyway, that the mining was still going ahead.

The human survivors were more difficult. They had to be taken back to their own towns and villages, so they were divided into groups that came from the same areas and the same sides of the mountain. It was now that the decision had to be made of how to get them home safely.

They had suffered enough so it was decided that Sunstar would make one more journey to the council and ask again for the faeries to help. Meanwhile, they went to find the food store and realised that indeed the trolls had been planning this for a long time. There was enough food in the store to last a good six months. The decision was made for some of the food to be given to each of the humans that were left and the rest was to go back to the castle, to the food store, in case there was indeed a siege.

It was Silas that arrived with an army of faeries just as the survivors were sitting down to have a much-needed rest. Silas looked around at the devastation and said to Maldwyn, "Well you do not do things by half, do you, my son? Please give me your counsel and tell me how many lives were lost and how we can help."

After listening to the tale that Maldwyn had to tell them, Silas said, "It would appear she is getting stronger and the only reason she may need extra gems would be to produce extra magyk. We need to close this mine down totally."

Millie answered, "Please, ancient one, myself and my sisters can do that in a controlled way, once all the people are away from the mountain."

"Of course you can," he replied. "We will start evacuation of these poor souls back to their towns and villages; and then I suggest you continue the rest of your journey on the surface. This way should be quicker and less hazardous but with all the trolls about it is turning out to be more dangerous now."

Maldwyn bowed his head. "We will do as you say, Great-grandfather, we will find a route out of here, although we have no idea where we are in relation to where we were!"

Silas answered, "You are precisely one mile further back but two hundred feet deeper. There is a supply shaft through there." He pointed to a small opening that made them wonder how the trolls had ever got through it, it was so small. "Follow that and you will be safe, I hope, and Maldwyn, my son, try to keep out of trouble please."

***

The faeries started to make small portals; these were not dangerous as they were localised, just transporters really, but magykal ones. The type that Merlin had conjured up were interdimensional and very dangerous.

After everyone had gone, they sorted out their belongings. Maldwyn got his staff back and made their clothes normal again. All that was left to do was the collapsing of the cave walls so that they could never be used again. Maldwyn also realised that he had gone through the whole battle without his trusted staff.

Isla said, "We will do it, it is just a small melting of the rock in three places and that should be enough to block it forever. We will be very gentle; it will not bring the mountain down, so do not worry."

Stephann said, "But I thought..."

Millie answered, "You thought that the whole mountain would come down as it would have when we were with the other trolls."

"Yes," he answered.

"No, we can see what we are doing here and we can work together with control. The trolls were causing pain, separating us to cause stress, and we had no idea where or if there was any gold in that part of the mountain so the blast would have been enormous."

He nodded an understanding nod and quickly joined Maldwyn in the tunnel entrance. They started to walk up the sloping tunnel towards the surface and the fresh air, while the sisters stood near the tunnel entrance doing their best to control the fire blast. There was an almighty crash and a few seconds later they heard Isla's voice saying, "All that was better than I expected." To which the other two giggled.

The sisters caught up with the others. They knew that the trolls were safe as they had been put near the tunnel entrance, ready to get out when they woke up. They made their way slowly through the tunnel, as the air rushed at their sensors and the light hit their eyes, they pushed through some dense shrubbery, treading carefully in case they were on the edge of a precipice.

They had come out on what they thought was the opposite side of the mountain to the village and the castle. This was an area that none of them really knew. Only Talos had gone over that side but never this far to the north. They looked around to get their bearings, then Talos noticed Tiberius was not with them.

He went back through the bushes to look for him. Tiberius was having trouble with the winter sunshine; he had not been given his dark eye glasses that the trolls had taken and his eyes hurt. This was partially from being in the dark for so long and partially because he had never seen or felt sunshine with his own eyes.

Talos went to inform Maldwyn who immediately went into his bag and handed Tiberius another pair of sunglasses, so that he might join them and start the adventure on the next leg of their journey.

CHAPTER SIXTEEN:
THE HOUSE IN THE SKY

ζ

Tiberius was more than a little happy to be out in the fresh air, with the sunshine beating down on his face. He knew about the effects of the sun on his eyes and that it would take time, but it was not a permanent affliction and eventually his sunglasses would be able to come off.

They looked around and found they were on a large plateau. Both Talos and Tiberius said they had never been on that part of the mountain before. It seemed to them that they were not actually on a mountain at all but on the land below, or were they?

As the others moved forward Maldwyn said, "Please can you all come back to me. There is powerful magyk at work in this place and we need to stay together. There is something wrong. I do not think we are on the mountain any more."

Maldwyn looked around him then noticed Olivia was missing. His heart sank. Where was she? He shouted, "Olivia, Olivia."

The others looked around. They were panic stricken. Isla, who was Olivia's non-identical twin, said as if in a trance, "She's gone, she is there, she is with..."

Her words faded and she stared up into the sky. Talos said, "That is what Olivia was doing just before you shouted us. We all turned to walk back to you and then you said she was gone. What is happening Maldwyn? Where are we?"

Maldwyn looked distressed. Olivia snatched from him. How? Why? Just then Millie screamed.

Pyewacket had gone to stretch her legs and was standing at the side of Isla. They were both transfixed looking up slightly into the sky, but no one else could see anything.

As the company observed, the pair slowly started to fade and were gone in a matter of seconds. Stephann, Winston and Millie all shouted, "No," at the same time. This caused the sort of flux in the air to appear where they had been standing. Just for a split second they thought they caught a glimpse of a large house in the sky.

Maldwyn was at a loss to know what was happening. He turned to Winston who was one of the most knowledgeable faeries he knew. "What is happening, Winston? Where are they? I have tried but I cannot see them or where they went. It is impossible, it has to be strong faerie magyk."

Winston looked sad. "I do not know either, Maldwyn. This journey has been wracked with danger from the start. I wish we had stayed at the castle and taken our chances.

"I have heard of the house in the sky when I was a younglin but the stories were so vague, as no one has ever seen the house or managed to stay in the visible world to tell the tale. It would need a faerie far older than I to impart the knowledge to us about the house."

Maldwyn immediately started to open his locket. The mist that came from the locket was all that the company could see. Maldwyn of course could see his mother, Cassandra.

"Oh, my son, why have you brought me back so soon? You only have twelve visions of me then I am no more. Please use them wisely, my son."

Maldwyn apologised, then commenced to tell his mother what had happened. He beckoned to Winston to come to him and the mist. Winston did as he was asked and told the mist of the house in the sky that he did not know much about.

He looked at Maldwyn, then at the locket and said, "Your mother? Faerie magyk?"

"Yes," Maldwyn said. His mother tried to recall her memories which was difficult as she was there in spirit only, but eventually she said, "I think I may know who it is. It may be Nafalius. He was one of the wisest of faerie folk but only half faerie.

"I'm afraid my son that the fascination with humans has been going on thousands of years. There are more half faerie folk than ever before and Nafalius was no exception.

"He was born in the human world, and although he was said to have died in the human world, reports of his death were much exaggerated. We are not sure what brought him here or how he got here but humans with faerie blood through their veins have a habit of turning up in Nirvana at some time or another in their lives.

"The humans knew him as Nicolas Flamel and referred to him as a great alchemist. He lived for many years amongst us, then he started to go a little mad. He tried potions on people that caused all sorts of problems; he said he had once found the elixir of life but he had lost his notes when he crossed into this realm and he was trying to replicate them but to no avail.

"Why he would want to do this we never knew because the nature of the beast is that if you are half faerie and you come to Nirvana you will live a long life anyway. He was a very old man when he started to fade, and I do mean fade. This was because he had tried so many potions on himself that he had caused a reaction which could not be reversed. Sometimes he was whole and other times he was fuzzy around the edges."

"But where does the house come in, Mother," said Maldwyn.

His mother said, "Well he was given the house. A magyk woman, but no one knows who, gave him the house. The house has the ability to fade and move about but there was a price to pay, a price that he did not know about until he accepted the gift. He could go in to the house but he could never leave. Well he could but on two conditions: one that he died and someone took his place, and two, that someone else was willing to take his place while he was alive and take over the curse.

"But again, this is not what it may seem. There is a way around the house, a way to keep Nafalius in the house and also give it to someone else and get it grounded without them being trapped."

"But why would anyone be so cruel, Mother? It is inhumane to trap someone in a house for ever," said Maldwyn.

She answered once more, "Because they wanted to live forever; they wanted the elixir of life plus the knowledge of gold making that came with it. But he would not give it, as the person in question was evil and would have used the potion to their own ends, not to benefit others as Nafalius had done. He was doomed to live for ever in the house on his own."

Maldwyn felt a pang of sadness for Nafalius. "Can I help him, Mother, and help my trapped friends at the same time?"

"I believe you can, my son, your powers have grown more than you know, but you will need the help of your friends, all of them," she answered.

He thanked her as she started to fade but before she went she just managed to say, "I believe that the hag you seek and the one that entrapped Nafalius are one in the same, my son, and somehow she has managed to stay alive longer than she normally would have been able to."

She faded away and Maldwyn put the locket safe. He turned back to the others and told them what he had learnt. They sat silent for a while.

Winston who was one of the oldest and the wisest of the Seelie Court said, "I can only see one solution to this problem. Nafalius must stay in the house after his death and be entombed there while one of us takes the house as their own, and lives there for the rest of their lives until someone else wants the house.

"But Nafalius can never be taken from the house as that would entrap the person that had taken over from him, and the house would be lost once more; fated to fade and appear and trying to trap the next person to take over the running of it."

Maldwyn answered, "Do you know, Winston, I think you have got the right idea. That's what we have to do and it's all we have got so we can at least try it."

Tiberius asked, "But who will stay? And does that mean that someone has to kill this Nafalius?"

Winston answered soberly, "The house will probably decide who will stay and in answer to your second question I do believe so, I do believe that Nafalius will have to die."

They all thought for a while about the consequences of what had just been said, then Maldwyn said, "I believe it is time for action, don't you? Now let's see if we can get into the house before it moves again, that's if it has not moved already."

They walked to where the others had been standing when they disappeared. Maldwyn had instructed them all to keep close to him, but Winston had said that he did not think it would be enough and that they should all hold hands. This is exactly what they did and it turned out to be the right decision.

They were standing for approximately ten minutes before the outline of the house became visible; it was a shimmer in the sky at first. It looked like the vision you would get out of the corner of your eye from a reflection in a window – it was very strange. Then a more visible picture came into view but it was still not solid. They found themselves staring at the house: it mesmerised them with a strangeness, but at the same time by its beauty.

The next thing they remembered was the door as they entered it; they were still holding hands but as soon as they were inside and the door had closed, they released each other's hand and they came back to their senses.

Maldwyn looked around. There was Millie, Stephann, Talos and Tiberius, but standing with them and still holding onto Maldwyn, was a very handsome faerie with big brown eyes and long flowing blonde hair. Among humans the colour of the eyes and the colour of the hair would be a contradiction but amongst faeries it was not.

They stared at the person that they did not know and Maldwyn smiled. "Please, if you will permit me to introduce you to Christano, formally known as Winston the owl: a wise and good Seelie Court faerie."

Christano looked at his hands and felt his face. "Am I really back? Or is it the house causing us to have dreams?"

Maldwyn answered, "I cannot be sure, but I think a combination of the charm I gave you and the residual magyk left in the house from the one that turned you into an owl in the first place, has caused a reverse reaction."

Christano gave out his last owlish hoot, then tapped his feet. "Oh, I am so glad to be back. Do you think the same thing has happened to Sorona?"

Maldwyn was again not sure but he could see no reason for it not to have happened to Sorona as well. Talos, who had only heard part of the story, was not in the least surprised, and he supposed that the cat Pyewacket was now Sorona the Princess.

Tiberius and Millie were at a loss as to what had just happened, but Maldwyn promised he would explain later at a more appropriate time.

They still had their backs to the large white door and the sight before them was not what they were expecting – all of the large hallway was light and very white. The floor was covered in white marble and the large curved staircase was also painted white, with white spindles and rails, with a deep pile, pale blue carpet covering the centre of the stairs.

To break the brightness of the walls, they were adorned with rich tapestries and paintings of the countryside and mountain ranges. It was not at all what they expected. There were several doors leading off the hallway downstairs so they decided to investigate some of these.

Talos wanted to split up but the rest were against that idea and thought that staying together was the best policy at this time. The first room they went into was a sitting room/reception and like the hallway it was decorated in whites and pastoral shades; this was on a par with the Empress's palace for its richness of decor.

They had a good look around then moved onto the next room. Again, this was empty. It was a dining room with an extra-large table that could accommodate plenty of guests. This was a little disconcerting as they knew this house never had guests.

But as they moved onto the next one they thought they heard voices. They walked across the hallway to where the voices were coming from and opened the double doors to a library. It was no ordinary library, it was one that was so magnificent in every way that they were in awe of the knowledge that must be in there.

There was a fire burning in a large stone fireplace which would not have looked out of place in any one of the human's stately homes.

A man's frail voice croaked, "So you are here at last, and not before time, my mage."

They walked forward a few paces into the room which was very large indeed. An old man started to carefully stand up from a large comfy chair. He turned slowly and looked at them. "Come, sit by the fire," he said. "It is so cold out there. I presume it is winter, is it not?"

Maldwyn walked forward and bowed his head. "Yes, it is, my lord. May I be so bold as to ask if I am speaking to Nafalius?"

The old man eyed him up and down, then the company he was with. He answered, "Nafalius, Nicolas Flamel, Philippeus von Hohenheim or Thomas Brown. I have been known by all of those names during my lifetime, but Nafalius is my true name and my preferred one.

"Now I suppose you wish to know where your companions are. Well they are well enough and will be back soon with some refreshments for you all, so please sit."

As they sat there was chatter from the door and three excitable young women walked in smiling and carrying some drinks and food on large silver trays. Everything in the house appeared to be larger than life including its owner.

Christano shouted, "Sorona, my love, are you all right?"

She put the big tray down and ran to him. They hugged each other; it had been so long since they were able to do this, it was nice to be normal again and hold each other once more.

Sorona said, "We think it was a combination of Maldwyn's charm and this place once belonging to Sheela that broke the spell, Christano."

"Yes," he replied, stroking her hair and looking fondly into her eyes, "that is exactly what Maldwyn thought too. I am so pleased to see you and so glad it is over." Christano went quiet. "Maldwyn, we will stay like this, won't we? We are not going to go back to the way we were, once we leave, are we?"

This time it was Nafalius that answered. "First, my young whippersnapper, you will have to leave the house to test that theory, but I think you will stay as you are if you do leave. I do not think there will be any more fur or feather about you two, but you have got to find a way to leave. That is all."

Christano said while still looking at Sorona, "Well we had thought about that problem but you may not like it Nafalius."

Nafalius smiled. "Come, have some vittles with us and I will tell you what I know must happen."

They all sat down and once more all in turn they conveyed their stories to Nafalius; it seems that over the last two weeks they had told their story so many times. After they had all finished and also told Nafalius why they were on this journey, he said, "I suppose I had better now tell you my story while there is still time because I am dying.

"I was born in the human land in a place where the summers are hot and the smell sweet. The winters are called picturesque; the year was 1330 and my life was that of a bachelor, a workaholic, and until I met the love my life, my darling Perenelle in 1368, I was alone.

"I already had money from two bookshops that I owned and from them the means to do with alchemy, but I will not be going into that right now. Perenelle also had money as unfortunately she had the misfortune of having lost two husbands before she met me.

"We were quite well off and due to hard work and perseverance in the sciences we became wealthier still. We helped the poor where we could and also the church, but there always seemed to be something missing as far as I was concerned, something that I did not know, and somewhere that I needed to be."

Tiberius interrupted, "Or somewhere else you should have been, a feeling of restlessness."

"Yes, that is right," said Nafalius, "Ah, but I forget, you are half faerie too. Well I carried on with my work and I succeeded in quite a lot of things. I managed to make a stone that would in turn make for us the elixir of life. I started to take the brew but my darling Perenelle would not take it; she said she had seen enough of what life could bring and she did not want to live longer than her allotted time, no longer than God wished her to.

"It was hard for me when she died. I was a man obsessed with my work. I was not obsessed in a big way, just in a small way, but it was enough all the same to keep me occupied. While I was rummaging through some old dusty papers of my father's that frankly I had forgotten about, I came across something that made me start thinking of other realms.

"My father had in his possession when he died a locket, and a note written by my mother to give to me when I was old enough, but he never gave it to me and I never knew it was there. So, it stayed with my father's papers until I was a very old man. Then when I looked at the locket and read the papers I realised that the woman I had called mother since I was a child was not really my mother at all.

"It was a lot for a human to take in that there was magyk in the world, and even more for them to realise that they were part of it, but I always felt there was something else and anyway the spirit of my mother talking to me from the locket was proof enough.

"It was then, with the help of my mother, I made my own tombstone and this was no ordinary tombstone, it was my entrance to her world, to this world; there were certain runes and spells hidden within the text on the stone so that I could have safe passage to Nirvana when I needed it.

"I arranged my death in 1418 in the human calendar. My most trusted servant put rocks into my coffin and sealed it; He was justly rewarded with great wealth after my death; people wondered where all the wealth had gone, while my servant had a lot of it, he deserved it. He was faithful and had put up with me all those years and he did the final act that he could do for me, he helped me to disappear.

After everything had settled down, I used my last incarnation of my mother and the tombstone to get here."

They had all been listening intently to Nafalius as he told them his story but it still did not explain how he came to be in the house. He had a drink of his chocolate then carried on; his voice was weak by now and he looked tired.

"I lived for a long time in this world with the help of the elixir, but while on my travels to one of the villages at the edge of the forest, I met a young lady. She was so beautiful and her eyes were bewitching. We spoke and she said she also was going to the village and could she accompany me.

"She mesmerised me so much I don't think I could have said no to anything that she asked me to do. Before long she was on the subject of living longer and keeping her beauty; she said it was hard to lose your looks and she had heard of a faerie that could give her an elixir to make her stay young.

"She said she was going to find him and ask him for his help."

Maldwyn asked, "But how did she know the faerie was male; the normal assumption of humans is a female faerie, is it not?"

Nafalius answered, "Yes, I never thought of that. Anyway, we were about a hundred yards from the village, when she changed her mind about going there and said we might meet again some time and walked back along the path she had come down – it was very strange.

"It was two days later when I met her once more. She was friendly and asked if I found what I was looking for at the market. I said no, as I was looking for somewhere to live. I wanted a house but I said I may have to go to the other side of Sandina to find exactly what I was looking for.

"She said she knew of one that I could rent or buy and I said I would look at it. I followed her for about two miles. We rounded copse of small trees and there it was: my dream house. I should have known it was too good to be true."

Nafalius was getting weaker but still he wanted to tell his story and to continue even after they had asked if he had had enough for today.

Nafalius continued, "It was perfect. She asked me inside to take a look around and we had no longer got into the house when she shut the door and wanted to know about the elixir of life and asked me if I could get it for her. I told her I had forgotten the formula but she could see right through my lies.

"For some reason I could not lie to her, she was so beautiful. I cannot even start tell you how beautiful she was. Then she offered me the house in exchange for the elixir. Of course, I kept saying no, I did not know the formula but she never believed me, every time I told her this it was as if she could read my mind.

"The discussion got very heated, then her eyes went dark and her face started to change. She grew in stature and then she became the ugliest thing I had ever seen; she was so ugly she repulsed me and her anger took over. It was then I realised that I was never going to get out of this house. I was not a magykal person. I did not inherit much of the magyk from my mother, I inherited more love and science from my father."

He looked at Maldwyn and said, "I am an alchemist not a powerful mage. I was no match for her. She put a spell on me, a curse, whatever you want to call it, and here I have been all these years confined to a house that I could not leave, and with no company until now.

"And that is how it has got to be until someone decides to take my place, but I do not want anyone to suffer the way I have for this last two hundred years. I am tired now and I would like to sleep, please can we speak in the morning."

CHAPTER SEVENTEEN:
THE BURIEL OF NAFALIUS

ϟ

Nafalius was obviously fatigued; he laid back in his comfy chair and fell to sleep, so Millie put a blanket over him to keep him warm.

Maldwyn said, "I think we had better find somewhere to sleep tonight. Did you see any beds on your travels through the house?"

Sorona replied, "Oh, yes indeed, the house is most beautiful and well equipped for a human house."

Millie continued, "There are nine bedrooms upstairs with nine comfy large beds, more than enough for us. But be warned they are a bit dusty."

***

They woke up the next morning to the sound of birds singing and the sun shining in through the windows. It certainly was peaceful and would make any of the humans in Nirvana think they were back in their own land, that is if there was any memory of their own land.

They went downstairs where the three sisters had already started preparing food for their breakfasts, and Nafalius was still sat in his chair but looking a little less tired.

They went to greet him, then Sorona asked, "Who cleans for you? And where does the food come from? Your store cupboard is so well-stocked, Nafalius."

Nafalius smiled. "Ah, it is magyk, the faeries could not get me out of the house but they could help me to stay in it. That was by providing food and a cleaning sprite, but I am afraid to say that it is not perfect, the cleaning sprite does sometimes leave a little dust and cobwebs around the house, but in her own way she is also trapped even though she can leave."

Sorona gave a little laugh. "Yes, Nafalius, we notice the dust in some of the bedrooms."

After breakfast Nafalius spoke to them all in turn. They all told him that they had not had a good night as they heard noises and bangs. They were cold and there was a feeling of unease and oppression in the house.

Only one person said differently and that person told Nafalius that he had a comfy night with sweet dreams and the bed, well the bed was delightful, because this person had never slept in a bed of such quality in his life.

He had also told Nafalius that the house was everything and more than he would ever have dreamed of. He finished by saying, "In some weird way you are lucky, Nafalius."

Nafalius, after he had spoken to them all, asked for a glass of water which Isla promptly went to get. When she brought it back to him, Nafalius put some powder into the water and stirred it up.

Maldwyn asked, "What is that potion if you do not mind me asking, Nafalius?"

Nafalius smiled. "Oh, do not concern yourself, mage, it is of faerie origins and will make me better, I assure you.

"Now I have an announcement to make. All of you with the exception of one have had a very bad night, and that is what I expected; it is what was prophesied by one of my ancestors when I first came into the house."

He drank his potion, then sat back in his chair for a minute or two. "Now, where was I? Oh yes, your coming here and what will happen now was all prophesied as I said, although I did not know who you were or when you would arrive, and this prophecy must not be altered.

"The house has picked its next owner, and one that I think is a good choice, as the house will be loved and cared for once again."

Nafalius went a little dizzy, then commenced with his announcement. "The house was brought here from the human world by the person that cursed me. Where exactly it came from I do not know, but it was a much-loved house that much I could tell, which, was not the case when it came here to me.

"As I said the house has chosen someone and that someone is Tiberius! He will be the new owner of this house."

There were a few gasps. No one really wanted the house as they were worried about the enchantment but Tiberius would gladly stay in the house; he had been tormented by the Cyclops for so long, this was peace to him.

Maldwyn looked at Nafalius. He was slipping away. "What have you done, you silly man?"

He answered, "I have done what I was supposed to do, Maldwyn, so that the new owner could take over. Now listen, and you must listen very carefully.

"In the back kitchen there is a door that leads down to the beautiful chapel of peace; it has in the centre of it a tomb. I am to be laid in that tomb."

While he was speaking it had slowly dawned on the others what was happening. Tiberius said, "Is this the only way, my lord, there must be something we can do. I will gladly stay with you until your natural death if you will permit me."

The old man smiled. "You are still but just a boy but you have the making of a good man, Tiberius. The faerie has named you well, you are all good people.

"But I am a very, very old man and I am more tired than you will ever know. I do not know how much time is left, so if you will permit me to make a suggestion before you lay me in my tomb.

"You must think of a nice place to put the house. You must stand in the entrance hall and speak the destination out loud. Maldwyn will help you choose somewhere I am sure, somewhere that is nice, and somewhere that the house and you both will enjoy.

"The house will then go there, but first you must intern me, then the house itself will be grounded when it comes to its next destination and it will become a normal house for the first time."

"But..."

Tiberius tried to say something but Nafalius put up his hand. "My time is near, please just accept the gift, and there is one other thing you need to know. You cannot go with these friends of yours. You must stay with the house for thirty nights after the exchange. You can go out, that is not the problem, but you need to know that for the first thirty nights you must spend them in the house or you too will die."

Christano was puzzled. "What kind of magyk is this, I do not understand!"

"Dark magyk, for the spell to be broken the house must feel loved and wanted by the new owner. Alas, I have spent my time wanting to leave the house and wishing its destruction and also living with the resentment of it. I have never really appreciated what a beautiful house it was," said Nafalius

He slumped back in his chair and gasped. Sorona and Olivia were at his side very quickly. He said in a very weak voice, "Do not weep for me, children, all my punishment is due to my arrogance. I was a bragger, a boaster. I was proud of my achievements and wanted everyone to know about them. I never thought for one moment that they may be jealous of my longevity, that is how naive I was. Is there any wonder I was caught in a trap of jealousy and deceit? No, it was all of my own doing."

He closed his eyes and went to sleep and within the hour he was dead.

***

It was a sad time for them all. They had known Nafalius such a short time but they had grown to love and admire him. In those few hours the house and Nafalius had certainly had an odd effect on the people that had entered it the previous day.

The females in the company put Nafalius on the ground on a long sheet and commenced with the last office, the final act they could do for him. They washed him, combed his hair and beard and dressed him in his clean, best clothes, then finally put his glasses on. He looked to all the world as if he was asleep.

The men then picked him up gently, treating him with the reverence and dignity he commanded and put him in the coffin which they then carried in procession to the chapel.

They walked down the steps of the chapel and were struck by the sheer size of the room. It was aesthetically pleasing and eclipsed everything else they had seen in the house. It was a peaceful room indeed. There were flagstones to the central floor area where the stone tomb stood and this was surrounded by a beautiful green short cut lawn. The surrounding walls were like the ruins of an old church or monastery with arched stone window frames and a cloister that ran around three sides of the room.

The cloister had seating at regular intervals so that people could sit and pay their respects to the dead, or just sit and read or contemplate the world. There was ivy and white roses rambling up the stonework and the smell of the roses was intoxicating.

The roof of the room was a glass dome which had opening windows all around the side. Nafalius had apparently always left these windows open to let the birds in and out as they pleased. There was a tree at the end of the room near the far cloister; this tree was home to four different species of birds that all seemed to live together in harmony.

It was a tranquil place and one that Tiberius knew he would spend time in, reading or talking to Nafalius. They laid him in the stone sarcophagus and placed the lid over his coffin, then Maldwyn sealed the lid with magyk.

Christano then spoke the words of what would have sounded to humans like a mediaeval prayer; it was the last thing they could do for such a tormented man.

They walked back to the library in a sombre mood. Tiberius could not believe he had such a beautiful house and a face that no man ran from any more, but sadness came with this good luck that he had been given. Everything has a price, and he had to pay one of the biggest prices of all, knowing that his good fortune was the result of the death of a great man.

Maldwyn could see he was deep in thought. "Do not be sad, Tiberius. Nafalius lived a good long life before this happened and should have died long ago. This is what he wanted; the last two hundred years have been hell for him and torture. He was ready to die, he is happy now and with his dear Perenelle."

"I know," said Tiberius, "but did he really have to die now? And why did he give me the house? Why?"

Maldwyn answered him in a sympathetic way. "Because you were the one that was the most comfortable in the house, the one person that needed to belong. Just accept it, you were the chosen one.

"Now shall we get down to business? We really do need a plan. I do have one if you wish to hear it?"

They all said yes as they had nothing; they did not know what to do next or how to go forward with the house.

"Well we have to leave the house before Tiberius tells it where to go, otherwise we will be taken with it. So where to go? Can I make a suggestion about that also, Tiberius?"

Tiberius answered, "Yes please do, Maldwyn, I have only seen the cave system and where we are now and I do not know Nirvana. I have not been free long enough."

Maldwyn smiled. "There is a small piece of land near the castle; it only has a couple of acres but it is mine. I will gladly give it to you, Tiberius. I do not want it myself as there is nothing I can do with it. You can put the house there and get some livestock; live a normal life near people that care about their neighbours."

Tiberius looked worried. "How can I afford livestock, I have no job, no money?"

Maldwyn smiled once more. "I have already thought about that. I will write a parchment to the Empress Alyssa. She will give you work but I will explain that you will have to be back in the house every night before nightfall for thirty days or you will die.

"I will tell her some of our progress, but you can fill her in on the other bits and tell her that the trolls are on the move."

Tiberius answered, "I will, Maldwyn, I just want to come with you and help."

Christano could see sadness in Tiberius's eyes. "You, my friend, can help protect the castle and the Empress. I am sure they will put you in one of the fighting forces, you will play your part if required, believe me."

"That is good," Tiberius said. "I need to help, especially if that is to be my home."

"You will, my friend," he replied, "you will."

Maldwyn wrote his parchment and gave it to Tiberius. He told him to ask the house to go to Hubert's field near the forest castle. They then filled up their supplies (which were by this time looking meagre) and after lengthy farewells they walked out of the door ready to set out on their own journey once more.

The house gave no resistance and would never again do so. Tiberius shut the door and spoke to the house sprite. "Please, Mr Sprite, show yourself to me; if we are to live together I would really like to have your company."

There was a long silence then a small voice said, "The last owner did not want to see me, so are you sure about this?"

He smiled. "Oh yes, too long have both of us been alone, sir, I think we should be friends, don't you?"

The sprite answered, "All right then, but I have been told by other sprites that I am extremely ugly but the faeries on my mother's side tell me I am pretty. I took this job to escape torment, you have been warned!"

Tiberius answered, "I too, my little friend, have been the subject of torment, show yourself please."

The sprite answered, "I know of your troubles but once you have seen me you may tell me to disappear again; are you sure you want to see me?"

Tiberius answered once more, "Oh yes I said so, please let me see you and then I will make up my own mind whether you are ugly or pretty and we can move the house."

There was a small jet of pale blue light that appeared on the stairs, then a small creature appeared, but Tiberius was awestruck. The small creature started to grow to human size and was in fact a very beautiful woman. She was so beautiful, she was breathtaking.

She took his reaction wrong and said, "I told you I was ugly."

"On the contrary," said Tiberius, "you are the most beautiful creature I have ever seen. Is that your true form?"

"Yes," the spite said sadly, "I think I look normal but other sprites do not; they say I am ugly and they call me names."

Tiberius said, "You say you are half faerie, then you must take after the faerie side of the family. If the sprites think you are ugly then they too must be an ugly race of people, sorry no offence to your family but you are beautiful."

She said, "Yes I have been told that I look like my mother. I thought she was very pretty but my father did not and neither did his family. I think he put a spell on her to marry him as he wanted the rights to the land she owned. Well that is what my mother used to say before she died."

Tiberius held out his hand. She was dubious at first but eventually she took it and he walked her down the few stairs that led to the hallway and put her in front of the hall mirror. He said, "Look, look how beautiful you are. You are not ugly at all you are faerie.

"I too am half faerie and I was very ugly until my faerie grandfather helped me to get the looks back that I had before a curse was put on my mother when I was in her womb."

The sprite said, "I did not look in the mirror before, I was very frightened of what I would see but I am glad you have persuaded me to do so."

Tiberius asked, "What is your name, sprite? I cannot keep calling you sprite for the rest of our lives, can I?"

She turned to look at him as she told him, "My name, sir, is Mary-Mary."

Tiberius asked, "Do you mean Mary?"

The sprite laughed. "No sir, it's Mary-Mary, that's the way sprites are called but my mother was called Celestial. She was a faerie and I thought she was lovely but my father's family said that she was ugly."

He said, "Come now we have to put these things behind us, Celestial. We need to live here in this house in a new free life, and a new start. It is time to move the house."

She exclaimed, "You called me Celestial!"

He smiled. "Of course I did, that is your name from now on. We both have new names now, come, stand with me and I will move our house to its final home"

They stood together in the hall and told the house where to go. The house did as it was bid and within half an hour of landing in Hubert's field there was a contingent from the castle led by Dimone and Godwin. They had also brought a few soldiers with them not knowing whether the house belonged to friend or foe.

Tiberius went out to greet them and gave Dimone the parchment that Maldwyn had written for them. Dimone wanted Tiberius to come and have dinner at the castle that evening, but Tiberius had to explain that he could not leave the house after dark, well at least not for thirty days anyway, as it would mean that he would die.

Dimone understood about evil magyk and the consequences that it could have, so he asked Tiberius to come to the castle the next morning. He said he could meet Empress Alyssa and tell her the news of Maldwyn and his companions.

Godwin was impressed with Tiberius, as with Maldwyn's help he had regained his muscular physique and looked like he could be a good fighter. He asked him, "Are you any good with a stave, lad?"

To which Tiberius had replied, "Do you want to try me, sir?"

This was a good answer and Tiberius was to start training as soon as this thirty days were up. Godwin had told him that he would be a good asset to the army and he needed at the moment every man he could get.

All in all, it had been a life changing week for Tiberius.

***

Maldwyn and his companions watched as the house disappeared, then they gathered their belongings and started to walk along the mountain pass. They were higher and further over the mountain than they previously were, but they seemed to be just as far along the length of the mountain as they were before so therefore they had lost no distance.

They made good distance that day and were all in good spirits, but that night while the others slept Maldwyn sat by the fire with Christano. Maldwyn said, "It's strange, Christano, I used to think we chose the path we went down but now I belief fate nudges us down that path and it is not all our own choice.

"I was on my own, then I had a cat and an owl. Now I have a family. And they also appear to be going down their own path, Doras with Mark and Tiberius with this house and his new face. You and Sorona are back to your normal forms and Talos is now man-sized which he always wished for.

"And the three sisters, well the three sisters I think they have found their three husbands on this little trip and if I have my way they will come back with us to the castle and live a normal life never to be nomads again.

"Change is constant, but so much change Christano, so much, and in so little time."

Christano was silent for a while staring at the campfire, then answered, "Change will happen, Maldwyn, and at what cost. At the end of all this some of us may be dead, but for sure all of us will have changed.

"We can only hope that the changes are not too drastic and we don't let the blackness that settles in our hearts take over and make us bitter, but I fear it may not be the case with some others, it will depend on the trauma and the loss that the individual has to go through."

"Then we will have to help each other, Christano, and stop that from happening," said Maldwyn.

Maldwyn went to sleep that night thinking about the beginning of the journey when he met Doras and Stephann, and he had taken them to see the Empress. But then he thought was that the beginning of this story or was it when he found his beloved cat and owl, or did it go back even further to when he was born and his father had to bring him to Nirvana.

He realised that while he was glad Sorona and Christano were back in their natural form, he would miss them terribly when he finally got home.

CHAPTER EIGHTEEN:
CANYON OF SHADOWS

ᛗ

Their journey was unpredictable as no map had ever been commissioned of this part of the Morby mountain range. It was referred to as a mountain but it was in fact a range of mountains that loomed over a number of villages and towns over a large expanse of Sandina.

As they walked down the pass Maldwyn realised the enormity of the mountain range. To their right was a range of steep peaks and he thought that on the other side of those peaks was the path they were originally on before the trolls abducted them.

To the left was a long expanse maybe a mile or more. It had a number of rocky outcrops that loomed over the land, some of them as high as fifty feet. At the end they could just see another range of mountains; it was a strange configuration and not like anything that Maldwyn had seen or read about before.

As they walked they realised that the pass was coming to an end. There appeared to be a deep drop. As they approached this anomaly in the path they realised that it was indeed a drop over a cliff and below them was a deep canyon.

Olivia, being the more adventurous of the sisters, walked towards the edge. Maldwyn quickly followed her. Small pieces of scree were falling away from the place where she was standing near the edge, and Maldwyn gently pulled her back. "Please, lady, do not stand so close; I thought I had lost you once, please no more."

She touched his face with fondness. "Oh, my mage, you are always there to protect me."

"As I should be," he said.

Talos and Stephann volunteered to walk along the edge of the cliff to see if they could find a way down. So Christano thought it would be a good idea to rest and have a bite to eat.

They had just started their evening meal when Talos and Stephann arrived back at camp, and after they had eaten their food Talos told the others what they had found. "There is a narrow path about a hundred yards down to the left. This path goes all the way down into the canyon; it is very, very, narrow and we will have to be careful that we do not slip and fall over the edge. But unless anybody wants to do a little mountain climbing on the range to our right and try to get back onto our original path, then there is no alternative. The canyon is the only way."

"Of course it is," Maldwyn said. "It is the most sensible way I think. Only, there is something, something I cannot just put my finger on!"

Christano asked, "You are worried, Maldwyn! And you would be right to be, there is something about this canyon. I felt it as soon as I was standing near the edge of the cliff. It was a strange feeling, a feeling of being watched, and the shadows. Did anyone else notice the shadows? There seem to be lots of them fleeting about in different directions but nothing that you could actually see."

Stephann said, "If you are both having feelings that you do not understand then would it not be wiser to stay here until morning. After all it would be foolish to start across a dubious canyon with night approaching, especially when the two most magykal beings we have with us are nervous about it."

Maldwyn stared at Stephann. He suddenly said in surprise, "You are becoming more confident with your decision-making, Stephann. Changes are coming over you. But yes, I agree that it is a good idea. We will camp here and set off early tomorrow."

Millie asked, "What do you think it is, Mage? Do you think there is someone out there?"

Sorona was standing very still looking into the direction of the canyon. She looked worried but at the same time there was a concentration on her face, concentration that meant she was trying to reach out to whatever it was in the canyon, trying to see if she could work out what the shadows were but to no avail. "Whatever it is, it is dark. I do not like it at all. It has a closed mind. I cannot reach the creature."

"Neither do I like it, but that is the way we must go, my love," said Christano. "If only those damn trolls had not taken us from our path we would have been okay."

Talos was cynical. "We probably would have been accosted by some other creature anyway. These mountains are a hotbed of thieves and evil creatures.

"Do you think we would get over faster if I go to my natural size and carry you all, my stride is large?"

Maldwyn was not happy with this. "I do believe that it would make no difference, Talos. If it is dark magyk your size will not stop them. It is beginning to get dusk please all of you get some sleep, I think we may need it. Oh yes, we are up at first light."

They had a restless night with screams, screeches and noises all around them, but what they did not see was the eerie mist that floated up from the depths of the canyon and hovered as if it was a predator awaiting its prey.

The mist was like no natural mist: it was dark and malevolent with the stench of death intermittently hanging in the air.

Maldwyn was the first to get up, but he was restless and wary of what they were to face that day. Sorona had said it well when she said `it's like a dark veil hanging over us'.

One by one they all woke from their sleep and all were feeling a sense of apprehension. They had a drink and some oat biscuits that Nafalius had his house sprite cook up for them; they were nutritious and filling but most of all they lasted months so at times like these it was a quick fix of food.

They walked in silence along the edge of the cliff to where the track started at the base of the mountain. Isla gasped, she thought she saw something. Yes, she did, she saw a shadow, something moving at the base of the mountain. The trouble was no one else had seen it, then there was a dark thick concentrated mist but by the time she turned away to tell the others it too had gone.

Christano said, "We need to stay close. If I may make a suggestion, Maldwyn, we may be better if, once at the base of the cliff we use a rope to fasten us together so that we do not get separated."

He agreed and they decided to prepare the rope before they set off down the path. Each person had the rope tied loosely around their waist, loose enough to get it up and down over their heads. The rope was then left three feet long before the next person was joined to it.

When the rope was ready, Talos folded it and hooked it diagonally over his torso, then they set off down the new path.

When Talos and Stephann had found the path the previous day it had been dry but now even though there had been no rain overnight the path was wet and slimy. It was as if someone had prepared it especially for them. It was treacherous and more dangerous than ever. Christano and Maldwyn were worried but they were not the only ones, they all were unnerved by the state of it and Maldwyn was so worried he decided to put a spell on them all so that they did not fall. But this was only after Millie had slipped and was hanging over the edge of the cliff. She said it was as if someone or something was pulling on her legs and the more they tried to pull her up the more difficult it became. It was only through the combined magyk of Maldwyn, Christano, Sorona and Stephann that they managed to pull her free.

That was when Maldwyn decided to put a levitation spell on them all; it was only temporary but useful. Millie was obviously shaken up and everyone was concerned for her, but she was none the worse for her experience and carried on as if nothing had happened.

They continued at a faster pace down the pass. No one wanted to be caught out again by whatever it was causing this trouble.

Talos pointed down into the canyon. "Look, there is movement!"

But by the time everyone else had looked in the direction he was pointing there was, once more, nothing to be seen. Maldwyn knew something was down there, but what? Whatever it was, was indeed playing a game of cat and mouse with them.

As soon as their feet touched the ground at the base of the pass they could feel it. It was a very intense feeling that tingled through their very being; it was unnerving to say the least and not a good experience.

Talos quickly attached the ropes to everyone before they set out across the canyon, while Maldwyn finished the job with a spell to stop the ropes being tightened up around their waist, thus expelling their breath and causing unconsciousness or worse. They were all worried and it was obvious.

Olivia asked, "Why the spell, my mage? Is the rope not enough?"

He answered, "I am just concerned that whatever or whoever is down here may decide to use the rope as a weapon against us, my lady. I hope I am a formidable enough shaman that my spell holds against this creature; it seems very clever."

"I would not use the word clever, Maldwyn, I would probably use the word devious," said Christano.

They started to walk through the rocky outcrop that had sprung up at the base of the cliff. The distance to the other side appeared to be a lot further away than it had done when they assessed it from the top of the cliff. This was again concerning as it caused Maldwyn to think that the creature must have the power of illusion.

They walked on for roughly half a mile, or so they thought, until they reached a small cluster of high rocks that formed a sort of passage way through the canyon. There seemed to be no way around it or over it as more high rocks were forming a sort of barrier. This was the only way through that they could see and they felt they were being herded like cattle.

Maldwyn was not the only one that was feeling nervous about this passage way of rocks. Stephann, Christano and Sorona were also feeling the same way. Their senses telling them it was a trap and always just out of reach at the corner of their eye they could see shadows moving, just fleeting glances, but definitely something.

It was hard to tell how long the narrow gorge went on for because of all its numerous twists and turns that caused disorientation and unease. No one really had a sense of where they were or how far they had come, all hoping that around every corner there would be an end to all this.

As they walked slowly on they found that another strange mist was hovering above their heads; the air became heavy and thick and they all started to feel a little nauseated. They did what they could with their combined magyk but it was not enough. It was not long before they succumbed to being sick and having to sit down through exhaustion and pain.

Talos was the only one not affected and Maldwyn put this down to the fact that although he was made of flesh and blood he was not born of flesh and blood. Also he realised that the toxicity of the mist was being absorbed through the skin and the bronze man had the perfect barrier for protection.

Maldwyn said, "Talos, if we all fall to this malady you will be the only one not affected. You need to fake it and let whoever is doing this take you too. You will be our only hope."

He gave Talos a potion and a vial of water. These he made invisible to all but Talos.

"Put these safe, Talos, and when the time comes, use it on myself or Christano. We will then do the rest of the company. I have once more changed the appearance of our clothes and hidden my second pouch so that we may have a way out."

Talos agreed and was just going to ask more questions when Sorona fell. She was quickly followed by Millie, Isla and Olivia. The males were the last to fall, but one by one they all succumbed and fell prey to the strange mist.

Talos sat down and pretended to be fighting it, then he too laid down and closed his eyes but of course he was faking the unconscious state.

How long they lay there Talos did not know. He was just starting to think that no one had done this deliberately and that the mist was a natural phenomenon. All this was going through his mind when a tall figure came bounding through the mist. He was very tall and loomed over them like a giant; one by one he picked them up and walked away with them, as Talos was further away than the others he was the last.

The creature picked him up as if he was a ragdoll. The strength of this creature was obvious and Talos knew he would have a tough time trying to beat it in battle.

As soon as the creature put him with the others and Talos was sure he had gone, he opened his eyes. The others were at the side of him so that was good. He looked around. They were laid about on large cushions in a room that had low soft lights.

Talos thought the room was reminiscent of a human Bedouin tent. He had seen the Persian influence before so he knew what they looked like, but the drapes, the cushions and the oil lamps hanging from the ceiling were all of Indian origin. It was very strange to have these artefacts from mixed cultures all in the same room.

Whatever the creature was he was probably like Talos and Tiberius and had walked into the Vortex innocently, only to walk out again at the other side in Nirvana. But how had the creature acquired all these authentic soft furnishings? Talos was at a loss to know how the creature had done this.

When Talos was pretty sure that the creature was not coming back, he went over to Maldwyn, mixed the ingredients and used the potion. He gently lifted Maldwyn's head and poured the potion into his mouth. It took a few minutes and at first he thought it was not working but eventually Maldwyn opened his eyes.

Maldwyn looked around him and said, "And pray tell me where are we now, please, Talos?"

Talos said, "I think we are under the mountain at the far side of the mountain range, the one we were heading for. At least if my assumption is right the creature has already brought us most of the way. We only have to get up onto the mountain top and I think we are back on track."

"And escape from our very formidable captor," said Maldwyn.

He looked at Talos, with a smirk on his face. "You forget that bit I think, Talos, escape is paramount."

Maldwyn was indeed changed; he knew now how to make light of most problems. Maldwyn quickly brought Christano back to consciousness, then Stephann, Sorona and the three sisters. Maldwyn then asked Talos if he had managed to have a good look at their captor.

Talos answered, "I did but he was weird. His attire was similar to that of the Persian traders that I used to see anchoring at the island where I lived. But in some ways it was different. He had a loincloth, highly decorated in oranges and golds with his legs showing. His headdress was also elaborate and his face was like that of a monkey crossed with a lion. It is really hard for me to describe how he looked, Maldwyn."

Several voices said in unison, "A what?"

Talos smiled. He had forgotten that most of the creatures in Nirvana had never heard of, let alone seen a monkey, but they did know what a lion was.

Christano said, "I have read extensively about the human land and also visited a few times. I know what a monkey is and I think I also know what the creature is."

He turned to Maldwyn. "Do you remember talk of an ancient creature roaming Nirvana thousands of years ago? It used to disappear then re-appear again centuries later eventually to disappear for good and no one has heard of the creature since, not for over a thousand years anyway. It has now gone into the mythology of Nirvana."

Maldwyn said, "Yes I vaguely remember it. I will try to find the right book and look it up."

Maldwyn retrieved his pouch and from it he took a human mythology book, when Christano said, "Asura, I am sure that was the name."

Maldwyn answered, "I thought it was Kravyads but it is possible that it had more than one name. Some of these so-called demons do have several names in several different mythologies."

They looked through the books and found the creature. There was the picture and Talos was right it did look like a cross between a lion and monkey. He let the others see the picture and Talos once again said that the humanoid creature that came into the room was the one in the picture.

Talos was fascinated with the book: its glossy facsimiles of places and people and the words, the words were magnificent to Talos.

Talos asked, "Please, Wizard, explain to me what these words of yours mean and these things you call pictures. I have seen similar before but had no one I could ask about them."

Maldwyn smiled. "Talos, when we have completed our quest I will teach you to read and explain about the pictures and the drawings, and the books are yet more of the things that the humans brought with them to Nirvana.

"No, that is a falsehood, the enchanted creatures of the forest had these things in their culture but they were all hand made. Man has machines to make these, that is the difference."

Millie walked over to Talos and took his hand. "If you will permit me, sir, I would be honoured to teach you how to read."

Talos looked at Maldwyn not knowing what to say, but Maldwyn nodded `Yes' and Talos said, "That would be welcomed, lady."

Millie smiled and they sat holding hands for a while.

Christano spoke, "What does it say about the creature, Maldwyn? Is there anything useful in there?"

He answered, "Well, I will start with his names as he has many. They are Asura, Manushya-Rakshasi, Rakshasi, Kravyads, Nri-Chakshas and Raksha.

"He will go by one of these names but which one I do not know, to us it does not matter but we may find out later. Apparently, he is malicious and dim-witted and can play tricks easily. He has the power to change shape that is his greatest asset."

Christano asked, "Can I interrupt you there, Maldwyn. Unless the creature is born from ancestry of Nirvana he will not be able to change shape here."

Maldwyn replied, "That is probably why he is still in this guise, it is his true form and not his chosen one.

"He also can conjure up illusions such as mist and people, so be very aware of this trickery. He is said to have venomous fingernails and in battle he feeds on human flesh, raw flesh.

"Oh dear, that does not bode well. He also has fangs so we appear to be in a little bit of trouble. This creature comes from the mythological tales of India, a country in the place where humans come from. He is said to be a demigod, a half god.

"How he was created and by whom is of no consequence. All that matters is that he is real and we have to work out what we are going to do with him before he works out what he's going to do with us."

Christano, who was now looking at the book, said, "I am not sure, but I think he can be killed. It says that Shakti killed the Rakshasi, whoever Shakti is."

Maldwyn said, "I do not know how I know it but recently I have knowledge of things I did not have knowledge of before. Shakti means power, primordial energy, and is thought to represent dynamic forces that move through the entire universe.

"If that is what killed him then we have to conjure up some sort of force that would render him inert while we escape."

Talos said, "I still do not understand how he managed to get his hands on all these Persian drapes and cushions!"

Sorona was puzzled. "I do not know about this Persian, or what it is, but these cushions and drapes are faerie made."

Millie said, "No they are not, they are of Celtic design, like our ancestors used to have."

Stephann spoke before Maldwyn had a chance to. "I think, Maldwyn, we had better sit down and all describe what we are actually seeing. I only see a dank cave with sacking on the floor and bones for pillows."

Everyone looked concerned even Maldwyn could not see what Stephann was seeing. If he was right and there was no reason to think he was not, then the Asura was using his powers of illusion on them even now.

Maldwyn held his hand up and immediately his staff flew into it and became visible once again. Maldwyn pointed the staff around the room, its light shining on everything and everyone as he turned in a full circle. As he moved his staff around and up and down within the dim light of the cave, they could see that Stephann was indeed right.

They were in a cave. There was a dirty piece of sacking over the wall at one side; this supposedly was the door. And for the moment they would not be going through it. Stephann lifted the sacking off a small raised area on the floor that everyone supposed were beautiful embroidered pillars and they saw the gruesome truth.

They had been laying on skulls and bones of every size and shape and not all were animals, in fact most were human. It was a scary reality that they found themselves in but Maldwyn had an idea.

CHAPTER NINETEEN:
ESCAPE AND THE KAPPA

✝

The first thing Maldwyn had to do was make a magykal net. this he did and floated it above the door ready to be dropped on the creature's head. This was made out of chainmail that they found rusting on the floor near a dismembered body.

Maldwyn had manipulated the metal to form a large net, a bit like a fishing net but with the strength of magyk to catch their large fish.

He said, "Let us take stock of the situation. Christano, you said he was killed, or one of his kind was killed, by Shakti which we both think is a powerful force of energy. Well I was thinking, would all our powers put together: yours, Sorona, Stephann and myself, concentrated with the help of the staff, be enough to bring the creature to its knees?

"If we could manage to weaken the creature, then we could let the net drop onto him and hopefully make our escape.

"Trouble would be we do not know the way out, or what is on the other side of that entrance."

Sorona said, still with a small hint of a meow in her voice, "We can try, Maldwyn. It is all we have, and it is either that or finish up like these poor souls."

Isla informed them, "We have much power in our fire hands, Mage. If we all concentrated our efforts, along with you, that would surely be enough. The only downside is the creature would be a little scorched." She said this with a giggle.

Maldwyn agreed it would not hurt to do this and it may even be the extra power that they needed to accomplish their goal, as the energy in fire is great.

Talos was feeling a little left out. "And what do I do while you magykal beings do your stuff. I feel useless."

Maldwyn smiled. "Ah, but you are not useless, my friend, you are the brawn. Once the net has been dropped on top of the creature you need to use your considerable strength to hold our captive while we prepare a binding spell. That is if I have enough strength left myself, performing magyk at this level can weaken us all considerably.

"I suggest we have some water and a few of the biscuits Nafalius gave us. I do not think we will get any food off our friend, after all why should he waste it on us."

Stephann asked, "Do you think he will kill us all at once, Maldwyn? If he had the chance, I mean?"

"No, I do not, he will want to keep fresh meat so he will probably kill one at a time, and as unfortunate as it is I think he may have done this before, probably keeping the strength of the captives up by giving them what they thought was cooked meats, which was probably mice and rats or the scraps he didn't want from their companions," said Maldwyn.

Sorona felt sick. "So, in other words giving them a meal that is actually their relations or friends."

"Yes," he replied, "That's exactly what I mean. He can make you think anything with his illusions, even what you are eating. Now all we have to do is wait."

They must have waited three days before they heard the sound of someone coming down the passage. They lay down as if still asleep in the places they were in previously. The creature came in and was silent for a while as if he was looking around for one of them to stir. He grunted and walked back out of the room.

When they had thought he had gone they all got up again. Talos asked, "What do you think that was all about?"

Maldwyn was not sure but Christano thought he knew. "He may have drugged us with something that is deadly to him. It would have been very powerful so it was something that takes a long time to get out of our system when inhaled in the form of gas.

"He probably can't eat us until we are fully purged, so I think he may come back later or if not tomorrow."

"Then we will be ready for him," said Maldwyn.

They had to wait a further two days before they heard the creature coming down the passage once more. Thump, thump, his steps were heavy and his temper vile. Maldwyn had already warned everyone that they must take no notice of anything they see as it may not be real, but the reality was, they were in the cave with skeletons and a monster who wanted to have them for his main meal.

He told them that as long as they kept this in their minds they would be fine. The Asura creature lifted the sacking back from the doorway. Just for a moment some of the company thought they saw a beautifully carved wooden door, but soon as they forced that thought away from their minds, reality was all too real.

Everyone but Talos was standing facing the doorway ready for the Asura to step under the sacking door. Talos was standing to one side ready to hold the creature down as the metal net fell onto him.

The Asura faced them, confused at what was in front of him, but in the few seconds it had taken him to assess the sight before him, it was enough for the plan to swing into action.

It happened very quickly again as those sorts of things usually do. They fired as much magyk as they could at the creature and he fell to the ground, the net on top of him, and Talos then pounced and sat on the creature waiting for Maldwyn to bind him with magyk.

The only downside to the plan was one that had already been discussed, as Stephann pointed out the downside of a few burns on the creature was bad but considering what he had in store for them it was not bad enough.

Once he was secure, they made their way cautiously through the gap. It was unknown territory so caution was indeed the main plan. They followed the path until they came to a large chamber; the chamber had a long wooden table at its centre and a large seat at what they presumed was the head of the table. It was sparse with nothing there but a bed and a hook with a change of clothes upon it.

There was a sort of shower affair where the water source had been diverted to come out of the rock face higher up on the wall. Directly below it there was a dip in the bedrock with an outlet for the water.

Maldwyn commented that the beast did not lack sophistication. There were two passages that went from this chamber, one led to the canyon they had come from and the other led on to who knows where.

They set off down the passage that led further into the mountain. There was no other option, they had to find a way out if possible.

They walked on for over an hour but it seemed longer. They were just beginning to think that they were never going to get out when Christano spotted something.

He said, "Wait! What is that?"

They all looked in the direction that Christano was looking; there was a mark on the wall, a definite mark that had been deliberately carved into the rock face.

Christano had a closer look. "I think it is a mark from the world of men; it is definitely not faerie in origin."

Maldwyn examined the sign. "Now let me think what the meaning of the sign is. I have seen this before; the language is called Celtic and its writings are called runes. Yes, I am sure I am right this is Celtic writing.

"This sign." He pointed to the sign. "This means Ior or water beast. And this one ᛗ, this is URUZ or Ur or W means wild and fierce beast. And here, look." Maldwyn hurried on to a piece of wall further up the passage. "And this < means kaunaz which converted to their language is C or Q, and usually means child.

"Don't you see, the creature that put these marks in the wall is sending us a message; he's trying to tell us who he is and I think I know."

Maldwyn used this finger to magykally draw on the wall using the signs and putting the words at the side of them. When all was done they could see that the words were water beast, fierce beast, water or child.

"These runes have now got a meaning and they represent to me a creature but again one which I thought extinct and that creature is a kappa."

Christano said, "But I also thought they were extinct." He looked at the others who seemed puzzled. "They are tricky creatures, and you can never tell if they are telling you the truth or not. Some of them got through to the land of man where they caused havoc, but all the horror tales about them are not true; they are not cruel creatures and in the land of men are much maligned."

Stephann suggested, "I think that would account for the water that was in the beast's chamber. You said this kappa is a water child so I presume he needs to be in water to survive?"

Maldwyn said, "Yes, you are right Stephann he does, he has an indentation in the top of his head, some say it looks like an inverted crown. If he leaves the water for more than an allotted time he must carry some of his water in the crown: this sustains him until he can get back to water but not for long.

"If he is trapped down here there must be water, so we must look for that. He has obviously been watching us unless there has been a breakout before and the symbols were for those prisoners before us."

"But they do look fresh and sharp. I do not think they have long been made, Maldwyn," said Christano.

Maldwyn studied the runes. "You are right, my friend, as usual. We will continue down this path as it is our only option for now and see if it comes out near a water source."

They continued down the passage way for quite a while, before reaching a small cavern with a pool about twenty feet across. Maldwyn smiled. "Here is where the kappa lives."

An eloquent but grumpy dismembered voice echoed around the cavern., "Oh, you think I live here, do you, Wizard? You are not as enlightened as I thought you would be."

The voice made everyone jump even Maldwyn, but he still managed to gather his thoughts. "Do you have a name or should we call you Kappa?"

The voice said, "Kappa is my faerie name and has been for thousands of years, Wizard, so I think that will suffice, don't you?

"Anyway, names and niceties are not what we need to talk about at this moment in time. I need a promise from you, a promise that once made I know you will at least try to keep.

"If you follow the path through to the next cavern I will speak with you. He, the ugly one, can get as far as this but the enchantment that keeps him here has a barrier and he can come no further than this, so you will be safe once you get to the next cavern."

There was a splash and the voice disappeared. They all started to mutter at once and it was not straightforward to get into the next cavern. They walked along the passage for a few more yards, then they encountered a bend in the path. As they rounded that bend, they were immediately confronted with a very narrow passage. the walls were so close they could all just get through sideways: it was a horrible feeling.

It was over thirty yards in length and felt like it was never going to end. They were all a little nervous as they started to go through the passageway. Unfortunately, Talos was far too large to get through the gap, although there was no problem with his height, his sheer bulk stopped him from getting into the passage. Maldwyn had to use a reducing spell on Talos once again, but this time it was to make him thinner, a lot thinner.

As soon as he was through the gap, he turned back to his normal size which he was very pleased with; he did not fancy being so thin for the rest of his life. It only took a further fifty yards of walking before the area opened up to a magnificent cavern that was lit by some sort of magyk.

The pool was large and blue in colour. There was a small house at the far end of the pool against the opposite wall to where they were standing. This house was a bit like a beaver dam but much more sophisticated and much larger. There were flowers growing on a grassed area to one side of the pool and a breeze coming in from somewhere, but where they could not tell.

The cavern itself had been excellently executed to produce a calm ambience that made everyone feel relaxed; the whole thing was perfect.

The voice was back again. "Welcome to my home, Wizard. I do not have the opportunity to show it off very often."

Maldwyn answered, "It is a very excellent home, Kappa. Are you happy here?"

The voice then said, "Oh yes, of course I am. I have fish, rats, mice, an occasional assortment of bats and a good supply of sparkling freshwater. And the view, well the view is breathtaking, it really is."

Stephann was puzzled. "What view? We are in a cave!"

There was a laugh that lasted a long time. "Oh dear, you creatures can only think as far as you can see. Please cross the small bridge to my grass garden, a meal has been prepared for you and before you ask there is not a rodent in sight of it."

He laughed once again thinking it was funny that they may think he would serve a rat or two up to them.

They walked to the end of the pool and saw a small ornate footbridge. Maldwyn put one foot on the bridge to test if it was strong enough to take them; he decided that it was and started to walk across followed by the rest of the party.

The grassed area was a pleasant area with flowers growing along three sides and the pool to the fourth. A picnic had been set out on the grass and there were cakes, bread, jams and some sort of cooked bird with wine to wash it down, or hot chocolate for those who did not partake.

The whole scene was surreal and almost dreamlike. They all thought the same thoughts: is this real or were they being manipulated once again. Maldwyn took his staff and let it shine around the cavern. This was definitely not an illusion; it was real.

The laugh once again filled the cavern. "Oh, you creatures, no faith, no faith."

Maldwyn was annoyed by this time and said, "Do you blame us for being cautious, Kappa? We were nearly the main course for the vile one as you call him. And for goodness sake show yourself, will you? This is getting annoying."

The kappa laughed once more, then opened the door to his house and crossed some small steppingstones that led from his house to the back corner of the grassed area. He said, "Hello, and welcome. Please sit and enjoy the food my house Sprite has prepared for you. You are lucky, he only visits me one day a week and today was that day."

Maldwyn asked, "I wondered about that, about this cavern and the food."

"Yes," he explained, "I was the last of my kind and the faeries decided that they would like to give me a comfortable life until it finally expires which I hope will be a long time yet. This was on the condition that I would keep an eye on the vile one from this end and later when they realised the creature was trapping people, try to help them escape whenever I could.

"My brief was to try and rescue anyone that got this far into the cave system. They knew I could not and would not dare to show myself to that ugly vile thing as he would have killed me, and the faerie council are still awaiting to see if they can find any more kappa so that my race does not die out like a lot of others in the magykal community.

"The trouble is the creature has only ever captured single creatures or double on some occasions, so they never stood a chance against him. You are the first to be in a group and you are the first to make it out."

Talos exclaimed, "But we are not out, as you call it. We are here and I cannot see a way out!"

The kappa laughed again: his small beak chattering as he laughed. "This is only my house and garden, bronze man, you will see the way out soon enough."

They were all silent for a while as they had some food and drink. Only Talos and Christano decided to partake of the wine as the others had never tasted it and much preferred chocolate.

Eventually Maldwyn asked, "Why did the faeries imprison the Asura here?"

The kappa looked at him thoughtfully. "Have you ever heard of the portal of light, Wizard?"

"Yes," Maldwyn replied.

"Then you will understand that the portal can show up anywhere in Nirvana and anywhere in the land of humans. Therefore, any creature with strange magykal traits can walk through. They do not all have to be half faerie as some creatures do think.

"And so it was that this vile, ugly one came into our world thousands of years ago. It had taken the faerie council hundreds of years to finally capture the creature and when they did they barred him to the cave and the canyon where he now dwells," said the kappa.

"But why not kill him?" Millie announced.

The kappa answered, "You cannot kill a demigod with normal magykal means, but now they have learnt of a way it may be done. There is a stone, it has several names in the human world because of their storytelling, but here in Nirvana it has its true name: the magenta stone.

"This stone, put together with ancient magyk, and the cauldron that Dimone's father is custodian of will kill the creature but only when mixed with the magykal waters of the crystalline."

The kappa's words set them all thinking. It was Sorona who eventually asked the question, "But how do we find these things and are you sure it will work if we do?"

Maldwyn said, "You do realise that we are on a quest to save Nirvana from evil, don't you? We cannot deviate from that path, we are already way behind and way too late. We should have been nearly at the end of the mountain range by now."

The kappa replied more seriously now, all the frivolity gone out of his voice, "As I said, Dimone can try to arrange to get the cauldron with his father and I hear that Merlin has been resurrected in the castle, so if one or more of you can persuade him to tell you the whereabouts of the magenta stone then two of the main ingredients are here, if he has not destroyed it. I thought he hid it after Nafalius gave it to him"

Stephann was curious. "But where do we find the waters of the crystalline?"

"Why here!" the kappa said, looking quite pleased with himself. "When you go outside you will see."

Maldwyn smiled. "I wondered why the pool was not stagnant; it either had a good supply of flowing water or it was magykal."

The kappa laughed once again. "Or both. Now if you have finished your food please follow me and we will set you on your way, but please promise me that when this is over you will come back to defeat the vile one."

"We will," said Maldwyn.

They followed the kappa towards his house and before they realised that they were too big to enter they were inside and following him down the staircase. Somehow either the house had grown or they had shrunk and it was then that Maldwyn, Christano and Sorona realised that the kappa had a few magykal skills of his own.

They came out on a ledge that had a curtain of water flowing down in front of them. The kappa, and indeed themselves, appeared to be normal size again. They followed him to the left side. He said, "Do you like my view?"

They walked out from behind the curtain of water and before them was a view over the mountain. They could see for miles and miles and far, far into the distance. They could just make out the lake near the castle but not the castle itself. The kappa looked back at the waterfall and said, "You can go down the steps there and continue through and inside the mountain or you can carry on a little further and enter a cave. That cave takes you to some steps leading up to the top mountain pass. It is up to you which way you go."

Maldwyn thought for a while then said, "I think we may take the latter, I for one have had enough of dark caves.

"Thank you, Kappa, we may meet again." They turned and walked off towards the cave that had the steps to the upper mountain pass.

CHAPTER TWENTY:
THE GREEN MAN

↑

They did as they were told and it was not too long before they were once again on the top of the mountain, and in the fresh air.

They knew which way to go now that they had seen the lake and as long as the central mountain was on their left they just had to continue their journey to find the Green Man.

Sorona said, "Please, let us have no more adventures. I am glad we met Nafalius as we regained our true form but I for one have had enough adventures of that kind."

Maldwyn suddenly had a thought. "You have not lost your charms, have you?"

"No," they both answered together.

"Why?" Sorona asked.

He informed them, "You may still need the charms for protection and until the hag is dead the spell may be able to re-activate, but I am not sure."

Christano and Sorona both looked worried but knew that if Maldwyn said to keep the charms safe then they should do that.

They carried on, once more hoping that nothing untoward was going to happen at this stage of the journey. It was hard going as the pass was rocky and winding. It was as if fate once more had played its hand.

They found a safe harbour in the shape of some overhanging rocks that formed a cave-type structure but with no sides. It was decided that they should make camp there for the night.

The kappa had made sure his sprite had provided them with some extra provisions, but by now they were all used to smaller portions, so these provisions would last a lot longer than normal, and they still had the biscuits that Nafalius had given them.

The night went by with no further incident, but whether it was their expectations of trouble they did not know but a feeling of unease was coming upon them all again.

They once more started on their journey. The sun was out, the birds were singing and the sky was blue, so why were they all so tense? They had been walking for roughly three hours and the sun was getting higher when a man came walking towards them.

He was dressed in a long robe of green and brown leaves, just right for camouflage in the forest but not entirely right for a mountain pass. He stepped directly in front of them and introduced himself. "I am Vardo the hermit," he said, bowing his head with the palms of his hands together.

Maldwyn stepped forward. "I am Maldwyn, the wizard. I am pleased to meet you, Vardo. What brings you onto the pass?"

He considered Maldwyn and one by one he looked at the others. "I have come to seek you out. You are looking for the Green Man, so I hear?"

"Yes, we are. Do you know where he is?" said Maldwyn.

He replied, "Only if you can tell me what you want him for, Mage."

"More to the point, hermit, how did you know that we were looking for him?" said Maldwyn suspiciously.

The hermit looked puzzled as if Maldwyn should have known. "Ah that would be the kappa, or should I say his sprite. The kappa sent him to find me and that made me think to myself, why do you wish to see the Green Man? What has he got that you want?"

Christano answered the hermit, "We need to speak to him about the hag and that is all we will say, hermit. We do not know who you are, for all we know you could be one of Sheela's spies."

"I have told you, I am Vardo the hermit," he said as if that was enough, after all who would not believe him.

Sorona, seeing that the situation could get out of hand replied, "You can see why we are all wary of you, hermit. We have been captured three times along this path and we have never met you before and yet you expect us to trust you without question.

"But then we can see why you are worrying. If you really are protecting the Green Man then you do not know who we are or what we want with him. So yes, you do have to be cautious of this, we understand."

Vardo considered her for a while and the others, once again he was trying to work out what their nature was. "Well put that way I do see the dilemma. I will take this one to plea your case and if the Green one says it is okay I will bring you all to him."

Christano was not happy. "If Sorona goes then so do I."

"Very admirable, son of Shard, but the beautiful one will come to no harm with me," said Vardo.

Christano asked in a sharp manner, "How do you know my father's name, hermit?"

He answered calmly, "Because I have met him; we were young together. I never dreamt I would outlive him after all he was Seelie Court. I was at your naming, Christano."

Maldwyn smiled. "You are the great castle wizard, are you not?"

"Yes," he said. "Now if we are done, we must go."

He held out his hand to Sorona and she took it. They walked up the path a short way, then they disappeared. Christano was worried. He paced up and down trying to work out what was taking them so long to get back, but back from where, he was concerned and so was Maldwyn.

Maldwyn said, "Do not fret, Christano, they will be back soon enough. I believe with all my heart that she is safe."

"What do you know about this Green Man, Maldwyn?" asked Isla.

Maldwyn considered what he should say and how he should say it. "The Green Man is an enigma; he has been around for millions of years and there is one in every world. The forest cannot exist without him. No one knows where he came from or how, but like the faeries he has always been here.

"In a lot of cultures, he is the symbol of nature, of renewal and growth, of rebirth, but to be honest no one knows much about him except his guardian. I do believe now that the hermit we just met is the Green Man's guardian and I also believe that he is a powerful magykal creature that excels way above anyone in this company."

Millie said, "It is odd but no one ever told me about faeries or the Green Man, but I knew of their existence from being a child, we all did!"

"That is because he is woven into the very fabric of our existence," said Maldwyn. "I believe that he was one of the first ancient creatures that was created as our world was formed. I could be wrong but that is my feeling."

They were all listening, then Christano said, "That is all well and good, Maldwyn, and you are probably right but where is she?" Christano was worried.

The ladies made them a hot drink but just as they were sitting down to drink it they saw two people walking towards them. It was Sorona and Vardo the hermit.

Vardo sniffed the air. "Ooh is that chocolate? I have not tasted chocolate for, well I do not know how long. I have herbal and green teas now that I live in the forest. I must admit I do miss hot chocolate."

Isla smiled and offered a mug of hot chocolate to Vardo; he bowed his head and received it graciously then sat down to drink it.

Meanwhile, Christano had walked up to Sorona and put his arms around her. "I thought I had lost you. Where have you been? Where did you go to I mean?"

Sorona put her fingers to his lips and said, "Shush, my love, do not upset yourself, it is not like you. I do not know where all this emotion has come from.

"We have been to the forest to meet the Green Man. He is a wonderful person, Christano. He has invited us all to go there and he will discuss the problem with us and see if he can help," said Sorona.

Christano hugged her once more and took her to one side. I am sorry, Sorona, for the way I am acting but as a Seelie Court I am not used to such emotions. When I was changed for so long into an owl and also being in contact with humans for so long, it has caused a change in me, a change that is not normal for my race. We love intensely, that I can cope with, but these new emotions take some getting used to. How do humans manage them?"

Maldwyn shouted them over. "Come, you to. We have to pack up and go with Vardo."

One minute the group was walking down the mountain pass and the next they were walking in the forest. It was not the forest near the castle, it was another one, but they knew not where.

They all knew that it had taken a great mage to transport them all without a portal. No one, not even the faeries, knew how this was done.

The forest was warm with a cool breeze flowing through it: this gave it a calm feeling. It was a bit like you would feel in the summer when the days are long and barmy; it was indeed an enchanted forest.

They did not know how long they were walking as the beauty surrounding them was a lot to take in. Every tree and every blade of grass was a lush deep green. There were flowers growing in small clumps and smaller ones like forget-me-nots scattered around the forest floor. Birds were chirping from up high and small creatures darted in and out of the branches of the trees above their heads, while other creatures darted behind the base of the trees playing some sort of game.

They could hear the trickle of running water that appeared to be getting louder as if they were walking towards it; it was indeed a place of enchantment.

The ladies were swooning over the small animals. They had spent much of their lives living in caves or small houses at the edge of the villages and never dared to venture far in case their secret was found out.

Everyone delighted in the latest reaction of the ladies. They had all taken open spaces for granted up to now but they were starting to realise just what self-imposed imprisonment could do to people and creatures. It was astounding, how lucky they were to be brought up with fields and water and trees.

They eventually reached the clearing that was far more beautiful than the forest. It had everything the forest had plus a waterfall and clear blue skies above, with the occasional fluffy cloud here and there.

As they walked towards the pool below the waterfall they heard a rustling in the trees to the left of them. Vardo asked them to be still. Out of the forest stepped a pure black unicorn with a bright white horn. He was unusual and something none had seen before. Legends abound about the unicorn but in all the stories they were white not jet.

The unicorn cautiously walked into the clearing, then he stopped dead in his tracks realising they were there. Vardo held out his hand slowly. "Zeke, do not be alarmed, these are our friends and they seek to stop the defiler."

The unicorn walked towards Vardo and allowed his nose to be touched. Then in turn he went from one to the other of the party so that they could all do the same. He then walked over to the pool to drink clear freshwater.

Sorona was just going to ask about the colour of the unicorn when a tall man with green skin and a coat made of the finest silk walked out of the forest to greet them. He greeted Vardo, then Vardo introduced the company to him; the man of course was the Green Man.

He asked them to sit with him and take tea. There were a few seats and benches at the far side of the pool and a table set out with seed cake, chocolate brownies and tea.

The Green Man had a sip of his tea, then asked, "Now, I believe you require my help, Maldwyn? Please tell me what has happened on your journey and leave no detail out as it may be of importance."

Maldwyn started to tell their story but he kept being interrupted by some of the others. After roughly two hours the story was told and Maldwyn sat back in his chair and had another cup of tea.

The Green Man sat quietly for some time before he offered his thoughts. "You have had an exciting journey and that journey has not been without its dangers, but you have helped people on the way and that is a measure of your character, and the character of your companions.

"The path you all walk is, and will be, a difficult one and the outcome is not certain, but if I can help you along the way then I will. You seek the hag, the Frau. I will tell you what I know about her, which is not much. She is from the human folklore and how she got here we do not know but she has been here for thousands of years.

"I believe she is not the original Frau therefore she does not know of the land of men and because she is not the original she has overstepped her role in life and has grown mad; she sees herself as a powerful being, a being that should rule this land as her birth right."

He looked at the ladies. They were staring at the black unicorn. He said, "Zeke was once white, but no more. He is now black for ever so he stays with us to protect him."

Millie asked, "How? Who or what did this to him?"

He replied, "It was her, it was the Frau, the hag, she thought it funny to torture this poor creature and turn his heart black. She did this to Zeke over a long period of time. She was trying to get him on her side because of the magykal powers that a unicorn has, but instead of his heart turning black he was so grief stricken and forlorn with anguish and despair that his heart stayed light. It was his coat that turned black. There is nothing so pure as a unicorn.

"She had no use for him then, so she turned him loose in a crowded town where humans could see him. Some of them thought he would be worth money so they tried to capture him. It was only the intervention of the faeries that prevented his death. And all this just because he was a different colour.

"That town had started to revert back to man's ways in the human world, the ways of cruelty and deceit, ways of war and fighting. We think it was the hag's influence that caused this. The faerie council had to clean memories of this type of behaviour once again; she is a threat and her influence could overturn the peace that we all enjoyed in Nirvana.

"Ever since man first came here they have lived in harmony with the magykal creatures of this land and let us not forget it is not man's land it is ours and we let them stay here as long as they live in peace. So, as you will see we in this forest are very aware of the problem, now tell me how can I help?"

Maldwyn said, "We need to know the whereabouts of Sheella's fortress; we hear that you will know where it is."

The Green Man smiled at them. "No, but I have a rough idea. Sarah the banshee, she knows better than I the whereabouts of the hag's castle. If you have been told differently then it is gobbling whispers."

Olivia asked, "What are gobbling whispers?"

He laughed. "Oh, it is when a story is told and the more people in the chain the more the tale loses its true form and can take on a totally different meaning.

"I believe it is called something else in the land of humans and they have had wars start over it."

She said, "I see, and why goblins?"

He answered, "Because they can be a bit silly and hear what they want to hear." He said with a smile on his face, the irony of how a small Nirvana saying could be the cause of the full conversation was not lost on him.

"As I was saying it was Sarah the banshee that knows the whereabouts of the fortress. She was captured by the hag and she wants revenge. Sarah is very bitter over the events that happened to her.

"The banshee is a much-maligned race. They only apply their wail to people who have wronged them or when they are in danger, so really only people that deserve it. They are one of the kindest gently creatures in Nirvana.

"Some weeks before Sarah was found wandering in the woods, the hag had held her captive in her stronghold. Apparently, she had her men seek Sarah out so that she could capture her and hopefully persuade her to give her allegiance to Sheela's cause.

"Sarah refused and the hag decided it would be good to torture her and take her wail away from her. I have never heard of this before but somehow she can and somehow she did. She has changed a magykal creature into a normal human being: this is dark magyk indeed."

Maldwyn said, "This is extreme dark magyk she has tapped into, but how we can find out where she has obtained the magyk is another story, where to now?"

The Green Man beckoned to Vardo. "Please, Vardo, will you send a message to Sarah and tell her we would like to pay her a visit if she is receiving guests."

Christano asked, "Receiving guests? Is she not well?"

He answered, "She has not been accepting guests since the hag took her wail away; she is very sad as well as very angry and the torture she was subjected to changed Sarah considerably. We can only hope that one day we will get Sarah back in her true form."

They talked for a further hour before Vardo came back and announced that Sarah would see them. They finished their fourth cup of tea, gathered their things and followed the Green Man and Vardo into the forest.

As the Green Man passed the flowers and trees, it was as if they knew he was there and they all stood to attention like little soldiers waiting to be inspected. Everything seemed more alive and fresher: the flowers seemed to give off more sweet scent and the small animals ran around the Green Man's legs or sat at the side of the path as if they were forming a guard of honour.

They walked along the winding path until they reached another waterfall. This one was smaller than the first but just as beautiful. There was a two-storey house at the side of the fall; it was made of dull red-coloured brick and it had smoke coming from the chimney.

Stephann enquired, "Isn't the house similar to the houses that humans live in?"

"Yes, it is. Sarah was used to living in the town of Trask until the hag Sheela captured her. And anyway except for the creatures that never leave the deep forest these types of houses are common place after all these millennia," said Vardo.

"She has not trusted the town since, so we built her a new house where she could feel safe and recover from her ordeal."

Vardo and the Green Man said they would go in first. Vardo would come back to tell them if Sarah was up to having visitors. Vardo came out a few minutes later and said they were all invited to come in but they must take their shoes off; Sarah was very house proud.

The house was beautiful, not at all as you would have expected considering the old tales about banshees and especially the tales that humans tell. It was a very refined, neat and tidy dwelling with three rooms downstairs and three rooms upstairs. There were floral curtains and chair coverings with light white furniture.

Sarah herself was only small but she was slim and very pretty with hair as dark as jet. It was a fact that when she wailed her face distorted and to some she could look monster like, but in fact she never changed her form.

She invited them to sit and made them some cocoa. She offered them apple and blackberry tarts with cream. The Green Man decided to just have the tea; it was very rare that he ate anything.

They all had a lot of questions for Sarah but Maldwyn was made spokesperson for them all so that she was not being bombarded with questions from every direction.

CHAPTER TWENTY-ONE: SARAH'S STORY

Maldwyn had to be very diplomatic in his approach to Sarah. She was obviously a bag of nerves, so he started with, "Sarah, how did you manage to live in the town of men without being found out?"

She smiled a weak smile. "Well I looked human and my wail only comes out in real danger or anger, if I'm distressed or someone is causing me pain, but in certain circumstances I can use it against an enemy at will.

"When the hag sent her minions to the town to find me they came to the shop that I owned and took me by surprise. I had a small patisserie/tea shop in the Market Square; it was a lovely shop, and I also sold flowered tableware and crockery from the Leeming factory at Brunsk.

"I was doing very well until the day came when the trolls came over my threshold. You have got to understand that the town of Trask is on the very far reaches of Sandina and it takes a long time for any trouble to be reported back to the castle. Look at the unicorn incident that happened after I had left, that should have been reported right away.

"I gave the shop to my assistant as I knew I would not be going back there. It was common knowledge that I had been taken so they would have known I was a magykal creature, and the prejudice was rife until the council stepped in and cleared the human's minds. Sheela had put it about that if any magykal creatures lived in the town they had been told to grab their children and take them away. Most magykal creatures that were obviously from Nirvana fled before mayhem ensued. But now it is safe again, but she may still put her influences on the town once more so I will not go back.

"Clara my friend is a wood nymph. She sent her friends out looking for me and it was they who eventually found me wandering in the woods. The Green Man had felt the balance in the nature of the town going wrong and that is why the faerie council was called. Vardo very kindly went to get my belongings from the patisserie and my furniture and personal belongings from my small house behind the shop.

"The next thing was for the council to be informed of Sheela's intention, so that they could put things back to normal in Trask if that was possible."

Olivia asked, "But if everything is back to normal you could go back!"

Sarah's face changed; one moment she was content and speaking to them, the next she was looking at them with fear in her eyes. She said with a shake in her voice, "No. I can never go back. I will stay here forever; it is not safe out there."

Sarah was so frightened to reveal what she went through but she knew she had to or at least face up to her demons if she was going to help. She had to let them know what they were up against if they got captured by the hag.

Sarah sat back in her chair and tried to relax. "What I am about to tell you is traumatic for me but I think it will help if I share my burden with others.

"I was in my back kitchen in the town of Trask. The front door of the shop was locked and there was no one else in there but me, so you can imagine my surprise to hear a crash coming from the shop area. I went into the shop. I was wiping my flowery hands on my apron and thought my assistant had let herself into the shop to help me in the kitchen as she sometimes did.

"Can you imagine my surprise when I saw that the front door was on the floor and two massive trolls were standing in the shop doorway. I knew I had to escape so I distorted my face in preparation to let out a wail and hopefully make my escape, while the trolls were screaming with the pain in the ears. But plans go wrong and as I prepared to wail another troll attacked me from behind and stopped me from wailing.

"That was the last thing I remember as I was rendered unconscious and kidnapped to be relocated to a secure area. When I came around I was in the back of a wagon being pulled by black horses. The trolls were walking at the side of the horses. Luckily there were only two of them and they were arguing as usual: that race can never get on with each other.

"I saw my chance and waited until they were on another path with the drop to one side and a steep embankment to the other. The trolls had not tied me up as they thought I would be out for the duration of the journey so they did not give me a second thought. I looked around for the third troll but I could not see him.

"I sat up and wailed. The noise was so piercing that the trolls immediately put their hands over their ears and then collapsed. I moved to the front of the wagon, took up the reins and drove off down the path. As soon as there was a turning in the road I turned and went down a small dirt track where I knew there was an abandoned shack.

"But before going down the track I fixed branches to the back of the cart to cover my movements. I did not want them following me. Once I was at the shack I could rest and think what I was going to do next. I had used this place before in times of need but that was many years ago and time had taken its toll on the furnishings: nature had claimed everything.

"I did not have a plan but I knew I had to get word to my assistant Rachel who was also my friend. She knew I was a banshee as she too was holding the secret of being half witch.

"I lit a fire in the very dusty hearth which caused a little bit of smoke to come into the house. I needed to boil some water for a warm drink of herbs that was still growing wild outside the shack. I knew that the smoke from the chimney would alert one of my other friends, Clara the wood nymph, and I was right. It was not long before Clara came to see who was using the shack.

"Clara greeted me and after finding out what had happened she went to Trask in the dead of night to speak to Rachel. She told her to have the shop and asked if she would look after my cottage until I had somewhere else to live and could send for my furniture and personal belongings.

"Rachel was obviously upset but understood what it was like to keep running; she was worried for her own safety and wondered how long her freedom would last. Trask had not been a nice place to live over the past few months, especially for magykal creatures.

"I could not understand how things were getting so bad, after all Nirvana was our land and the humans were guests, and guests with conditions. I knew it would not be tolerated for long; eventually the faerie council would set the migration spell into the equation if they did not live peacefully and then they would be back in their world, a world they did not know.

"It was true that while the council did tolerate a lot, they did have their limits when the equilibrium of Nirvana was being disrupted.

"I had decided to head for the magyk forest where I knew the Green Man resided, then from there to the great forest to inform the council of the situation. I decided not to take the cart as this would have attracted attention. So I went on foot through the back lanes and fields that I knew so well, but I was not so lucky this time.

"That hag, she had spies all over that side of the mountain, and the dirt tracks, roads and woods were full of foul-smelling trolls and other such creatures searching for me.

"I cannot remember how it happened but the last thing I do remember was making my way through the undergrowth as stealthily as I could, then the next thing, I was waking up in what could only be described as an oubliette. I was in the dark and as far as I could see as I walked around the walls there was no door. I thought I was alone but then from the centre of the oubliette there was a weak voice that said Gastak."

Sorona sat forward in her chair and was going to say something at the mention of her father's name, but Maldwyn indicated for her to be silent for now.

Sarah held her hands to her face: she was in distress. She did not want to face telling the rest of the story, it was too painful. She needed to get out of the room: there was too many people for her to cope with at this time.

"I am sorry but I need to be on my own for a while. I cannot tell you my story, it is bringing back too many painful memories. I will go into the other room and meditate for a while. I may be able to come back and tell you the rest of my story later."

Sorona could not wait and said in an anxious voice, "But, please you must tell us about this Gastak, please I beg you."

Maldwyn walked towards Sorona and held her hand. He said, "Not now, Sorona, not now." He knew what she was going to ask, she was hoping it was her father.

Vardo said, "We should let Sarah be for now, she will come back."

Sarah walked into the kitchen, closed the door and sat down at the table. She had tears in her eyes; it had caused her great distress to talk about her ordeal and that was only the start of it. She sat there trying to put it out of her mind but could not. She closed her eyes and started to relive the full ordeal.

Sarah heard the voice in the oubliette. She jumped realising someone was in there with her and asked, "I do not understand, what is Gastak?"

The voice replied, "I am, that is my name, what is yours?"

It had taken a few minutes for Sarah to realise she was expected to answer. "Oh, sorry I am still a little dazed from whatever they did to me. My name is Sarah."

"Thank you," he said. "If you do not mind my asking could you tell me what your special gift is?"

Sarah was taken aback with this question; she decided to be a little coy about it. "I am sorry, I do not fully understand what you are asking me!"

There was a laugh, it was a kind laugh, the person or creature, whatever it was, had a very pleasant voice with an intellect shining through that made Sarah think he was very well-educated. "You would not be here if you did not have a special gift, my lady."

"Who exactly are you?" asked Sarah.

The creature or man she did not know which because she could not see him, lifted his palm and the light shone around him. "Let us start again. I am Gastak, I am Ghillie Dhu, I am guardian of the trees. I have been a naughty boy; therefore they have punished me by putting me in here and separated me from my wife Emily and our friends."

"What did you do that was so bad?" Sarah asked.

He laughed again. His laugh was so gentle, it put Sarah at ease and he said, "I tried to escape, of course, so they thought a little beating up and a spell in here would do me

250

the world of good. But I will not try again as they have informed me that my wife will take the punishment next time for anything that I do."

Sarah was curious about this man. "How long have you been here?"

"I do not know, months, but how many I cannot say." He went into a kind of sadness when he said this and he was deep in thought, "We only hope our daughter Sorona has survived. We left her with a guardian as soon as we knew this hag was looking for her, but we have had no news of them or our friends' children."

Sarah was sorry for him. "I am sorry, sir, I have not heard anything. I live in Trask, or should I say I did. Because we are so far out we are the last to hear any news and the other towns are the last to hear anything about Trask also." She then told what she knew about her own capture.

"Where exactly are we and are we in this oubliette to die as I see no way out." Sarah said this with panic in her voice.

He pointed to the wall behind him with his hand. About two feet up the wall was the way out: a door locked from the outside.

"Not an oubliette then!" she replied.

"No," replied Gastak. "But I know we are in a fortified compound at the far end of the Morby Mountains; she is mad, she is crazy, she has gone from wanting to be the most beautiful creature in Nirvana to wanting to be the Queen of Nirvana. She is pure evil and we can see every creature in Nirvana enslaved if nothing is done about it. I do not know who you really are, Sarah, but I do know that you are in danger if she has brought you here.

"We are being held as hostages, well that is what we are presuming as there is no other reason for her to keep us alive. But you, you must be special or you would be dead by now.

She has work for you and she wants you to join them and if you do not you will suffer greatly."

"Never," said Sarah with venom in her voice. "I would rather die than join forces with her and my special gift as you call it is a wail."

He lifted his head and looked straight at her. "You are banshee? Then you are in danger, you will be needed on her front lines to disable the enemy, her enemy. Be very careful, banshee, that she does not turn you, her methods of torture are nasty indeed."

Sarah was just about to answer when the metal door opened with an almighty creek. Someone shouted, "You." It was a troll and he was pointing his fat finger at Gastak.

"I said you now, or you will be left in here forever."

Gastak got up and walked towards the troll and the way out. "Please, Sarah, be careful, you could be a powerful ally for her."

Gastak left and the door was slammed shut behind him, leaving Sarah was once more in the dark alone.

The next few times the door opened was for the reason of putting food and water inside the cell. She had to feel her way about the room once the door was shut. The smell was overpowering and she decided that the best thing to do was to stay near the door as the far end of the large round cell had been used for personal habits.

The hag had provided nothing in the way of facilities. Eventually they came for her, large trolls with muffs over their ears to protect them from the wail in case Sarah decided to use it. They bound her hands together as soon as she had climbed up and out through the door. The light hurt her eyes, but as she tried to cover them with her bound hands, they pulled on her chains and made her walk. She stumbled as she went, the light so bright.

When her eyes finally became accustomed to the light she found she was being walked across a courtyard of a fortified mansion. There were stables on one side, wooden buildings on the other, which she could only presume were the trolls' quarters and straight-ahead of them was the house. Every time she tried to turn around to see what was behind her she was pulled forward with the chains.

The house was where Sarah was being taken. They approached a big wooden door but they suddenly stopped and knocked on the door instead of going in as Sarah thought they may have. It seemed that the trolls were not allowed in the house but other creatures were. Sarah could only imagine it was because they were too foul and dirty. A man came to the door wearing a bright yellow coat from neck to foot. Sarah thought he looked ridiculous but of course he did not.

The yellow coated creature said, "Is this her? She's not much to look at, is she? Okay, I'll take her now, you lot go about your business and get that prison cleaned out, will you, it stinks. Dirty trolls."

He was a very angry little creature and did not care if he insulted anyone or not. Sarah thought it best to keep her mouth shut for now. The door they had just gone through was the side door. This led to a small staircase on her left that went down into the bowels of the house. As she was dragged down the stairs with the chains Sarah could hear screams and pleas for mercy echoing around the lower levels and then silence: it was very unnerving.

The creature in the ridiculous yellow jacket muttered, "That's mercy for you, a lot kinder when they have gone."

Sarah now understood that the poor soul had been killed which considering his screaming probably was a mercy killing. At the bottom of the stairs there was a long corridor cut out of the bedrock below the house, with rooms going off at either side; these rooms had heavy iron doors and most had locks and chains on them, these were in fact cells.

The creature pulled hard on Sarah and she fell over. He walked up to her and hovered like a vulture over carrion. "And who said you could have a rest, you little pig?" He punched her in the ribs then pulled at her chains; as she was standing up he kicked her once more but this time in the abdomen. He laughed. "You don't rest until I say you can, pig."

Sarah let out a scream but kept her wail still under control. Her body was aching but she got up as dignified as she could and carried on walking. They passed a large alcove with bars across the front of it and the door made out of bars also. A man came up to the bars and said loudly, "Be brave, Sarah, be brave, we need you."

It was Gastak. The yellow coat scowled at him and said, "Do you want to go back in the pokey or better still does your lovely wife want to go?" He laughed as he pulled on Sarah's chains and carried on down the corridor.

The very end room was where they were going and as they walked in Sarah wished she was back in the oubliette. It was a very large room with all sorts of strange mechanisms and tables along either side. There was a couch and a small table in the centre near the back of the room. She was dragged down to stand in front of this couch: it was all so surreal.

There was a woman sitting on the couch. She was slim, looked in her twenties and was so very beautiful, but all this said there was an evil expression on her face, an evilness that could only be earned over years of evil deeds, an evilness that has to grow inside someone over many millennia.

The woman's smile was sickly sweet. It tried to say sorry, trust me I am your friend, but in actual fact it said if I say so they will make you suffer beyond belief. Sarah was under no illusions about how this interview would go or what would happen to her if she did not comply.

Sheela stood up to greet her. "Come, my dear, and sit with me. Klaus bring Sarah a chair. I would ask you to sit on the couch with me but you are a little dirty, my dear."

There was no way in her present state that Sheela would ever have let her sit on that couch with her and Sarah knew it. A wooden chair was brought by Klaus; the yellow coated creature pulled Sarah onto the chair as hard as he could, hoping it would hurt her.

Sheela smiled in a sickly way once more. "Now, now, Klaus, be a little more gentle with our guests, will you please?"

Sheela clicked her fingers and another minion brought her some tea. She offered Sarah some but she declined. Sarah asked, "Can we disperse with the niceties and tell me what you want with me."

Sheela's face grimaced. Just for a moment Sarah thought she saw her true form but she composed herself and smiled. "Now, now child, do not be so confrontational, alas it will do you no good now. I have a proposition for you and I hope you will consider it seriously." Sheela spoke slowly as if she was trying to control herself.

"I want you to come and join us in our fight for freedom, freedom for Nirvana. You would be a great asset to our little band and we would afford you all the luxuries that the house could offer you. But I will let you think about it for a while; it is a big decision after all."

She clicked her fingers and Klaus pulled on Sarah's chains once more. He pulled her up off the chair violently and she was taken back to where Gastak and his party was being held captive. She was put in the cell opposite them with the open bars in front.

Klaus laughed as he locked her in. "Now, my little song bird, see how we honour you with an upgrade in living accommodation."

He beckoned for her to put her hands to the bars and he unlocked the chains. After Klaus had gone, Gastak asked, "Are you all right, Sarah?"

She looked up and realised she was in the cell opposite to him; she had not realised it when she was first put in there. "I am fine, thank you, Gastak. I must think about getting out of here. I think I am going to be in for worse than I've had today."

He answered, "It is not possible to leave this place. Magyk cannot be used within the walls unless someone from the outside uses a stronger counter spell. Then we could probably all get out but be warned she is a formidable adversary, Sarah. We will need a strong force to bring her down."

CHAPTER TWENTY-TWO:
TORTURE AND FREEDOM
↑ ↑

Gastak had fallen silent for a while. He was thinking of Sarah being alone; at least he had his wife and his two companions to give him council. Then, as if he was trying to alter the conversation, he said, "I would like to introduce you to my wife, Emily. And our good friends Sefton and Thea. I am sorry, Sarah, but there is no way out. We have tried it and suffered greatly; we have endured torture and starvation.

"We are only alive because she wants to draw our beloved Sorona here and kill her before she goes to war against Nirvana."

Sarah thought for a while. "I am pleased to meet you all and I am so sorry I have been so preoccupied. I have not really introduced myself correctly. Gastak has probably already told you I am Sarah."

Sarah was concerned: she wondered if the faerie council knew about what Sheela had in mind. "Surely the council will not let this happen? I still cannot believe this is actually happening here in Nirvana. The humans of Trask are all acting so strange; they are looking for magykal creatures, as if we were something to be feared, as if we were something that needed to be exterminated."

Emily spoke in her soft gentle voice, "The humans of Trask and the towns this side of the mountain have been under the hag's influence for many years now. The anger and

257

evil has grown like bindweed in their hearts, squeezing and squeezing until only bitterness is left.

"They are probably to be pitied in many ways as they cannot fight the hag; they do not have the strength of will. There are a few that offer resistance but they are soon stamped on. I suppose it is not their fault and we must not be unkind."

Gastak smiled. "My dear wife." Gastak took his wife's hand in his. "My dear wife will see the best in everyone, even me. She does not believe that these humans are to blame but the fear that is being put inside their hearts is the thing that we must blame, and ultimately the hag. We can keep going around in circles all day talking about the same issues but it will not solve anything."

Thea who had been quiet up to now said, "Our children will send us a message of that we are sure. When the time comes we will be ready and we will all escape, then we can start the fight proper against this evil hag."

There was a laugh that was nasty sounding. Sarah looked around the passage and across at the other cells but she could see no one.

Sefton grunted, "You are slime, do you think that you will get away with it? We know you are the hag's man planted to take our secrets back to her, you are no prisoner." He looked across at Sarah, "I am sorry, Sarah, we should have told you earlier, do not trust the pixie."

A very disgruntled voice said, "I am not pixie and well you know it. I am gnome and proud of it."

Emily was very cross with the gnome, she commented, "Yes, and a gnome that has betrayed his people and will suffer the consequences once this is all over, that is if you survive with all your deceit."

The gnome laughed again. "Ah well, I suppose I had better find something better to do then than stay here in this dark dank cell; at least I can go and get a bit of comfort, that is more that can be said for you; prisoners. At least I am with the victor and not the loser of this war." The gnome opened the cell door and walked along up the corridor laughing.

They settled down for some sleep. Sarah was tired although it was still early afternoon. The others rested so that they did not disturb Sarah while she slept, but they too were trying to conserve their energy; the lack of food and water was taking its toll on all of them.

It was very early the next morning when they came for Sarah. Gastak shouted at the guards to leave her alone. They banged on the cell threateningly, shouting abuse at them.

Sarah was taken to the room she had been in the previous day. She was worried at the way the guards pushed and pulled at her, and realised she was not being taken for just a talk this time.

Sarah was pushed into the room and kept being pushed until she was standing about five feet in front of the sofas. Sheela walked out of the door at the back of the room. She never looked at Sarah. Her head was held high and she was wearing a pure white dress, her hair long and golden; she looked so beautiful and serene. It was hard to imagine that she was really an ugly evil old hag under that disguise. She sat down on the sofa and made herself comfortable, playing with her dress so that it covered all of the seating.

She said, "Now, child, I hope you have thought about joining us a little more seriously than you did yesterday; you really would be better off joining us in our little quest for freedom, you know it is the right thing to do."

Sarah was defiant and did not answer. Sheela asked, "Now tell me, are you banshee?" She looked at Sarah then said, "Yes you are, I can see it in your eyes. You may as well give in now and save us the trouble of torturing you: it is so tiresome." Sheela yawned as if she was bored and in reality, she was.

All this time Sarah was standing defiant; she would not talk even with torture, she was not going to give in.

"All right then," said Sheela in a calm voice. Then she screamed at the guards, "Take her, muscles first, then bone. I don't care, just get her out of my sight and get her to talk and to join us any way you can. We need your wail, Sarah, and if we don't get it no one else will."

They took Sarah across to a mechanism a bit like a rack but this was different. It started by crushing the muscles in your legs and arms, it manipulated them, tormented them, it hurt the muscles until every nerve in your legs ached in every way possible; then if you didn't give in they could start breaking your bones. The mechanism was also capable of stretching a body and these were the screams that Sarah had heard when she first came into the house.

Sarah was fastened to the machine; the guards took great delight in tightening her bonds, splitting her skin and making it bleed. Sarah could not stand the pain. She screamed and the more she screamed the more they turned the screws on the machine. Her muscles were in agony; they were burning, they were ripping and she did not know what to do. Then came the breaking of her legs, first the bones at the bottom of the leg then the top, then the next leg. She screamed and screamed, then she fainted.

The tortures she went through were enough to kill a mortal man but for a magykal creature such as Sarah the pain was the same as a mortal could feel, but she could take a lot more and Sheela knew this.

Sarah awakened to the sound of Sheela laughing. Her body was aching, but there seemed to be nothing wrong with her bones or muscles, no broken bones, no ripped muscles and no cuts to her wrists: she could not understand it.

Sheela said, "I have mended you; after all I need you to be able to walk then we can do it all over again tomorrow, won't that be nice? Take her back to the cells."

Sarah was dragged; she still could not walk properly, her legs felt like jelly and the aching was excruciating. If this was the plan for tomorrow to do it all over again, she had to find a way to get out.

The guards dropped her on the floor of her cell. She eventually managed to get up and crawl onto the meagre bed that was in the corner and there she lay; for how long she did not know, she was in too much pain to move.

Gastak and his companions were worried about Sarah, very worried. They had all had to endure some sort of torture from time to time during their captivity but only Gastak had been subjected to any of the machines or apparatus.

They shouted words of comfort but Sarah did not hear them; she was deep inside herself, deep in pain and in despair. It was then she decided that she would never give in; even if it meant her life, it would be worth it. Nirvana could not ever be ruled by such a vile evil creature.

She was left alone the next morning, but by the afternoon Sheela decided she wanted more sport, so she sent for Sarah once again. She had Sarah brought to her and she asked once more if she was banshee and if she would join them in the fight for freedom. Sarah once more said no and this time the torture got worse, much worse.

Sheela was so angry that again, just for a moment, Sheela disappeared and the hag formed in her face. Then she smiled, pointed her arms towards Sarah and moved her fingers in a wave formation, while Sarah doubled up with pain in her abdomen and chest. Sarah screamed, the pain was unbearable; it was as if the hag had got part of a hand inside Sarah's body and was twisting and crushing her from the inside.

When she had had enough and she got bored of this sport she released Sarah from her clutches and ordered the guards to take her away again. They took her back to her cell and threw her on the floor. She was broken; how much more could she take, but Sarah realised the more they did this to her the more she would be defiant. She was a creature of Nirvana not a human that gave into the first sign of pain.

Emily tried very hard to use her magyk to help Sarah but it did not work; the spell that prevented magyk being used by others was strong, there was nothing any of them could do.

Later that day they came for Sarah again. Sarah begged them not to take her; it was heart-breaking for the others to hear her pleading. This time Sheela was adamant that Sarah would join her but again Sarah said she would not, she was more defiant than ever.

Sheela was angry. She was angrier than any of her minions had seen her for a long time. she instructed the guards to throw Sarah into the hole with the Surl. Even the guards were horrified as the trolls were scared of this creature.

Sarah was dropped into a black hole in the floor. She could hear something coming towards her but never saw what it was; the stench from the creature was so bad and she was so frightened that she fainted. This was a good thing as Sarah did not know what the creature was doing to her.

She was dazed and could not work out what had happened or where she was. She was confused, what had happened? Then Sarah tasted blood; she spit it out on the floor – her mouth tasted of blood but where was it coming from?

Emily shouted to her but she did not answer. She could not talk. Her arms, legs, fingers, toes were all bleeding and all had puncture marks. The puncture marks had rings around them as if some sort of tiny suckers had been put on her body with a needle in the centre.

She realised then as the memories came flooding back that the creature in the hole was slug like in appearance and had tentacles; she then supposed that these tentacles had suckers on them. Sarah fell asleep. She slept until morning, then as she sat up and tried to make sense of what had happened, she realised something was wrong: she realised that part of her was missing.

Sarah had stopped bleeding but she could still taste the blood in her mouth. It was then that she realised what the creature had done. She tried to wail but nothing came out; the creature had taken part of her, he had taken the living instrument out of her throat that was her wail. Her vocal cords were intact, it was just the extra cord that the Surl had taken.

Sarah was devastated. She started to cry and sobbed and sobbed. The others in the cell opposite felt so sorry for her. Gastak shouted, "Are you all right, Sarah? What have they done?"

She swallowed hard and drank a small amount of the stale water that had been left the night before, then she spoke slowly to her companions and she told them what had happened. "We have to get out of here. I cannot stand any more. I am not banshee, the Surl has taken all that I am, and all that I was, he has taken my very being. I will have to live the rest of my life as a nothing."

She cried again. Sarah was upset because to take that part of her body was like taking someone's right arm away.

She carried on sobbing for a few minutes, then she suddenly stopped. Hatred came into her mind. She said, "Tell me about the hag and tell me about your children." She could hardly speak; her voice was croaking and she was angry.

Emily answered, "Sheela's spies have told her that our daughter is on her way with a small band of misfits, but I believe they are more than they seem. If the children have done as we have asked them, then they are with the greatest mage Nirvana has ever known."

Sarah said, "Myrddin? But I thought he was dead!"

"No," she answered. "The son of Myrddin, of Merlin, that is who is coming. There is an old prophecy and that prophecy talks about the son of Merlin saving Nirvana from great evil. I have been around a long time, long enough to remember being told of the prophecy. All is not lost yet."

"So, you believe that this mage is on his way here to battle with Sheela, with the hag. Now can you please tell me about the use of magyk in this place?" said Sarah.

Thea was the one that answered Sarah. "We cannot use magyk because of the spell and barriers that Sheela has put on this place, but someone from the outside could break the spell if they were strong enough and they knew that the spells came from a dark place, a place that any decent magykal creature would ever go to."

Sarah thought for a while. "I am going to try and escape. I know magyk cannot work but that does not mean abilities cannot, does it?"

The others were all puzzled by what Sarah had said and really could not answer her. Sarah had to explain herself. "There is one thing I inherited from my father that is unusual for any creature let alone a banshee and I am hoping that this ability still works in this place."

Sarah walked up to the bars at the side of her door. She stood sideways and started to climb through the bars, her body flattening so that it was less than the distance between the bars; she got out the other side and walked across to the others.

She smiled and said, "Did you like my party trick? When it gets dark I am going to get through the bars on the window and see if I can get help. I am only sorry I cannot take you with me. It is not magyk, it is an ability I was born with and I tried so hard to keep this ability to myself because this is one thing she could not take away from me. Therefore, she would have killed me if she had known."

Gastak said, "That is why she gave us those metal bunks and you have wood. It's because I could blend into the wood and surprise the guard and overpower them while he was looking for me."

Sarah smiled. "So, you can still do that, can you, Gastak? That is very good. It is a pity that she knew your ability as you could have used it to your advantage."

Gastak smiled. "Oh yes, because like you it is not magyk but part of my genetic makeup; they cannot take it away from me unless they kill me."

Sarah wobbled as she felt dizzy. She fell onto the bars. Thea put her arms through the bar to steady Sarah. "Are you all right, Sarah? What did they do to you?"

Sarah broke down and cried once again which would normally have resulted in a wail as she was very distressed, but it did not as that particular ability had gone. "They took my wail from me, they put me in a pit, a hole in the ground and there was something in there but I must have fainted. I woke up here with wounds on my body and my wail gone. I also feel very weak. The creature was like a slug but with tentacles.

"That vile thing, that Surl, must have had its tentacle right inside my mouth ripping my very soul away." She cried again: it was very distressing for her.

Emily was upset and so was Thea. "When we get out of here we will ask the faerie council to help you; there may be a way to repair the damage," said Thea.

Sarah thanked them and went back to her cell.

That night, when the others were asleep, Sarah made her escape through the bars of the window. It was a long painful drop but nothing compared to what she had been through, and what she may go through now she was of no use to the hag. She went from doorway to doorway keeping in the shadows until she eventually reached the main way into the complex.

The perimeter wall, on the side where the gateway was, across the front had peep holes in them in the form of slits. This was the only way that Sarah was going to get out of the complex but it was a very high drop on the other side. She knew she could break her legs or arms or worse; it would all depend on what she landed on.

She climbed up onto the high landing walkway that formed a gantry and made her way to one of the slits. She put her arm through, then her head, then the rest of her body and she fell. The fall was roughly about fifteen feet but luckily for Sarah she landed on the top of the tree, which bounced her down through its branches till she eventually fell on the floor. She was not badly hurt just bruised and with a small sprain to her ankle.

Sarah ran as fast as she could considering her injuries until she was clear of the hag's house or fortress. Sarah continued through the undergrowth in the woods until morning, when she was found collapsed by some wood nymphs. Her friend Rachel had sent them to look for her.

CHAPTER TWENTY-THREE:
A CUP OF TEA
↑ ↑

Sarah went back into the other room to sit with her guests. She was still upset from her recollection of the time she was in Sheela's lair. Sarah looked at her guests. "I do apologise," she said, "I have just been reliving the experiences I had while I was a guest of the hag and it was very painful for me. I cannot forget the pain and the humiliation I was subjected to."

She sat quietly for a while then she turned to face Sorona and Stephann. "There were people in the cell opposite mine that I think will be of great interest to the two of you. Their names were Gastak, Emily, Sefton and Thea."

Sorona started to cry. "Are they all right? What kind of condition are they in, psychologically I mean? They are children of the forest and are not meant to be in a prison."

Sarah answered, "I cannot repeat what happened to me, but know this, your parents are in good spirits and in decent health albeit a little thin. Do not fret they are quite all right. I saw them and I spoke with them, all of them.

"I met Gastak in the oubliette. He said he had been a naughty boy; he had tried to escape and the hag had put him in there for ten days as a punishment. He did get out before me but he did tantalise his guards so much they got angry. They threatened to put his wife Emily into the oubliette if he continued."

Sorona laughed between her tears. She was so grateful to hear their parents were not dead and so was Stephann. Sorona said, "I am so relieved, as I believe Stephann is also, to hear that they are still relatively safe. Thank you, Sarah, it gives us hope and my father well, my father is always a joker; he gets himself into such trouble.

"I can imagine him setting out to upset the guards and making a joke about his punishment, but he would never subject myself or my mother to any harm."

Sarah smiled a tired smile. "As I said, I am not going to tell you what happened to me, what I had to endure. But I can tell you this, she has a torture you would never believe, and the creature that she put me into the hole with was a thing of nightmares. I have never seen or heard of such a creature before, but the evilness of it and the stench, it must have come from hell and to do to me what it did, to take my wail away, it was a creature without compassion."

Sarah started to cry a little, she had said too much. The memories came flooding back; it was more than she could bear to relive it all once again.

The Green Man was standing in the doorway and had heard what Sarah was telling the others. Maldwyn was just about to ask Sarah what the creature looked like when the Green Man said, "Sarah, this creature, it had taken your wail, how?"

Sarah cried, she put her head in her hands. "It's hard," she said. "I remember the stench, it was..."

"It was putrid, like something dead or rotting," the Green Man replied.

"Yes, yes," Sarah answered anxiously.

Sorona put her arm around Sarah to comfort her and Maldwyn addressed the Green Man. "Do you know what this vile creature is, Green Man?"

He looked at Maldwyn gravely and at his visitors to his forest. He turned to Vardo and whispered something in his ear. Vardo left quickly and disappeared down the path.

The Green Man sat down at the table. He poured himself a cup of tea and asked everyone else to sit. He said, "Let us have a nice cup of tea and while you are drinking it I will tell you about the Surl."

"Yes, that is what the troll called it," said Sarah.

He looked at her with compassion in his eyes. "I am sorry you had to go through that, Sarah. It is a blessing that you were rendered unconscious as you may have died if you had not; he is a foul creature indeed.

"He should not even be in this realm. He was banished many thousands of years ago to the dark or veil where minor demons live. If she has brought him here then what else has she done? And more to the point how has she done it?"

Maldwyn asked, "Where does this creature come from originally? Is it a creature of Nirvana?"

The Green Man replied, "Yes, many thousands of years ago there was a young merman. He was handsome, very handsome, and was sought by many females of every race. He finally mated with an ugly, aged old witch from deep inside the mountain. She had put a spell on him so that he would love her; he did not see the ugly witch, he only saw the beautiful maiden that he was to marry.

"They married and she had a child but as she was giving birth to that child she had to go into her natural form. She was so ugly and so evil that the merman could not bear it and when the child was born it was hideous. The creature had the look of a sea creature with tentacles like a Kraken but the body of a sea slug, and although not greatly intelligent, it was a sentient being but with all the craftiness and evilness of its mother.

"The abomination should never have been born but the council would not hear of its destruction; it goes against their highest law killing a younglin. The father, seeing how he had been tricked, tried to kill his offspring but he was stopped by the council.

"The Surl soon grew full-size and he was spoilt by his mother but soon the killing started. He would take great pleasure in bleeding his victims and then taking from them their greatest asset. If he killed a faerie he could take their magyk; he could do nothing with it as he was not a magykal creature just a creature of spells and potions, which he could not prepare as he had no hands to do that with, or the intellect.

The council were horrified but still could not bring themselves to destroy the Surl as he was still too young. So, they banished him to the upper veil where he would stay forever, never to come back.

"The witch was so grief stricken at losing her offspring that she killed the merman and in turn the council had the witch killed. The creature was born out of trickery but at the same time out of love and the desire for a child by the witch. The love that the witch felt for the merman was true but how she came to have the Surl was by pure trickery.

"It was not the Surl's fault to be born but the creature will not stop his evil ways, therefore the Surl is at fault and now it is old enough it must be destroyed."

Maldwyn asked, "Why kill the merman if she loved him so much?"

The Green Man smiled. "She blamed him, she blamed him for having faulty genes, she blamed him for not having enough love for her or their child. But alas he did, he loved the kind sweet gentle girl that he married but he did not love the evil ugly old hag that tricked him.

"She performed magyk on her own body so she could reproduce; this was because she was very old and well past childbearing years, she already had a child. The council and I myself think this is what caused the deformity in the child. But the witch had to blame someone as witches are not known for blaming themselves and the only person she could blame was the father.

"There are seven realms to death and the upper level 'the veil' is where the Surl was banished to, and there it would stay wandering its fields and waters not able to harm any living thing any more. There should never have been a problem, it should have stayed there.

"It is dark magyk indeed that the hag has tapped into; for her to have the skills to bring someone back from the veil, then she has more power than we originally thought she had."

No one had been taking much notice of Stephann, after all he was a quiet person and listened more than he talked. They were discussing a lot of things concerning Sheela and no one noticed that Stephann had taken himself across to the window and was looking out into the forest: he was deep in thought.

It was Christano that sensed something was wrong. He walked up to Stephann and sat with him; as he looked into Stephann's eyes he could see tears. The Seelie Court then realised that because Stephann was male all the attention had been put on his beloved Sorona and no one had given Stephann a second thought.

Stephann's parents too were being held hostage and his sister was miles away in the other direction, so there was no one for Stephann to confide his fears to, no one for him to protect, only Sorona and she had Christano. Sorona was the only one in the group that could understand the aching that he felt inside, but Isla also felt for him and tried to comfort him.

Christano looked at his friend. "Stephann, I have come to think of you as my brother and I see your pain. We as a group have not been considerate to you; we have been caught up with Sorona and her parents, this I am truly sorry for, my friend."

Stephann continued to stare out of the window, then he said, "Christano, I am worried that as soon as she realises my parents have no value to her the hag will kill them. I do believe that my parents could have escaped by now unless their strength has waned and they are not able to change, but knowing my parents they will stay with their friends to the bitter end with no concern for their own welfare: they will not leave them.

"But what if she decides they are worthless, Christano? And they do not have the strength to escape? I am so worried."

"Escape? What do you mean escape?" said Christano.

He replied, "Oh, I see, you do not understand. If they were strong enough they could have got out by trickery."

Christano asked, "Stephann, can the others hear this please, it may save all our lives, any little bit of intel we can have would be good."

Stephann nodded and they went back to the others. Christano quickly told them of this conversation which made the company feel bad for their neglect of their friend. But after a suggestion of yet another cup of tea from the Green Man they sat down to listen.

Maldwyn asked, "Why did you not speak to me, Stephann? This kind of emotion should not be bottled up; it is not good for you. You are a magykal creature, bottling sadness and worries up the way you have could cause all sorts of problems."

Sorona said that she felt selfish and was so sorry for her omissions. But after all was said and people had time to apologise, the Green Man asked, "Now, Stephann, if you please, tell us what you mean by your parents escaping?"

Then Stephann told them something else about Bucca that they did not know. He said, "As some of you know and some of you don't, we are called Bucca and this means we can take other forms. No one except other Buccas know what we really look like, our true identity is a closely guarded secret. We also have the power of persuasion and in some ways it is quite complicated, but it means we can alter events by slightly manipulating people's way of thinking, normally humans.

Many hundreds of years ago Bucca would go into the land of men. They would be invisible and befriend someone in trouble and that person alone would be the only one that could see the Bucca. The problem was that sometimes before the Bucca could help that person they could be deemed as being crazy and put into an asylum, and that is why my race stopped doing this; we stopped interfering and trying to help man and came back to Nirvana which was our home. Unfortunately, we got a bad reputation in some parts of the human world.

"Manipulating the situation is something we no longer do, but in certain circumstances, like being in jail unlawfully, we could do it. Our gifts are not magykal they are abilities, a bit like Sarah's wail, but some magyk does come into the equation when we make ourselves invisible to all but one person. That said it can be done but if as Sarah has suggested there is no way you can use magyk in Sheela's fortress, then that way out would be out of the question.

"My parents being much older than Doras and I, have more abilities as we are still quite young, we are still learning. My father can think bad thoughts and then he will turn into a cave troll. He can do this very easily; it used to be his party trick when we were younglin but his two favourite guises are a dog or a mouse.

"My mother can turn herself into a horse or like my father a large dog or a mouse. She can also, if need be, turn herself into a troll but she would need the help of my father as she finds it very difficult to have bad thoughts. In the early days if they had wanted to, they could have escaped, so the only reason I can see why they would stay is for their friends, to see if they could escape together. I have no doubt that Gastak and Emily would have done the same for them. The only problem is that they cannot use their magyk because all four creatures together would be a formidable foe for most of Sheela's guards."

By this time Isla had positioned herself at the side of Stephann and was holding his hand. She too felt bad as she had not realised just how deeply these events had affected Stephann; it was true that because he was male everyone had assumed he was coping with it, but obviously this was not the case. Bucca are passionate creatures and feel others' pain.

Maldwyn asked, "So unless we lift the spell preventing magyk being used in the fortress other than Sheela's, your parents and Sorona's cannot conjure enough magykal power to escape. Is that correct?"

"Yes, especially if they are not resting and have had no food and drink. They will be weak and magyk would be almost impossible without this embargo let alone with it," said Stephann.

Sarah had been listening intently. "I do believe you are right, they would be too weak to use magyk. The cells are very oppressive making them weak in the spirit and the mind. If they could have got out I do believe they would have done so, but as you say together."

The Green Man said, "Let us think about our assets, or should I say your assets as I cannot leave the forest.

"Firstly, we have Gastak the Ghillie Dhu. He is very strong and has an infinity with trees, especially birch trees. He like myself can command branches to bend and hit the enemy. But his greatest asset is one of camouflage as he can meld with the tree or anything made from trees and no one would tell he was there.

"Then we have Emily the Peri Truckle. She is very beautiful. She is magykal and throughout her history has been persecuted for her beauty by wicked spirits such as the hag. The greatest asset is magyk. She is blessed with strong magyk and as yet, I suspect, has never tapped into it as there has never been a need.

"Then there is Sefton the Bucca. He is capable of transforming himself into many amazing characters and a variety of forms. I also believe that your father has not experimented with all that he can do with his shape shifting, Stephann. But I think his greatest asset is that after he has transformed, say into a troll, he could probably work his magyk and make other trolls through the power of suggestion do what he wanted them to do.

"Then we have Thea also Bucca. She is the female of the species and therefore stronger minded than the male. She may not be able to turn herself into as many shapes and forms as the male but her power of suggestion is greater, so that again is her greatest asset.

"Then we have Christano the Seelie Court. He is a very magykal creature indeed and one with great strength; your greatest asset, Christano, is the ability to fight relentlessly in battle and win.

"Then we have the Elementals; three combined have tremendous power over fire. You alone could get into Sheela's lair without anyone else as you alone have the fire burning inside you, that is an ability not magyk. When you three are together, and you are in danger or angry or fearful for your friends or your own life, you are unstoppable. Your greatest asset is one of unity, the bond you have with each other and fire.

"Next we have Talos. You, my friend, are also a great asset to this little band of fighters. You bring strength and your tough skin prevents even an arrow from penetrating it. But again, your greatest asset is the fact that you can grow two hundredfold until you are the height of a small mountain.

"Then we come to you, my mage, you alone, Maldwyn, are the key to it all; you have magyk inside you that you do not even know about yet. As the son of Myrddin you are more than equipped to lead this battle and join in the fight of your life, to rescue the ones who are being held hostage.

"But as the son of Casandra your magyk is even stronger. Your mother was also the daughter of Silus, his first born, and you are her first born. You are more faerie than you realise and eventually you will become very powerful and that is why you had to have a meagre upbringing with few privileges.

"It will not be long, Maldwyn, before you understand the true power of what is inside you, and you may at times have to hold back, but it may take longer than we have. So again, magyk is Maldwyn's greatest asset."

Maldwyn said, "That is why Silus has always treated me civilly when he has insulted others; he is my natural grandfather and not many times removed as he professed."

"Yes," said the Green Man, "he is a lot older than he says he is.

"Now we have Stephann, again your best asset is the same as your parents, but I suspect that since you have been with Maldwyn your magyk has grown.

"Now I think you should all get some rest now, and, Maldwyn, you should meditate and try to find one of the spells that your father has hidden inside you. You can stay here with Sarah where you will be undisturbed.

"The rest of you should follow the unicorn. He will take you to a small dwelling in another part of the woods where you can rest."

While the party went out of the house to go to their new abode, Maldwyn sat down on the easy chair that was near the window and attempted to meditate. He had not done well with this before; as a child his father Hubert had tried to teach him the art of meditation but he had failed miserably.

Sarah went for a walk with the Green Man to discuss her experiences. She had been in the magyk forest for months but had always thwarted the Green Man's attempts to get her to open up about her experiences.

The Green Man was attentive and tried to absorb all that she was telling him. Like the unicorn before her, she had been badly tortured and to some extent her spirit broken, albeit not all of it. They walked to the waterfall and sat down. Sarah felt better for the counselling that the Green Man had given her, but she was still sad to think that part of her may never come back. It was a part of her that she never used, well hardly ever, but all the same it was part of Sarah.

Maldwyn had succeeded in his meditation attempt. When the Green Man and Sarah came back from their walk, he told them he had achieved quite a lot and he was ready to face Sheela no matter what the consequences would be to him personally. Maldwyn seemed to think that he had found spells from deep inside the psyche that would counteract anything she could throw at him.

***

The unicorn once more made the journey to the small house with Maldwyn so that he could join his companions and get some much-needed rest.

Maldwyn felt sorry for the unicorn; he stroked his muzzle, then instinctively put both his hands at either side of his head and applied a little pressure. The unicorn tried to move but Maldwyn stayed firm. He closed his eyes as he uttered spells under his breath, then something remarkable happened; the unicorn calmed himself and very slowly started to turn white until he was whole again.

Stephann had been looking out of the window and observed what was happening; he was in awe of Maldwyn's powers. Maldwyn turned and walked towards the house, but all of the friends had walked outside as soon as Stephann had alerted them to Maldwyn's magyk.

Some had tears in their eyes at the beauty of the unicorn; he flicked his head, nodded at Maldwyn, then trotted into the forest, a happy creature indeed.

***

The next morning, they were up bright and early because the house sprite had been given instructions to get their breakfasts for seven thirty.

After breakfast they made their way back to Sarah's house as these were the Green Man's instructions. They had no sooner knocked on the door when they heard a commotion behind them. They turned around and Vardo was standing there with a contingent of faeries.

Newton was standing at their head and he said, "Good day Maldwyn, I hope you are well, and I trust you and your party are all ready for a fight; it is time to make plans and rescue the hostages.

CHAPTER TWENTY-FOUR:
FAERIE COUNCIL

ᛏᚠ

Maldwyn greeted his kin with surprise in his eyes. "What are you doing here, Newton? I did not send for you! What is happening; is there news from the castle?"

Newton said gravely, "Do not concern yourself, my brethren, the castle is safe for now. We have come to help you lay siege to the fortress of the hag Sheela.

"Vardo has told us that you all have skills but you Maldwyn will need help, ancient help with the expelling of the hag's magyk embargo. You are more powerful than you realise, but for now a little help will make your magyk stronger, while you are learning how to use it."

Maldwyn bowed his head in thanks and looked at his small friend that was still curled up asleep on his ring. He said in his mind to Sunstar so that no one else could hear, 'not this battle, little one, I want to keep you for the castle, you are our insurance, our surprise.'

Sunstar lifted her head and looked at Maldwyn, then she curled up again and went back to sleep.

Newton then asked, "Do you have an apprentice, Mage?"

Maldwyn smiled. "Well, yes and no. I have someone in mind but have not asked him yet."

"And is that someone with you right now, Mage? And is that someone, Bucca by any chance?" replied Newton.

Stephann, hearing the conversation, exclaimed, "Me?"

Maldwyn laughed. "Stephann, I have spoken many times about this; you knew the decision was coming."

"I did hear comments, but I thought you were in jest! I am Bucca, no Bucca has ever been chosen as a wizard's apprentice before," said Stephann.

Newton, being a faerie and male, was very serious most of the time. He said, "What better creature to be a wizard than a magykal one. You already possess more magykal powers that the average apprentice! Come, while the others seek out a place to hold the war council, we will walk and I will tell you what is required of you at this stage and during the forthcoming battle."

Stephann was curious. "Why did Maldwyn not tell me, sir?"

He answered, "Because all wizards' apprentices have to be vetted by the council, after all, the powers you learn will be great and we do not want evil to take over in Nirvana. Look what has happened now with the hag. The apprentice of any wizard must have a pure heart. Especially you, as you already possess natural powers and you are morph-mage, a shapeshifter!

"Every apprentice has to be worthy, sometimes a wizard's own son is not deemed to be a worthy wizard: that can cause great tribulations in a family.

"And sometimes as in Myrddin's case the apprentice can come from a very lowly existence, from a family of very meagre means."

Stephann's eyes opened wide. "Myrddin, he was an outcast?"

Newton actually smiled. "No, that is not what I meant. He came from a very poor family; his father was a tinker and his mother had to take washing and sewing in for the would-be gentry of the area. It is a little-known fact amongst humans as stories have built up over the years about Myrddin.

"His beginnings were indeed humble but his parents were honest folk and Myrddin was a worthy apprentice.

"You may be the first Bucca to be given the honour of a wizard's apprentice but you may not be the last.

"Do you have a lady?"

Stephann blushed. "Well I do have one in mind."

"And is she worthy or willing to take on the role of a wizard's lady?" asked Newton.

Stephann, still blushing, answered nervously, "I, well I have not actually made my true feelings known but I believe she is aware of them."

Newton studied Stephann for a while. "Dare I ask who she is, Apprentice?"

Stephann stood proud and straight. Newton had called him apprentice and many thoughts were going through his mind. How would everyone take this? And how would his parents take the news? "Thank you, sir, I will do my best to be a good apprentice and live up to the name, and the lady in question is Isla, she is one of the elementals."

Now it was Newton's turn to be surprised. "Well your children will be very interesting beings anyway, Apprentice, but you have chosen well. Now I suggest you take her to one side and tell her who you are and how you feel before we go any further.

"Now for the battle. During the battle, unless Maldwyn tells you otherwise, you will stay at his side, his right-hand side, and you perform your magyk to the best of your ability. Maldwyn will lead you and guide you, so do exactly as he says and no harm will come to you.

"Now as I suggested before, go and ask your lady, preferably before the battle, so that your mind is free to concentrate on the business in hand."

"I will, sir," he answered.

Stephann walked with Newton back through the forest to the small cottage they had been using. Sarah had told the Green Man they could use her house, but he declined the invitation saying that it was her home not a lodging house or war room.

She went with them to the new dwelling ready to take part in the war council and if need be to go back and face Sheela, even though the thought scared her.

As Stephann walked towards the small cottage he saw his beloved Isla talking to her two sisters. He beckoned her to come and speak with him. All three of the ladies giggled like little school girls, then Isla walked towards him.

As she approached he looked so worried she walked up to him and held both his hands in hers. "What is it, my lord? You seem troubled!"

He looked at the beauty standing before him. "I have something to tell you and something to ask you, my lady." He was embarrassed as he was new to the affairs of the heart; he had only realised recently that ladies seem to know how to handle these affairs better than men.

Isla was concerned. "Then you must speak at once if it troubles you so, it is better to be shared."

Stephann squeezed both hands. "Lady Isla, I have had the honour bestowed upon me of becoming Maldwyn's apprentice."

She smiled. "That is good, I cannot think of a better person, my mage."

He looked at her shocked at the word mage. Sensing his shock she told him, "You will have to get used to it from now on as that is what your title will be when you pass your apprenticeship."

He was silent for a while thinking about this. "There is also something else, my lady, something I do not know how to say, but here goes. The life of a wizard is fraught at best of times but as an apprentice it seems to me that it could be worse.

"Oh dear, I do not know how to say this. Lady Isla will you have a blessing with me or marry me, I am happy with whichever your beliefs are."

Stephann had started to waffle, then it was her turn to squeeze his hands. She let his hands go and put them either side of his face, stood upon her tiptoes and gently kissed him. He knew right away that she meant yes and they both started to laugh.

They walked back over to the cottage to inform her sisters that she was now engaged, and not only that but she was engaged to a mage-in-waiting.

Isla was the first of the sisters to get engaged, even though they had lived several lifetimes they dared not let anyone know of their powers, therefore marriage was out of the question. Now it seemed they were being welcomed with open arms and they had all found potential husbands, even though Talos and Maldwyn had not plucked up the courage to ask the ladies yet.

Stephann and the ladies walked into the cottage in mixed moods; they were all happy for Stephann and Isla but, and it was a big but, they were all going into battle and did not know how it would work out for all of them.

***

The war council sat around a large table that had been conjured up by the faeries. They had a map of the area surrounding the small fortress or the big house as Sheela liked to call it; they were going to surround the house and then attack simultaneously from every side.

The trouble with that plan was that there was no way that this could happen. Yes, there were four sides to the complex but on three sides there was only solid brick walls, no windows, and no way over, just very, very, high walls. The house was a solid structure of dense hard brick and those bricks on the outer wall were several feet thick.

The only way in was the front entrance and that was difficult. Sarah had told them that behind the front wall there was a walkway where guards patrolled the perimeter and had orders to shoot arrows at anything that moved. The place literally was a fortress, unless they could somehow bring down the magyk veil that protected it.

They decided that the only way in was by the front entrance but that was camouflaged and could only be accessed through magyk or if you knew what you were looking for. Sarah confirmed that it was an underground entrance, a tunnel affair under the front facade.

To anyone looking at the wall that would be what it looked like – a solid wall with no entrance and no doorway, in fact no way to get in. This was because the entrance sloped down and then went under the wall.

"Ingenious," said one of the faeries. "What a strategy, even without its magyk protection it would be hard to get through such a tunnelled affair; we would all get caught in a trap and be like baited animals."

Newton said, "There has got to be another way, we just have not thought of it yet."

The discussion went on for a long time. There were several strategies that were put forward but none of them were going to be good enough to get them in safely. There would be too many casualties on their side before they even got inside the complex, leaving hardly anyone left to fight.

Stephann suddenly stood up and addressed Newton. "Why did you not come before? Why did we have to go through all those things on our journey that were dangerous? Why?"

The faeries went quiet and Newton did not know how to answer, then eventually he said, "We were waiting for her to tell us it was time. If we had contacted you too soon we could have warned Sheela that we knew of her plans and of the betrayer."

Stephann repeated his question, "Why?"

Maldwyn was proud of his apprentice. He had only had the position for just over an hour and he was already a formidable force. Newton was getting angry and he ignored the question and started to carry on talking to the council as if Stephann was not there.

The Green Man had been listening. He asked in a gentle voice, "The mage-in-waiting has a valid question, Newton. Are you not going to answer him?"

Newton was not pleased; male faeries can be cunning when they want to be and usually they have an agenda when they are helping anyone else other than faeries. He knew he had to answer, and after a few of the other faeries gave a little nod to him as if giving their permission, he did give an answer of sorts. "We have a spy in her camp and have had for some time now.

"We knew that the hag's forces were on the rise and we were quite aware of the things that were going on in and around Nirvana, and we do not need things reporting to us. Well not all things like unrest concerning the population of the towns and villages.

"We needed to wait and see where the hag was getting her power, and who was helping her. It was no good taking her down if we have not got the source of the power, the puppet master, the mole as humans like to call them."

Sarah interrupted him, "So I went through all that for nothing. You, the council and all your faerie brethren knew about her powers and you could have prevented all the deaths and torture that myself and others went through."

Newton could see things getting out of hand and he was getting angry that the faerie council was being questioned. He said, "You have to understand, it was for the greater good..."

Newton was cut short again as Sarah ran out of the house crying and into the woods. The Green Man followed but as he went through the doorway he turned to the rest of the faerie contingent and said gravely, "I will require a full explanation from you and the council when I get back. How low has the council sunk? Tricks and deceit like these you have carried out on humans before and I have said it is wrong but that banshee, she is your own! What politics are you playing?"

The Green Man was angry and even Vardo, his trusted guardian had never seen the Green Man angry in all the centuries he had known him; it was not in the Green Man's nature unless it was something very grave indeed.

There was an awkward pause from the chatter that had been around the room and everyone stared at Newton as if it was he who was to blame and not the full council; this is because Newton represented the council.

They eventually settled down and started to talk about the siege once more. No matter what had happened or what had led to this point the problem was still the same. Sheela the hag, the Frau Berchta, she had to be stopped.

Ideas about how to get into the fortress were flying about but once again nothing was settled. It was Talos who came up with the best idea. He suggested that the eagle squadron may be able to gain access where they could not. Maldwyn had told him about the castle and how the eagles had nowhere to live and the Aerials had started to train them so that men could ride on their backs. Talos could not see why they could not go over the wall as it was virtually impossible for anyone to get under it or through it.

Christano had been quiet as he was ashamed to call himself faerie but at that moment in time he became excited. "I think that is a very good idea, Talos. I am sure they would help! What do you think, Maldwyn?"

Maldwyn said excitedly, "Yes, why didn't we think of that before? I think if the Aerials agree then we could start making proper plans to get into the fortress, and as the Aerials are not governed by magyk, there should not be any reason why they should not succeed.

"I know Keatin has been experimenting with some sort of aerial device that you can drop onto your enemy. It is strictly organic so therefore does not impede on the restrictions given out by the council. It is flour and water, glue, fat and feathers, anything to get the enemy off guard."

Newton asked, "You really think this will work, Maldwyn? But what if they fire arrows at the Aerials as they are flying over, then the eagles and the men could all be killed."

Talos had the answer to that. "What if some sort of armour was fitted to the underside of the eagles that would make them impenetrable to any arrow fired from below, a bit like the breastplate I used to wear."

Christano said, "Yes that would work I think the armour would be stronger if it was magykally made, but as that is out of the question, I still think that traditional faerie made armour will be stronger than anything man can make. Could that be arranged, Newton?"

"I do not see any reason why not. I will get someone onto that straightaway. And if you want to write a parchment to the castle, Maldwyn, then we will deliver that on our way through to the forest of Sandina," said Newton. "By the way, we are sure none of these things that the Aerials are to drop are anything like the ones that they use in the land of men? Those are banned."

Maldwyn reassured him, then started to write the parchment they needed to get the ball rolling, and then they could start planning how exactly they were going to do this and when. But Maldwyn was still puzzled about what Newton had said concerning some sort of puppet master. He decided he would talk to Christano and see if he knew anything.

Maldwyn and Christano went outside to talk and Talos went with them. Talos was an outsider and as such sometimes felt a little left out but he had a lot to offer, especially during the forthcoming battle. Maldwyn and Christano wanted to show Talos he was as much a part of the team as they were.

As they walked they saw the Green Man and Sarah walking back along the path. They stopped and Maldwyn asked how Sarah was. She had stopped crying but she was still upset to think that she had gone through being captured and tortured and had that thing, that Surl, rip her wail from her throat with its tentacles. It was too much, far too much to think that the faerie council allowed her and others to go through this knowingly.

The five of them walked over to the waterfall and the Green Man asked one of the wood nymphs if she would bring some tea and cakes. After they had discussed Sarah's plight and the plight of Sorona and Stephann's parents, the subject came around to the puppet master. It was a strange term to use especially by a faerie, but they assumed he had used this term for the other creatures in the room so that they could understand what he was telling them.

Maldwyn asked, "What is he on about, Christano? Have you got any idea? Can you throw any light on this situation?"

Christano answered, "Before I left to guard my dear Sorona I did hear about a problem with one of the faeries. They were worried that she was turning bad as she was looking into things that no faerie and no living being should be looking into. I do not know who she is but I know they were worried, very worried that she had purpose to all this and that purpose would be detrimental to everyone in Nirvana.

"But when Silas came to take the Cyclops' face off of Tiberius, he seemed very angry about the person that had done this to him as a baby, and I fear the person he is calling the puppet master and the person that did that terrible deed to Tiberius may be one and the same.

"It is very rare for a faerie to go bad. Yes, they can be devious, yes, they can be cunning and that is where the Seelie Court are different; we are very different as our feelings are out there, we do not keep them deep inside our chests. We love openly, and we confront anarchy openly. We do not keep it inside where hatred lives and breeds. I believe that is also how wizards are taught, is it not, Maldwyn?"

Talos said, "So it may be the same faerie that put Tiberius through a life of hell from the time he was born until the time we met him?"

Maldwyn answered instead of Christano. "I believe Christano is correct in his assumption; it is very rare that a faerie goes bad, so it is an easy supposition to say it is the same one. But I fear the faerie council has probably given her too much room in their attempts to capture her dealing in the dark arts. I am now wondering if she has evaded them and they do not know where she is, and that is why they want to storm this fortress as they think she is held up in there."

Sarah asked a question, "But who is she? Who were they talking about? They have someone on the inside and I know for a fact it is not Emily or Thea as they too have been tortured. No there has to be someone else in there, someone that I have not seen. It is either someone working there in full view, or someone that is hiding, but how? How would you hide yourself in such a place? I could not find anywhere to hide once I had attempted to make my escape."

"A sprite, a sprite could get around the castle very easily and as long as it did not use its magyk there would be no problem. Flying is part of their ability and so is hiding; they do not need magyk for that. Then all they have to do is fly over the wall and send a message using magyk back to the faerie council. Yes, I think it is a sprite," the Green Man said.

Sarah said, "I did not see one while I was there."

"Well," said Maldwyn, "I suppose we should go back into the war council and see what they have come up with. They are not going to tell us the truth about why things have been allowed to get this bad, but I suppose they will tell you, Green Man, so we will have to leave it at that."

The Green Man looked very sullen once more and said, "Yes they will definitely have to tell me. They should have told me before they did anything. The faeries think they rule Nirvana and everyone thinks that the faeries rule Nirvana, and they do, but if anything happens the like of which is happening now, I am the ultimate force that they must tell, as I am nature and anything that threatens the equilibrium of nature is my business."

CHAPTER TWENTY-FIVE: SHEELA'S LAIR

They went back into the war room just as the council were sitting down. They joined them and in the absence of Newton, Maldwyn was asked to take the chair.

Maldwyn said, "The plan to use the Aerials is good and it may be our only hope, but I still think all the magykal beings need to group together and gather at a safe distance from the fortress, at least let us try to bring down the magykal barrier.

"If we all send our magyk out at the same time, hopefully something should happen. Even if we don't take it down completely, at least we may weaken it and the rest can be done once we are inside.

"If it does not work then we send in the Aerials and at least if we have weakened the magyk they will stand a better chance of success. It is, I feel, more cautious to try the magykal way first.

"Has anyone else anything more to put forward, any more ideas? This is a difficult situation and we need as many options as possible."

One young faerie, that had an ancient name that no one could pronounce, made a suggestion of making Golems and sending them into the tunnel once they could find the entrance. Maldwyn, Christano, Sorona and Stephann almost simultaneously said, "NO."

They knew from experience and their encounter with Mark that Golems felt pain, even if it was not physical it was psychological and that is what made them angry and turn on their makers. They decided it was not right to put more Golems through that dreadful ordeal.

They made their case and the older faeries conceded that making Golems would be a bad idea, and they were also unpredictable. Many Golems had been made and then had to be destroyed in the past. And if what Maldwyn and the others were telling them was true, then all Golems that are made and were made were sentient beings and should be treated as such.

Another of the older faeries said, "When this is all over, Maldwyn, we must meet this Mark to ascertain his intelligence. We know of a Golem living in the mountains and he was a peaceful docile creature but if what you say is true and the Bucca female, no matter how it happened, has transferred the good parts and intelligent parts of her true love, then this is something new. I personally have never heard of such a thing."

Stephann said, "When all this is over and we have rescued our parents then you can meet Mark, my brother, my sister's husband. But first my parents should meet him and then with my parents present you can interview, Mark. Would that be conducive to the council?"

The faerie nodded and so did the rest of the council and that was the end of that conversation.

The younger faerie whose name was unpronounceable added, "As most Golems are weak minded anyway unless something weird has happened, as with your sister and husband, then I suppose it would be a bad idea because if Sheela has the magyk that we think she has, she may turn the Golems on their makers and that would never do."

Maldwyn and the company of friends agreed with this reasoning and were relieved that no more Golems would be fashioned and made to work for anyone in Nirvana, due to their being unstable.

***

All that they could do over the next few hours was wait for Newton and the army of magykal creatures to arrive back in the Green Man's woods. The magykal woods were so very beautiful and well, magykal.

They all enjoyed the woods and the waterfalls as they walked and marvelled at the beauty of the trees, the flowers and the small animals most of all Sorona was enjoying Sarah's company. She had not had the company of an adult female for so many months. Empress Alyssa did not count as she was the Empress, and Doras did not count at the time because she was a small girl. It was only after she had met Mark that she became a woman and became interesting to talk to.

Sarah said, "I wish that when this is all over I could go back to the world outside. This place is so beautiful but it is a place for damaged souls and recovery; it is a place of dreams and we cannot live in dreams for ever."

Sorona held her friend's hands. "I know it is hard for you, especially when you heard how the council have omitted to help, but the very fact you opened your heart to us and the Green Man means that you are healing.

"I hope that after the siege and we have all survived, that you will, if you want to, come and live with us in the great forest. Our faerie town is vast and I am sure we can arrange a nice shop and a house for you."

Sarah looked at Sorona with tears in her eyes. "You are like your parents, so caring. I may consider that offer, we will see."

They once again all met up by the waterfall where the Green Man provided tea once more; it seemed that most of the Green Man's time was spent sitting at the waterfall drinking tea but of course that was not the case.

When the Green Man was alone and he was sitting there contemplating his small world around him, he was actually meditating, his mind linking to every tree, every plant and every blade of grass throughout Nirvana. The Green Man had the ability to be everyplace at the same time but without others having knowledge of him being there. He was in the very air that they breathed; he was in truth nature personified.

It was a few hours before Newton came back and by his side was Silas, although he would not be going into battle with them. There was also an army of two thousand strong faeries and other magykal beings.

They made their way back to the cottage to talk about strategies. One leader from each of the magykal groups sat at the war council, they then would disseminate the information to their own people.

They decided that Maldwyn was probably right and if they at least tried to take down the magykal barrier it may help them to get into the fortress.

The plan was simple. All magykal beings would stand at a safe distance and cast the same coordinated spell at the fortress to try and weaken or bring down the magykal barrier. But it was decided that the Aerials would be used as well.

Keatin said that his Aerials were ready and they would fly over the walls in three waves. "The first wave, if the council so wished it, would drop all sorts of concoctions onto the enemy to put them off their guard. Then during the ensuing confusion, the second wave would fly over, swoop down and drop as many warriors as they could into the central courtyard, then fly up and go back and pick some more up.

"Meanwhile, the third wave would drop more men and if there was still more, they would drop the fourth wave. The object was to confuse the enemy and drop as many warriors as they could in the central courtyard area: confusion was key."

Newton thought this was a good idea and said so, but Keatin wanted them to be sure what they were letting themselves in for and added, "It can be dangerous, it is up to the warriors to be ready to jump on, then when on target roll off the eagles as soon as they are just above the ground. I hope this is helpful to you, but I just need you to know that jumping from an eagle and hitting hard ground is not an easy feat."

Newton said, "It is very helpful and I suggest that the faerie warriors would be better placed for that particular exercise as they could jump from higher up on the eagles, then they could fly off for their next pickup with less fear of being shot with an arrow.

"I believe that this plan can work, Keatin. The warriors can do as much damage as possible to the trolls within the complex, and their job will be to get to the tunnel, open the main gates and make the passage for the rest of us as safe as possible."

Maldwyn and the others in the room agreed. Maldwyn was still wondering how his beloved castle was faring with all this upheaval, so before he went any further with the plans for the siege on Sheela's fortress he asked Newton, "What news of our beloved, Empress Alyssa? She is well, I hope, Newton?"

Newton answered, "She as usual is well and preparing, as they all are, for the oncoming battle if it happens. The castle is in a state of lockdown and there is a good security system in place to get in and even to get out. The chief security officer of the army appears to know when anyone breathes the wrong way; he really does have everything under control, Maldwyn.

"There have been three spies caught and no more are expected as the lockdown is tight. Your friend, the former Cyclops, Tiberius, is learning the craft of controlled disciplined fighting very well. Godwin is pleased to have him as part of the army; he is very strong. There is talk of him becoming part of the Empress's personal guard, he is that good.

"The sleepers are contributing their knowledge and strategies in readiness for the onslaught of battle. Sheela and her minions will not find it easy. But that said they all need as much help as they can get and it is hopeful we will all be back to help if we are needed. Therefore, this must be a swift rescue as we all need to get back to the castle and the forest."

Maldwyn thanked Newton for the information, then he asked, "What of the outer reaches? Any news of those?"

Silas answered this question. "Some of the villagers have been attacked and the wizards taken or killed. It is worrying. Her magyk is too strong for such a creature; she should not have the magykal strength that she has.

"But because of the spies that we caught in the castle and our own hidden within the fortress, we now know our presumptions were right. I am ashamed to say that one of our brethren is to blame for Sheela's power."

Christano asked gravely, "May I ask, Silas, who is it sir? Is it the same one that afflicted Tiberius as a foetus in his mother's womb?"

"Yes," the ancient one answered. "It is that situation that alerted us to her. We knew that for some years she had been interested in things she should not have been interested in, and we always knew she was a little unstable, but we never dreamt she would go this far," said Silas.

"When we confronted Bertha she denied it. We then kept her under observation as we were not happy. She escaped our hold on her and fatally injured two of our most powerful brethren; she is indeed strong with magyk. We searched her dwelling and found hidden places with books and mathematical equations that she should not have had.

"Sheela may not know yet of all the worlds that Bertha does, but we feel she is helping the hag for self-interest and eventually will kill her and take over herself. Who knows what she is capable of. She has been to the human world once that we know of. She could have been many times and she could go again using the magyk that she now has, and if she did she would wreak havoc on that world and try to rule it herself."

Sorona spoke, "Is Bertha her true name, Grandfather? As my mother used to talk about a very unsavoury faerie called Baga-Bertha."

One of the other faeries around the council table answered, "Yes that was her grandmother. She was half witch half faerie and that could be where she got her information about dark magyk as Baga-Bertha was the mother of the Surl."

Sorona was puzzled. "How can that be? I thought the Surl was her only child, if you can call it a child."

"No," he answered. "She played the same trick on a faerie a good hundred years before the merman incident. The child was taken from her and brought up by the father. She was normal but her child Bertha apparently was not. Both Bertha's mother and father had an early demise by faerie standards and we did not think anything of it at the time, but

297

now we are having second thoughts, and thinking that somehow because they tried to stop their own daughter, Bertha, she killed them.

"We now suspect Bertha poisoned them both. She takes after her grandmother: she is pure evil."

The Green Man said, "I think it is now time for the faerie council to start sharing some information, don't you? Your affairs have spilt over into everyone's lives and could have been handled much better, Silas."

"Yes, we know that now, but at the time it was faerie business and we wanted to—" Silas was cut short by the Green Man.

"You wanted to keep it within the faerie brethren, I know that, Silas. I have heard it all before. You may be the majority in Nirvana but you are not the rulers, everyone has a say. We rely on you to police good and evil, not engage in keeping silent bad deeds just because the perpetrator is faerie."

Newton stood up and slammed the table with his hands angrily.

The Green Man said calmly, "Remember who you are offending, Newton. I do not vent my authority likely and never will but you are pushing me to my limit; it is the poor innocent creatures of this land that will suffer for the council's omissions."

Silas was angry with Newton. "Newton sit down, the Green Man is correct. We handled the situation badly, now we must clean it up. It is our fault. We are very lucky that the other creatures here today are helping us, so let us get on with the business at hand.

"We know that tomorrow the hag will not be in the fortress. She and a dozen or so of her trolls are going to a village where they have heard there are magykal beings that may be able to help her in her cause. We have removed these beings from the village and in fact they are here with us now, ready to fight. But while she is away we should attack, then we only have Bertha to deal with, unless she lets the Surl loose."

Maldwyn said, "Does that mean that the Surl is Bertha's uncle?"

Silas looked at Maldwyn. "Yes, I suppose it does, my grandson, I never connected it, really we just see it as a nasty creature. But now you have brought it to my attention that is probably how she controls it: they come from the same gene pool."

The Green Man had calmed down a little. "It seems you have not thought about a lot of things, Silas. Please just learn from this and sort yourselves out, it seems that you all have become too complacent. And by the way do you know about the explosive substance that some of the humans are experimenting with in the town of Theme?"

Silas was shocked. "No, we did not." He looked at Newton and Newton was just as shocked as Silas. The Green Man nodded his head from side to side and as he left the room he said, "Well I rest my case, Silas."

Vardo followed him saying, "I have never seen the Green Man angry before. This is twice in one cycle. Nature will suffer if this keeps happening. Please sort yourselves out before Nirvana has a famine, the last thing we want is the Green Man to go into a depression."

Newton said, "Have we really been that bad and that blinded by our own arrogance, Father?"

"It would appear so, my son," said Silas. "But I suggest preparation now and rest, as in ten hours we fight. But before that send two of your best faeries to sort out the town of Theme and if need be wipe the knowledge from the minds of everyone in that town about this explosive substance. If humans remember that part of their history, then Nirvana will be doomed."

***

There was only one way in and out of the wood, even for the faeries, and that was with Vardo. There was such a lot of creatures to get out of the wood that Vardo had to do it in three journeys.

He had taken them just a little further back from the tree line that faced Sheela's fortress. There was a small clearing to the left of them and that was where the eagle squadron was going to land and pick up the faerie warriors. Some of the warriors, in fact most of them were Seelie Court and relatives of Christano.

Seelie Court were the best and toughest warriors of the faerie kingdom and when in battle they were fearless.

After they had all gathered at the site, the ones that had been chosen to join the Aerials went to the clearing to wait for them. The faeries had produced lightweight breastplates for the eagles, but there was a concern that these would fall apart as magyk was used to forge them and magyk did not work in the fortress, well only the hag's magyk.

Silas reassured them by saying, "I do not think that the spell works in that way. It has to be magyk performed within the compound. Plus, the breastplates were made in the traditional way, with traditional materials; it was just that they were made quicker by using magyk instead of every piece tentatively forged by a faerie craftsman. No, I do not believe they will fall apart."

The army, as that was what it was now, lined up against the tree line, weapons in hand. All the magykal beings with extra skills in magyk lined up in front of them. They were ready to cast their spells and try to bring down all, or at least part of the magykal barrier.

The Aerials waited in the clearing until the magykal beings had finished casting their spells. On Newton's command the first wave stepped forward. In their ranks were Maldwyn, Sorona, Christano, Stephann and Newton. They waved their arms in the air chanting and concentrating all their powers towards the fortress. Everyone there felt the tingle of the extreme magyk that was coming from these beings; it was awe-inspiring and at times frightening.

One by one as they expelled their energy they stopped and fell back to sit down and rest as the amount of intense magyk they were using was exhausting. Only Maldwyn carried on for a further ten minutes after the last of the other magykal beings had given up, but Maldwyn too had to fall back and rest.

Maldwyn was surprised to find that he soon recovered. He recovered a lot quicker than the others; he was not seriously tired, in fact he felt invigorated as if he had just been bathed in a rejuvenating bath of light.

He walked around the others touching them, helping them to get their strength back. As he passed Newton, Newton said, "I told you, Mage, that your powers were beyond your understanding. Now do you believe me?"

Maldwyn considered the question then replied, "Yes, I do now, faerie."

Newton, feeling stronger, gave the command for the eagles to go. They took to the sky one hundred strong. To start with these were the eagles and riders that would drop confusing concoctions on top of the guards. Exactly two minutes after they had set off, Newton ordered the second wave, which were two hundred strong; these were the ones that had the faerie warriors on their backs.

They went high into the sky, too high for the arrows to reach them, then at the last minute they swooped into the courtyard of the fortress, and when they were about eight feet off the ground the faeries jumped, some of them onto the trolls and some of them onto the floor, but luckily none of them were injured.

As soon as these eagles got back to the clearing the next wave had already set off, carrying more faerie warriors. They kept on in this way until there was five hundred strong warriors on the ground.

Then as planned a hundred or so warriors broke away from the main fighting and ran down the passageway to the front of the stronghold. They were fighting their way along the passage to open the main gates for the rest of the army to get through.

The trolls did not know what had hit them. The faeries were unyielding in their ferocity and hatred for the trolls, showing them no mercy and brutally dismembering them and killing them: they did not intend to take any prisoners.

Newton gave the order and leading the charge he ran from the tree line towards the fortress and into the tunnel; there were small hatches in the top of the tunnel that started to open as they came in. The faeries that were already in there had not noticed the open hatches at first.

Out of these hatches trolls dropped down to attack the intruders. Others dangled from the hatches with hatchets and swords in their hands trying to hack off the heads of the intruders, but to no avail, as they were pulled down to the floor by the larger faeries.

It was a bloody battle, but the faeries won out, and by the time they came out of the tunnel there was not one troll living and the way was clear for Sorona to walk through and find her parents.

TWENTY-SIX:
BERTHA AND THE RESCUE
↑ ⚡

Maldwyn with Sorona, Stephann, Christano and Talos walked into the compound behind the fighters ready to test their magyk. Immediately the very muscular Seelie Court faeries joined them as their guard.

Sarah was not with them. Silas had wanted her to stay with him back in the magykal woods as he and the Green Man thought it would be too traumatic for her to re-enter the compound.

Sarah had told them where to go and how to get there. They made their way straight across the compound to the house, through the door to the left and down the steps to the dungeons.

Sorona could hear voices and she thought she recognised one of them, so she broke ranks and ran down the corridor between the cells in a frenzy, hoping to find her parents. The people that were speaking were in the cell right at the far end on her right; she rushed up to the cell and put her hands on the bars and shook them. She sobbed, she could see her parents and they were alive.

Sorona tried as hard as she could to use magyk on the bars but to no avail, the only thing she managed to do was bend them a little, but they would not break or move and the door would not open.

Maldwyn, seeing anxiety in Stephann's face, said, "Go Apprentice, go to your parents and let them know that you are all right."

Stephann smiled a weak smile, nodded, and also ran down the corridor to find his parents. By the time Maldwyn had walked down to the group of magykal beings, they were all crying and talking on top of each other; it was a very emotional sight with everyone trying to talk at the same time.

Maldwyn strolled up to the bars and said, "Please, Sorona, can you stand back with Christano and Talos. Apprentice, if you will be so kind as to stand on my right side we will see if our combined efforts can release your parents."

Stephann did as his mage commanded and so did Sorona. The Bucca parents were confused to hear their son being called apprentice! Surely, they had heard wrong, he was Bucca! He could not be an apprentice to a great mage! That was beyond explanation. No mage had ever taken a Bucca child as his apprentice; it had always been unthinkable.

Stephann stood at Maldwyn's right-hand side and emulated what his mage was doing. They rolled up their sleeves, held their arms straight out in front of them, then waved and chanted the opening spell in unison, and they concentrated all their powers on the cell door but to no avail.

The door started to vibrate and shake but it would not move, while they had weakened the magyk, it was not totally in their power yet to perform magyk as it should be performed.

Maldwyn said, "Stop, Apprentice, please stand back. The rest of you in the cell get down low and hide behind the bench."

The parents in the cell did as they were told turning the bench on its side to act as a type of shield. Maldwyn had finally had enough of all this not being able to do magyk nonsense; what he was about to do went against everything that he should be able to do, as his powers should not have allowed it. But after the magyk he had used on the unicorn, he now felt powerful enough to fight Sheela's spell, if only in a small way.

***

Maldwyn lifted his arms, pulled his elbows back and in one concentrated effort pushed his arms forward, hands open making a movement as if he was grabbing hold of the cell doors and then pulled back. The door immediately came off its hinges and flew to one side landing at the bottom of the stairs at the top of the corridor.

The four adults were unscathed if a little shaken by their ordeal; there was much hugging and weeping with everyone wanting to know the other story. Sorona's parents were asking her how she and Christano had taken their true forms once more.

Stephann's parents could see that he was unscathed but they were worried about their daughter Doras. Was she all right? Was she safe? Then the next question was how it was that Stephann was the apprentice to a mage.

Maldwyn said, "Doras is quite safe I can assure you of that, but we must get on, tempus fugit, and we will answer all questions later. For now, you must stay here, and you too Talos. I do not want Bertha to know about you quite just yet. I need you to look after everyone while we go to face Bertha.

"Christano, if you and your brethren will come with me, I think we should go and find Bertha now."

Stephann stepped forward. Maldwyn looked at him with fondness and he put his hand on Stephann's shoulder. "Not this time, Apprentice, you are not ready."

Stephann was just about to argue when Maldwyn continued, "And you vowed to obey me without question, Apprentice."

Maldwyn took off his ring and whispered something to Sunstar, then he gave the ring to Stephann. "Guard your family and take care of Sunstar. Put the ring on until I get back. She will let you; you will have no trouble from her, she knows you are the apprentice. I do not know how powerful Bertha is and the last thing I want her to know is the ancient magyk that was used on both Talos and Sunstar. But that said, if we falter then you can do your worst and Sunstar and Talos will help you."

Maldwyn smiled at them as if he was going for a walk in the park, but truth be known he did not know if he would be coming back. He did not know how strong Bertha's magyk was. Is it possible that he could win the battle that was ahead of him? It seems that Newton was right, he had powers far beyond his own expectations. But were these powers enough when evil confronted him?

Christano and his brethren followed Maldwyn into Sheela's torture room. They were just in time to see Bertha emerge from the hatch that was the Surl's hiding place. The Surl was already out and staring at the intruders, trying to work out if he should attack them or not.

The smell, as well as his looks, were obnoxious but at the same time Maldwyn felt pity for the creature. He was born out of love, albeit a twisted love, and this was why he was born so deformed.

Once Bertha was all the way out of the hole she closed the hatch; she turned in their direction not realising that they were in the room.

She was standing at the side of the Surl and stroked his slug-like head. "Oh uncle, see who has come to see us, the would-be victors. How nice it is to see you, Wizard. I have heard such a lot about you, and who is this that you have brought with you?"

She laughed a piercing laugh; she was very much like her grandmother. "Oh Uncle, you will gorge yourself today with both wizard blood and faerie! How is that for a treat?"

She looked at them for a while, none of them saying a word back to her, then she continued, "Ah, I was wrong, Uncle, these are not just faeries these three are Seelie Court. How nice will that be for you, Uncle."

The Surl was standing upright on his back end; he reached at least seven feet and his tentacles were just as long; they were splaying all around him, the stench worsening by the minute. As he was standing upright it seemed to be coming from a hole in his underside: probably an old injury.

Bertha was not afraid at all, if anything she was confident that she would be the victor and nothing would stand in her way, after all she had dark magyk.

All the time Maldwyn had been listening to her he was performing a spell around himself and the Seelie Court; the spell was a barrier that made them impervious to the smell, the slime, and the tentacles of the Surl. Maldwyn only hoped that this barrier would hold, then at least the Surl would not be a problem to them.

Maldwyn said, "So Bertha, you have come a long way since you killed your parents; you must be very proud."

Her smile turned to rage then back to the sickly smile once more. "How do you know my name, Wizard, how?"

Maldwyn smirked, at least at this moment in time he did have the upper hand as he knew her true name and this is what he could use against her. "Silas knew your name as soon as he started taking the mask from the poor Cyclops; the mask you put on when he was but in his mother's womb. How cruel are you to maim a small baby in such a way. You will regret the day you did that, of this I am sure."

Bertha was angry and just for a moment she was speechless and did not know how to answer the charges, then she said, "I was betrayed, that creature's father was my betrothed and he betrayed me with a mortal woman. I will have my vengeance, I will! How dare you and Silas interfere? The child deserved all he got and so did the mother; she watched the thing she had given birth to grow into a monster, as my grandmother had to with my uncle: it was poetic justice."

Maldwyn felt a certain amount of pity for Bertha. She had obviously been under the influence of her grandmother for quite a while without her parents knowing it, otherwise she would not have been as bad as she was. "I pity you, Bertha, the hatred you must have inside you. You must know that your grandmother tricked the merman and that creature, your uncle, was not born out of love he was born out of weird love and that has weird consequences. When potions are used to make someone love you there are always consequences and your uncle was that consequence.

"But the poor Cyclops was born out of true love and the faerie you said you were betrothed to, well you were not. You just hoped that he would ask you to be with him and when he did not you killed him and hurt the mother and child, that is a heinous crime, Bertha, to afflict the unborn is unforgivable."

Bertha screamed at Maldwyn, "He was mine. We played in the forest when we were young, we grew up together. He was faerie! How dare he take a common human for his mate? Yes, I killed him and I would do it all over again."

Maldwyn was not really surprised at the hatred that was within Bertha but he was puzzled. "You were either a small child or not even born when your grandmother died. How could you know what you know about her and your uncle?"

She laughed once more, then said venomously, "I was born, but only very small, but not too small that I could not listen to the words of my grandmother before they caught up with her." She fell silent and screamed at Maldwyn once more, "Die, my grandmother died? No, Wizard, she was murdered and everyone in Nirvana will pay for that; they will pay for the murder of my grandmother."

"But why your parents, Bertha? What had they done to you?" he asked.

She screamed at him once more, "Because they tried to turn me against her. She told me in her writings what they were doing and she told me what to do, so as a dutiful granddaughter, I am doing what she wants me to do.

"Do you know that my mother and father killed my real grandfather just because he did not agree with them being together?"

One of the Seelie Court answered, his name was Ristof. "You are wrong, Bertha, your parents did not kill your grandfather. Your grandfather died and although it could not be proved we all knew that she was the one, your grandmother was investigated for the crime."

Bertha was angry now, "Do not lie to me, faerie, you know nothing."

He answered calmly, "Yes I do, your father was my friend and I know that your grandfather was dead long before he met your mother, so you see they could not have done this deed."

Bertha was fuming by now. "You lie, and you are trying to make me feel sorry for what has happened and win me over so that you can kill me! Do I look stupid, faerie?"

"No, I am not, why would I? I just want you to know the truth before you die, as die you will," said Ristof.

Maldwyn looked at him with horror. "Now does anyone need to die, Ristof? Please can't we just—"

Maldwyn was cut off as Bertha sent them backwards with her first attack, at least the barrier had saved them a little. Bertha kept throwing spell after spell at them. Maldwyn and the Seelie Court gave as much back. The Surl stepped in and tried to protect his kin but he was knocked backwards at every turn, as he was not magyk enough and could not get past the barrier that Maldwyn had put up.

While the others kept Bertha occupied, Christano ran past the witch, opened the hatch, grabbed the Surl and threw him into the pit. The Surl screamed as he landed on his back; it was a gurgling scream that echoed around the fortress.

Bertha turned, her attention on Christano. He quickly closed the hatch and started to defend himself. The others circled her one on each side. Maldwyn was bleeding from his arm. The Seelie Court called Strachan had blood oozing from his left eye and an open wound to his torso. Ristof also had a head injury but to the back of his head. He got that as he fell back and hit his head on the floor. Only Christano was wound free at this moment in time. They kept firing spells her way one after the other, all in unison hoping they would weaken her but it seemed futile.

Maldwyn had a thought: if he said the shrinking spell under his breath it would render her small enough to battle, but just as he was about to do this his father Merlin came to him; it was as if he was speaking in Maldwyn's head. "Search your mind, my son, search for the mind door. You need to solve this problem. You do not have to use magyk. Do not show your hand, my son, the spell is too dangerous to use now, at this moment."

All the time Maldwyn was thinking these thoughts he was helping the others by firing spells at Bertha. Maldwyn thought about Emily and knew she was a faerie of renowned skill in archery. While trying to concentrate on the spells, he used a different part of his mind to concentrate on sending a message to Emily.

The telepathy must have worked as Emily grabbed the bow off one of the guards that were lying on the cell floor. She went running up the stairs to the room where Maldwyn and the Seelie Court were fighting Bertha.

Gastak and Sorona chased after her wondering what was happening and if she was going to put herself in danger. When she got to the top of the stairs, Emily raised her bow, concentrated and fired. As she did so Maldwyn pushed Ristof out of the way. The arrow grazed his arm but hit Bertha firmly in the heart. She fell to the floor and no sound came from her, no murmur, she was silent. Only the wailing of the Surl could be heard as it sensed the death of his blood kin.

There was a dark mist that emanated from her body, It floated about for a few seconds, then disappeared into the hatch and back into the Surl from whence it came. They all surmised that whatever this was it was part of the Surl or part of what he had become. They knew it was time to destroy the creature as he now was something that he was not before.

Maldwyn went over to the body of the witch. He looked down at her: all the evil gone from her face. "At least you are at peace now, Bertha, you will have no more worries, my child."

Maldwyn turned to the warriors. "The Surl must be destroyed before Sheela gets back. The evil within will die when it dies as it is part of him and cannot live without him. If we leave the Surl alive the evil may leave him again and choose another host and if it is Sheela we are all doomed.

Ristof immediately disappeared and came back moments later with Silas and five other elders. This would mean that with Christano, Strachan and Ristof that made nine. This was the magykal number they required to kill the Surl.

The rest of them started to walk back to the courtyard and left the faerie contingent to dispatch the Surl; it was sad but he had become what his mother had wanted him to be and that meant he could not be allowed to live any longer, as his evil influence would be too dangerous if it were allowed to grow.

Stephann walked up to Maldwyn. He took the ring from his finger and gave it back to Maldwyn. "You are bleeding, Mage! Are you badly hurt?"

"No, not as bad as those poor souls." Maldwyn nodded at the dead comrades lying in the courtyard.

Sorona said, "Will that be an end to Sheela now that Bertha and the Surl are dead?"

Emily answered her daughter, "No, my daughter, Sheela is evil and had started her campaign of death long before Bertha approached her. We still have to face her, and believe what I say, she will be very angry when she arrives back and finds out what has happened."

"And what of the dead?" asked Thea. "Our dead?"

"The faerie dead including Bertha and the Surl will be transported back to our forest and will have a traditional faerie funeral pyre as befits them. The trolls, well they will stay here where they fell. They chose their side and deserve no more," said Emily.

They walked through the devastation outside; the carnage was not as bad as it could have been. The faerie dead came to eleven in total but the trolls were over one hundred. The rest of the trolls lay where they fell, wounded, awaiting their mistress's return and certain death for failing her.

Silas shouted to Maldwyn just as he was going into the tunnel to leave the complex. Maldwyn stopped and turned to Silas. "What is it grandfather, is there something wrong? Has the Surl not been dispatched?"

Silas replied, "No, my grandchild, just a question. We have dispatched the Surl and prepared both he and his niece for transport but we found something!"

He handed Maldwyn a book; it was written by Bag-Bertha to her granddaughter Bertha. Maldwyn opened the book and it was an interesting read; it was full of reasons why Bertha should follow her grandmother and become evil. It told ridiculous lies about the betrayal of Bertha's mother and her father and the Faerie community as a whole. It told of the merman and his great lust for Bag-Bertha and then how he left her when she was having his child.

The hatred in the book was intense and as Maldwyn read the book he looked at Silas. "I think, Grandfather, that you should destroy this work of fiction, it may be used again. Its dark secrets and writings could influence others in the future, I have not read it all and even I was starting to feel sorry for Bag-Bertha; there must be some magyk at play between these lines. Someone as young and vulnerable as Bertha could easily be influenced by it once more."

"I thought you would say that, my grandson, and with that in mind I would like you to do the honours and destroy the book. It will be good practice for your skills," said Silas.

Maldwyn was puzzled, it was after all just a book. Surely, he could destroy it with no problems. Maldwyn thought of the spell he would need and focused his attention on the book but it would not be destroyed. He knew then what his grandfather had meant and he knew that he must draw from his inner self, his new-found power, to destroy this book that was protected by evil.

Maldwyn tried four different spells and numerous ways of uttering them until he eventually managed a spell that disintegrated the book. It disintegrated the book so finally that there was nothing left to see and that was the end of that.

Now they had to join Vardo who was waiting for them in the tree line and go back to the magyk wood to tell the Green Man all that had happened.

CHAPTER TWENTY-SEVEN: REUNION

↑ ≶

They rendezvoused once more at the edge of the tree line. Vardo was waiting for them, waiting to transport them to the Green Man's wood. They were all much relieved to be there and in one piece, but there were regrets for the fallen.

The Green Man and Sarah were waiting for them. It was an emotional time for Sarah when she realised that the Surl was dead; her emotions once more overwhelming her and she started to sob.

The Green Man stroked her head and as if he had put a spell on her (which he had) she stopped crying, took a deep breath and carried on listening to the sombre tales of battle the others were telling.

Sarah did not feel sorry for the Surl or for Bertha. It was unbecoming of her race to hold a grudge but she felt glad for the revenge that had been meted out to these creatures; in fact, Sarah was very happy.

The Green Man listened intently to all the encounters, then he decided to speak once more before they left. "As soon as you are refreshed I suggest that you go back to your homes and make ready for battle. I have already been warned from the cave Aspy that—

The Green Man was stopped from speaking by Silus. "Excuse me! The what?"

The Green Man was not pleased but he understood that some of the creatures would not know what an Aspy was, but he really thought that Silas ought to. "A cave Aspy, have you really never heard of one, Silas?"

Silas shook his head. The Green Man carried on, "You do surprise me! The Aspy is a small creature that lives in different environments all over each of the worlds that exist. Their purpose in life is to police the qualities of the ecosystem to which I am privy and to also give me or the Green Man in whichever world they live a regular update. This way I know when anything is going wrong and more to the point who is causing it.

"Now does that answer your question, Silas?"

Silas was not happy. How could these creatures exist? How could they exist without him one of the leaders of the great council of faeries not knowing about them? Silas was silent, thoughts running around his head.

The Green Man smiled. "You think you know all the creatures in Nirvana, Silas? There are creatures here in my wood that you cannot even start to imagine exist, creatures that are under my protection. The last of their kind. You only have to ask and you can speak to them. If they agree that is.

"The faerie council are not as all-knowing as they think they are, Silas, and you and the council need to get out there and see what is going on around you, otherwise another Sheela or another Bertha will happen in the future, that is if any of you have a future, because this battle is not over yet.

"Why do you think the humans were so easy to sway over to Sheela's way of thinking? It is because magykal creatures have taken to the shadows. You as the faerie council should have been in the forefront of these humans' minds, minds that you should have guided like you would guide a child. Yes, they have been here for thousands of years now but they are still infantile in their thinking. Silas, they need guidance.

"If you do not mind me saying so it was not a wise decision to leave the humans to their own devices. Eventually that will lead to the very thing that was banned when they first came to this world, technology, and it will be technology that will kill this world.

"Please, Silas, do not let this happen, go amongst the humans, live amongst the humans, let them take your counsel, help them make decisions. If they are wanting to build roads let them build roads, but as you said from the start when Myrddin brought the first humans to this world, limit them. The rise of vehicles and firearms as these will lead to decay, so watch them ensure they do not go that far, but help them make their lives easier.

"Their lives have changed. Their small villages have turned to towns. They have produced goods in the factories that they have built. Help them but at the same time watch them."

Silas answered in defence of his people's decision, "It was decided long ago to let them get on with it. We thought it best but what can we do now things have gone too far?"

The Green Man nodded his head from side to side. "You are faerie, Silas, you can alter their way of thinking to some extent. You did it when their ancestors first came here. They lived together and they pick each other as life partners because of love. They have forgotten about their different religions and different races; they look upon each other as brothers and sisters without prejudice and in this way war has been averted.

"Consider the problem and do something similar again, Silas. You are not suffocating their thoughts. The only thing you are doing is helping them to live in peace without loss of life. Sarah lived among them for over a hundred years until this hate and racism raised its head once again. Humans are fickle and tend to follow the person that is the strongest. Yes, there are some out there that will follow the lame dog, the one in need, but not enough of them exist."

"I will talk to the council after all this is over," said Silas.

"Please do," he replied. "Now as I was saying the cave Aspy informed me that Sheela went to the caves to see where her diamonds were. Apparently, Sheela told her aid Klaus that Bertha needed the diamonds so that she could start making a weapon. She did not know what the weapon was as Bertha had not confided in her just yet but when she got the weapon that would also be the end of Bertha. This was what Sheela had planned.

"She was in the diamond cave and was screaming at the trolls because her plans had been thwarted. She was so angry she killed three of them just out of rage. She then set off for the goldmine at the other end of the mountain. Apparently, the trolls had three sisters in captivity. The sisters were going to find the gold for her and then forge the gold that was found into ingots so that it could be transported back to her fortress.

"I presume she meant you three ladies? I am afraid she will be in for a further disappointment when she gets there!" The Green Man smiled. He was pleased that Sheela would be dealt such a blow but on the other hand he was worried what she would do.

Christano added, "Yes and when she gets back to her stronghold she will be even more upset. We are in for trouble and it could come quicker than we were thinking."

Vardo then addressed the assembled group. "Please, when you are all refreshed I will escort you in groups to your various destinations. You need to get back to your abodes to offer protection to your people."

They all agreed and started to pack what few belongings and weapons that they had brought with them ready for departure. They then assembled in small groups. The first to go were the faeries. They could appear and disappear at will

318

but not in the Green Man's domain; they had to be invited and taken there by Vardo.

The faeries had a predetermined destination that they always used if they wanted to see the Green Man or when the Green Man wanted to see them. Vardo took a group of twenty-five faeries; they followed him, walking closely. They could feel the magyk emanating from Vardo. It was like a magyk fog all around them. He brought them out on the edge of the forest near Maldwyn's house.

There was a villager that was out rabbiting with his son. He was startled by the sudden appearance of the faeries. He had fallen on hard times and his butcher's shop was on the verge of closing. He was out trying to find food for his young family and the villages.

Silas walked over to talk to the man and his son. After the man had nervously explained his plight, Silas said, "We are very sorry that as your guardians we have failed you, but this will all change after we have defeated this hag. We realise we should never have let it get this far and I apologise to you. We will in future offer protection against anyone that tries to overthrow the peace in our world. But alas for now we have to fight, and we have to go back to the forest to make our plans."

Silas handed the man a small pouch containing a powder. "Take this, my friend, spread it on your counters and in your windows and the small amount of meat that you have will increase enough to feed your community. But ensure everyone gets a share? Charge half the price to the people that can afford it and nothing to the ones that are in dire straits. This magyk will last for five weeks. You can use it twice weekly and then it will be spent, but by that time I am sure we will have resolved the problem and things will be back to normal."

The man accepted the pouch of powder or magyk dust, as that is basically what it was. "Thank you, sir, we are out of food now and we only have the stores of grain and the cold store with some vegetables left, but it is still winter and this meat will help greatly.

"The Empress wants us to go to the castle and take all our stores with us but with respect I do not feel she realises how many there are. She could not possibly fit all of us into the castle along with the other villagers that she has already taken in.

"We are a town now not a village, although we are still known as a village we are a lot larger, and we cannot sustain ourselves at the moment, it is impossible, but neither can we go to the castle and put a strain on their resources. They have to keep their strength up to fight this hag."

Silas listened to what he had said. "I think we have a lot of work to do to make up for the years we have neglected you, my friend. When this is over we will have counsel and you shall be at its head; we will discuss infrastructures and roads and we will leave a guardian in each town and village. What is your name, sir, so that I will know you later?"

"My name is John Markham, sir, and this is my son, Nigel."

The boy Nigel was about nine years old and said to his father, "I told you, I told you, Father, that the faeries would not forsake us. I told you."

Silas looked at the boy. "Unfortunately, we had and we are so ashamed. Through our own pride and ignorance, we did forsake you without realising it, but that will change my boy, I promise you, and your faith in us will not go unnoticed, Nigel Markham."

Silas gave the boy a pendant made out of pure silver. "This is a good fortune talisman. I want you to wear it always and you will grow strong and be a good leader of your people."

That said he clicked his fingers and the talisman appeared around Nigel's neck. "Now we must get back, but after this is over we will help."

The faeries disappeared leaving the man and his son staring in amazement. What they did not know yet was that in the future young Nigel Markham was to become a great leader of his town and the husband of a future Empress, the daughter of Alyssa and Dimone.

***

Maldwyn and his group were the last to leave. Vardo dropped them off just outside the cave where Doras and Mark lived. Doras was hanging the washing out in a small garden she had created across from the cave door. There was a small road running between their cave and the small garden; it was a road that was open to all travellers and she could not block it.

She turned when she heard someone talking. She saw it was her parents so she dropped the pegs and the washing and ran to her mother and father and then Stephann. She was ecstatic to see them and also relieved to see that they were safe.

Thea said, "You look well, Daughter, and so much change in you too, you are now a young woman, a young married woman I believe. When Stephann told us what you had done it was hard for us to take it in. You are the only Bucca girl in living memory that has ever brought a handmade creature to life. But look at you, you are a young woman and you are special as is your brother. We thought you would stay a child forever: you liked it so much."

Her father said, "We feared the worst when Stephann arrived on his own. We thought you were expired, my daughter." Sefton hugged his daughter once more, pleased that she was not harmed.

Then something strange happened, all four hugged and appeared to meld into one creature; the shape was unrecognisable and shimmered. This was yet another thing that people did not know about Bucca.

Sefton started to speak again but Doras said, "No, Father, I don't want to speak any more out here in the garden. Let us go inside and you can meet my husband Mark. We will sit have a nice drink of tea and speak of what has happened to you and to us." She grinned a girlish grin. "We may even have a little party."

Thea looked puzzled at her daughter. "A party? What do you mean, Doras?"

Maldwyn said, "I think Doras has picked up some human traits while she was at the palace, Thea. I do apologise it is probably my fault."

Thea smiled at Maldwyn. She knew exactly what must have happened with her daughter and her son being exposed to the human children's ways. They followed Doras inside the cave house to meet their son-in-law, Mark.

Mark was carrying a wooden bowl he had made. He was coming outside to show Doras that it was finished but stood dead in his tracks. Who were all these people? He was just going to say something when Doras said, "Be still, my husband, there is no danger here, come." She held out her hand and he stood beside her. "This is my husband Mark. Mark this is my mother and father."

Her father said, "Well it is very nice to meet you, Mark, or should I say son?"

Mark's face beamed and he started to feel tears in his eyes. He said, "I have never had a family let alone a mother and a father. I am so happy, so happy."

Thea looked at Mark and said, "You look after Doras and we will look after you, Mark, that is all we ask."

Mark looked at Doras. He had been thinking and he looked very worried. "Do they know, Doras, about me? I mean, do they know what I was?"

Thea touched his hand. Her touch was gentle like her daughter's and Mark trusted it. "Yes, Mark, we do know. We know that as a foetus you were Golem but when you were born you were Mark. That is all we need to know."

Mark smiled, he really was happy now but with all the troubles that were going on around them both he and Doras wondered how long this happiness would last.

Mark went into the kitchen area and made some tea while Doras fetched the cakes that were baking in the oven; she had been baking before she went out to hang the washing on the line. Mark brought in the tea and set it on the table followed by Doras carrying the cakes which Maldwyn immediately increased in number.

They all sat down and the rest of the introductions were carried out, then Stephann said to his sister, "And this is Isla, my betrothed." Doras nearly choked on a bite of the cake she had just popped in her mouth.

She looked at the group standing in front of her then she said with a grin, "And I suppose that you, Talos, are betrothed to Millie, and you, Maldwyn, well you have found your Olivia at long last."

The people in question blushed, even Maldwyn. Stephann grinned, then said to his sister, "Well, they have not exactly plucked up the courage to ask the ladies yet."

There was a silence in the room, you could have heard a pin drop. Then Thea started to laugh and everyone joined in. Emily said, "Yes, and it looks like we will also have a blessing if I am reading my daughter and her champion right."

Sorona was just about to say something to her mother when her father Gastak said, "I would not bother Sorona or you Christano, it is obvious to everyone and to be honest you are a good choice for each other, you have our blessing."

Sorona and Christano were very happy about this; at least now they did not have the awkwardness of having to tell Sorona's parents that they were betrothed.

It was decided that they were all going to stay the night, then set off for the castle in the morning. Maldwyn removed their bedrolls from the pouches they were carrying and was going to make room for them in the sitting room but Doras said, "Maybe some of you could stay on the first floor but it needs checking out before we make that decision."

Stephann was puzzled. "I did not think there was a first-floor, just this one!"

Doras answered her brother, "Well neither did we, but one day I asked Mark to move that heavy plate dresser that was in the corner, the really dirty one. I was going to clean it and put some of the plates on it that we found in the cupboard. I had also dropped one of my favourite hair combs behind it.

"He moved the dresser and there it was, the large door that you see before you. It leads to a room upstairs but it is so dark when we opened the door we decided to wait until Maldwyn got back and ask him to investigate for us as we were not sure what was in that room. We could both feel the magyk and it was worrying."

Maldwyn suggested that he, Stephann, Doras and Mark should go and investigate the upstairs room while the rest of them stayed downstairs and relaxed for a while. They cautiously followed Maldwyn. The stairs were wide and very high; the staircase turned slightly at the top and there was a small landing with just one door leading from it.

Maldwyn put his hand on the door handle. It was a very intricately carved door handle and looked and felt like silver to Maldwyn, which was odd considering this was just a cave.

Maldwyn opened the door and stepped inside. There were no windows to this room so Maldwyn whispered the illuminating spell and immediately the room lit up as if the sun was coming through a large window.

He walked further into the room and they followed him in. There was all manner of things in this large room. There was furniture richly carved with carvings that could only be faerie. There were drapes of velvet with gold fringing and tassels to the pelmet and tiebacks. Richly carved chairs and a large ornate cabinet lined the walls, with beautiful ornaments of porcelain, bronze and silver.

As Maldwyn walked around the room he saw another door hidden behind a large bookcase. He had been looking at the books in this bookcase, some of which were again faerie in origin but some were also of human origin. Books that told of the history of man, very old books that were probably brought through with the first refugees, but Maldwyn put the thought of the books behind him as he wanted to see what was behind the door.

The door was locked and Maldwyn could not get in so again he had to use magyk to allow access. Maldwyn slowly turned the doorknob. This one was round and appeared to be some sort of crystal, probably with a built-in magykal locking spell, as crystal is a good conductor of magyk.

He held the others back and said, "This room was obviously locked for a reason, so let us not be too hasty and go barging in just in case there is danger." After a few seconds of surveying the room looking for magyk, looking for spells, Maldwyn said, "Right, we can go in. I do not think there is anything in here that is harmful to us."

The sight before them was magnificent. This room was larger than the previous one and the items that were in the room far exceeded the ones in the previous room for their beauty and style.

The walls were very high and whoever had created this cave had painted these walls with a shimmering cream iridescent colour, which again Maldwyn thought must be burglar proof as there were paintings and tapestries hanging on these walls. Some of these were of human origin but most were faerie.

They walked along, removing the dust sheets from the furniture only to reveal plush sofas and chairs covered in red velvet and blue velvet; a large table and sideboards were amongst the furniture that was in the room. This furniture and all the soft furnishings that went with it would not be out of place in Empress Alyssa's castle. The furniture really was fit for a palace or faerie castle.

There were several chests lined up side-by-side in the middle of the room. These also were magnificently carved and again obviously faerie made. They started to lift the lids on the chests; they were full of beautiful bedding and clothes again fit for royalty. These were not the trappings of a normal family. This strange house and its contents did not belong to any gentle mountain giant nor did it belong to any common creature. This cave belonged to someone that was hiding their family treasures but why?

Doras went to the last chest but she could not lift the lid: it was heavy. Mark walked up to her and bent over to help lift the lid. It suddenly came up as if it was as light as a feather; both their hands were touching at this point and that was when the lid seemed to lift with no effort as if it had a mind of its own.

Maldwyn who was looking at a painting at the other end of the room sensed the magyk and turned. He said, "Stop, just wait before you put your hands in there." But it was too late as they pulled their hands out of the chest two rings with faerie markings flew out and placed themselves on both Mark and Doras`s fingers.

Maldwyn said, "Please tell me you can remove these rings, please."

They tried to remove the rings and they came off easily. They handed them to Maldwyn and he suddenly stumbled back as memories flooded into his mind.

"Oh my, oh my," Maldwyn said as he sat down on one of the nearby chests.

"What is it? Are you all right, my mage? Has something happened?" said Stephann.

Maldwyn smiled. "Oh, far from it, my young apprentice, in fact everything is good. Let us see what else is in the chest and I will tell you all when we go downstairs. I think Emily will be more than interested in this."

CHAPTER TWENTY-EIGHT:
THE JOURNEY BACK

ᛏᛗ

They went back down to the others and Maldwyn sat down near Emily to tell her what they had found and what it all meant.

But Doras started to tell everyone excitedly what they had found. After she had told the story about what had happened and what they had found up to the point of the rings coming off of their fingers, Maldwyn had to take over the conversation as he was the one that had investigated the chest more thoroughly.

Maldwyn said, "The top of the chest as everyone there saw, was full of goblets, plates and jewellery, some made of gold but most made of silver and obviously faerie made, as were a lot of the items in both rooms. After I removed a few of the plates and goblets and put them to one side, I lifted the cloth that they were laid on and underneath I found gold, faerie gold, over half a chest full.

"The other thing that was there was some sort of spell, that is what I was feeling. It was waiting for the right person so that it could give them the memories of the people who put all these treasures in this cave, and it would seem that I was the right person. These memories came flooding into my head.

"This will be of special interest to you Emily as it was a faerie family that owned these items and made this cave to hide them in. Also, the faerie family were of royal blood. They

328

were in fact Bertha's mother and father. They knew that their daughter had been poisoned by her grandmother and after her death they also knew that she had found the book, the diary of her grandmother. Try as they may, they could not stop the young Bertha from carrying out evil deeds, but they did not want her to have the money and the means to practise more evil after they were gone.

"They knew that their daughter had designs on killing them both as her father was a seer. He knew also that there was nothing he could do about it; their fate was in their daughter's hands. If she decided not to kill them then that would be their fate but he knew in his heart that their daughter, their sweet lovely daughter, was now an evil witch.

"They decided to gather up all their belongings, everything that was of value to them, and also of monetary value to their daughter. They gathered it all up and brought it to this cave which her father had been preparing in secret, so that Bertha would not know where they had hidden their treasure.

"They set spells and locks in place to ensure that only the right person would find the treasure and use it to make a better life for themselves."

Maldwyn looked sad and was deep in thought. Olivia walked over to him and touched his hand. "What is wrong, my mage? You look so sad."

He replied, "If I am ever blessed with children I would like to think that they will not be evil, but as children do not know what their parents' true nature is, parents do not know what their children's true nature is also: it is so sad."

Stephann asked, "Then does the treasure belong to you, Maldwyn? Or do we need to send for Silas so that he can give it back to the faerie nation?"

Maldwyn smiled. "No, we do not, this treasure, in fact everything that you find in this cave belongs to Doras and

Mark. They were the ones that were first allowed to see the door at the base of the stairs. They are the ones that opened the magyk up initially, therefore the treasure belongs to them."

Doras was excited. "You mean all that is ours? We are wealthy! We can build a fine house and have a garden and animals!"

Doras was so excited, she was beside herself, and Mark picked up on her happiness. He put his arms around his wife and bestowed a kiss on the cheek. This is what they had been talking about while the others were fighting their battles, that when this was all over they hoped they could get a house near civilisation where people would accept them.

There was much chatter over the next hour or so about the treasure, about the house, about the battles they had won and the battles they had lost, then it was time for bed.

Maldwyn had decided that they would all spend the night downstairs in the best parlour and Doras and Mark could keep to their own bedroom. They were a weary bunch that went to bed that night, very tired but with good heart, and while not ready for the battle ahead they had come to terms with the fact that there was going to be a battle.

After breakfast the next day, the ladies set to work putting everything safely away in the house and making sure that all the food they had was packed into their packs and pouches. Doras and Mark did not want to leave their home but after Maldwyn had explained about the threat they would face if they stayed from Sheela and the mountain trolls, they capitulated and packed up some of their personal belongings ready to go with them.

If the things in the upstairs room that belonged to Bertha's parents now belonged to herself and Mark, then Doras did not want to leave them alone in case they were taken. She could not believe that it was all theirs and that they were rich now and could afford to have a proper house built. Maldwyn reassured her that everything was theirs and suggested that Doras and Mark went into the upstairs room and filled a small pouch with a handful of silver and gold coins. Doras did not want to be a burden on anyone, especially now that they had money to buy things, money of their own. They could also help her parents and Stephann.

When they were all standing outside the cave and the door was locked, Maldwyn waved his arms and muttered a spell; this spell built a wall in front of the house so that anyone passing on the mountain road would think it was just an ordinary rock face.

The company walked across to the garden that Doras had worked so hard on over the past few weeks. They walked down the garden path that ran through the centre of the little plot until they reached the cave entrance, that would lead them down to the mountain pass overlooking the great lake.

Chatting amongst themselves they did not realise that Vardo had arrived to take them to the castle. As he spoke they all turned, even Maldwyn had not realised the mage was behind him. "Would your company like a quicker journey to the castle, Maldwyn?" He grinned.

Maldwyn had never seen Vardo smile before and it was strange to see a smile on the old wrinkled face, but it was acceptable and Maldwyn thought Vardo should do this more often as he had learnt to do. It also made Maldwyn think about how lonely he was before and how lonely Vardo must be: the life of the wizard was not one of sharing with another.

He smiled back at Vardo and said, "How did you know we were ready to start our journey back, Vardo?"

"Oh, it was not me I assure you, I do not have that particular trait. It was the great man himself that foresaw this event."

They walked back up the small garden path and followed Vardo as he walked along the road in front of the cave that Maldwyn had just sealed, then they evaporated into thin air only to reappear near the house of Tiberius and Celestial.

Vardo did not wait for goodbyes. He turned and vanished as quickly as he had arrived.

Tiberius was just coming back from the castle. He was smartly dressed in his guard uniform and was walking tall and with confidence. He quickened his pace when he saw a group of travellers outside his home, worried for his beloved Celestial, then he saw Talos and realised his friends had come back to the castle.

Talos on the other hand did not recognise his friend in his smart new uniform and as he had never been to a castle before he was ready for a fight in case they were challenged, but Maldwyn seeing the signs said, "Talos, do you not recognise your friend, Tiberius?"

Talos looked again, then with a tear in his eye the big bronze man walked towards his friend. "Oh, my friend, I did not recognise you! You look so well." And they embraced like brothers. Both men had gone through a transformation for the better, with the help of Maldwyn.

Tiberius was happy to see them all. He had not known them long but as with everyone that he had met on this journey, he looked upon them as his family. Tiberius had indeed changed, but then again so had they all. His demeanour was a far cry from the young man that only a few short weeks ago would have challenged anyone in his path through anger and loneliness.

Thanks to these people Tiberius had not only had a name given him, but he had a new face, and a purpose in life: a new house and a wife to be. He said, "Please, come in and meet Celestial. Do you remember she was the house sprite? But then you never did meet her, did you? Anyway, come along and you can tell me all about your adventures and introduce me to your new friends. I am presuming that these are the parents you were seeking?"

Mark was curious. He walked up to Tiberius and looked into his face. "So, you are Tiberius? We have a similar thing in common; we were both made whole by this company of friends and given new life."

Tiberius looked at Mark. "And you must be Mark. It is remarkable you are fully human and a good-looking specimen too! You would make a good soldier."

Mark smiled. "As you are Tiberius. It is hard for me to really understand what you must have looked like with one eye!"

"No, three eyes, my friend," said Tiberius.

This made everyone laugh as they walked down the path and into the house. It was nice that Tiberius could now laugh at himself without feeling bitter. They walked through the gate and down the long path to the house. Tiberius had wasted no time putting a fence around his property, a property that Maldwyn had kindly given him. He had not yet cultivated the grass into a garden or obtained any animals but that would come, but not just yet.

Maldwyn told Doras, "I think your husband has found a brother and friend, Doras, in Talos and in Tiberius."

She nodded and smiled at the thought of Mark actually making a new friend; it was the next step in his rehabilitation from Golem to human.

They settled down in the parlour while Tiberius went into the kitchen to find Celestial and help her make the cocoa and bring some cakes in for their guests. The house was still the same as when Nafalius had lived in it. They had not changed a thing, but then why would they? Nafalius had just lived in the house, the furniture and everything in it was put the way the house sprite wanted it. He had left her to do what she wanted, but there was one exception, the house was now cleaner and brighter and had no oppressive feel to it.

They came back with two trays and Celestial set them down on the table. After introductions, Maldwyn said, "Come here, child, let me look at you."

Celestial walked towards the mage and he studied her face, then picked up her hands and turned them over looking at them intently. "You are a sprite! But how strange, if you do not mind me saying so, you are quite beautiful, Celestial. Every sprite I have ever known has been, through the eyes of humans, quite ugly, as I suppose we are to them. I suspect you have faerie blood in you, my dear."

She answered shyly, "Yes, my father said I was ugly as I look like my mother and she was faerie. And I also have the magykal traits of both races and if I choose to be I can be invisible as all sprites can, and I can be small or tall: I can be any size I wish. But I also possess the magyk of the faerie race and that is what is unusual to sprites, and that is why my father does not like me. As well as the fact that I look weird to him.

"But my Tiberius said I am as lovely as the evening stars, so I am happy that he does not think me ugly."

Talos looked at his friend. "Tiberius, I did not hear you say that you and Celestial were sweet on each other, a small omission on your part I think."

Tiberius was just about to answer when Emily, who had been listening intently, said, "Please, Celestial, sit with me. I wish to talk to you about your mother. I may have known her and how it came to be that she married your father."

The whole exercise of Emily talking to Celestial was to give her confidence and reassurance, as Emily knew only too well that sprites were cruel; they were paid well for their duties and usually worked as house sprites but to hear them talk they were slaves and never got paid for their services. They were not a nice race of beings.

But to hear Celestial talk about the way her father treated her and her mother was cruel and beyond belief. Emily suspected that Celestial's mother died of a broken heart as can happen with sensitive faerie females.

Celestial was different. She had the work ethic of a sprite and therefore the mental strength, but luckily the beauty and nature of a faerie.

To be polite Maldwyn had a drink of cocoa with the rest of them, but he knew he must go to the castle as soon as possible to let Empress Alyssa know that they were back.

He was only there about an hour when he said, "I am sorry, Tiberius but I must make my way to the castle to see Empress Alyssa. She and the war council must be given the news we have about the towns at the far end of the kingdom and also the hag's strengths and weaknesses. We must also tell them the strength of her army, well the army that we have seen. I feel there is a lot more somewhere that we are not seeing a lot more that we are missing, but I would like you to come with me please, Talos."

"Yes of course I will come with you but I do not really know what to do in a castle, Maldwyn," said Talos.

"You will be fine. I will also make arrangements for the rest of you to meet the Empress as she will need to know your stories. Every one of you may be able to tell her a little bit more and we can build up a proper picture of what is really happening out there and what we may or may not face."

Emily said seriously, "Yes, I think there are many things we could tell her, Maldwyn. Things about the fortress. We were there a while and went into different places; each time they moved us we were all taking notice of our surroundings. We saw many things and we saw much of her army, but we will tell that information to the council, then you can all hear it."

Maldwyn nodded. "I will convey this message to the Empress and we will arrange a conference."

After Maldwyn had gone the company spent a pleasant day with Tiberius and Celestial, and that night when Maldwyn returned from the castle, after their evening meal they all went into the chapel to pay their respects to Nafalius. Maldwyn once more resided over the proceedings and said an ancient prayer which brought a tear to Celestial and Tiberius.

They then dispersed to the bed chambers that Celestial had given them for the night. Only Maldwyn and Olivia were left in the chapel. They sat in the cloister on one of the stone benches – it was so peaceful. Olivia said, "It is hard to believe that war is waging and a battle is to be fought when we sit here in this place that is tranquil and pleasing."

She looked around her, then stared at the roof. "This will be magnificent in the summertime when it is open and the blue sky is allowed to pour down through the roof. I wish one day to live in a house with a chapel such as this: I can think of no better place to meditate and read."

They sat for over two hours before Maldwyn said it was time that they got some sleep. He walked Olivia to her bedchamber where her sisters were waiting for her, but just before she entered Maldwyn plucked up the courage to kiss her.

Olivia looked at him with fondness and said, "No one has ever kissed me before, Mage, and I must admit it was pleasant." She grinned.

Maldwyn blushed and she could just see this on the cheeks that were showing between his hair and his beard. He said, "I have been putting this off because I was scared, my lady, but may I have your hand in blessing or is that far too presumptuous?"

Olivia held his hands gently and said, "No, my mage, it is not too presumptuous, and yes I will give you my hand and thank you."

She turned and walked into her bedchamber to tell her sisters that she too was betrothed. It was just a pity that the excitement of the betrothal was overpowered by the threat of battle.

Maldwyn had told them that the Empress was expecting them at the castle by nine a.m., so by eight thirty they were ringing the bell outside the castle ready for their meeting with Empress Alyssa.

CHAPTER TWENTY-NINE: MEETING THE EMPRESS

↑†

Millie and the bronze man, Talos, were talking a little way behind the others. They were getting quite animated and excited. Olivia turned to face her sister and said, "Is there something the matter, Millie?"

"No sister," she said, "on the contrary Talos has asked for my hand in union and I have said yes. So now we are all betrothed."

Her sisters ran to her in excitement with everyone congratulating them. Doras suddenly said, "But does that mean that you, Maldwyn, plucked up the courage to ask Olivia?" Doris was grinning and so was Stephann.

"I may have done, but we have more pressing business, we can talk of this later," said Maldwyn, trying to take the attention off of himself.

Hubert let the company into the castle as per his instructions and they were taken straight through to the cabinet room where Empress Alyssa and her war cabinet, including the sleepers, were waiting for them. After the introductions she asked Emily, Thea, Gastak and Sefton if they could start the proceedings by telling them what they saw while they were in Sheela's stronghold.

Sefton told the first part of the story with the others filling in all the details that were important. "When we were first taken to the fortress we were put in the oubliette. We thought that was it for us and we would meet our deaths there. It was dark and we could not see any way out, so in the end we all decided that we would die with dignity and not scream to get out, the way most people do when they are in an oubliette.

"We do not know how long we were in there before the light shone in and blinded our eyes. We had not seen daylight for many days, but how many we do not know. We were very hungry and thirsty as when they put us in the oubliette they had left us with four containers of water and we did ration ourselves, so by the time the light went on and they took us out of there, we were badly dehydrated.

"The large troll that came to take us out, pushed us to the edge of the wall and another one pulled us up two or three feet through a door in the side of the wall. It was so well concealed that we had not seen it. We walked past rooms that had open doors. There must have been over a hundred beds in each room one on top of the other. They were the beds that soldiers usually sleep in, in their barracks."

Thea who was listening intently said, "How do you know how soldiers sleep? You have never been a soldier, my love?"

He replied with a grin on his face, "Because as a younglin I wanted to be a soldier but I thought they would not accept me because I was Bucca. Anyway, we digress, my love, there were at least fifty rooms all with these types of beds and all were occupied by trolls as far as we could see but they were asleep. Well that's what we thought but Gastak—"

Gastak interrupted, "I think they were all under enchantment. After all they would not need feeding and the hag hated the foul smell of the trolls, she said as much when we were captured. Why they work for her we did not know as she treats them like vermin. It would suit her very well to keep them in a deep sleep until she needed them to fight for her."

Sefton took up the tale once more. "We were taken to the torture room where one by one we were put through hell, and she made the others watch: it was the worst of times."

Alyssa felt sorry for them. "What information could she possibly want from you? She wanted your daughter and she had escaped, so why torture you? Was it just for the sheer pleasure of it?"

Emily told her, "She did not want anything. She did it to show that she was the powerful one, that one day we would all obey her, but she did not realise, and she still does not realise, the dissent that will start when the masses are threatened. She is so evil. I am sorry, Sefton, I will let you carry on with our tale. I just had to let the Empress know what she was like."

Sefton carried on once more. "When we were finished in the torture chamber she paraded us around the square, dragging us if we fell in pain. We were open to ridicule and abuse from the trolls. We had things thrown at us, and they swore at us and kicked us. But we saw something!

"We saw Bertha come into the fortress. She had many, many warriors with her. They were dressed in black clothes and all had their heads covered with some sort of full headdress. It was impossible to see what kind of creature they were, even their hands were covered. There must have been at least a thousand of them. And then came the Surl. It was being carried in some sort of cradle between two stout horses.

"They marched into one of the buildings, the opposite one to where we had seen the sleeping trolls. The hag snarled at us with that hateful laugh of hers. She told us that this was what awaited our beloved countrymen and she would make sure everyone was under her before the end of the year and those that did not conform would be dead.

"We went back into the building where the cells were below the torture chamber and that is where you found us. But Gastak did do a little more intel gathering." Sefton gave a little laugh and looked at Gastak.

Gastak also laughed but Emily and Thea were obviously very cross with them both. Whatever it was that Gastak had done they did not think it was funny at all.

Gastak took up the story. "If I may, Empress, I will tell you what Sefton meant by that comment."

Alyssa nodded and Gastak carried on, "I thought, well we thought that if I tried to escape and I was not successful at least I may be able to see what was happening inside the fortress. My dear Emily and Thea disagreed as they can always see the danger that the male of the species try to ignore.

"We had wooden bunks and a wooden table in the cell. This was good as I am a Ghillie Dhu and my nature is to blend with any tree or if I so wish wooden furniture and structures. It is not magyk as we could not use magyk, Sheela had blocked it, but more the nature of the Ghillie. Sefton and Thea could turn themselves into different creatures, but the smallest one, a rodent, the hag had already thought about and she had set magykal alarms around the cells so if any rodent dared to come into the cells they would be instantly killed."

Alyssa had never heard of this. She had heard of a Ghillie Dhu but was not familiar with their traits. So Gastak walked up to the heavily carved door that they had entered through earlier and moulded himself into it. No one could tell that Gastak was in the door and some of the council thought he had by some magyk walked through it to the other side, until he opened his eyes and stared at them, which was the weirdest thing that any of them had ever seen.

Gastak slowly reappeared out of the door and was once more a man. He said, "You see because I am one with the wood, and I protect the trees, I can melt into any wood and become invisible and this is what I did. I became part of the table in the centre of the cell. When the guard came and opened the cell door he could not find me and as he looked under the bunk I made my escape and locked him in the cell. But I never managed to escape. The next guard, he managed to catch me as they seem to walk about in pairs but that was the plan; I wanted to see what was going on around us and what she was planning: what were her strategies and her manpower?

"If we were rescued, as we were, then this information would be vital. On one of my little jaunts around the fortress, it took them quite a while to catch me and I did manage to get into the part of the fortress where the strange-looking warriors had been taken and they too were sleeping just like the trolls. But this part also had heavily armed rooms, rooms full of weapons but not only weapons for causing death straightaway but weapons of torture as well: portable torture weapons that she could carry with her and use on the enemy on the battlefield.

"I eventually had to come to a halt with my escape attempts as the last time I was put in the oubliette, and that was the time when I met the banshee, Sarah. I was threatened that if I tried it again my darling Emily would be tortured severely so I had to take this as a real threat and stop what I was doing.

"That is as much as I can tell you, Empress."

Alyssa looked gravely at her husband. She was worried, as were they all, that their strength of numbers was too weak to stave off the enemy's forces, but this was all they had so they had to make sure that they used all their assets to the fullest advantage.

Godwin asked, "How can we hope to beat them knowing what forces they have. We do need a different strategy to the one we have at the moment, Empress."

Alyssa answered calmly, "And we have Lord Godwin, we have. We are ready for her and the element of surprise is no more: we know she is coming.

"We have the sleepers and the extra wizards from the outer lands, also the Aerials and our Navy as well as our Army. She just has a rabble of thugs that are neither trained nor articulate in the ways of fighting.

"Lord Desmy has procured some extra manpower and secret weapons from the Merpeople and we will take them by surprise if and when they come the way of the great lake.

"Lord Keatin has also perfected his aerial strategies for the dropping of devices on the enemy without the eagles being in danger. And Silas has promised that by the end of the week armour will be ready for all the eagle squadron. And the Seelie Court army will be flying with the Aerials and have also perfected a way of diving and jumping onto the enemy. Is that not right, my Lord Keatin?"

He allowed himself a little smile. "Yes, my Empress, the humans call it parachuting. But we seem to think that according to their history books this involves a large jellyfish looking canopy that floats down from the sky depositing them safely on the ground."

Alyssa allowed herself a smile. She was part human herself but their ingenuity would never cease to amaze her. Were there really such devices, it sounded incredible. "This I would like to see, my Lord Keatin, it sounds quite wondrous."

He replied, "I will accommodate that request at some point in the future, my Empress, if we can work out the design of such a structure."

Dimone asked, "What of you, my Lord Godwin, are the Army's plans forthcoming?"

He answered, "They are coming along, my lord, we have reinforced the side doors, tunnels and the main gate. The battlements are patrolled at all times by soldiers plus two wizards and two sleepers. The rooms with windows on the first two levels are also under constant guard and we are taking the precaution of having sleepers in those areas due to the fact that the spells may be cast on the living, and as you know sleepers cannot be affected by spells, therefore if all fails, the sleepers will prevail.

"My men are training hard and have become more organised and stronger as a fighting force. I am ashamed to say that in times of peace we do become soft and do not keep up our training."

"As do we all!" said Desmy.

Dimone told them, "Then we will have to ensure this does not happen again and that full training and readiness is the normal state of affairs from now on."

All the commanders said in unison, "Yes, my lord, we understand."

Dexter, who was one of the sleepers and also one of the greatest strategists that had ever lived, said, "We have moved those who wish to come into the castle from the outer towns and villages, and we have filled the storehouses full of produce and the cold store is now full of meat. Everyone is on the alert for spies and all entrances have been covered and there are certain factors in place for most eventualities as they happen.

"Have you any further strategies to suggest, Maldwyn?"

"We have a couple but I wish to keep them secret at the moment, my lord. The more people that know about them, the more chance there is of the information being passed on to the enemy," said the mage.

Merlin smiled, he knew about the dragon, Sunstar. And he also had come across tales of a large bronze man when he was on his travels in the land of men. It did not take a genius to work out that when Maldwyn himself introduced him as Talos that this was the bronze man of the fabled stories from the island of Crete. Merlin supposed that Maldwyn had used the reducing spell on the big man.

The war council went on for many hours and there were accounts from all the heads and commanders in the castle, and then there was a heartfelt speech from Silas about the virtues of helping man to live a happy and productive life in Nirvana. It seemed he had seen the errors of the faerie ways.

After the council was over and rooms had been found for their extra guests either in the castle or with Celestial and Tiberius, Maldwyn went to meet with his beloved Alyssa. And he asked for Olivia to go with him.

When they arrived at Alyssa's private chambers Dimone had just joined his wife a few moments before. Dimone opened the door for them and invited them in. Alyssa had been expecting them.

"Come sit down, my mage," she said. "And you too, Olivia, I must admit I never thought to see the day when Maldwyn would sit in front of me asking for a joining permission, but here we are."

Olivia did not understand why Maldwyn had to ask permission for a blessing/marriage. Alyssa seeing the puzzlement in Olivia's eyes thought that she had better explain. "You look puzzled, my lady. Maldwyn is the court wizard and as such cannot leave the castle to go on a journey or take up blessing with anyone unless he has sought the permission of the ruling Romanova.

"It is for security reasons more than anything but it is not usually a problem and it will not be this time."

Olivia considered this, then asked, "So all future partners are seen as a problem, Empress? With myself and my sisters being elementals, is that the problem?"

Alyssa smiled. "No, my dear Olivia, you are not. In fact, you are the perfect partner for my Maldwyn, and before you ask I have known Maldwyn since we were children. We played together always, well Maldwyn and Dimone and I. He is as a brother to me."

Olivia was still puzzled. "Could I be so bold, Empress, as to ask why you refer to the ruling emperor or empress as, what was it, Romanova?"

Alyssa replied, "Of course I can explain that. The first humans that were brought to this world were from a place that was in turmoil through internal fighting and war. The Czar of that country or the Emperor as we would now call him, was put to death along with his family but one child escaped and her name was Anastasia.

"She escaped with some relatives. Merlin helped them, brought them to Nirvana and Anastasia became the first Empress of Sandina. Her last name and that of her father was Romanova and from that day forward the leaders of this place have always been known as the Romanova, in memory of the ones sacrificed to save our founder Anastasia.

"Does that give sufficient explanation, my lady? It is only a brief explanation but I think it says it all."

Olivia nodded. "That is a good explanation, Empress, and I thank you for giving it to me. I understand the meaning of tradition."

Maldwyn had been sat patiently waiting for the ladies to finish their conversation. "Well, Alyssa!" He grinned. "Does Olivia pass muster? Can I keep her?"

Olivia looked at him. He was laughing, and so was Alyssa. She realised he was joking when he said 'keep her' like you would if you found a stray cat or dog. They all laughed but Maldwyn could see that Olivia was puzzled when he called the Empress by her first name. Maldwyn then explained that he called the Empress Alyssa in private but it would never do for him to call it her in front of anyone else.

Alyssa still smiling asked, "When will the ceremony be, Maldwyn?"

"I think we will wait until after the battle as we all know that is imminent and I think we shall concentrate our efforts on that," said Maldwyn.

Alyssa had other plans. "I am sorry, my mage, but I think it is a wrong decision. Tiberius, Talos and Stephann are all to have blessings as soon as possible and I think you should also go down that path.

"A blessing of four couples could be held together in the chapel tomorrow night. There would be no problem with that."

Maldwyn said, "Five."

Alyssa looked puzzled. Why was Maldwyn saying five? Then he carried on, "Sorona and Christano have already asked for a blessing ceremony tomorrow night."

Alyssa was surprised. "They do not want a faerie blessing?"

It was Olivia that answered the question. "They will have one of those after the war ends and if we can win, which we hope we can; for now, I believe you are right, that we take our partners in life for the few hours of peace that we have left."

Maldwyn was going to ask about the ceremony and as if his question was pre-empted Alyssa gave him the answer. "You are all very honoured as Merlin will be officiating at this event. I just need to tell him how many."

Maldwyn answered with a grin, "I think he will already know, my Empress."

She agreed, then added how pleasant it was for her to see Maldwyn smile and laugh so much. This had not happened since he was a young man and then he lost his adopted father Hubert and went from apprentice to wizard overnight. this had a profound effect on Maldwyn and he never smiled much after that.

Alyssa was very fond of him and, as she had already said many times, she looked on Maldwyn as her brother, and although Maldwyn thought he was protecting her, much of the time Alyssa was protecting him.

CHAPTER THIRTY:
THE KILLING OF DESMY

↑

It was getting late by this time and Alyssa thought that Olivia needed her rest, after all tomorrow she was going to be paired with her life partner. Maldwyn agreed and he walked Olivia to the chamber that she shared with her sisters.

When they reached the chamber door, Maldwyn said good night. Olivia bowed her head and he gently kissed her on her forehead. "I will see you tomorrow, my lady." He smiled as she walked inside to tell her sisters of the conversation she had had with the Empress.

Alyssa had also left the sitting room and she and Dimone went to find Merlin to inform him of the forthcoming events. They had to tell him that there were more blessings than were originally planned but as Maldwyn had predicted he already knew.

***

The next day was a hive of activity. The palace was once more humming with the excitement of the five forthcoming blessings.

There were dresses for the ladies and appropriate attire for the men, each one of them picking their own individual styles from their cultures. There were so many wizards in the castle that there was no problem making these quickly ready for the ceremony. There was also no shortage of food and drink or anything else for that matter: as long as the basic materials were there they could 'within limits' be increased by magyk to accommodate the amount that was needed.

The proceedings, as with Alyssa and Dimone's wedding/blessing, was not just for five people. In the end it was six as Maldwyn had suggested that Doras and Mark join them in a proper ceremony, as they were slightly cheated a ceremony with them being forced into it by the consensus of the group at the time. And as Maldwyn also pointed out Doras would love to get dressed up and party as she still had a girlish way about her.

The ceremony and the subsequent festivities went off without a hitch, but because of the threat of a siege at any time the party did not go on for long and by ten thirty most of the guests had either gone or were leaving to go to their respective rooms in the castle.

All with the exception of Talos, Isla, Christano and Sorona, who along with Sorona's parent Gastak and Emily, decided to take up the offer of a room at the house of Tiberius and Celestial.

There was to be no honeymoon period for the couples as the next day was back to normal as usual. The palace was again a hive of activity but this time with everybody making sure that the defensive measures were all in place and as impenetrable as they could be.

The merpeople decided, after consultation with the palace, that they would set nets across the lake to trap any boats that decided to come that way with ill intent. They set nets between the Morby mountain and the cliff wall at the other side of the lake. The only thing was the net was so long that they had to put supports every ten feet or so to make sure they were secure.

That done there was nothing else to do but wait, wait to see if the attack was actually going to happen.

It was just over two weeks later on a cool starry night that a disembodied scream was let out across the water. The scream resonated through the half of the castle that overlooked the lake. It was an eerie and frightening sound: the scream was that of pain, of torture, of fear, of death.

The castle immediately went on to high alert and a team was assigned to go out and find out where the disembodied scream had come from. Someone was in danger and someone was in pain, they had to find out who.

It did not take them long to find the source of the incident but who made the sound was still not clear. The jetty that was in a hidden position at the entrance to a cave at the back of the castle, was where the fleet of ships was kept, to be precise it was where four ships were kept as this was all the ships Sandina had.

Strewn across the large jetty there were boxes knocked over. It looked like there had been a struggle. They checked from ship to ship and found all the guards on all the ships were unconscious and one ship had its captain's cabin wrecked: the lock had been forced.

The captain of the patrol ran back to the castle to inform the council of their findings. Alyssa suddenly looked around the room in panic realising someone was missing. "Where is Desmy?" she asked anxiously.

The question was fired at anyone in the room that could answer it but truth be known no one could, no one had seen Desmy since earlier that day. He was not feeling well and put it down to something that he had for his lunch.

Dimone said, "We need search parties right away and lots of them, as many men as we can muster before more torture is inflicted on Desmy."

The commander of the search informed the council that search parties had already been deployed and they had also informed the merpeople so that they could search the bottom of the lake.

There was no way that anyone that captured him could get away as the immediate area was fully guarded. The problem was how did they get in? All the commanders went to help as did the wizards and Dimone, in fact any available man that was willing to search was put to the task. The only ones that were not deployed were the men guarding the castle inside and out. They were kept at their posts just in case the plan was for everybody to look for Desmy and leave the castle un-guarded.

They searched until just after daybreak and still they found no trace of him. How had the intruders got away? That was when one of the sleeper wizards offered his help. Casey had once been the castle wizard and was also a scryer. If anyone could find Desmy he could. It only took Casey a few minutes of scrying to find the invaders. They were indeed still within the castle area. They were in the cave behind the ships and the jetty.

There was an underground cave at the far end that no one knew about. To get to it you needed to dive into the water and swim under the rock face. Then you came out in a big cavern, and this was where the perpetrators had been held up since before the lockdown on the castle.

This was also where their base was, where they thought they could sabotage the castle defences from and one by one pick off the leaders.

Once this hideout had been found it was not as easy as they thought it was going to be to get the trolls into custody. They battled with the Trolls for quite a while until three of the merpeople came to help; seeing that the trolls were stood at the side of the water they dragged them with their feet and held them down until they were dead. They immediately looked for Desmy, but they were too late, Desmy was dead.

They managed to capture a further six Trolls that, being the cowards that they were, had found a hiding place in the cave. How they had found their way into the cave was yet to be discovered, but the aftermath of the fight between the guards and the trolls left four trolls dead, six injured and five guards with lacerations and bruising.

Desmy, his body laid on the rocks at the side of the water, had been tortured badly, but they knew he would not have said anything, he was too strong for that.

There was a silence that came over the area as the realisation hit everyone in the cave. They stared in disbelief at Desmy's body. Desmy had been the first casualty of war and the irony of it all was he had lost his life for nothing, because the trolls could not do anything with the information even if he had given in to the torture. They were prisoners within the castle walls just the same as everyone else was and could not get the information out.

The trolls were taken down to the dungeons where two of the sleepers kept an eye on them while it was decided what to do with them. Everyone had more pressing things on their minds, namely the burial of Desmy.

His body was taken back to the castle and laid in the Great Hall so that people could pay their respects to a great navigator. It was decided that Desmy would be buried the next day with military honours and be placed in the same graveyard as all the other great leaders of the castle forces.

At Desmy's funeral everyone, except the guards that were keeping the castle safe, paid their respects. Even the merpeople did something they had not done in unison for centuries. Using their magyk they came out of the water on two legs so that they could pay their respects to their friend Desmy.

This was one of the highest honours that any merman or mermaid could make as they went through an extremely painful transformation to do this.

Zamor, the sleeper wizard, was a distant relative of Desmy's and now his only relative was devastated by the news. He always thought that his bloodline would continue but it was sad to think that the last of that line was lying dead in a coffin in front of him.

Zamor was sad but at the same time proud of his nephew many times removed. Desmy certainly was well thought of and loved in his community and the Navy was what he had made it but the question was who would take over?

Zamor touched Desmy on his face and then suddenly said, "There is a maid called Susie. Where is she? I must see her."

Susie was found and brought into the private room with Zamor, Dimone and Alyssa. She was worried that she had done something wrong but she had not.

Zamor said, "Do not be frightened, child, I am a distant relative of Lord Desmy. How well did you know him?"

Susie looked puzzled. "I am sorry, sir, I do not understand. Lord Desmy was very kind to me always, as I was an orphan he adopted me in a way. He would come to the family I was put with when my mother died giving birth to me. He would bring gifts and give them money to help with my clothes.

"I knew that the lady that brought me up was my mother's sister and not my mother and I assumed that Lord Desmy carried out many charitable deeds for the orphans."

Susie, while making herself clear was getting things a little back to front: she was very nervous.

Alyssa walked over to her, held her hand and said, "How do you feel about the death of Lord Desmy?"

Susie cried, they could see she already had red eyes from crying. "I looked upon him as an uncle and the news was not welcomed, my Empress."

Zamor said, "I am pleased you loved Desmy as a family member, Susie, because he was your father!"

Susie did not know what to say. She cried more at the thought that he never told her.

"When your mother died he probably could not cope with the loss and you would have required a mother, so he must have asked your aunt to have you as the life he led was not one for a young girl."

Susie nodded, she understood. "Now," he said, "with the Empress's permission I would like you to take me to your aunt and we will make arrangements for your father's funeral, and after this is all over the Empress will decide what would be best for you. You are of course a lady now."

***

Because of the nature of Sandina and its meagre military forces there had never been much need for hierarchy in any way. The commander and his men were enough, that is all that had been needed up to now, but they were slowly realising now that the time had come to deploy those military forces that were sloppy and untrained. Therefore, there had to be some changes made and those changes were to start with creating chains of command.

They had what were called Groups that were each in charge of a few men, but not the designation that some worlds used.

The day after the funeral the war council met in the castle to decide who was going to take Desmy's place and be in charge of the Navy. This was not a problem that was going to take long to decide as Desmy had already put a candidate forward before his death.

There were four Groups, one in charge of each ship. Desmy had always stayed with the Royal ship and he considered the Group that led the men on that ship to be the most proficient and the one he would leave in charge if he ever became too ill to carry out his duties. The name of that Group he had discussed with Zamor and Dimone and had made it very clear that this group alone was the best in his fleet.

The council sat around the table procrastinating about the problem, and it was taking far too long to Dimone's way of thinking. He butted into the discussion as there were more serious things to think about at the moment and this matter needed to be cleared up urgently.

Dimone spoke in a clear voice. "Can I make one thing clear, the Navy will have its own commander, so any thoughts of one of you taking the reins," he cast a glance at Keating and Godwin then carried on with what he was saying, "is out of the question. You have enough to do in your own expertise without setting on more work, especially at a time like this.

"Also we need someone that knows about the Navy."

Zamor answered, "My great nephew Desmy used to talk about a Group called Richard. He has been in the Navy from a lad and started off as a cabin boy. Desmy told me that the man has good leadership skills and the men look up to him. He already does a lot more than he should and helped Desmy out with a lot of his duties. Desmy could rely on this man to get the work done if he had a prior engagement, and this was the man he was looking to when he eventually decided to retire."

Dimone said something in Alyssa's ear and Alyssa made an announcement. "Well I think we should see this young man! Will someone please go and find him and we will vet him and see if he is suitable to stand in Desmy's shoes."

It had taken some fifty minutes to find the young man. He was in the cave with the designated commander of the search looking for secret entrances and clues as to how the trolls may have got into the castle grounds.

***

Richard walked into the room with an air of confidence, thinking that the council required an update on the troll situation.

Alyssa said, "Come, Richard." She stood up and held out her hands in greeting. He looked horrified. Did the Empress really want him to touch her person? He looked at Dimone who nodded for him to come forward and greet the Empress in the traditional way.

Richard walked forward slowly and reluctantly he held out his hands in greeting. Alyssa clasped them in hers, he said somewhat nervously, "My Empress, you wish to see me?"

Alyssa felt him shaking. "Please, Richard, sit at the side of my Lord Keating, we have some questions for you."

Richard did as his Empress wished him to do, but he was not very comfortable with it all. They had many questions that he answered eloquently and with knowledge and confidence, but still he did not know what all this was about.

Dimone had a question. "This may seem disrespectful as Desmy has only been dead a short while but did he ever discuss with you any changes he may have had in the pipeline, anything at all?

"I only ask because he once said he had new thoughts on the order of things in the Navy and was wanting to put some hierarchy in place."

Richard was stunned and unsure of what he should say: he was like a frightened rabbit, his confidence starting to wane. "Yes, my lord, he gathered all four Groups together and we discussed the order of things; it was decided as a group of Groups, oh that sounds odd I do apologise."

"Exactly, that is what we are trying to alter," commented Dimone.

Richard carried on speaking, "We decided that the order of things was not conducive to the modern Navy so we came up with some new ideas.

"There would be the commander of the Navy then the Group, which would have his name altered to the Group captain as he would be pilot of the ship. Then there would be the Navigators, then the Sailors and finally the Cabin. My Lord Desmy reasoned that if one person was ill or had to leave for any reason there would always be another to take their place, either permanently or temporarily, a person who was skilled and knew what to do in that post.

"But if the commander fell ill there would have to be interviews of the four Group Captains to see who would move up the ranks to commander."

It suddenly dawned on Richard what he was doing in this room. His eyes widened and he looked shocked, very shocked. "You don't mean?"

Alyssa smiled. "Yes, we do, my Lord Richard."

He was speechless. How? Why? No it could not be that he, Richard from a normal family was to be a lord with all the status and monetary value that it entailed. Everything was running through his mind at a great pace. How would he cope? Was he good enough to do this job? And eventually he thought, could he buy his mother a new house?

All the responsibility would be a great burden at times as it was for Desmy, and with a war pending how would he manage? Could he do the job?

Richard suddenly realised everyone was looking at him and Alyssa was talking to him; he turned his attentions to concentrating on what his Empress was saying. "My Lord Richard, are you all right, sir? You look much shaken."

He fumbled for the appropriate words that he wanted to say but what could he say? He took a deep breath. "Thank you, Empress. I really am honoured but do you think I am the right person for the job? I mean I am only a Group."

Alyssa smiled, she was a kindly person, "Why Lord Richard, you are as modest as Desmy was when he was first approached to do this job. It was his expertise he learnt over the years and the mistakes that were made, that made Desmy the person we knew. But tragically we have lost him early and at such a time as he was needed; someone else does have to take his place and they are very big shoes to fill, my Lord Richard. But I have no doubt in my heart that you can do it."

Keatin addressed Richard. "Desmy was not always a force to be reckoned with, his slight arrogance and stubbornness were not always there, these were traits that he acquired along the way, these were traits that made him a great leader of his men. Do you know the battle plan, my lord?"

"Yes I do, but all the Groups also, not only I," he answered.

Keatin laughed. "Then you will be perfect for the job, my boy, and we know from Zamor that Desmy thought you were the best to take over his job. Did you know he was looking to retire after this war and apparently you were going to be his replacement?

"Now, my Lord Richard, I suggest we have a recess and you go away, get appropriately dressed as befits your position and introduce yourself to your men, and make it clear to them that there will be some changes in the ranks."

Alyssa said, "I think we should disperse now and a meeting, to discuss the new rankings once it has all been worked out and where we are going from here, will be scheduled for eight p.m."

Dimone kissed his wife's hand and disappeared with Richard to guide him in his new duties.

He went with Richard to his quarters, situated in the back near the men, but as he was a Group they had a room just off the dormitory where the men slept.

Dimone spent a further hour with Richard as they were going through the rudiments of his position and his duties. They then made their way into the men's living quarters to inform them about the changes that were to be made in the chain of command of all the military organisations.

When Dimone made the announcement, there seemed to be a sigh of relief that came from three of his colleagues. They were the other three Groups and were very pleased that they were not picked for this post at such a crucial time in Nirvana's history.

A reluctant Richard had to speak to his men before giving them the rallying speech to try and get them ready for war. He read out from the list he had made with the help of Dimone: these were the names of each man and their new designations.

Some of the men were surprised with their new roles, but for some it was a foregone conclusion, like the Navigator and the pilot, they all had their jobs and knew them well, only now they all had a second, an apprentice, someone that could take over if they were incapacitated.

The sailors were warned that if the war came from land alone then they would be expected to fight with the rest of the people in the castle and leave any watery defences to the merpeople.

CHAPTER THIRTY-ONE:
THE BATTLE
ᛏ ᛞ

Richard's first day in post was to be an eventful one. The day started as usual and by nine a.m. everyone knew their new titles and what was expected of them, but that said everyone also knew that there were going to be mistakes and there were going to be things to sort out that they had not even thought about.

The war council met as they did every morning but little did they know that this was going to be the last time before the battle for the castle.

The day started off well enough with everybody going about their business, bustling around making sure that last-minute preparations were made just in case today was the day. It was about halfway through the afternoon when it happened.

There was a massive thud on the gate and when the gate guard looked out of the hatch he saw in front of him a very large troll. The troll was an angry-looking beast with two deep scars down one side of his face. He growled at the gate guard, "I have a message for your Empress, let me in now."

The guard, whose name was Harry, was not taking any chances. He told him to wait to which the answer was a growl and another thud on the gate. Trolls are not known for their patience and this one had an ugly temperament to match his face.

Harry hurried along to tell Hubert what had happened and that there was a troll at the gate wanting to see the Empress. Hubert smirked and said, "So it begins. Does he seriously think we are going to let him in to see our beloved Empress? The creature is a fool. I will go and let my Lord Godwin and my Lord Dimone know of the creature's presence."

It was not long before Godwin was at the gate. He and about twelve of his men stepped outside the gate to talk to the troll. It turned out that the troll had a parchment for the Empress but he was supposed to deliver it to her and her alone.

Godwin told the troll that it was not going to happen, so the troll gave it to Godwin to deliver to the Empress. Why should he care anyway? He did not want to see the puny human.

The troll was not happy but, after he gave the parchment to Godwin, he then turned and walked away from the gate as if he had just delivered a birthday card and not a declaration of war.

Godwin hurried back into the castle. He went to the war room where Alyssa and her husband Dimone were waiting. Godwin handed them the parchment and Alyssa read it. She started to smile, then she laughed and handed it to the others to read: she obviously found it very funny.

Godwin said, "I cannot believe this hag. she wants us to hand over the castle and the Empress and everything in it, plus all the lands of Nirvana including the magyk forest. Does she take us for fools? Does she really think we are going to give up without a fight? She has had a sample of what we can do. Does she not believe it? Is she that deluded?"

Alyssa who was a gentle soul answered him, "Yes I do believe she is deluded. She is deluded into thinking that she is the rightful ruler of Nirvana when really there is no ruler. People look to me and say I am the ruler but I am only the custodian of the castle and I am here to counsel the human subjects that live within its lands. I do not profess to be its ruler, just the guiding hand for those that need it. The faerie council are the real rulers, they let the humans stay here.

Godwin asked, "How do we answer this, my Empress? And how do we get the message back to them?"

She looked at him and smiled once more. "What we do or should not do is send someone out with the answer, that would be a grave mistake as she would kill them on sight. She would not let them go as we let the troll go. No Godwin, I think the war has started. As from now and we must ready our subjects and let them know that the siege will happen at any time."

Everyone started to get ready for the battle. It was not going to be easy and people would die but they had to defend the castle at all costs. Once the castle had fallen then all the human population would be under the influence of the hag, and eventually that would mean the magyk forest.

***

They did not have to wait long. Because they had not sent a messenger back with an answer, Sheela got angry and she sent troops to storm the castle. The first the people knew of the castle being invaded was the noise, the loud noise of creatures of all description including trolls charging the castle from three sides.

The largest of the creatures were carrying battering rams which they used on the great door but to no avail. At first, Sheela's forces did not expect the magyk spells that had been put over these areas by the sleepers, in fact they did not expect the sleepers as Sheela did not know about them.

The noise was booming. The adults and the children in the castle that were not going to fight had been taken down to the dungeon areas for protection. Alyssa refused to go. She was going to stay and fight with her people and no one, not even her darling husband, was going to tell her any different.

Grappling hooks were thrown to the upper parapets to try and get a foot hold but again to no avail. The first wave of the attack had failed and no one in the castle had to lift a finger but they knew this could not go on. Sheela was strong and if she started using her dark magyk there would be no going back, she would get into the castle.

The next wave came at ground level, rushing at the castle trying to climb the walls, battering the doors at what they thought were the weakest part of the walls. There were thousands upon thousands of creatures.

Sheela knew she had to do something. She got into her chariot that was driven by the hounds of hell and headed for the castle, going straight overhead so that she could see the soldiers and the defenders in the courtyard. As they looked up she tried throwing spells down at them, but the wizards and the sleepers had put a barrier over the entire castle. It was a vicious air attack and she kept at it to try and weaken the barrier. Unfortunately, a number of people were killed and injured as she managed to penetrate the magykal barrier that had been put up.

She laughed and screamed abuse at the people below and at Alyssa, saying that she was personally going to torture her and take great pleasure out of it. Sheela turned and came back across for a third strike at the castle when the eagle squadron came to the rescue. The eagles flew straight for Sheela and at first she was surprised. They managed to wound a couple of her hell hounds, but once she realised what was happening she also managed to put a magykal barrier around herself and the hounds and retreated to rethink her strategy.

All this time her troops had been on the ground trying to get into the castle. The magyk could not hold them indefinitely so it was decided that hand-to-hand combat was the only thing.

The plan was to keep the marauders outside the castle walls by any means necessary. They were going to use spells and crossbows and the eagle squadron was to fly overhead dropping rocks and missiles that were made up in the kitchens on the enemy.

But the use of catapults and battering rams that were tinted with dark magyk was too much for the main gate, and as its collapse became imminent it was decided that hand-to-hand combat was the only way forward.

The one thing they did not want was the inner doors of the castle to be breached. So, all protection was put on these areas and smaller entrances and windows around the castle; there were already safeguards in place but it was realised that some extra protection would not be a bad thing.

The castle army which included the sailors, as there was no threat at this time from the lake, along with the wizards, ran out into the thick of the troll army ready to fight and die if need be. The sleepers who could not leave the castle stood on the parapets casting spells and offering protection to their combatants. They put hexes on the enemy, concentrating on groups of five at a time until they collapsed in pain and eventually died.

The battle raged on for half a day, spells flying everywhere and hand-to-hand fighting with the cruellest of weapons in the hands of Sheela's army. The trolls had moved on from clubs and whips and they now had the added advantage of the Morning Star, pikes and flails at their disposal. These were the weapons that they had been trained with in the fortress grounds.

These mediaeval weapons in the hands of the trolls produced carnage beyond belief: no one was safe. Sheela had been complacent when it came to putting a magykal barrier around the weapons. Yes, she had made them sharper and more deadly with magyk but she never thought that anyone would be powerful enough to alter the shape of these weapons.

Five of the sleepers were casting spells as fast as they could. The weapons the trolls were holding were turning into rats, mice and birds but the weapons that the sleeper Mylo targeted turned into pretty bunches of flowers. He thought this hilarious, and it was true that the look on the faces of the trolls was a treat to see amongst all the carnage.

The cruellest of Sheela's soldiers were the black hooded warriors that Gastak had seen within the fortress walls. They were the ones that Sheela had trained in a separate area of the fortress. No one knew who they were but they were in fact misfits: a cross-section of human, faeries and creatures that never seemed to quite fit into their community.

They were easy pickings for radicalisation to Sheela's warped perception of the world and she used them to her advantage. These elite warriors she held back, after all in her eyes the trolls were dispensable and a casualty of war that served her purpose. But her elite forces were her guards. These were the warriors that would ensure her victory and after the victory they would ensure that she was protected against would be assassins.

It was late evening before Sheela sounded the retreat so that she could take stock of how the battle was going and how the enemy's defences were holding. The fighters from the castle carried their dead and wounded back through the castle gates along with some of the gross weapons that had been used by the enemy.

The wounded were taken to the Great Hall. This had been turned into a hospital, but the dead were taken to the army's Drill Hall where they were laid with reverence side-by-side ready for identification and the hero's burial when this was all over.

As Alyssa, Dimone and the battle-battered Maldwyn looked down from their vantage point at the top of the castle at the place where the carnage had taken place, Alyssa could not help but feel sorry for the trolls.

"Look how many troll souls died out there today," she said. "None of their kin appear to care! It is a sad state of affairs when they cannot take the time to carry any of their dead away."

Dimone was just about to answer his wife when a small contingent of trolls appeared at the edge of the battlefield and started to walk towards their dead. At first, as they started to pick the bodies up, they thought maybe the trolls were not bad after all and were taking their dead for burial but they were wrong.

They picked the bodies up, threw one over each shoulder and walked towards the edge of the battlefield. It was a part that should be out of the way of the fighting, where they dropped the bodies in a pile, one on top of the other, as if they were rubbish. Then they walked away grunting and laughing to once again reunite with their fellow trolls and their mistress Sheela. It was as if these trolls' lives meant nothing, even to other trolls.

It was one of the worst scenes that any of them had ever witnessed, for a race of beings to treat their kin in such a way was unthinkable.

Dimone said, "Now that we have a chance to breathe. I think we should send a message to the faeries. They do not know that the battle has started and we could really do with their help for when the next wave comes.

"The creatures we have seen so far are bad enough but I cannot remember seeing any of Sheela's elite soldiers and that is worrying. She is holding them back, so that when we get tired and our soldiers cannot fight any more, she will send them in for the slaughter and I am afraid she will win. We need reinforcements and we need them fast."

Maldwyn thought for a while. "I do not really want to send Sunstar and she knows this, we may need her sooner than we think. Several times while I was out there fighting I sensed she wanted to get off the ring and join in the fight, but I told her to be still. The problem is she is our only secret weapon and we do desperately need the faeries."

Alyssa said, "I will go to the sleeper Casey, he was a scryer and I need to learn how to scry, so hopefully we can send for the faeries together and I will have my first lesson."

She went to find Casey who was guarding the far side of the castle battlements. He had already taken three arrows as he was in an odd position that was open to attack. Of course, Casey was already dead so therefore technically could not be killed, he just said that the arrows were annoying.

Alyssa knew, as they all did, that without the magykal help of the sleepers the castle would have fallen by now, but even they had their limitations. One of their skills would be fighting with the enemy if the castle was breached as they could kill but not be killed. They were a good ally to have on your side.

Alyssa found Casey talking to one of the soldiers. He had just treated his painful wound but the soldier's wound was so deep it was impossible for the magyk of a wizard to heal it completely. So, Casey was patching him up so that he could be taken down to the Great Hall, where Jessica the gentle had turned into a Phoenix and was healing as many people as she could.

"Ah, Empress! You have come for advice. No! You have come for my help?"

The thing with the sleeping wizards was that they seemed to know everything, and it was a little disconcerting when you approach them with a problem and they knew what it was you wanted.

"Yes," was the answer, "I need you to use your scrying skills, my mage, and contact the faeries as we are in desperate need of more fighters."

Casey smiled. It was odd, very odd, seeing a dead person smile. It looked more like a grimace as not all of the sleepers had regained that particular skill.

"Empress, do not concern yourself that task is already in hand. I sent for the faeries over one hour ago."

"Ah." Alyssa was visibly disappointed. "I was hoping to have a few lessons on scrying, my lord, but never mind I will have to have lessons later from one of my grandfathers."

"Of course you were, please forgive my haste, Empress, but I saw the urgency in the act and it needed to be done at once."

It was not long before Sheela laid siege to the castle once more, only this time she had her elite soldiers with her. Sheela, like most mad tyrants, was a coward and sheltered in the tree line near the forest, watching as her army did her bidding.

She sent in the trolls and the other creatures that she considered low life, with the battering rams to batter the walls and to hopefully gain access through the gate, while her elite force was trying to get through the magyk that surrounded the castle, with grappling hooks and arrows that were as black as their hearts.

There were thousands of them; it looked like the battle was lost before it had really begun. The sleepers were constantly renewing the magykal barrier while the archers on the parapets of the castle fired on the elite soldiers. They knew the trolls were a threat but it was these fiends from hell that posed the biggest threat: these soldiers, warriors dressed in black and firing black arrows tainted with dark magyk.

They were striking fear into the hearts of the people in the castle and that was causing mistakes to be made. The sisters of fire were on the battlements behind the magykal barrier but it did not stop one of them being wounded.

As they rained fire down on the army below, one of the black arrows managed to penetrate the barrier. None of them saw it coming so they did not move out of its way, and it hit Olivia in the left side of her chest just missing her heart. She fell to the ground unconscious.

The sleeper nearest her immediately tried to heal the wound but dark magyk is hard to heal and she was taken to the Great Hall for treatment: maybe Jessica could help her. Isla and Millie were full of rage and while they did not let the full beast out they did produce more fire energy than they had ever done before. The fire storm they produced was both terrifying and at the same time awe inspiring, to think that such small slim women could produce that kind of rage.

At the same time as this was happening the gate collapsed and the trolls rushed in. The fighting was getting bloody now and more people were dying. The barrier started to collapse and this time it was the turn of the elite solders to join in the battle.

The order came from Dimone that the great doors to the castle must be defended and Sheela's army must be pushed back at all costs. Dimone along with Maldwyn, and their company of friends, were in the thick of it fighting and pushing, trying to get the enemy back outside the gates so that Maldwyn could safely release Sunstar.

Talos had offered to become his proper size but Maldwyn had said no. He could tell everyone after the battle that his father had put the spell on Sunstar but he did not want it to be known that he also had the knowledge to perform the spell.

Just as all seemed lost they heard the familiar popping sound that came as the faeries appeared out of thin air. Christano shouted above the noise of battle, "Oh, you got here then, Newton?"

Newton grinned and shouted back, "You do not think we were going to let you have all the fun, Cousin, did you?"

The faeries charged the enemy and with their combined efforts managed to push them back to the front of the castle. The noise was horrific and the smell of blood was beyond words. They were fighting over the bodies of friends and foes: it was a gruesome sight to behold.

They were now getting the upper hand on the enemy but Sheela, seeing it was starting to go bad, called her elite soldiers back to the tree line where they were re-grouping for a further attack using all the dark magyk that Sheela could muster. Their black armour was impenetrable to arrows and swords. This would be a fight indeed.

Now that Maldwyn had the enemy where he wanted them he whispered to Sunstar. She lifted her head, flew off into the sky and grew to her full magnificent size, casting a shadow over the land below.

For the first time in over a thousand years she felt the wind on her wings and the sun on her back. She flew higher to start with, giving herself a few seconds to bathe in nature's gift to her: the sky.

She felt invigorated and she was now ready for battle. She looked down at the battlefield which looked like a child's toy below her, the creatures like small ants running about. She turned and nose-dived down to the enemy's army, raining fire as she went. This was what she was born to do: she was happy, she was Draco.

Maldwyn called for the castle's army to retreat behind the castle walls and let Sunstar do her thing. She rained fire down for nearly an hour flying back up into the sky, then diving once more onto the enemy, raining down more fire, causing even more damage, killing even more creatures. The dead lay piled up on top of each other.

Up to this point Sunstar had managed to avoid the black arrows from Sheela's elite soldiers but just as she was about to retreat into the sky once more an arrow hit her square in the chest. Sunstar started to fall and everyone in the castle gasped. They had been watching the spectacle and shouting support for Sunstar but now what they feared the most was about to happen before their very eyes. Sunstar looked as if she was dying.

But this dragon was the last of her kind and she had one more trick up her sleeve! She was not going to die without a fight and she had something within her that not many people knew about, something that was more spectacular and could win the war for the humans and the faeries. She had her Draco children.

It was more complicated than it looked when it happened as dragon lore is very mysterious and magykal, but to keep her race alive she had to make the ultimate sacrifice.

CHAPTER THIRTY-TWO: FAREWELLS

⇈

Maldwyn was beside himself with grief, even he did not know what was going to happen. He was distraught at the thought of the last Draco dying, and in the back of his mind there was still hope that by some miracle she would survive.

Maldwyn then thought about Starburst, the ultimate backup was Starburst. Merlin had told him that so maybe Sunstar would survive after all if she put that into play, whatever that was.

Sunstar recovered herself enough to control her dive. She aimed for the elite army that were guarding Sheela. They were still firing the black poisonous arrows at Sunstar's breast hoping to kill her before she attacked them. She was hit by a further ten arrows before she could make the ultimate sacrifice, her death.

She started to fall quickly now, but at the same time for those creatures watching, time seemed to slow down. It was the strangest thing as everyone saw the battle that Sunstar was having in slow motion. When she was a few yards from the ground she suddenly became encapsulated by a bright white light which started to lift her back up into the sky, higher than she had been before.

Once she was out of reach of the arrows the ball of light with Sunstar still in the centre started to explode like a firework, as small orbs of light fired off from it to form a perfect circle around the dragon.

These orbs of light grew and grew then each one burst open to reveal a fully formed dragon, not quite as big as their mother but big enough to cause some serious damage to their enemies.

The central ball which had been Sunstar faded and eventually fizzled out; there was nothing left she was dead. She had indeed made the ultimate sacrifice so that the young Draco within her could live. The young that she had shielded for so many years were now twelve magnificent perfect specimens of dragon.

They were ready to do battle against the men that killed their mother and their revenge was swift. They did not just rain down fire on the men but they also swooped down hitting them with their claws, picking them up in their talons and flying higher and higher up into the sky only to let the elite soldiers drop from a dizzy height to their death. The screams were bloodcurdling but the dragons showed no mercy.

Sheela turned her chariot, whipping the hounds of hell so ferociously that they whimpered as she tried to make her escape, but she could not outrun the young dragons, they were far too quick for her. They landed on the ground circling her and within seconds Sheela and the dogs were dead, ripped apart and scattered as if they were nothing more than rag dolls with the stuffing taken out of them. It truly was a horrific sight to behold.

There was a deathly silence as the last screams died down. Maldwyn walked out of the gateway and stood on the path that led down to the woods. The silence was welcomed after two days of battle but it was an eerie silence, it was the silence of death.

The young Draco all turned and gently walked towards Maldwyn forming a semicircle in front of him. Everyone in the castle was afraid but these dragons had saved the day. Would they really harm the mage?

Alyssa and Dimone followed Maldwyn out of the castle and stood at the side of him. Maldwyn addressed the Draco, "Who will speak for you? Who was the first to Starburst?"

A white dragon walked forward. He was pure white as all the others were pure red; he was the first born from the light and therefore had the purest and wisest soul. Maldwyn started to approach him but Alyssa touched Maldwyn on his arm. "I must do this, Maldwyn, it is my responsibility."

As the small figure of Alyssa walked forward to speak with the Draco her people thought how brave she was, she was true Romanova.

Alyssa said, "May I approach you, my champion?"

The dragon bowed his head and said, "You may, my Empress."

The onlookers did not realise that these creatures could talk and some were quite surprised as they did not realise the intelligence that these creatures had.

Alyssa, Maldwyn and Dimone walked back with the Draco to his sisters and there they stood for some thirty minutes speaking with them. Then the three walked back to the castle to start clearing some of the mess up and getting people back to their homes, but the Draco stayed where they were to await the servants of the castle to bring them food and refreshments.

Then the Draco could sleep until Alyssa and the council could work out where the they were going to live, as no more would they be persecuted but would instead become part of the community of Nirvana as the savours of their world, as heroes. Things would have to change and the faerie council knew this.

Everyone, over the next few hours, spent their time clearing up the mess and the carnage that had been caused during the battle. There was more than a few that felt nauseous through the clearing up process and a few that were literally sick, but the stench and the sight of battle was odious.

Alyssa along with Maldwyn and Dimone made their way to thank the sleeper wizards, and one by one as their thanks were given and Alyssa touched their hands, the wizards would fade. They carried on walking around the castle thanking the sleepers until all but one had vanished. The last one of course was Merlin.

He was left until last through respect for him as the oldest wizard, and as also he was the one that had done the most to help them to their victory by giving Maldwyn the gifts he had given him. They briefly talked about Sunstar and the young that she now had given to Nirvana and Alyssa assured him that Sunstar would not be forgotten.

He then gave Dimone and Maldwyn a locket. They knew straightaway that the lockets were the magykal ones similar to the one that Merlin had given Maldwyn with his mother's facsimile inside Maldwyn's locket had a facsimile of Merlin and Dimone's had a facsimile of Marlon.

These lockets may not be opened in their lifetime but if not they were there to give to their children: a parting gift from their sleeper wizard relatives. Alyssa touched Merlin's hand and in doing so, as with the others, she sealed his fate and he faded.

In the castle graveyard near to Desmy's grave a mausoleum appeared and inside were twelve well-respected wizards in their last resting place.

Maldwyn had no idea that Olivia had been injured. He was weary, as were they all, but before he did anything else he wanted to see if his wife was all right, so he made his apologies to Alyssa and Dimone and said he was going to find the three sisters, and that he would be back to help them with the clearing up as soon as he had spoken to his wife.

It was at that moment when one of the servants came running up to Maldwyn and said, "Your wife is asking for you, my mage."

Maldwyn was immediately concerned and asked, "Is she hurt? What has happened?"

The servant bowed his head. "I am sorry, my mage, but your wife was injured with one of the black arrows while she was on the parapet. She is doing better now; one of the sleepers attended to her until Jessica the Gentle could tend her wound. Jessica the Gentle has worked her magyk and your wife is much better but she is asking for you. Could you please come as there is a complication and Jessica needs to speak to you?"

Maldwyn looked at Alyssa and Dimone. "I must go, my Empress, and see what injuries my beloved Olivia has sustained. I can only suppose that there was so much going on, on the field of battle, that I did not sense her injured body."

Alyssa was concerned. "Of course, you must, Maldwyn, go and tell Olivia I will come to see her in a short while, as I will all the wounded, but first we must ensure that the castle is once more safe."

***

What people had not seen in the heat of their battle was exactly what other people were doing around them and in other parts of the castle.

Alyssa's powers had started to come into their own and she was doing just as much as the sleepers to keep the trolls and the other creatures out of the castle. There was a troll that was five times her size and weight, she held out her arms and just thought about what she wanted to do, picked him up in the air and slammed him against the wall, killing him instantly. Her power now truly advanced.

She did this time and time again, trying to keep the enemies out of the castle and stop them from killing her people. Now she knew what it was to have blood on her hands, but to save her people she would do it all again.

The three sisters were doing their bit on the parapets throwing as much fire at the enemy as they could.

Talos was using his strength; while the enemy was fighting with weapons he was fighting with brute force, ripping the weapons from their hands and breaking them in two over his knee. He also was picking the enemy up and throwing them about like they were rag dolls just as Alyssa had done, but he did it physically.

Tiberius had been trained well with the sword. He had used one before but during his training with the Empress's army he realised he was holding the sword wrong and doing all the wrong things when fighting with it. He learnt well and he learnt fast and many of the enemy laid on the ground after he had finished fighting with them, but he too was injured and fell during the last part of the battle, his arm nearly severed.

Stephann was no longer a boy but a married man and the apprentice to the wizard. He was using Maldwyn's staff with great gusto. It did not take Stephann long to learn the ways of the staff, and it did not take the staff long to learn the ways of Stephann. He fought alongside everyone else, hitting out where he could but using the staff to throw people across the courtyard injuring many.

Mark also used this brute strength, as Talos had, his rage and anger greater than most when one of the trolls tried to grab his beloved Doras by the hand and drag her away.

Emily, Gastak, Thea and Sefton also fought in the battle as did Celestial. Everyone that was in Maldwyn's party, and everyone that he had met along the way on his quest to find Sheela's fort, did their bit in the battle for the castle, as did the military forces.

All the household servants down to the cook were fighting with weapons that they had to hand. The head cook was raining hot cooking oil down on the enemy and throwing pans at them, in fact anything he could find to hand he would throw at the enemy.

If it had not been for the battle being so serious, the sight of the cook fighting the way he did would have been quite funny, especially as he was shouting abuse also at the trolls and at the hag Sheela while he was doing this. He was fearless in his resolve.

The Seelie Court warriors were flying over the enemy on the giant eagles and jumping from a great height into the midst of the battle. The rest of the eagle squadron were flying overhead, dropping rocks and other projectiles onto the enemy, making their mark on the battle field.

The faeries were also getting into the thick of it, jumping off the parapets, landing on the trolls, pulling their heads back and their arms, breaking them and firing their arrows into the mob. They were also a force to be reckoned with. Everyone had done what they could do to keep the castle safe.

Everyone was doing their bit. Sheela and her army did not stand a chance. She thought she would win this battle but she was wrong. The determination of the humans and the magykal creatures of Nirvana to live free went far beyond any magyk that the hag could muster.

After the battle Alyssa, Dimone and the commanders of the forces quickly went around the castle and the perimeter of the castle to ensure that people were all right and that it was safe, but now they had the problem of disposing of all the dead bodies.

***

The next day was a day for the dead. These were the heroes of the castle, the people that had fallen in battle. They were buried in state alongside the sleepers in the castle graveyard. No dead went back to towns and villages to be buried. They were all buried in the castle graveyard and a few weeks after the battle Alyssa was to have a memorial put on the site, with beautifully carved seats where people could come and sit, to reflect and talk to their loved ones that have passed.

Olivia was feeling much better the next day. The only thing was she had a scar and because it was a black arrow that had dark magyk on the tip, the wound would never heal and the scar would always look dark in colour. It would not bother Olivia much but over the years she had to have treatment on the wound from Jessica the Gentle to stop it from getting infected. It would never truly heal.

There were over fifty people in all with similar wounds to Olivia and none of them would ever truly heal.

***

It had been a week since the battle when the war council met once more in the war room. It was not for the planning of war as that was now not required but for the planning of peace, and of what needed to be done and how they were going to do it.

The first thing on the agenda were the Draco. There were twelve of them and they were all sat outside near the path leading down to the forest. What would they do with them and where would they live?

Silas and Seth were late for the meeting but it was for a good reason; they had found somewhere for the Draco to live. There was a field with several caves just below Sorby Hill. It was ideal as the eagles lived on Sorby Hill and the gnomes did their mining under Sorby Hill. The gnomes were quite eager to have the dragons there as they could protect their mining interests against any would-be humans that wanted to take over.

After consultation with Starburst (the male dragon), they agreed to live there and over the years that followed the dragons could be seen flying with the eagles through the skies of Nirvana.

They discussed many things at the meeting but the one thing that Maldwyn would not let them forget was his promise to the Kappa to rid Nirvana of the Asura. The faerie council said they would deal with this one as it would probably need the combined magyk of several faeries.

They were to speak to Dimone after the meeting and ask if he knew the whereabouts of his father, the Tuatha de Danaan, and try to persuade him to help them by using the magykal cauldron. The problem would be the magenta stone or as it was commonly known the philosopher's stone. This could not be obtained as it was destroyed by Merlin and Nafalius, and this was the reason why it may take several extremely magykal faeries to think of something to substitute for the magenta stone.

Doras and Mark built a house in the field next to Tiberius and Celestial, while Stephann and Isla along with his parents extended Maldwyn's house and went to live there.

Olivia and Maldwyn lived in the palace; Alyssa gave them a set of rooms that overlooked the lake at the opposite side to the Morby Mountain. It was a set of rooms that was big enough to bring a family up.

Talos and Millie bought a cottage on the edge of the woods next to the village which was now a small town. Talos had no trouble with the villagers as everyone in Nirvana accepted everyone else for what they were.

Emily, Gastak, Sorona and Christano all went back to the magykal wood to live amongst their own people.

The first of the friends to have a child was Tiberius and Celestial; they had a boy and called him Sammy after the faerie father of Tiberius.

All in all, it was a good time to live in Nirvana and Silas and Seth kept a promise to the human population, to be there for them to guide them and help whenever they could.

Each of the couples went on to have many children between them, except Alyssa and Dimone who just had one girl whom they called Anastasia.

Anastasia grew up to be a very beautiful young lady with the common sense of her mother and the practicalities of her father. She would eventually rule as Empress over the human population of Nirvana and she would have a very special someone by her side. This man as a boy once met a group of faeries on the edge of the forest when he was out rabbiting with his father, the young boy's name was Nigel Markham.

EPILOGUE:

The path these individuals started down was a lonely one.

They all thought they knew their fates, and they all thought they were walking the right path, but along the way they met kindred spirits and when they came to the forks in the path, they had chosen them together and decided which one they would take.

They had protected each other from harm and loved and laughed together, making for new friendships and bonds that were unexpected.

We think in our hours of despair that we are alone but if we look deep enough into our hearts and are selfless in our resolve to others, we usually find friends and even family in strangers.